PRAISE FOR WEIRD

"Not just H. P. Lovecraft
Jones' Shadows Over Inns
its predecessor, the stories in this anthology draw inspiration from
Lovecraft's classic novelette of alien miscegenation, 'The Shadow Over
Innsmouth,' but avoid Cthulhu Mythos clichés."
PUBLISHERS WEEKLY

"Jones has brought together some of the industry's top-notch authors…
This collection is strongly recommended for Mythos fans. Due to the
overall quality of the writing, though, it is strongly recommended for
everyone else, too."
HELLNOTES

"Fascinating and recommended."
ALL HALLOWS

PRAISE FOR SHADOWS OVER INNSMOUTH

"If you love Lovecraft then this anthology is a must-have. Story after
story presents you with situations and characters that Lovecraft himself
could have created. I'm hard-pressed to think of another effort that stays
so true to the original."
SCIENCE FICTION CHRONICLE

"Shadows Over Innsmouth is a very strong anthology, buttressed by
some outstanding art by Dave Carson, Martin McKenna and Jim Pitts."
THE SCREAM FACTORY

"Fans of Lovecraft's Mythos will enjoy the stories."
SF SITE

"Shadows Over Innsmouth is good, slimy fun."
SAN FRANCISCO CHRONICLE

"A fascinating idea for a horror compilation."
LANCASHIRE EVENING PRESS

"This is an intelligent, witty anthology."
THE GOOD BOOK GUIDE

"Lovecraftians will rejoice."
BOOKLIST

WEIRD SHADOWS OVER
INNSMOUTH

WEIRD SHADOWS OVER INNSMOUTH

Edited by STEPHEN JONES

Illustrated by
RANDY BROECKER
LES EDWARDS
BOB EGGLETON
ALLAN SERVOSS

TITAN BOOKS

WEIRD SHADOWS OVER INNSMOUTH
Print edition ISBN: 9781781165294 • E-book edition ISBN: 9781781165300

Published by Titan Books
A division of Titan Publishing Group Ltd
144 Southwark Street, London SE1 0UP

First Titan Books edition: October 2013

1 3 5 7 9 10 8 6 4 2

A CIP catalogue record for this title is available from the British Library.

Printed and bound in the United States.

For NATE
in the year of his spawning,
and those Great Old Ones
MIKE *and* PAULA
for putting their trust in me.

TABLE OF CONTENTS

INTRODUCTION

WEIRD SHADOWS...

AROUND THE END of the 1980s, I had a brilliant idea for an anthology.

To celebrate the centenary of the birth of supernatural fiction writer Howard Phillips Lovecraft in Providence, Rhode Island, in 1890, *Shadows Over Innsmouth* would use the author's 1931 novella 'The Shadow Over Innsmouth' as the literary touchstone for a number of established authors to expand upon his concepts and create a loose, fictional history of the decaying Massachusetts seaport in the story and its ichthyoid denizens, the Deep Ones.

I was so certain that the book would sell that, for the only time in my career, I went ahead and started commissioning stories from authors without a publisher's deal. Luckily, most of the writers I contacted shared my enthusiasm for the project, and before long I had compiled mostly original stories by an impressive line-up of names, including Ramsey Campbell, Brian Lumley, Basil Copper, Neil Gaiman, Kim Newman, Brian Stableford, Michael Marshall Smith and others, including Lovecraft's seminal 26,000-word story itself.

In the way these things sometimes work out, most of the stories I found myself accepting were from British authors, and in the end

I decided to limit the book's contributors to those shores (after all, Lovecraft himself was an avowed Anglophile, so it seemed somewhat appropriate).

Then I started showing the manuscript to publishers on both sides of the Atlantic. Although many expressed their enjoyment of the book, not a single one made an offer to publish it. A year turned into two. H. P. Lovecraft's centenary came and went without creating more than a ripple, and still I couldn't find a publisher.

Finally, I gave up. Reluctantly, I explained the situation to the contributors (who were all very understanding) and released them from their contracts to sell their stories elsewhere. It didn't come as much of a surprise that many of them found new markets almost immediately.

And that, I thought, was that. At least I had learned a hard lesson—never commission an anthology without first getting an agreement with a publisher.

Then, while I was attending the World Horror Convention in Nashville, Tennessee, I was approached on the final day of the event by Dwayne H. Olson, who had heard that I had a Lovecraftian anthology I could not sell and wanted to introduce me to Phil Rahman of Minneapolis small press publisher Fedogan & Bremer.

Just as August Derleth and Donald Wandrei had initially set up Arkham House to ensure that Lovecraft's fiction remained in print between hardcovers following the author's premature death in 1937, so F&B was founded to preserve Wandrei's work, although it also quickly expanded into a publisher of "widowed" Arkham-style books as well. *Shadows Over Innsmouth* fitted their avowed objective almost perfectly. Phil was enthusiastic about the book, and a proposed deal was done before the evening was over.

The only problem was that I had already released all the contributors from their contracts. So, over the next couple of months, I contacted all the writers and got them to sell their stories back to me again.

Shadows Over Innsmouth was finally published in 1994 in a beautifully illustrated hardcover edition. It was launched with a fish-themed signing party at the World Fantasy Convention in New Orleans and became the first book from Fedogan & Bremer to sell out and be reprinted. There was an attractive trade paperback edition from Gollancz in Britain, a cute two-volume set published in Japan, and (after rejecting it all those years earlier) Del Rey eventually added it to their handsome series of Lovecraftian paperbacks in America. More recently there has been a stylish Greek edition, and we've also sold rights to Russia and Germany. Now that first book (along with this follow-up volume) has been reissued by Titan Books as part of the publisher's prestigious series of Lovecraft paperbacks. The reviews have been mostly positive, and the original edition was even nominated for a World Fantasy Award.

Not bad for an anthology I couldn't even sell initially.

The thing was, though, it *wasn't* a Lovecraft anthology. Well, not in inspiration, at least. With *Shadows Over Innsmouth*, I was trying to emulate one of the most talented, hard-working and perceptive editors in the weird fiction field—August W. Derleth (1909–1971).

As much as I admired Lovecraft's cosmic themes and eldritch horrors, it was actually the pulp thrills of Derleth's pastiche collection *The Mask of Cthulhu*, his novel *The Trail of Cthulhu* and, especially, the anthology *Tales of the Cthulhu Mythos* that I was attempting to recapture. Lovecraft himself had occasionally encouraged other writers to develop themes from his stories in their own work, and I attempted the same with a fictional history of Innsmouth.

And so the years passed, and I began wondering... if *Shadows Over Innsmouth* had used Lovecraft's 1920s-set story for its inspiration, what would happen if we moved on a step further? The answer can now be found in *Weird Shadows Over Innsmouth*, where several of the contributors to the original volume, along with a number of additional authors from both sides of the Atlantic, put their own spin on the dark history of Innsmouth and its batrachian followers of Dagon.

Using an early, discarded draft of Lovecraft's story as a point of departure, once again as the decades pass, the fishy Deep Ones spread out from the east coast of the United States to cast their scaled shadows across the rest of the world in unusual and often unexpected ways.

And in case you were wondering, yes, this book had it's own set of problems, although nothing like those that assailed the earlier title.

But if you are a Mythos fan who has enjoyed both of these volumes, then rest assured that I am already thinking about those *Weirder Shadows Over Innsmouth*…

Iä-R'lyeh! Cthulhu fhtagn! Iä! Iä!

Stephen Jones
London, England

DISCARDED DRAFT OF
' THE SHADOW OVER INNSMOUTH'
by H. P. LOVECRAFT

[PP. 1–6:]

IT WAS IN the summer of 1927 that I suddenly cut short my sightseeing tour of New England and returned to Cleveland under a nervous strain. I have seldom mentioned the particulars of this trip, and hardly know why I do so now except that a recent newspaper cutting has somehow relieved the tension which formerly existed. A sweeping fire, it appears, has wiped out most of the empty ancient houses along the deserted Innsmouth waterfront as well as a certain number of buildings farther inland; while a singularly simultaneous explosion, heard for many miles around, has destroyed to a vast depth the great black reef a mile and a half out from shore where the sea-bottom abruptly falls to form an incalculable abyss. For certain reasons I take great satisfaction in these occurrences, even the first of which seems to me a blessing rather than a disaster. Especially am I glad that the old brick jewellery factory and the pillared Order of Dagon Hall have gone along with the rest. There is talk of incendiarism, and I suppose old Father Iwanicki could tell much if he chose; but what I know gives a very unusual angle to my opinion.

I never heard of Innsmouth till the day before I saw it for the first and last time. It does not seem to be mentioned on any modern map, and I was planning to go directly from Newburyport to Arkham, and thence to Gloucester, if I could find transportation. I had no car, but was travelling by motor coach, train, and trolley, always seeking the cheapest possible route. In Newburyport they told me that the steam train was the thing to take to Arkham; and it was only at the station ticket office, when I demurred at the high fare, that I heard about Innsmouth. The agent, whose speech shewed him to be no local man, seemed sympathetic toward my efforts at economy, and made a suggestion that none of my other informants had offered,

"You could take that old bus, I suppose," he said with a certain hesitation, "but it isn't thought much of hereabouts. It goes through Innsmouth—you may have heard about that—and so the people don't like it. Run by an Innsmouth man—Joe Sargent—but never gets any custom from here, or from Arkham either, I guess. Wonder it keeps running at all. I suppose it's cheap enough, but I never see more than two or three people in it—nobody but those Innsmouth folks. Leaves the Square—front of Hammond's Drug Store—at 10:00 a.m. and 7:00 p.m. unless they've changed lately. Looks like a terrible rattletrap—I've never been on it."

That was the first I ever heard of Innsmouth. Any reference to a town not listed in the guidebooks would have interested me, and the agent's odd manner of allusion roused something like real curiosity. A town able to inspire such dislike in its neighbours, I thought, must be at least rather unusual, and worthy of a sightseer's attention. If it came before Arkham I would stop off there—and so I asked the agent to tell me something about it.

He was very deliberate, and spoke with an air of feeling somewhat superior to what he said.

"Innsmouth? Well, it's a queer kind of a town down at the mouth of the Manuxet. It used to be almost a city—quite a seaport before the War of 1812—but the place has all gone to pieces in the last hundred years or so. There's no railroad—the B & M never went through there, and the branch line from Rowley was given up years ago. More empty houses than there are people, I guess, and no business to speak of.

Everybody trades either here or in Arkham or Ipswich. At one time they had quite a number of mills there, but nothing's left now but one jewellery refinery.

"That's a pretty prominent proposition, though—all the travelling salesmen seem to know about it. Makes a special kind of fancy jewellery out of a secret alloy that nobody can analyse very well. They say it's platinum, silver, and gold—but these people sell it so cheap that you can hardly believe it. Guess they have a corner on that kind of goods.

"Old man Marsh, who owns the thing, must be richer than Croesus. Queer old duck, though, and sticks pretty close around the town. He's the grandson of Capt. Obed Marsh, who founded the business. His mother was some kind of foreigner—they say a South Sea native—so everybody raised Cain when he married an Ipswich girl fifty years ago. They always do that about Innsmouth people. But his children and grandchildren look just like anybody else so far as I can see. I've had 'em pointed out to me here. Never saw the old man.

"And why is everybody so down on Innsmouth? Well—you mustn't take too much stock in what people around here say. They're hard to get started, but once they do get started they never stop. They've been telling things about Innsmouth—whispering 'em, mostly—for the last hundred years, I guess, and I gather they're more scared than anything else. Some of the stories would make you laugh—about old Captain Marsh driving bargains with the devil and bringing imps out of hell to live in Innsmouth, or about some kind of devil-worship and awful sacrifices in some place near the wharves that people stumbled on around 1850 or thereabouts—but I come from Panton, Vermont, and that kind of story doesn't go down with me.

"The real thing behind all this is simply race prejudice—and I don't say I'm blaming those that hold it. I hate those Innsmouth folks myself, and I wouldn't care to go to their town. I suppose you know—though I can see you're a Westerner by the way you talk—what a lot our New England ships used to have to do with queer ports in Asia, Africa, the South Seas, and everywhere else, and what queer kinds of people they sometimes brought back with them. You've probably heard about the Salem man that came back with a Chinese wife, and maybe you know there's still a colony of Fiji Islanders somewhere around Cape Cod.

"Well, there must be something like that back of the Innsmouth people. The place was always badly cut off from the rest of the country by salt marshes and inlets, and we can't be sure about the ins and outs of the matter, but it's pretty plain that old Captain Marsh must have brought home some odd specimens when he had all three of his ships in commission back in the 1830s and 1840s. There certainly is a strange kind of a streak in the Innsmouth folks today—I don't know how to express it, but it sort of makes me crawl. You'll notice it a little in Joe Sargent if you take that bus. Some of them have flat noses, big mouths, weak retreating chins, and a funny kind of rough grey skin. The sides of their necks are sort of shrivelled or creased up, and they get bald very young. Nobody around here or in Arkham will have anything to do with them, and they act kind of offish themselves when they come to town. They used to ride on the railroad, walking and taking the train at Rowley or Ipswich, but now they use that bus.

"Yes, there's a hotel in Innsmouth—called the Gilman House—but I don't believe it can amount to much. I wouldn't advise you to try it. Better stay over here and take the ten o'clock bus tomorrow morning. Then you can get an evening bus there for Arkham at eight o'clock. There was a factory inspector who stopped at the Gilman a couple of years ago, and he had a lot of unpleasant hints about the place. It seems they get a queer crowd there, for this fellow heard voices in other rooms that gave him the shivers. It was foreign talk, but he said the bad thing about it was the kind of voice that sometimes spoke. It sounded so unnatural—slopping-like, he said—that he didn't dare go to sleep. Just kept dressed and lit out early in the morning. The talk went on most of the night.

"This man—Casey, his name was—had a lot to say about the old Marsh factory, and what he said fitted in very well with some of the wild stories. The books were in no kind of shape, and the machinery looked old and almost abandoned, as if it hadn't been run a great deal. The place still used water power from the Lower Falls of the Manuxet. There were only a few employees, and they didn't seem to be doing much. It made me think, when he told me, about the local rumours that Marsh doesn't actually make the stuff he sells. Many people say he doesn't get enough factory supplies to be really running the place, and that he must be importing those queer ornaments from somewhere—heaven knows where. I don't believe that, though. The Marshes have been selling those outlandish rings and armlets and tiaras and things for nearly a hundred years; and if there were anywhere else where they got 'em, the general public would have found out all about it by this time. Then, too, there's no shipping or in-bound trucking around Innsmouth that would account for such imports. What does get imported is the queerest kind of glass and rubber trinkets—makes you think of what they used to buy in the old days to trade with savages. But it's a straight fact that all inspectors run up against queer things at the plant. Twenty odd years ago one of them disappeared at Innsmouth—never heard of again—and I myself knew George Cole, who went insane down there one night, and had to be lugged away by two men from the Danvers asylum, where he is now. He talks of some kind of sound and shrieks things about 'scaly water-devils'.

"And that makes me think of another of the old stories—about the black reef off the coast. Devil's Reef, they call it. It's almost above water a good part of the time, but at that you could hardly call it a real island. The story is that there's a whole legion of devils seen sometimes on that reef—sprawled about, or darting in and out of some kind of caves near the top. It's a rugged, uneven thing, a good bit over a mile out, and sailors used to make great detours just to avoid it. One of the things they had against Captain Marsh was that he used to land on it sometimes when it was fairly dry. Probably the rock formation interested him, but there was talk about his having dealings with demons. That was before the big epidemic of 1846, when over half the people in Innsmouth were carried off. They never did quite figure out what the trouble was, but it was probably some foreign kind of disease brought from China or somewhere by the shipping.

"Maybe that plague took off the best blood in Innsmouth. Anyway, they're a doubtful lot now—and there can't be more than 500 or 600 of them. The rich Marshes are as bad as any. I guess they're all what people call 'white trash' down South—lawless and sly, and full of secret doings. Lobster fishermen, mostly—exporting by truck. Nobody can ever keep track of 'em, and state school officials and census people have a devil of a time. That's why I wouldn't go at night if I were you. I've never been there and have no wish to go, but I guess a daytime trip wouldn't hurt you—even though the people here will advise you not to take it. If you're just sightseeing, Innsmouth ought to be quite a place for you."

And so I spent that evening at the Newburyport Public Library looking up data about Innsmouth. When I had tried to question natives in the shops, the lunch room, and the fire station I had found them even harder to get started than the ticket agent had predicted, and realised that I could not spare the time to overcome their first instinctive reticence. They had a kind of obscure suspiciousness. At the YMCA the clerk merely discouraged my going to such a dismal, decadent place, and the people at the library shewed much the same attitude, holding Innsmouth to be merely an exaggerated case of civic degeneration.

The Essex County histories on the shelves had very little to say, except that the town was founded in 1643, noted for shipbuilding before the Revolution, a seat of great marine prosperity in the early nineteenth century, and later on a minor factory centre using the Manuxet as power. References to decline were very few, though the significance of the later records was unmistakable. After the Civil War all industrial life centred in the Marsh Refining Company at the Lower Falls, and the marketing of its products formed the only remaining bit of major commerce. There were very few foreigners; mostly Poles and Portuguese on the southern fringe of the town. Local finances were very bad, and but for the Marsh factory the place would have been bankrupt.

I saw a good many booklets and catalogues and advertising calendars of the Marsh Refining Company in the business department of the library, and began to realise what a striking thing that lone industry was. The jewels and ornaments it sold were of the finest possible artistry and the most extreme originality; so delicately wrought, indeed, that one could not doubt but that handicraft played a large part in at least their final stages of manufacture. Some of the half-tone pictures of them interested me profoundly, for the strangeness and beauty of the designs seemed to my eye indicative of a profound and exotic genius—a genius so spectacular and bizarre that one could not help wondering whence the inspiration had come. It was easy to credit the boast of one of the booklets that this jewellery was a favourite with persons of sophisticated taste, and that several specimens were exhibited in museums of modern craftsmanship.

Large pieces predominated—armlets, tiaras, and elaborate pendants—but rings and lesser items were numerous. The raised or incised designs—partly conventional and partly with a curious marine motif—were wrought in a style of tremendous distinctiveness and of utter dissimilarity to the art traditions of any race or epoch I knew about. This other-worldly character was emphasised by the oddness of the precious alloy, whose general effect was suggested in several colour-plates. Something about these pictured things fascinated me intensely—almost disproportionately—and I resolved to see as many original specimens as possible both at Innsmouth and in shops and museums elsewhere. Yet there was a distinct element of repulsion mixed with the fascination; proceeding, perhaps, from the evil and silly old legends about the founder of the business which the ticket-agent had told me.

[P. 17:]

The door of the Marsh retail office was open, and I walked in with considerable expectancy. The interior was shabby and ill-lighted, but contained a large number of display cases of solid and capable workmanship. A youngish man came forward to meet me, and as I studied his face a fresh wave of disturbance passed over me. He was not unhandsome, but there was something subtly bizarre and aberrant about his features and vocal timbre. I could not stifle a keen sudden aversion, and acquired an unexplained reluctance to seem like any sort of curious investigator. Before I knew it I found myself telling the fellow that I was a jewellery buyer for a Cleveland firm, and preparing myself to shew a merely professional interest in what I should see.

It was hard, though, to carry out this policy. The clerk switched on more lights and began to lead me from case to case, but when I beheld the glittering marvels before me I could scarcely walk steadily or talk coherently. It took no excessive sensitiveness to beauty to make one literally gasp at the strange, alien loveliness of these opulent objects, and as I gazed fascinatedly I saw how little justice even the colour-plates had done them. Even now I can hardly describe what I saw—though those who own such pieces or have seen them in shops and museums can supply the missing data. The massed effect of so many elaborate examples was what produced my especial feeling of awe and unrest. For somehow or other, these singular grotesques and arabesques did not seem to be the product of any earthly handiwork— least of all a factory only a stone's throw away. The patterns and traceries all hinted of remote spaces and unimaginable abysses, and the aquatic nature of the occasional pictorial items added to the general unearthliness. Some of the fabulous monsters filled me with an uncomfortable sense of dark pseudo-memory which I tried

[P. 21:]

the taint and blasphemy of furtive Innsmouth. He, like me, was a normal being outside the pall of decay and normally terrified by it. But because he was so inextricably close to the thing, he had been broken in a way that I was not yet broken.

Shaking off the hands of the firemen who sought to detain him, the ancient rose to his feet and greeted me as if I were an acquaintance. The grocery youth had told me where most of Uncle Zadok's liquor was obtained, and without a word I began leading him in that direction—through the Square and around into Eliot Street. His step was astonishingly brisk for one of his age and bibulousness, and I marvelled at the original strength of his constitution. My haste to leave Innsmouth had abated for the moment, and I felt instead a queer curiosity to dip into this mumbling patriarch's chaotic store of extravagant myth.

When we had brought a quart of whiskey in the rear of a dismal variety store, I led Uncle Zadok along South Street to the utterly abandoned section of the waterfront, and still farther southward to a point where even the fishermen on the distant breakwater could not see us, where I knew we could talk undisturbed. For some reason or other he seemed to dislike this arrangement—casting nervous glances out to sea in the direction of Devil Reef—but the lure of the whiskey was too strong for him to resist. After we had found a seat on the edge of a rotting wharf I gave him a pull at the bottle and waited for it to take effect. Naturally I graduated the doses very carefully, for I did not wish the old man's loquacity to turn into a stupor. As he grew more mellow, I began to venture some remarks and inquiries about Innsmouth, and was really startled by the terrible and sincere portentousness of his lowered voice. He did not seem as crazy as his wild tales would indicate, and I found myself shuddering even when I could not believe his fantastic inventions. I hardly wondered at the naive credulity of superstitious Father Iwanicki.

THE QUEST FOR Y' HA–NTHLEI

by JOHN GLASBY

I N THE AUTUMN of 1927, the United States Federal Authorities were approached by Professor Derby of Miskatonic University concerning certain incidents occurring in the seaport town of Innsmouth as told to him by a Robert Olmstead. It had been known for some time that a trade in gold articles existed between Innsmouth and the neighbouring towns of Arkham, Rowley and Ipswich, such items occasionally turning up as far afield as Boston.

However, Olmstead further claimed that illegal immigrants were also present in the town, that a large number of murders had been committed and several people known to have visited Innsmouth had unaccountably disappeared, leaving no clues as to their vanishing.

Acting on this information, two Federal investigators were sent to Innsmouth to look into these claims. When neither man returned, it was decided that an armed raid was to be organised to determine the truth behind the stories of smuggling, murder and the disappearance of a number of individuals.

What happened in February 1928 was never released to the public. The testimony of three agents who accompanied this force into Innsmouth, given in three official reports, has been kept under lock and *key on the orders of the Federal authorities. All subsequent inquiries as to the contents of these reports have been met with the same answer. There never were such documents, the raid was merely to arrest certain individuals for tax evasion, and any suggestions to the contrary are simply pure invention and speculation on the part of the newspapers of that time.*

Until now, it has proved impossible to establish whether such reports do indeed exist and, if they do, what is set down in them. The account that follows is based upon photographic copies of the TOP SECRET documents, which have lain in the archives of the Federal Building for more than seventy years.

How they come to be in my possession is not only irrelevant but also highly dangerous for certain individuals, including myself. Likewise, the name of the person who obtained them must be protected since, were it to become known, he would certainly face a long period of imprisonment or, like those in Innsmouth, simply vanish off the face of the Earth.

It is true that the events described herein occurred more than half a century ago, that they are so bizarre that few will believe them, and that others will describe them as a deliberate hoax. Yet all were written within two weeks of the raid on Innsmouth by sober, competent agents, all of whom were warned of dire consequences should they speak about the incident to any member of the public.

The decision to publish them now, more than seventy years after the event, has been taken because it is deemed essential that the world should be aware of the lurking horror that may, at any time, emerge and overwhelm mankind.

I

NARRATIVE OF FEDERAL AGENT JAMES P. CURRAN: FEBRUARY 27, 1928

My first acquaintance with Innsmouth was in early January, 1928. Prior to that I had never heard of the town, nor could I find it marked on any map or listed in any gazetteer. My superiors had instructed me to accompany a colleague, Andrew McAlpine, from the Treasury Department, to Arkham where we were to question a certain Robert Olmstead who wished to give specific information concerning the town.

The drive from Boston to Arkham took the best part of an hour and, with McAlpine at the wheel. I spent the time going through the file that had been given to us. Apparently, Innsmouth was a small seaport town on the north coast of Massachusetts, isolated from, and shunned, by its neighbours. Once a flourishing port, it had decayed and degenerated over the last half century and was now a backward community which kept itself to itself.

Rumours concerning Innsmouth were legion. There were reports of smuggling and the importation of certain natives from some island in the South Seas during the mid-19th century, presumably part of the slave trade. There was certainly a small, but significant, trade in gold items for many of these pieces were on show in Arkham, most of them produced at the Marsh refinery situated on the banks of the Manuxet River.

Reports of murder and unexplained disappearances were also catalogued in the file, although whether these were on the scale believed by residents in Arkham and Rowley had not been verified. More recently, during the preceding autumn, two agents from the Treasury Department had been sent to Innsmouth to report on tax evasions and possible contraband passing through the town. Neither agent had returned and this had brought things to a head as far as the Federal authorities were concerned.

The decision to raid the town had been taken at the highest level and a date set for February. Very little accurate information on conditions inside the town was available. However, an urgent telephone call to the Bureau from Professor Derby of Miskatonic University had resulted in our being ordered to go to the Federal office in Arkham, to interview Robert Olmstead, who claimed to have recently escaped from Innsmouth and who had important information for us.

Olmstead turned up at the office a little after 2:00 p.m. that afternoon. He wasn't at all what I had expected. Approximately twenty years old, he gave an address in Cleveland and my first question was why he had travelled such a distance just to visit Innsmouth.

Initially, he seemed oddly evasive and kept fidgeting in his chair for a full two minutes before replying. The gist of his response was that he was attempting to trace his ancestral history back to Arkham and had discovered that, prior to moving there, his maternal family had originally come from nearby Innsmouth.

"Are you aware that Innsmouth has been under close surveillance by the Federal authorities for some months?" I asked.

He shook his head. "I know nothing about that," he declared. "My only reason for going there was to trace any of my maternal relatives who might still be living in Innsmouth."

"Then if that was your only reason," McAlpine put in, "why did you have to flee for your life as Professor Derby has informed us?"

I could tell at once that Olmstead was hiding something from us; that something had happened there which he either didn't want to tell us, or was sure we wouldn't believe.

Then he cleared his throat nervously. "I spoke with one of the inhabitants, Zadok Allen, who told me things about Innsmouth which the townsfolk don't want the outside world to know. He warned me that if they suspected I'd spoken to him, they'd kill me rather than let any of this information get out."

"Then I think you'd better tell us what you know," I said.

"You wouldn't believe a word of it," he muttered.

"Try us," McAlpine said.

Moistening his lips, he went on. "First you have to know there are no religious denominations left in Innsmouth except for one. All of the others were shut down sixty years ago by Obed Marsh who ran the town then. Seemingly, he brought back some pagan religion from some island in the South Pacific, along with a large number of natives. Now they're all members of the Esoteric Order of Dagon."

"Dagon?" McAlpine inquired.

"Some kind of fish deity. They all believe he lives in some sunken city in the deeps off Devil Reef."

I nodded. "We've come across people like this before. Weird cults in the bayou country. But it seems to me that what you're suggesting here might be something more than that."

"Take my word for it," he said, and there was no doubting the earnestness in his tone. "This is far worse than anything you've come up against before. This heathen worship is bad, but there's even worse than that in Innsmouth."

"Worse?" I prompted, as he hesitated again.

"Much worse. I've seen them and even those I saw aren't as bad as those they've got hidden away in the big houses on Washington, Lafayette and Addams Streets. You can hear about it from the people in Arkham. They call it 'the Innsmouth look'. It comes from the time when those foreigners were brought into the town by Obed Marsh.

"Seems he called up others from the sea off Devil Reef and forced the folk in Innsmouth to mate with them. Call their offspring hybrids, or whatever you like, but they change. Bulging eyes, wide mouths, ears that change into gills. They often swim out to Devil Reef, maybe beyond, and when their time comes, when the change is complete, they leave Innsmouth and go down into the really deep water and remain there for ever in their sunken city they call Y'ha-nthlei."

I threw my colleague a quick glance at that point. Closing the file in front of me, I said, "Well, Mister Olmstead, thank you for your information. We'll certainly pass it on to the proper quarter. It will then be up to our superiors as to what action, if any, needs to be taken."

When he had gone, McAlpine and I sat looking at each other in silence. I had little doubt that something had occurred in Innsmouth to have frightened Olmstead so much that it had sent him running for his life along the abandoned railway line to Rowley.

Once our report had been sent to the Bureau, we heard nothing more until I received orders to report to a Major Fenton, a war veteran, in Boston where I was to place myself under his command.

He turned out to be a short, stocky man in his late forties with dark hair already showing signs of grey.

Taking me aside, he said gruffly, "I'll expect the fullest co-operation from you. You'll already know something of what's been planned. I also understand you know a little about Innsmouth."

"Only what I've read in the preliminary file and what I've learned from Robert Olmstead," I told him.

Without making any further comment, he signalled to one of the officers accompanying him.

A map was spread out on the table and he motioned me forward. "This is the road from Arkham." He traced the outline with his forefinger. "As you see, it enters Innsmouth along Federal Street and continues all the way to the town centre. That's the route we'll take. At the same time, a second force, including the Marine Corps, will enter from the west, while others will go ashore and come in through tunnels which were used for smuggling in the old days."

"And if some of the inhabitants try to escape by boat?" I asked.

He gave a grim smile. "We've taken that possibility into account. Three ships will be patrolling the shoreline. They'll take care of anyone attempting to get away by boat."

Leaning forward, he stabbed a finger at the map. "One other thing. There may be no truth in this but we do know there's been a lot of activity here, near Devil Reef. For more than a century, contraband has been landed on this reef. It's a dangerous place for vessels but apparently the old sea-captains brought natives and other illegal goods there before ferrying them ashore. More importantly as far as we're concerned, there's a two-thousand-foot drop there down to the ocean floor."

He paused, as if for dramatic effect. Personally, I couldn't see what he was getting at.

"I don't believe half of this myself," he continued, almost apologetically, "but from scraps of information we've gathered from a couple of Federal agents who did return from Innsmouth, there's talk in that town of some sunken remains on the seabed in that region."

"What sort of remains?" asked one of the officers.

Fenton looked across at me. "You've read the file which was given you some weeks ago. You'll know that every Christian religion has been outlawed in Innsmouth. Everybody there belongs to this weird cult, the Esoteric Order of Dagon. They actually worship this god and believe a sunken city lies at the bottom of the sea, just off the reef. A city they call Y'ha-nthlei, where this Dagon lives."

"Surely you don't believe that, sir," said the officer.

"I only believe what I can see, Lieutenant. Nevertheless, someone in the government seems to take it all seriously. A submarine has been ordered to dive down towards the sea bottom and take a look. If there is anything there, they have enough torpedoes on board to blast it to Hell and back."

Two days later, I was in a convoy of ten Army trucks approaching the outskirts of Innsmouth. It was now dark and the vehicle moved without any lights showing. Each of us had received specific orders before we set out. We would stop at the end of Federal Street and from there proceed to the building which housed the Esoteric Order of Dagon, where half of our force would then move off to occupy the Marsh mansion on Washington Street.

Reaching the end of Federal Street, we disembarked. A few dim streetlights shone along its length but nothing showed in any of the once-grand Colonial buildings as we passed, moving from one shadowed doorway to the next. Within five minutes we were within sight of our objective. The building stood facing an open space covered in rough grass. It boasted several massive pillars with the name still visible above the pediment. Its original use as the Masonic Temple still showed where the set square and pair of compasses of that Order, although partially obliterated by time, were still visible.

Sending twenty men to watch the rear of the building, Major Fenton led the rest of us towards the front door. Not bothering to check whether or not it was locked, he gave the order to smash it down. The rusted hinges yielded readily and, switching on our torches, we rushed inside. A sharp, fishy stench met us, catching horribly at the back of my throat.

In the torchlight we saw that the large lower room was empty apart from a long table flanked by two high-backed chairs.

Then, without warning, a door at the far end of the room suddenly burst open and a horde of dark figures poured into the room. For a moment, I stood absolutely still, abruptly shocked by what the wavering torchlight revealed. I had expected the citizens of this town to offer some resistance to our invasion, but this was something neither I, nor any of the others, had been prepared for.

Only their apparel was normal. They moved forward with a hideous hopping, slithering gait and there was something bordering on the ichthyic, or batrachian, about their leering features. Huge, bulging eyes glared unwinkingly at us from beneath sloping foreheads. Their skin, what little we could see of it, appeared scaled and the wide mouths reminded me of frogs. I think we had all anticipated finding some signs of degeneracy among these folk, but nothing like this.

How such monstrosities had come into being, I was unable to guess. Certainly, the tales of mixed breeding with another race seemed to have some basis in fact.

Uttering guttural croaking sounds, utterly unlike human speech, they threw themselves upon us. Several were clubbed with rifle butts as they attempted to force us back towards the door. Five minutes later, it was all over. Six of them had been killed and the rest were securely tied up. We had lost two men, their faces and chests ripped to shreds by webbed, taloned hands.

Leaving three men to watch the captives, the rest of us followed Major Fenton through the far door. Here there was a flight of stone steps leading down below street level with a faint light just visible at the bottom. The sight which confronted us there was one which shocked all of the warmth from my limbs.

The room was large, even bigger than the one above, decked out in tattered tapestries, all depicting some repellent forms of marine life; giant, octopoid creatures, malformed denizens of the deep and, worst of all, creatures which had the shape of men but with webbed hands and feet and features not dissimilar to those creatures we had just encountered!

The light came from several burning brands set in metal brackets around the walls and by their light we made out the huge altar at the far end, flanked by two massive statues. One was clearly male, the other female—but beyond that they bore no resemblance to anything I had ever seen before.

"What in the name of all that's holy is this place?" Fenton muttered hoarsely, speaking to no one in particular.

Somehow, I forced myself to speak. "I reckon it's obvious, Major.

This is their temple where they worship this heathen god—Dagon. God alone knows what rites they hold down here."

Fenton's face twisted into a scowl. "Put a light to it," he ordered tersely. "I've seen enough."

By the time we left the building the flames had taken a firm hold. Through the billowing smoke, we emerged into the street. Already, the sound of rifle fire was coming from several positions around the town centre. Since our orders had been to fire on these people only as a last resort, it was clear that other units had run into serious trouble.

Fifteen minutes later, after fighting our way through a group of yelling figures who attempted to block our path, we linked up with the force which had been sent to raid the Marsh house on Washington Street. They, too, had captured several of the hideously disfigured hybrids. Three of their men had been killed and five wounded during the attack.

After collecting a number of the alien artefacts from the house as evidence, we returned to where we had left the trucks, herding the prisoners on board. For the most part they offered little resistance, but I noticed that the men ordered to guard them kept their distance. I could guess how they were feeling and doubted if any of them would ever be the same after what we had uncovered in Innsmouth.

II

TESTIMONY OF FEDERAL AGENT WILLIAM T. DARNFORTH: MARCH 2, 1928

Acting on sealed orders from the Federal Bureau, I proceeded by train to the small town of Rowley, situated some seven miles west of Innsmouth. My orders were to place myself under the command of Lieutenant Corlson of the Marine Corp. I knew very little concerning Innsmouth, only that a number of Federal agents had disappeared when visiting the town and our task was to enter the place under cover of darkness, proceed to the town centre where it was believed that a number of tunnels, used for more than a century for smuggling contraband into Innsmouth, had their exits.

From the Lieutenant I gathered that our attack would be co-ordinated with that of a further force moving in from the south. Some resistance was expected and we were to maintain radio contact for as long as possible with two other squads who would be entering the tunnels from the beach. Any of the inhabitants who attempted to flee the town through the tunnels would be trapped between ourselves and those men coming in from the sea.

The first part of our task was accomplished without any serious incident. Small groups of the townsfolk made half-hearted attempts to prevent us advancing along Rowley Road and Dock Street but these scattered for cover after a few shots were fired. As we entered Federal Street north of the bridge across the Manuxet, however, we encountered a larger force and here we were compelled to take cover before we finally succeeded in driving them off.

The bridge was the first real obstacle we had to tackle. It was evident at once that it had received no repairs for many years and we had no idea how secure were the ties across the gorge. But now we had progressed this far, there was no turning back. Two at a time, we crossed the decaying structure until we were all safely across.

By now, a number of fires had been started and the conflagration was spreading rapidly inland from the decaying warehouses along the waterfront, lighting up the sky in that direction.

Reaching the town square we dispersed to search for the hidden entrances to some of the tunnels reputed to exist. It was unlikely they would be well concealed since few visitors ever came to Innsmouth and, from what little information we had of the place, those who did were watched closely. It was not long before we stumbled upon one of them, covered with a thin layer of earth and coarse grass.

There was an iron-runged ladder fastened to the circular side. It didn't look particularly secure, testifying to the fact that the tunnel had probably not been in use for several decades. Lowering ourselves down, we used our torches to delineate our surroundings. The tunnel was larger than I had expected, fully ten feet in height and only a little less in width.

Pools of stagnant water lay everywhere, oozing from the muddy ground and running down the slimy walls. Weird echoes came from somewhere in the blackness ahead of us, and not all of them could be put down to sounds of our own making. I struggled desperately to keep my emotions under tight control for there was something about those faint, elusive sounds which set my nerves on edge, lifting the small hairs on the back of my neck.

Then, still some distance ahead, I made out other noises, more distinct, that increased the tension in my mind. Low, throaty mutterings and occasional piping whistles which seemed oddly out of place down there. In addition, there were faint splashing sounds like objects being dropped into water.

Corlson had also picked them out for he gave a hissed order to halt. In the ensuing silence we could now hear the noises distinctly, although it was impossible to pinpoint their position accurately.

Waving an arm, the Lieutenant signalled us to continue. A few moments later, the torchlight showed where the tunnel turned abruptly to the right and, rounding the bend, where the beams from our torches illuminated the area ahead, we all saw the full horror which dwelt within those accursed tunnels which burrowed like gigantic wormholes through the rock!

It was a scene out of a nightmare. Lit by a nauseous green radiance which came from countless luminous algae encrusting the rocks, a vast grotto lay spread out before us. Large stalactites hung from the roof, finding their distorted reflection in a vast pool of sluggish water.

But it was not this that sent me staggering back against the Lieutenant. It was the sight of the indescribable creatures that flopped and floundered around the edge of the black water.

Fish-headed monsters, which belonged only in the mad visions of a deranged mind came surging out of that pool as we emerged onto the slippery, treacherous rocks at its edge. Somewhere there had to be an outlet to the sea for common sense told me such monstrosities had never evolved on the land.

Several of the men with us seemed on the point of running but Corlson shouted a sudden, urgent command and, somehow, succeeded in bringing them back to their senses. Military discipline reasserted itself. My own actions were instinctive. Bringing up my revolver, I fired several shots into the midst of the slithering creatures. Steeling themselves, the marines opened fire as the Lieutenant signalled to them to spread out and take cover.

How many of the hideous ocean dwellers there were it was impossible to estimate, but in the face of the withering rifle fire they were forced to retreat, diving back into the water and disappearing beneath the oily surface. When it was all over, we went forward to examine the bodies. Two of them were still alive with only minor wounds and these were trussed up and left with two men to guard them while we moved on.

Apart from the tunnel along which we had come, three more opened out from around the walls. Checking his compass, the Lieutenant pointed to the one on our left.

"That way," he said decisively. His voice shook a little. "The others seem to lead deeper into the town."

Moving cautiously into the tunnel, now fully aware of the danger that lurked beneath Innsmouth, we went forward in single file, our weapons ready for any further attack. Every man among us had been visibly shaken by our recent experience. Normal degeneracy and inbreeding such as was common among small, isolated communities living in the bayou regions and other townships such as Dunwich, we had expected. But these creatures were something completely different. At that moment, some of the odd stories I had heard from one of the few agents to have spent some time in Innsmouth and left to tell the tale, began to assume something approaching the truth.

In places, the tunnel we were following widened out into larger spaces but here we found nothing more abnormal than driftwood and splintered wooden cases which had evidently been left there to rot by bygone smugglers moving contraband into the town from ships lying off Devil Reef.

Everywhere there was a fishy stench. We had first noticed it on entering the grotto, but now it grew stronger and more pronounced and I guessed we were nearing the sea. On occasions, we passed other tunnels branching off from that which we were traversing but only darkness and silence lived in them.

Then, almost an hour after we had lowered ourselves into the depths, a sound did reach us from directly ahead. It began as a faint slithering noise, followed by hoarse croaking gutturals, which bore no resemblance to human speech. Corlson uttered a sharp warning and we immediately switched off our torches, pressing ourselves hard against the slimy, moisture-running walls as we struggled to pinpoint the exact location of the sound.

Soon it became obvious that a large party of creatures were moving rapidly in our direction and, a moment later, I picked out more normal sounds superimposed upon the obnoxious mutterings—the shouts of men—and guessed that part of the force which had landed on the beach were close on the heels of these unnatural abominations.

A couple of minutes later, stabbing torchlight showed along the walls of the tunnel, highlighting the large group of Deep Ones now almost upon us. In the confined space of the tunnel with a squad of our own men at the rear, we were unable to open fire on the creatures. Using their bayonets and the butts of their rifles, the Marines clubbed most of them as they struggled to break through our lines. Caught between the two forces, they were speedily overcome. The pitched battle lasted for less than ten minutes.

At the end of that time, seventeen prisoners had been taken, the remainder lying dead on the floor of the tunnel. Three of our force had been killed, their throats slashed.

Linking up with the group from the seaward end of the tunnel, we moved back to where we had left the other prisoners with their two guards. Here we came upon a scene of utter carnage.

It was all too clear what had happened. Those creatures which had escaped us by diving into the pool had returned and clearly in overwhelming numbers. The captives were gone but more than a score of the creatures lay dead on the rocks where the guards had cut them down before being overwhelmed. Of the two men, however, there was no sign. Evidently they had been overpowered after their ammunition had run out and had been dragged into the water.

Corlson gave a muttered oath as he surveyed the scene. "I should have foreseen this might happen," he gritted. "God knows, there must be hundreds, if not thousands, of those creatures somewhere out there in the deep water."

I tried to reassure him. "You weren't to know this might happen," I told him. "None of us were given any warning of the scale of this—

infestation. They're like rats in the sewers."

For a moment I thought that, in his anger at what had happened to his men, he was about to give the order to shoot those captives we had. Then he regained his self-control, rigid discipline took over, and he signalled us to make our way back to the surface.

Once in the town square, we paused to take stock of the situation. Large fires were now burning out of control at several sites, but the streets radiating from the square seemed oddly deserted. Either the majority of the citizens were now concealed in the deep cellars across town or had somehow succeeded in fleeing Innsmouth.

Sporadic firing could still be heard but for the most part the town seemed deathly quiet. Over towards the sea, the entire waterfront was now a mass of flame, the conflagration spreading rapidly inland as the fire consumed the ancient wooden buildings.

Corlson gave the order to his men to convey the prisoners to the trucks waiting at the north side of Innsmouth.

Once they were gone, he turned to me. "I reckon you'll have to put in some kind of report to the Federal Bureau, Darnforth."

Nodding, I said, "Whatever I put in it, there aren't going to be many who'll believe a single word. I can't believe most of it myself. All of those nightmare creatures living here or coming up out of the sea! It's against all nature."

"We've got those captives," the Lieutenant retorted grimly. "People will have to believe the evidence of their own eyes." He threw a swift glance to where the last of the men were disappearing along Federal Street. "But what in the name of God are those—*things*? Where could they possibly have come from? One thing's for sure, they're not normal inhabitants of this town, no matter how much inbreeding there may have been in the past."

"I guess the only way any of this makes sense is if you believe in the stories that have been legion in this area concerning Innsmouth for nearly a century," I told him. "If it wasn't for what I've witnessed tonight, I'd have said they were nothing more than pure myth and superstition. Now I know different."

Corlson took out a pack of cigarettes, offered one to me, then nodded. "You seem to know a little more of this whole affair than I do," he muttered, blowing smoke into the cold, still air. "Just what are these odd tales?"

I shrugged. "All I really know is what's given in the file I got and what little I picked up in the last couple of weeks, talking to folk in Rowley. Seems some sea-captain, Obed Marsh, brought back this pagan religion from some uncharted island in the South Pacific back in the 1840s and, somehow, converted almost the whole town. Most of the creatures in Innsmouth are hybrids as a result of enforced mating with these natives and with those others, the Deep Ones, who supposedly live in some sunken city—Y'ha-nthlei —that lies on the ocean bottom off Devil Reef."

"So these Deep Ones also interbred with the town's inhabitants?" Corlson sounded incredulous.

"So they reckon. And they all worship this sea deity—Dagon."

"God Almighty. This is far worse than anything we've come across before." He rubbed the back of his hand across his forehead. In spite of the chill, he was sweating. "So what do you figure the government will do with these prisoners?"

"Keep them all locked up somewhere is my guess. Somehow, I doubt if much of this will ever be released to the general public."

When we pulled out of Innsmouth five hours later, many of the old buildings and all of the wooden warehouses along the waterfront were still burning. More than three hundred of the citizens had been taken prisoner.

Later, we heard they had been transferred to special, isolated camps where they were to be interrogated and kept under constant observation. No details as to the exact whereabouts of these camps were to be released.

III

CONFIDENTIAL REPORT OF FEDERAL INVESTIGATOR WALTER C. TARPEY: MARCH 5, 1929

Following special orders received on February 12, 1928, I proceeded by train to Boston, Massachusetts, where I was informed that the government had decided to launch an armed raid on a small fishing port named Innsmouth, some distance along the coast from Arkham. Reports of bootlegging and smuggling of illegal immigrants had apparently been received from several quarters and my orders were to join a submarine, which was to patrol the coast of an island known locally as Devil Reef. This mission was to be co-ordinated with a land raid upon the town and our task was firstly to prevent any inhabitants escaping by sea (this in conjunction with three vessels of the coastguard) and second, to dive into the deep water off Devil Reef and carry out a survey of the ocean bottom in that region.

It was late afternoon when we were piloted out of the harbour and heading out to sea. Conditions inside the submarine were Spartan and cramped, with little room in which to move. We rode on the surface, accompanied by the other three vessels, the convoy heading north within sight of the coast.

Commander Lowrie had seen service during the war, as had several members of the crew. Apart from myself, however, no one on board knew any details of our mission when we set out, Lowrie having been given sealed orders not to be opened until we were at sea.

Once we arrived offshore from Innsmouth, three of the crew were ordered above, one to man the machine-gun and two others to act as lookouts for any of the townsfolk attempting to escape by boat. With Lowrie's permission, I accompanied them, struggling to maintain my balance against the rolling of the vessel. There was an unusually heavy swell between the shore and Devil Reef, the latter an irregular mass of rock about two miles from the distant harbour.

The night was very still but bitterly cold and I was glad of my thick parka. Despite the darkness, the sky was clear and it was just possible to make out a scattering of lights in the town and at least three fires had been started among the shadowy warehouses that stood along the waterfront.

A sudden hoarse shout from one of the lookouts near the conning tower brought me swiftly around. He was pointing urgently, not in the direction of the town, but out to sea. For several moments, I could make out nothing in that direction to account for his actions. Then, dimly, I saw numerous black shapes in the water, heading towards us from Devil Reef.

Somehow, O'Brien managed to turn the unwieldy machine-gun. Not a moment too soon, he opened fire, swinging the weapon expertly from side to side in a wide arc. Several of the shapes disappeared beneath the waves although it was impossible to determine whether they had been hit. Others still came on and, for the first time, I made out something of their outlines. Those I could see were not even remotely human in appearance. More like fish, but with humanoid bodies and legs, they came surging through the water in a relentless, black tide.

"Get down below!" Somehow, I managed to force the numbness of shock from my round and get the words out. "You can't possibly stop them all, even with that weapon."

The men obeyed me instantly, lowering themselves quickly through the hatch. Closing it swiftly, O'Brien stared at me in the dim light, an incredulous expression on his bluff features.

"What in the name of all that's holy are those things?"

Before I could reply, there came a clamorous hammering on the hull. It sounded as though there were hundreds of them battering against the tough steel.

Moments later, we heard the Commander's voice giving the order to dive. Hanging on grimly to keep my balance, I experienced a sudden chill as we began to descend. With an effort, I made my way forward.

Here, I found Commander Lowrie at the periscope. He turned and listened grimly as I briefly explained what had happened and what we had seen. Strangely, he didn't appear as surprised as I had expected when I described those creatures, which were now attacking the submarine. It was almost as if he had anticipated something of the kind.

"I've read my orders," he said harshly. "Clearly there's some truth in the odd tales which have come out of Innsmouth over the years. Some of them speak of hybrid creatures spawned in the town during the last century and others of the Deep Ones, denizens of some city on the sea bottom. Seems they can exist both on land and in the water."

"Surely that's not possible," I said.

"I'm just going by what I've been told. Obviously there's something out here that defies common sense. But until I find out otherwise, I have to accept these stories, no matter how weird they may seem."

"What are our orders?" I asked. The battering against the hull had now diminished appreciably. "Most of those creatures seem to have dispersed now we're going down."

"We're to remain at a depth of eighty feet and head west, skirting that reef and head into open water. Then we go down as far as we can and, depending on what we find there, I'll have to make a decision regarding firing the torpedoes we have on board."

"Then you reckon there may be something down there which has to be destroyed?"

"Maybe." He paused, then added as an afterthought, "I've been in the Navy for nearly thirty years and I've seen some strange things in that time, believe me."

He motioned towards the search periscope, which, unlike the normal one, had a wide angle of vision. "We have a very powerful searchlight mounted forward on the hull. Hopefully, we'll be able to use this periscope to see something of what's down there."

"You won't have much latitude," I remarked.

"No, but in the circumstances, it's the best we can do."

Levelling off at eighty feet, we edged slowly ocean-ward, skirting the reef to the south.

"We have a hydrophone operator on board," Lowrie explained, "and he's listening out for obstacles since we don't know accurately how far that reef extends below the surface."

Twenty minutes later, we had safely navigated the southern edge of the reef and were soon in deeper water. Now, the submarine angled more steeply downward and Commander Lowrie remained at the search periscope, using it for the first time underwater in an attempt to pick out anything visible in the beam from the searchlight.

In this manner, we proceeded to within thirty feet of the ocean floor, then assumed a more even keel. Motioning me forward, he indicated I could take a look at the scene outside. At first, even with my eye pressed hard against the lens, I could see very little. The searchlight beam, powerful as it was, scarcely penetrated more than ten feet into the inky black water. Then something suddenly flashed across my field of view. I caught only the barest glimpse of it before it vanished, but that had been sufficient to recognise one of those creatures we had spotted on the surface.

It was followed, an instant later, by another and this time I almost cried out at the sight. Whatever it was, I doubted if that creature could ever have been human. It seemed octopoid in outline with tentacles rather than two arms, yet the rest of the body was almost like that of a man!

Beside me, I heard the Commander issue a terse order. The next moment, we began to descend once more and now, through the periscope, I was able to discern the sea-bed some thirty feet below. It sloped gradually downward but two minutes later a black, almost straight line of utter darkness appeared directly in front of us, stretching away in an unbroken line in both directions.

I recognised immediately what it was; the dark abyss at the edge of the shallows around Devil Reef, a fathomless chasm the depth of which we did not know.

Sucking in a deep breath, I relinquished the periscope to the commander and heard his muttered exclamation as he, too, saw it.

"How far down is it possible for us to go without cracking the hull?" I asked.

"Certainly not more than three hundred feet," he replied. "More than that I wouldn't like to attempt."

"That's still a good distance above the bottom if the reports about the depth of this area are accurate."

"I'm well aware of that, Agent Tarpey. There's nothing in my orders about going to the bottom. There are ten torpedoes on board this vessel. Once we reach the designated position, these are to be fired straight down and then we get out of here."

"How long before we reach that position?" I inquired. The feeling of claustrophobia, which had made itself felt the moment I had come aboard was now beginning to tell on my nerves. A small number of the men also appeared to be similarly affected.

Lowrie checked his watch, holding it close to his eyes in the dim light. "Another twelve minutes," he said briefly. He called Lieutenant Commander Westlock and gave him orders for the torpedoes to be made ready for firing.

While this was being done, I returned to the periscope. Not that I expected to see anything even though the vessel was now descending slowly, but at a steeper angle than before, into the inky blackness of the abyss.

Yet there was something.

At first, my vision refused to take it in. A wavering phosphorescence far below us. I knew that certain deep sea creatures emitted a fluorescent glow—but what I saw covered a vast area and would have required a shoal of millions of such creatures to produce such an effect. Furthermore, there seemed to be an odd regularity about the masses of palely glimmering light. Although it seemed impossible, to me they held ineffable suggestions of structures utterly unlike anything I had ever seen. Squinting, I struggled to imbue them with some form of normality.

How high those alien configurations loomed above the distant ocean floor, it was impossible even to guess, for the glowing radiance seemed to come only from the lowermost regions. But even this was sufficient to show the sheer alienness of their overall outlines.

Had they been nothing more than amorphous masses, it would not have offended my sense of perspective to such a degree. But there were vast bulbous appendages and oddly truncated cones, which intermeshed in angles bearing no relation to Euclidean geometry and I felt my eyes twist horribly as I tried vainly to assimilate everything in my field of vision.

But even this outrage of nature was not the worst. Just before I removed my eye from the periscope, I saw something black and monstrous outlined against the flickering light of that vast city far below. To describe it as tentacled or winged would be to ignore completely the quintessential horror of that slowly ascending shape. I had seen pictures of giant squids reputed to haunt the midnight depths of the ocean but this was far larger, far more abnormal, to belong to that class of creature.

Hearing my sharp exclamation, Commander Lowrie thrust me hurriedly to one side and took my position at the periscope. Clasping the handles in a white-knuckled grip, he turned it slowly. Then, without moving his head, he barked, "Increase the angle of descent. Ready all torpedoes for immediate firing."

Once his orders had been carried out, he turned an ashen face in my direction. He seemed to have some difficulty in finding the right words. Finally, he muttered, "What in God's name is that down there?"

"Y'ha-nthlei, perhaps," I replied. "I can't think of anything else. God knows how old that place is. And don't ask me what that—*thing*—is. All I know is that it's coming this way and the sooner we get this over with and surface, the better."

I could not analyse the reasons for my certitude that whatever that monstrous creature was, we were its target and there was not a moment to be lost if we were to extricate ourselves from this horrible predicament. From what little I had seen, I knew that monstrosity was ten, maybe even twenty, times larger than the submarine and if it succeeded in reaching us, it could drag us down into those alien depths with ease.

In front of me, Lowrie stood, tensed and rigid, at the periscope. I knew he was seeing exactly what I had seen and I firmly believed that the mere sight of that incredible horror might have driven a lesser man over the edge. But he did not flinch. His features set into a mass of grim determination, he waited until he judged the torpedoes would find their mark, then gave the order to fire.

From where we stood, there was little to indicate that the torpedoes were on their way. Five minutes passed with complete silence inside the submarine. Then there came a slight, but distinct, shudder as the detonation waves hit us.

When I stepped forward at Lowrie's gesture to take my last look through the periscope, I was trembling all over. At first, my eyes refused to focus properly. Sucking in a deep breath, I forced myself to remain calm. Slowly, everything became clear.

That frightful distortion of nature I had seen only a few minutes earlier was gone although I thought I caught a fragmentary glimpse of something amorphous dwindling into the depths. As for that vast city, the torpedoes had clearly done their work for here and there were irregular patches of blackness like scars on the overall phosphorescence. Nevertheless, large areas still shone with that sickly radiance and it was evident that, although Y'ha-nthlei, like that creature which had risen to attack us, had been badly damaged, they had not been totally destroyed.

By the time we surfaced, there was no sign of the Deep Ones who had earlier swarmed over the hull. To the west, Innsmouth was burning. The shells of those Colonial houses built of stone would remain as smoke-blackened monuments to the night's raid but almost all of the wooden structures would be reduced to ashes by morning.

I must end this report on a warning note. Innsmouth must remain under close surveillance and a continual watch kept on the ocean just beyond Devil Reef. That which is merely injured, may rise again!

BRACKISH WATERS

by RICHARD A. LUPOFF

DELBERT MARSTON, JR., Ph.D., D.Sc., was the youngest tenured professor on the faculty of the University of California. He was widely regarded as a rising academic star, not only on the University's premiere campus at Berkeley but throughout the huge multi-campus system and, if the truth be known, throughout the national and international community of scholars.

Tall and dark-haired with a touch of premature grey at the temples, he was regarded as a catch by female faculty members who competed vigorously for his attention. He dressed conservatively, held his tongue in matters of both public and campus politics, drank single-malt scotch whiskey exclusively, and drove an onyx-black supercharged 1937 Cord Phaeton. Perhaps it was Marston's otherwise thoroughly conventional lifestyle that caused his vehicular preference to be regarded as a sign of high taste and acceptable self-indulgence rather than one of eccentricity.

He had the Cord serviced regularly at an exclusive garage on the island of Alameda, the owner of which establishment catered to fanciers of the three marques formerly built in Auburn, Indiana—the Auburn, the stately Duesenberg, and the tragically short-lived

Cord. The Auburn Motor Car Company, or what was left of it, was now producing Lycoming aircraft engines and B-24 Liberator bombers for the Army Air Forces. Once the war was over there was no predicting the future of the discontinued automobiles, but in Marston's estimation their prospects were poor.

On the night in question—the night, at any rate, that would initiate the series of events destined to lead to Delbert Marston's apotheosis—the sky above the San Francisco Bay Area was black with a cold storm that had swept down from the Gulf of Alaska and attacked the Pacific Coast with fierce winds and a series of hammering downpours of pelting rain laced with occasional hints of sleet. Such weather was not uncommon in Northern California during the winter months, and the winter of 1943–44 was no exception; the onslaught of wind and water was regarded as anything but freakish. The Bay Bridge was swept by an icy gale but the Cord held the roadway with a steadiness unmatched by vehicles of lesser quality.

Professor Marston was accompanied by an older colleague, one Aurelia Blenheim, Ph.D. Grey-haired and dignified, Professor Blenheim had served for some years as Marston's mentor and sponsor. It was her spirited championing of his cause that had persuaded the Tenure Committee to grant him its seal of approval despite what was regarded as his almost scandalous youth. Marston's intellectual equal, Aurelia Blenheim had found in the younger academic the friendship and platonic camaraderie that her lifelong celibacy had otherwise denied her.

"I don't know why I let you talk me into spending an evening with this squad of eccentrics, Aurelia." Marston braked to keep his distance behind a superannuated Model A Ford that looked ready to topple over in the gale.

"Why, for the sheer pleasure and mental stimulation of bouncing off some people with unconventional ideas. Besides, the semester's over, most of the kiddies who have managed to stay out of the service have gone home to Bakersfield or Beloit or wherever they came from. What else did you have to do?"

"You've got to be kidding. The Oakland Symphony is doing an all-Mahler program, the San Francisco Ballet has a Berlioz show, and the opera is offering *The Marriage of Figaro*. And we're going to meet a bunch of wackos who think—if you can call it thinking—as a matter of fact, Aurelia, what in the world is it that they do think?"

Aurelia Blenheim shook her head. "Come now, Delbert. They have a lot of different ideas. That's the fun of it. They don't have a body of fixed beliefs. Attending one of their meetings is like sitting in on a First Century council of bishops and listening to them debate the nature of the mystical body of Christ."

"I can't think of anything less interesting."

They had reached the San Francisco end of the bridge now and Marston manoeuvred the Cord through merging traffic and headed south. A rattletrap Nash sedan full of high school kids pulled alongside the Cord. The driver lowered his window and yelled at Aurelia, "Why don't you put that submarine back in the water where it belongs, grandma?"

Aurelia Blenheim turned to face the heckler and mouthed some words that remained unheard and unknown to Delbert Marston. The expression on the face of the heckler changed suddenly. He raised his window and floored his gas pedal. The Nash sped away. Three kids in the backseat stared open-mouthed at the grey-haired professor.

"Aurelia," Marston asked, "what did you say to them?"

"I just gave them a little warning, Delbert. Best keep your eyes on the road. I'll get us a little music." She reached for the radio controls on the Cord's dashboard. Although the radio had added to the price of Marston's Cord he had ordered it installed when he purchased the Phaeton.

The sounds of Franz Liszt's 'Mephisto Waltz' filled the Cord's tonneau.

A particularly dense sheet of rain mixed with a seeming bucketful of hailstones crashed against the Cord's roof and engine hood, adding the sound of an insane kettle drum concerto to the music.

"There's our exit sign," Aurelia Blenheim shouted above the din.

Delbert Marston edged into the exit lane and guided the Cord off the highway and onto a local thoroughfare. Aurelia Blenheim navigated for him, giving instructions until she finally said, "There it is. You can park in the driveway."

The house stood out like an anomaly. Curwen Street and its environs—still known as Curwen Heights—had once been among San Francisco's more fashionable neighbourhoods. Victorian homes had reared their turrets and cupolas against the chilly air and damply cloying fog. Families who claimed the status of municipal pioneers, direct descendants of the leaders of the Gold Rush and survivors of the earthquake and fire of 1906, had erected gingerbread-encrusted mansions and filled them with children and servants. Carriage-houses and stables were discreetly placed behind the family establishments.

But the passing decades had brought changes to Curwen Street and Curwen Heights. Urban crowding had driven the wealthiest families to Palo Alto, Burlingame and other lush, roomy suburbs. The construction of the Golden Gate Bridge and Bay Bridge in the 1930s had opened the unspoiled territories and sleepy villages of Marin and Alameda Counties for the use of daily commuters. Key Route trains brought workers from Oakland and Berkeley into the city each day.

Marston switched off the engine and half-blackened headlights, and climbed from behind the steering wheel. He exited the car and helped Aurelia Blenheim to do the same. He carefully locked the vehicle's doors and escorted her to the front entrance of the house. In the darkened street and with storm clouds blackening the sky it was difficult to see anything. Even so, the house had the appearance of a one-time showplace, long since fallen into disrepair. Blackout curtains made the windows look like shrouded paintings. Marston searched for a doorbell and found none. Instead, a heavy cast-iron knocker shaped like a gargoyle signalled their arrival.

The door swung open and they were greeted by a rotund individual wearing thick, horn-rimmed glasses. He peered owlishly at Marston, then dropped his gaze to Aurelia Blenheim.

"Dr. Blenheim!" He took her hand in both of his and pumped it enthusiastically. After he released her she introduced Marston. The rotund youth identified himself as Charlie Einstein, "No relation," subjected Marston's hand to the same treatment Aurelia Blenheim's had received, and ushered them into the house.

Voices were emerging from another room, as was the odour of fried food. In the background a radio added to the din.

Charlie Einstein led Marston and Aurelia Blenheim to a high-ceilinged parlour. Men and women sat on worn furniture, each of them holding a plate of snack food or a beverage or both.

Einstein clapped his hands for attention and conversations wound down. The radio continued to play. Einstein said, "Ben, would you mind?" He gestured toward a Philco console. "You're the closest."

A painfully thin and painfully young-looking man in a Navy uniform reached for the Philco and switched it off. "Nobody was paying attention anyhow," he said. He turned toward Marston and Aurelia Blenheim. "Aurelia, hello. And you must be Professor Marston."

Del Marston nodded.

"Ben Keeler," the sailor said. His spotless winter blues bore the eagle-and-chevron insignia of a petty officer. He shook Marston's hand. "We've been hearing about you for weeks now, sir. I'm so pleased that you could finally make it to a meeting."

Charlie Einstein set out to fetch beverages for Marston and Aurelia Blenheim. Keeler pointed out the others in the room, giving their names. Marston nodded to each.

One of them was a thirty-ish woman whose mouse-brown sweater was a perfect match for her stringy hair. She was sitting next to the fireplace, where a log smouldered fitfully. "This is Bernice," Keeler announced. "Bernice Sanderson."

The woman looked up at Marston and Aurelia Blenheim. It was obvious that she knew Blenheim; they exchanged silent nods. "So you're the famous professor." She glared at Marston. "The sceptic who doesn't believe in anything he can't see for himself. You've got a lot to learn, Professor."

She turned away.

Keeler took Marston by the elbow and steered him away. "Sorry about that, sir."

Marston interrupted. "Please just call me Del."

"Fine." The sailor grinned. "You know, I was an undergrad at Cal until we got into this war. I'm accustomed to calling professors, *Sir*." He reddened. "Or, *Ma'am*, Professor Bleinheim."

"Aurie."

"Yes." Keeler turned a brighter shade of red. "Anyway, once the war is over I plan to go back and finish up my degree."

Marston nodded. He saw that Keeler wore an engineer's rating on his uniform sleeve. "Good for you," he said. "There will be plenty of need for good engineers in the post-war world."

"Yes, sir," replied Keeler. "In fact—"

He was interrupted by Charlie Einstein carrying a tray with two steaming cups on it. "I know Aurie likes these things and she told me that you did, too, Professor."

"Del."

"Right. Hot rum toddies. Good for a night like this."

When Einstein went on his way, Ben Keeler resumed. "I'd hoped to have you as my faculty adviser when I get to grad school. If I'm not being too pushy, that is."

Marston shook his head. "I'm flattered. Sure, come and see me when the war's over. I envy you, Ben, serving in the Navy. You just went down and enlisted when Pearl Harbor was attacked?"

"I thought it was the right thing to do. In fact, I'd have thought that a man with your credentials would have a commission. If you don't mind my saying so, Professor. Del."

Marston sipped at his rum toddy. "They turned me down. Said I couldn't march right, and besides, they wanted me to hang around and lend my expertise when they had problems for me to play with. Said I was more valuable as a civilian than I would be in the Navy."

Keeler nodded sympathetically.

Marston breathed a sigh of relief. The rum couldn't be that strong and fast-acting, it was just careless of him to mention not being able to march right. He'd been born with minor deformities of both feet. They'd never kept him from normal activities, in fact he felt that they helped him as a swimmer. But the Navy doctors had taken one look at his feet and told him to go home and find a way to contribute to the war effort as a civilian.

Still, the Navy had accepted him as a consultant, calling upon his expertise as a marine geologist and hydrologist. He'd received a high security clearance and worked with naval personnel whenever he wasn't busy teaching. He looked around, observing that nearly everyone in the room was young. Aurelia Blenheim had persuaded

Marston to attend a meeting, but this looked more like a party. There were plates of snack food scattered around the room and bottles of soft drinks. There was a low, steady hum of conversation. Marston spotted only two girls among the crowd, discounting the acerbic Miss Sanderson. Outnumbered as they were by males, they were twin centres of constant attention and manoeuvring.

A fireplace dominated one end of the room. A young man of neurasthenic appearance wearing a baggy suit and hand-painted necktie had stationed himself in front of it. He held a brass bell and miniature hammer above his head and sounded the bell.

"The twelfth regular meeting of the New Deep Ones Society of the Pacific will come to order." He looked around, clearly pleased with himself. Conversation had ceased and he was the target of all eyes. "We have a distinguished guest with us tonight, Professor Marston of the University of California. If anyone can shed light on the problem of the Deep Ones, I'm sure Professor Marston can."

Now attention shifted from the young man to Del Marston. What a farce this was turning into. Marston mulled over suitable forms of revenge against Aurelia Blenheim.

"Professor Marston," the young man was babbling on, "perhaps you'll be willing to address our little group?"

Marston was holding a thick sandwich in one hand and a soft drink in the other. He put them on a table and said, "I'm afraid I'm not quite prepared for that. Maybe you'll tell me a little bit about your group, starting with your name."

"Albert Hartley, Dr. Marston. I'm the President of the New Deep Ones Society of the Pacific. Our members are dedicated to unravelling the mystery of the Deep Ones. Hence our name." He giggled nervously, then resumed. "And Dr. Blenheim says that you're the leading marine geologist in the region."

"Dr. Blenheim flatters me. But tell me about your New Deep Ones Society. Does the name refer to the fact that you are all deep thinkers?"

"Now you flatter us," Hartley replied. They had settled onto chairs and sofas by now, the boys clustering around the girls while Albert Hartley tried to hold their attention. "The Deep Ones," (Marston could almost hear the capital letters) "are strange creatures who live on the sea-bottoms of the world. People have known about them for thousands of years. They're in Greek mythology, Sumerian mythology, African mythology. And in modern times authors keep writing about them. But nowadays they have to disguise their books as fiction."

"Why?"

Hartley looked startled. The room was silent.

Then somebody else made an ostentatious demand for the floor. Del Marston recognised the new speaker as Charlie Einstein. The ponderous Einstein blew out a breath. "There are people in the government who don't want us to know about the Deep Ones. People in every government. You wouldn't think that the Nazis in Germany and the Reds in Russia and the Democrats in Washington could agree on anything while they're fighting this huge war and all, but they have secret meetings in Switzerland, you know. The Japs are there, too."

"You mean the war is a front for something else?" Marston asked. "Cities getting blown up, soldiers dying in foxholes, aerial and naval battles, people suffering all over the world—it's all a put-up job?"

Einstein shook his head, his too-long, dirty-blond hair falling across his face. "Oh, the war is real enough, okay. My brother is in the Army, he was at Tobruk in North Africa and was wounded and he's back in England now, in the hospital. The war is real, you bet, Dr. Marston. But the big shots who are running things still have their secret agreements. You'll see, when it ends, nothing much will change. And they really don't want us to know about the Deep Ones. Lovecraft wrote about them, too. In fact, he was writing about them even before that Czech guy, Karel Capek, wrote his book *War with the Newts*. They're everywhere. Lovecraft was a New Englander and he knew about them, they have a big base at Innsmouth, in Massachusetts."

"But that was just fiction." Marston tried to calm the excited youngsters. "Foolish stories about monsters. As silly as Orson Welles' radio play about Martians. There are problems enough in this world without having to invent more."

"Oh, no. Oh, no." Einstein shook his head. His fleshy jowls shook with emotion. "And another thing. There's the 1890 Paradox."

"The what?" Marston could barely keep from laughing.

"The 1890 Paradox," Einstein repeated. "Karel Capek was born in 1890 in Bohemia, in what is now Czechoslovakia. Howard Phillips Lovecraft was born in Rhode Island. And Adolf Hitler was born in Linz, Austria. You can't call that a coincidence, can you?"

"Of course I can." Marston frowned. "Millions of people are born every year. You can pick any year out of history and find musicians, authors, politicians, scientists, generals, philosophers, all born that year. Of course it's a coincidence."

"Then what about their deaths? Lovecraft and Capek both wrote about the Deep Ones, both exposed their intentions, and both died within a matter of months! Explain that for me, if you can, Dr. Marston."

"I can't explain it. There's no explaining to do. Out of all the millions of people born in 1890, I imagine that tens or hundreds of thousands would have died in—what year was it that your two writers passed on?"

"Lovecraft died in 1937, Capek in 1938."

"And Hitler?"

"You know he's still alive. That's because the stars were right for those births in 1890, and they were right for the two deaths in 1937 and '38. As for Hitler—he's no menace to the Deep Ones. It wouldn't surprise me if he's in league with them. Malignant beings have a long history of making alliances with humans willing to sell out their species for personal gain, like vampires offering their sort of undead immortality to their human servants. And the Deep Ones have a lot to offer their allies. Long, long life for one thing. And incredible pleasures obtained through their unspeakable rites. That's what the Deep Ones have to offer."

"And we believe they're here, Dr. Marston." This from Albert Hartley, taking back the centre of attention. He was interrupted by a middle-aged woman who entered the room wearing a housedress and apron. "There's coffee and cocoa on the stove for anybody who wants them," she announced.

Hartley looked exasperated. "Thanks, Mom. Not right now, please." The woman withdrew.

"They're out in the Bay, even as we speak," Hartley resumed. "They have a whole city down there. When people disappear, when you hear about people jumping off the new bridge to Marin, the Deep Ones are involved in that."

Marston frowned. It was hard to take these kids seriously but he had promised Aurelia Blenheim and he was going to do his best. "I think the jumpers are suicides."

"That's what you're supposed to think. The Deep Ones, they're amphibians. Lovecraft said so in his writings. They look like regular people at first. They grow up among us, they could be anybody. Then as they get older they start to show their true nature. It's called the Innsmouth Look. They start to resemble frogs or toads. Eventually they have to go back to the sea, to live with their own people."

Marston picked up his abandoned sandwich and took a bite. Mom Hartley made good snacks, anyway. The sandwich was spiced salami and crisp lettuce with a really sharp mustard, served on hard-crusted sourdough. Marston had a good appetite, and besides, chewing earnestly away at Mom Hartley's salami sandwich gave him an excuse not to answer young Albert Hartley's wild assertions.

Now a girl sitting surrounded by boys spoke up. "My name is Narda Long, Dr. Marston."

Del Marston nodded.

"We don't think that there has to be war with the Deep Ones." Narda wore her medium-brown hair in curls. Her face would be pretty, Marston decided, in a few years when she shed her baby fat. It would help her figure, too. For now, she filled her pink blouse and plaid skirt a bit more amply than she might, but in this crowd anyone young and female would get all the attention she wanted.

The room was filled with a buzz. Apparently the New Deep Ones Society was divided between those who thought they could make league with the wet folk and those who considered the amphibians the implacable enemies of land-dwellers.

"If we'd just make friends with them, I'm sure they'd leave us alone. Or even help us. Who knows what treasures there are in the sea, on the sea bottom, and we probably have things here on land that would help them."

"That's right." The boy sitting next to Narda Long agreed. "We have these battles and we go shooting torpedoes around and we set off depth charges, we're probably ruining their cities. No wonder they're mad at us."

"What can you tell us about the Deep Ones, Dr. Marston?" The only other non-hostile girl in the room, a freckled redhead, asked.

Marston shook his head. "I think you invited the wrong person to your meeting. You need a folklorist or maybe a mystic. Somebody from the Classics Department might be good. I'm just a marine geologist. I study things like underwater volcanism and seismology, and their effect on shore structures and the way bodies of water behave. It's all pretty dry stuff."

Nobody got the joke.

The debate went on, the let's-be-friends-with-the-frogs group versus the it's-a-fight-to-the-finish group. Finally Del Marston looked at his watch and exchanged a signal with Aurelia Blenheim.

"I'm sorry but I have to teach an early class tomorrow," she announced. "You know, we old folks can't stay up as late as we used to, not if we're going to go to work in the morning."

"Thanks for getting us out of there," Marston addressed Aurelia Blenheim. "Another five minutes and I was about ready to take a couple of those young blockheads and knock their skulls together."

Aurelia Blenheim laughed. "They weren't that bad, Delbert. They're young, they can't help that, and a certain amount of foolish passion goes with the territory."

"I suppose so," Marston grumbled. "And a couple of them even seemed moderately intelligent. The only one who seemed sensible was the young sailor—what was his name?"

"Ben Keeler. You weren't just impressed by his hero-worshipping attitude, by any chance."

"Not in the least. Sincere and merited admiration is never misplaced and is always appreciated."

"What a lovely aphorism." Aurelia Blenheim leaned forward and switched on the Cord's radio. The Phaeton had cleared the Bay

Bridge, the structural steel and giant cables of which would have interfered with reception. A late-night broadcaster was rhapsodising about the progress of General Clark's forces in Italy and the successes of Admiral Nimitz's fleet against the Japanese. The announcer must have been local because he went on to talk about Nimitz's pre-war connection with the University of California in Berkeley.

When the news broadcast ended Marston switched to a station playing a Mozart clarinet piece. "You don't really think those kids have something, do you?" he asked his companion.

"I try to keep an open mind."

Marston asked, not for the first time, how his friend had first encountered the New Deep Ones. As usual she referred to a vague relationship between herself and Mrs. Hartley. "We went to school together a million years ago. I was in her wedding. Poor Walter, her husband, was on a sub that went down in the Pacific. She carries on and I try to keep her spirits up."

"And you really do have a class in the morning," Marston commented. He drove through Berkeley, dropped her at her home on Garber Street and returned to his home on Brookside Drive.

He refused further invitations to attend meetings of the New Deep Ones. His feet were bothering him and walking had become difficult and uncomfortable if not downright painful. And he was having problems with his jaw and teeth. He consulted his dentist and his medical doctor alternately. Each reported that he could find no source for Marston's difficulties and referred him to the other.

Marston worked at his office on campus, solving problems brought to him from local naval installations. He reduced his social schedule until he was a near recluse, moving between his bachelor's bungalow and his office on the university campus. He met requests for his company with increasing abrasive refusals until the day he realised he was excluded from faculty cocktail parties and all but the most compulsory of campus events.

The conversation he had in part overheard, in part contributed to, at the meeting of the New Deep Ones preyed on his mind. Several times he sought out Aurelia Blenheim, by now not only his longest-enduring acquaintance but virtually his only friend. Over a cup of coffee or a glass of wine he queried her about Selena Hartley, young Albert's mother. At least Aurelia Blenheim had revealed her friend's first name.

Her maiden name had been Curwen. She was a native San Franciscan, descended from the founder of Curwen Heights. She had married Walter at the height of the tumultuous Roaring Twenties and had struggled at his side through the years of the Depression to preserve their relationship and to keep the old house, built by the original Eben Curwen during the previous century, in the family.

Beyond that, Aurelia Blenheim had no information to share with Delbert Marston.

Naval Intelligence had ferreted out Japanese plans to send submarines against the West Coast of the United States. To Marston this made no sense. Earlier in the war, after the Japanese had decimated the US Pacific Fleet at Pearl Harbor and had conquered the Philippines and Wake Island, it would have made sense. But the Japanese were being forced back by General MacArthur's island-hopping campaign and General LeMay's fire-bombing of the home islands.

An anti-submarine net had been strung across the Golden Gate in 1942, when a direct attack by Admiral Yamamoto's forces seemed imminent. The attack had never come, but the Navy had been spooked by their intelligence and Marston was called on to help design a new and improved underwater defence line. Knowing the Navy, the war would be over before the new defences were built and the defences would be outdated before another war could make them useful, but Marston was not one to shirk his duty.

He spent his days touring the Bay and the Golden Gate in naval motor launches, alternating the excursions with long days at the desk calculator and the drawing board. His nights he spent in his living room, looking out over Brookside Drive, listening to music, and drinking scotch whiskey. It was almost impossible to find good single malt nowadays, far more difficult than it had been during the laughably ineffective Prohibition of Marston's youth. He shuddered at the thought of having to switch to blended swill.

As walking became increasingly painful he spent more hours in the University pool. Even sitting in an easy chair or lying in bed he had to deal with discomfort, and the ongoing changes in his jaw and teeth made eating a nasty chore. He was losing his teeth one by one, and new ones were emerging in their place. He'd heard of people getting a third set of teeth, it was a rare but not-unknown phenomenon. His own new teeth were triangular in shape and razor-sharp. Only when he had slipped into the waters of the pool did the pain in his extremities ease, and even his mouth felt less discomfort.

Yet he was drawing unwelcome glances in the changing area at the pool. He altered his routine, suiting up at home and wearing baggy clothing over his trunks until he reached the locker room. There he would doff his outer costume and plunge into the water, staying beneath the surface as long as he could before rising for air. As time passed he found himself able to stay under for longer periods. He ascribed this to the practice of almost daily swims.

One day he stayed under for a period that must have set his personal record. When he surfaced he was the centre of attention. One of the other swimmers muttered, "Say, you must have been down there for five or six minutes. How do you do that?"

Marston growled an answer, then hastened to his locker, pulled his baggy clothing on over his wet body and dripping suit, and headed for home.

That night he drove to the Berkeley Marina. He parked his Cord, looked around and ascertained that he was alone. He walked to the water's edge, disrobed, and slipped into the Bay. The water was icy but somehow it eased the now-constant ache in his legs and feet. His hands, too, seemed to be changing their shape in some small, subtle way. They were uncomfortable, as well. He wondered if he was developing arthritis.

He swam out toward Angel Island. He had no way of knowing just how far he had gone or how long he had remained submerged, but he felt that it must have been fifteen or twenty minutes. He broke surface and realised that he was not out of breath. In fact, he had to force himself to inhale the fog-drenched night air. His neck itched and he rubbed it with his hands, feeling horizontal ridges of muscle that he had never noticed before.

He looked around, searching for landmarks, but the enforced

wartime blackout precluded the use of bright lights in the cities that lined San Francisco Bay. He made out the silhouette of Bay Bridge against the sky, then that of the Golden Gate Bridge. He turned in the water, recognising the forbidding fortifications of Alcatraz. Without inhaling again he ducked beneath the surface and swam back toward the Berkeley shoreline. In time he waded from the cold, brackish waters of the Bay. By contrast, the night air felt warm against his body. He shook like a dog to rid himself of water, pulled on his clothing, and drove home.

In the Brookside Drive cottage he drew a polished captain's chair to an open window. Through the window he could hear the soft gurgle of the nearby stream that gave the thoroughfare its name. Odd, Marston thought, that he had never noticed this before. The sound brought with it a melancholy, pleasant feeling. He thought of putting a record on the turntable, had even selected Handel's 'Music for the Royal Fireworks', and pouring himself a scotch while he listened to the recording, but instead brought a pillow from his bedroom and placed it on the living room carpet.

He lay down in darkness and closed his eyes, letting the sound of the stream fill his consciousness. He fell asleep and dreamed of dark waters, strange creatures and ancient cities beneath the sea. He awoke the following morning and staggered to the mirror in his bedroom. He brushed water from his hair.

By the end of May, in normal times, the university's spring semester would have ended and the students departed, leaving Berkeley a quiet suburb of Oakland instead of the bustling community of scholars it became during the academic year. But in wartime the military had set up accelerated programs for the education of junior officers, and the University of California was on a year-round schedule.

Delbert Marston's assignments from his naval superiors had changed as well. The computations and design of the anti-submarine defences were completed and construction was well under way. The data provided to Marston now was peculiar and the requested analytical reports were more peculiar than ever. In Europe the long-anticipated cross-channel invasion had taken place and Allied forces were pushing the *Wehrmacht* back toward Germany. In the Pacific Japanese troops were resisting with fanatical dedication, whole units dying to the last soldier rather than raise the flag of surrender.

But as the Office of War Information reminded the American public, the conflict was far from over. The Germans had developed flying bombs and rocket weapons and were using them against Allied forces in France and Belgium, and sending them to wreak havoc in England. If they could develop longer-range models, even the US would be in danger. A Nazi super-scientist named Heisenberg was rumoured to be developing a weapon of unprecedented power that could be delivered to New York by a jet-propelled flying wing bomber. The whole thing seemed like a scenario from a Fritz Lang movie.

Still, Marston made his way to his office each morning, labouring on feet that sent agony lancing up his increasingly deformed legs. Once at work he found it hard even to hold a pencil, relying on an assistant to take dictation rather than try to write up his own notes. He seldom spoke with anyone save his naval superiors and assistants.

His only pleasures were his solitary, nocturnal excursions beneath the surface of the Bay. He no longer bothered with the fiction of breathing air once he entered the Bay, relying on water inhaled through his now wide mouth and expelled through the gill slits in his neck once his body had extracted its oxygen content.

He saw shapes beneath the water now, sometimes dark, sometimes sickly luminescent. At first he avoided them, then he began to pursue them. He couldn't make out their appearance well, either, although as time passed he began to develop more acute vision in the dark medium. From time to time one of the shapes would swim toward him, then flash aside when he reached out to touch it.

One night he found one of the creatures drifting aimlessly a few feet beneath the surface. He swam to it and saw that it was more or less human in outline but clearly not human. He reached for it and it did not flash away. Once he grasped it he realised that it was dead, its flesh horribly torn as if it had been caught in the propeller of a passing ship. Even as he studied the strange cadaver two more shapes flashed into sight and snatched it from his grasp, moving first out of his reach and then out of his sight.

But he had touched the remains. The flesh was white and stringy, the skin as smooth and slick as that of a giant frog.

Despite the changes he was undergoing he managed to maintain the pretence of normality, taking his meals, filling his Cord Phaeton with precious, rationed gasoline, sending his laundry out to be done, keeping his modest lodgings in order.

Late one Saturday afternoon he nearly collided with Aurelia Blenheim while pushing a shopping cart in the aisle of the grocery store nearest his home. He was shocked at her haggard appearance. How long had it been since their last meeting? How could she have aged so badly? He thought of his own changed appearance and wondered if he looked as worrisome to Aurelia as she to him.

The expression on Aurelia Blenheim's face showed shock and deep concern. "Delbert," the elderly woman exclaimed, "are you all right?"

"Of course I am."

"But you look so—are you certain?"

"Yes," he growled. He should have turned and left the store the instant he spotted Blenheim, but he had failed to act and now he was caught. "I'm just a little tired," he explained. "Very tired, in fact. The war. So much work."

"I'm coming to your house," Blenheim asserted. "I'm going to make dinner for you. You're not taking care of yourself. You're headed for the hospital if you don't get yourself together. You should be ashamed!"

When they reached Marston's cottage he turned his key in the door lock and stood aside to let Aurelia Blenheim enter first. Marston carried the bag of groceries Blenheim had helped him select. She had even loaned him a few ration stamps and tokens to complete his purchase.

The selection of foodstuffs was far more extensive than the Spartan diet Marston had been living on in recent months. In fact he occasionally supplemented his nourishment during his nocturnal swims in the Bay. That body was densely populated with marine species that throve in its cold, brackish waters. Marston became ravenous when he came upon the abalone, eels, crabs, clams and small octopods that lurked in the silted seabed. When he came upon one he would devour it raw, fresh, and sometimes living. His new teeth could pierce the shell of a living crab as if it were paper.

Just inside the doorway Aurelia Blenheim bent over and picked up a buff-coloured envelope. "Here's a telegram for you, Delbert."

He took the envelope from her and opened it. The message was typed in capital letters on strips of buff paper and glued to the message form. The telegram came from a Captain Kinne, commanding officer of the Naval Weapons Station at Port Chicago, a village on the shore of Suisun Bay, an extension of San Francisco Bay fed by the Sacramento River.

The message itself was terse. It directed Marston to report to the commanding officer's headquarters first thing Monday morning. In traditional naval fashion Marston was told to show up at or about 06:00 hours, on or about July 3, 1944. Marston had never heard of anyone in the Navy arriving after the designated time and date with the excuse that he had arrived "about" the indicated time.

Aurelia Blenheim steered Marston into an easy chair and carried the bag of groceries into his kitchen. She had visited the Brookside Drive cottage before, although months had passed since her last visit. Marston put some light music on the turntable, an RCA Red Seal twelve-inch recording of 'Vltava' by the tragic Bohemian madman Bedrich Smetana.

With astonishing speed Blenheim produced a tempting bouillabaisse. The odour coming from the kitchen was mouth-watering and the flavour of the marine stew proved delicious. The only problem, for Marston, was that everything seemed overdone. He would have preferred to consume the aquatic creatures uncooked.

After dinner they relaxed in Marston's living room with glasses of pre-war brandy. Jokingly, Aurelia Blenheim asked why Marston's mother hadn't taught him to take better care of himself. When he reacted to the question with frowning silence the older woman set down her glass and took his free hand between both of hers. "I'm sorry. I didn't mean to upset you."

Marston drew away. Of late his arthritis had become worse. The last joints of his fingers and toes had curled downwards and his finger- and toenails seemed to be turning into claws. He worked to keep them trimmed but they grew back rapidly. The small triangles of flesh between the bases of his digits were growing, also, a change that proved helpful in water but embarrassing in public.

Desperate to draw attention away from his increasing physical abnormalities, Marston said, "No, I'm afraid she didn't."

Blenheim frowned, "Who didn't what?"

"My mother. She never taught me to take care of myself. She never taught me anything. I never knew her. My father told me that she loved to swim. They lived in Chicago and she would swim in Lake Michigan all year round. She joined a group, they called themselves the Polar Bear Club, and they would plunge into the lake every New Year's Day, no matter how cold it was, even if it was snowing. But that was just a stunt. They used to get their picture in the Chicago *Times* and the *Tribune* and the *Sun*. But Mother took it all very seriously. The photographers loved her, she was the only female Polar Bear."

He took a deep draught of golden liqueur.

"She was an immigrant," he resumed. "I never knew where she was born. Father just said it was a cold country. I was born on December 25th, you know," he changed the subject. "I was a Christmas baby." He said it with bitterness. "Father brought Mother and me home from the hospital on New Year's Eve. The next day Mother insisted on her annual plunge with the other Polar Bears. They used to run out into the lake, throw themselves into the surf, frisk for a few minutes and then come running back out of the water. But Mother swam out. Snow was falling, Father told me, and visibility was poor. Mother just swam out into the lake. They sent search parties after her but they never found her."

"I'm so sorry," Aurelia Blenheim said. She started again to reach for his hand, then drew back, avoiding a repetition of his previous withdrawal. After a moment she said, "Did your father ever re-marry?"

Marston shook his head. "He raised me alone, as best he could, until he was gunned down when I was six. I had no other relatives and I wound up bouncing from one orphanage to another until I went out on my own."

"But you've made such a success of yourself, Delbert. I never knew about your childhood. How sad. But look at you now, a tenured professor, a respected member of the community. I'm so proud of you, and you should be proud of yourself."

She insisted on clearing the dishes and cleaning up Marston's kitchen. She returned to the living room and said, "You know I live nearby. I'll just walk home, it's such a warm evening. Please promise me you'll take better care of yourself. And let me know how things work out at Port Chicago. As much as the Navy lets you tell me, of course."

He stood on his lawn and watched until she disappeared. He returned to his house and filled another snifter of brandy, then sipped until it was gone. The summer evening was long and he was in agony by the time full darkness descended. Then he left the house and drove to the marina. He parked, disrobed at the water's edge and slipped into the Bay.

Monday morning he rose early and drove to Port Chicago. The naval base consisted mainly of warehouses and barracks. A railroad spur ran onto a pier that extended into the Bay. Even at this early hour he could see crews of coloured stevedores in Navy fatigues working to move munitions from railroad cars to the hold of a ship moored to the side of the pier. The stevedores were supervised by white men in officers' uniforms.

A guard had demanded to see Marston's identification and the telegram summoning him to the base. Once satisfied, the guard directed Marston to the headquarters building, a wood-frame structure badly in need of fresh paint. Once inside he was escorted by a smartly uniformed WAVE into the commander's office.

Captain Kinne looked as if he had stepped out of bandbox. Every crease in his uniform was knife-sharp, every button glistened.

Marston of course wore civilian garb, the academic uniform of tweed jacket, flannel slacks and button-down shirt. He had replaced his customary striped necktie with a scarf that concealed his gill-slits and added a pair of oversized dark glasses. He stood in front of

Captain Kinne's desk wondering whether he was expected to salute or shake hands. The WAVE introduced him and Kinne looked up at him. "You're Marston, eh?"

He said, "I am."

"All right, I just wanted to get a look at you. Tell a lot about a man with one look. You'll do. What happened to your hands, Marston? Some kind of tropical disease? Jungle rot?"

Marston started to answer but Kinne went on.

"Jaspers," he addressed the WAVE, "take Mr. Marston down the hall. Give him to Keeler." He turned back to Marston and nodded curtly. "Go with Jaspers. Keeler will tell you what to do. Thanks for coming."

The WAVE, obviously Jaspers, led Marston to another office. She halted and knocked at the door, then turned the knob and opened the door a few inches. "Mr. Marston is here, sir."

She gestured and Marston stepped past her into the office. He heard Jaspers close the door behind him. He found himself in a smaller office now, surrounded by charts and manuals. The man who stood up to greet him wore a set of summer khakis with the twin tracks of a Navy lieutenant on the collar.

"A real pleasure to see you again, Dr. Marston. After that little party in Curwen Heights I was afraid you wouldn't want anything to do with us."

"Ben Keeler?" Marston said. "You've certainly risen fast. You were a junior petty officer the last time I saw you."

Keeler grinned. "Petty Officer Third Ben Keeler, Lieutenant Benjamin Keeler, same fellow. ONI put me in that EM's uniform to check out the New Deep Ones Society. They were pretty worried at one point, those kids were getting too close to the truth and the Naval Intelligence wanted them steered off. That was my job. I still attend their meetings, by the way. If you ever want to come by again, I'd love some moral support. Just don't blow my cover."

"All right," Marston smiled. "I wouldn't want to get you in trouble with Naval Intelligence."

"And they're just a bunch of harmless eccentrics, you know," Keeler added. He walked around the desk and put his arm on Marston's shoulders. "Take a walk with me, Dr. Marston. There are some things you need to see, and then some questions I'll want to ask you."

Marston acceded, determined not to show the pain that he knew he was in for. At Keeler's side he made his way along the pier. A freighter stood in the middle of Suisun Bay, black smoke pouring from its stacks. It would clear the Golden Gate before noon, Marston knew, *en route* to the soldiers and marines fighting the Japanese in the Pacific. An empty ship had already taken the place of the freighter on one side of the pier, while another, opposite it, received pallets and crates of munitions.

As they moved past work gangs Keeler took salutes from ensigns and petty officers supervising the stevedores. The latter continued to work as Marston and Keeler passed.

At the end of the pier they halted. A breeze had kicked up and the surface of Suisun Bay had turned choppy.

Marston gestured back toward the work gangs they had passed. "All of the stevedores are Negroes, all of the officers are white," he commented. The question was implicit.

"That's Navy policy," Keeler said. "Not very long ago the Navy was trying to get rid of all its Negroes, even though they were just messmen and laundry workers. Filipinos make better workers. But there's too much pressure from Washington, finally the service gave in. And these coloured stevedores are pretty good, as long as you keep a close eye on them."

They turned to face the buildings of Port Chicago. "What we're concerned about, Del, is a very special cargo that we're going to ship out this month."

Marston nodded, then waited for Keeler to continue.

"It's a very special bomb. It's coming in by train next week, and Captain Kinne wanted to get your help in handling it."

Marston shook his head. "What do I know about bombs?"

"Oh, we have plenty of people who know about bombs," Keeler grinned. "We need somebody who knows hydrology and submarine geology to keep this baby safe."

"What is it, something bigger than the ones LeMay is dropping on Japan? The closer we get to the home islands, the easier it's' going to be to hit 'em."

"No," Keeeler shook his head. "This is something different. Look, everybody knows that we're close to finishing off the European war. Ike took a big risk with the Normandy landings but that was a big success and Patton and Montgomery are rolling through France. Italy's out of the game. And the Russians are closing in on the Nazis from the East. It's just a matter of time now."

"And in the Pacific, too, don't you agree, Benjamin?"

"But we're taking terrible losses. The President is up for re-election this November and those casualties are going to hurt him. He's put pressure on the War Department and the Navy Department to give him this bigger, better bomb. We figure once we drop a couple of these babies on Japan, maybe one on Tokyo and one on Kobe, even the fanatical Nips will cave in. Washington doesn't want to have to invade the home islands, don't you see. That's what this is all about, Del."

There was a moment of silence as a zephyr swept in from the Bay, bringing the smell of brine and brackish waters with it. Then the wind shifted and the clatter of tools, the sound of voices, the roar of donkey engines came to them from the ships and the railroad cars.

"And there's another thing," Keeler added. "You know Uncle Sam didn't much care for the Bolshies when they first took over Russia twenty-five years ago. President Wilson even sent some troops over there. The government doesn't like to talk about that any more now that Joe Stalin is our buddy but you know we took sides in their civil war and we picked a loser."

"That was a long time ago," Marston put in.

The combination of the choppy Bay and the increasingly brisk breeze whipped up a spray of salt-flavoured water that pelted onto the pier and onto Keeler and Marston. Keeler pulled a bandanna from his uniform trousers pocket and wiped his face, frowning. Marston licked his lips. He felt hugely refreshed.

"The US wouldn't even recognise the new government in Russia until Roosevelt came in, and there are still a lot of powerful men in Washington who don't trust Stalin and his gang. They want to get this new bomb and use it before the war is over as a warning to the Reds not to get too big for their britches."

He hooked his arm through Marston's and the two men strolled back along the pier, returning finally to Keeler's office. Keeler said, "Will you get to work on this, Del? Captain Kinne has already worked it out with his counterparts, you'll be excused from your other duties until the special bomb is safely out on the ocean, on its way to a bomber base in the islands. We need your analysis and your recommendations about the seabed and waters from here to the Farralons. And we need your report before that ship moves. The bomb is coming in next week, and we need to get it out of here on the *Quinalt Victory*. Our Negroes will be working on the *Bryan* most of the time, that will serve as cover for the bomb going out on the *Quinalt*."

Keeler opened a safe and extracted a pass for Marston. "This will get you anywhere on the base," he said. "Guard it, Del, it could be dangerous if it got away from you."

Marston accepted the pass, slipped it into his pocket and left.

He spent the next few days alternating between Port Chicago and the University campus in Berkeley, studying the physical layout at Suisun Bay and existing charts and studies of the area. He could hardly hold himself back from examining the seabed in person, but he resisted the temptation until he felt ready.

Then he drove from Berkeley to Port Chicago after dark, parked the Cord, and walked out to the pier. The work here went on around the clock, seven days a week. There was no way he could use the pier without being observed, so he informed the young officer supervising the loading work of his intentions.

At the end of the pier he left his clothing, climbed down a ladder, and slipped into the water.

The Bay water was cold and dark and as it welcomed him he felt the aches leave his body and limbs. He had always been a strong swimmer; now, the webbing between his fingers and between his toes turned him into a virtual amphibian. His eyes, too, had developed a sensitivity that permitted him to manoeuvre in the dark, brackish water.

He spotted a huge dark-green crab scuttling toward a large rock on the seabed. The creature didn't have a chance. Marston's new, powerful jaw and strong, triangular teeth crunched through its shell. The living meat was sweet and the juices of the crab were more delicious than the finest liquor.

Marston saw human-like forms swimming nearby and pursued them. Ever since his encounter with the dead creature he had wondered about these beings. They might be a species of giant batrachian hitherto unknown to science, far larger than any recorded frog or toad; perhaps they were survivors of a species of amphibian that had evolved aeons ago only to disappear from most of the world.

He swam after them and they permitted him to approach them but not to establish direct contact. They swam with the current created by the waters of the Sacramento River as it emptied into Suisun Bay. They looked back from time to time as if to encourage Marston to follow them, but the speed and stamina with which they swam far exceeded even his enhanced abilities.

Finally he gave up and swam back toward the loading pier and the two ships at Port Chicago.

He climbed the ladder, then drew himself onto the pier. The young ensign he had spoken with earlier greeted him with a shake of his head. "I was getting pretty worried," the ensign said. "Do you know how long you were gone, sir? And do you realise how cold the Bay is, and how tricky the currents can be?"

Marston didn't feel like talking with this youngster but he managed a few polite words. Yes, he knew exactly what he was doing, he had never been in danger, there was nothing to worry about but he appreciated the ensign's concern.

During the brief conversation he had been pulling his clothing back on. He had purchased new shoes, as wide as he could find, to accommodate his newly altered feet. Even so, it was fiercely painful to force his feet into them.

He repeated his activities each night. The underwater creatures gradually grew accustomed to him, permitting him to approach ever more closely, permitting him to accompany them farther and farther from Port Chicago. It was clear to Marston that they communicated with one another, mainly by means of subtle gestures made with their broad, webbed, clawed hands. Marston inferred that they had a language as sophisticated and complex as any spoken by land-dwellers.

Now that he was affiliated with the Port Chicago base Marston had discontinued all contacts with his former associates in Berkeley. He did not worry about running into Aurelia Blenheim at the grocery as he now relied entirely on a diet of creatures he encountered during his nocturnal explorations of the Bay's waters.

He maintained a relationship with Lieutenant Keeler and though him with Captain Kinne, furnishing reports and recommendations as required of him. He resented every meeting he had to attend, every conversation he had to conduct; in fact, he found himself living for his submarine excursions and suffering through each hour he spent walking on land, breathing with his gradually atrophying lungs instead of his gills.

On Friday, July 14, Keeler demanded that Marston attend a meeting with Captain Kinne. Also present were two high-ranking officers, one from the Navy and the other from the Army, the latter with Army Air Force insignia on his uniform blouse, and the commanders of the Negro stevedoring gangs.

Captain Kinne's WAVE secretary, Jaspers, ushered Marston into the commanding officer's area. When the meeting participants were assembled they were joined by a pair of armed shore patrolmen and the doors were securely locked.

"The bomb will arrive in forty-eight hours," the Army officer announced. A major general's paired silver stars glittered on his uniform shoulders. "We will deliver it to the loading pier, then we need a sign-off from the Navy and our job is finished."

"And ours begins," the naval officer took over. His uniform sleeves bore the broad gold stripes of a rear admiral. "Captain Kinne, are your men ready to get the bomb stowed in *Quinalt Victory* Monday evening? ONI insists that we do the loading at night, but it must be finished in time to catch the late tide out of the Golden Gate." The admiral cast a sharp look at Marston. "Dr. Marston has provided all the information we'll need to get *Quinalt Victory* safely out of the Bay and on her way by midnight?"

The utterance was worded as a statement but spoken as a question.

"We have everything, sir," Keeler furnished.

"All right. Let's go over the complete plan again," The admiral growled. "There must be no slip-ups, I can't emphasise that too much."

They spent the rest of the day going over the details of unloading the special bomb from its railroad car and loading it into the hold of the *Quinalt Victory* without a hitch. A squad of white-jacketed messmen served coffee and rolls at mid-morning and a full meal at noon. No one left the meeting for any reason. Marston was able to pass up the coffee and rolls but by lunchtime he was forced to consume a few sips of beverage and half a sandwich. This disgusted him.

When the meeting ended he drove into Port Chicago. He had seen the town fleetingly each day but today for the first time he parked his Cord and walked through the streets. He found a motion picture theatre and purchased a ticket. They were running a long program, the dramatic film *Lifeboat* with Tallulah Bankhead and Canada Lee, the lightweight *Bathing Beauty* with Esther Williams, a newsreel and a chapter of "Crash" Corrigan's old serial, *Undersea Kingdom*.

Once inside he settled into a seat and unlaced his shoes, finding a modicum of relief for his aching feet. He leaned back and studied the neon-ringed clock mounted high on one wall of the auditorium. Most of the patrons were servicemen in uniform, whiling away their off-duty hours. None of them were coloured, of course. Negroes were excluded from the theatre and from the town's plain restaurants. They had to find their own entertainment, or make it.

Marston ignored the images on the screen and closed his eyes. Images of undersea life swam through his mind, the peace and serenity of the submarine world contrasting with the pain and violence that dominated the world of the land-dwellers.

After a while he opened his eyes and glanced at the illuminated clock-face. Even in the long July evening, darkness would have fallen by now.

He drove back to the naval base, showed his pass to the gate-guard, and parked as near to the water's edge as he could. He carefully locked the Cord and walked to the base of the pier. A special guard had been placed there, and even Marston's special pass could not gain him access to the pier.

Instead he walked back to his car, unlocked the door and climbed inside. He disrobed, left the car again, and walked undiscovered to the edge of the Bay. He slipped into the Bay and swam away from the shore.

He made his way to the cold, flowing water that he knew came from the Sacramento River. The river water had less flavour than the Bay water. With a start Marston realised that he had never experienced the richness of the Pacific. He turned to swim with the current. His anticipation of the new experience filled him with an almost sexual excitement.

When he reached the submarine net at the mouth of San Francisco Bay he paused briefly, then pulled himself through it into the ocean. He was terrified but soon calmed himself. He had undergone a rite of passage, he felt, had experienced a sea change. He would explore farther in later days, he decided, but for now he felt emotionally drained and physically exhausted.

He turned and began the long swim back to Suisun Bay.

He had seen fewer of the human-like creatures than usual on this night, but as he approached Port Chicago they became more numerous. He was beginning to learn their language and felt eager to converse with them, find out who or what they were, but they kept their distance from him this night, and instead of joining them he continued on his solitary way.

In time he recognised the submerged landmarks that told him he was at his destination. He had been swimming along the sea bottom, insulated by fathoms of brackish water from the world of men, immune from the noisome companionship of air breathers and land dwellers. He rose slowly toward the top of the water. He was shocked as he breached to realise that he had spent the entire night under water. The brilliant sun now blasted down from a bright blue sky.

He made his way to his Cord, drove home and slept around the clock. He awoke Sunday morning and spent the day in seclusion, sustaining himself with alcohol and music. After dark he made his way to the nearby stream and stood in it, letting its waters soothe his feet. He went home and slept, dreaming once more of an undersea city, and rose late on Monday. He hadn't realised how far he had swum on Friday night, or how exhausted the effort had left him. Still, the experience had been an exhilarating one and he looked forward to spending even more time beneath the surface, to travelling farther into the ocean.

When he reached Port Chicago on Monday the transfer of the bomb from railroad freight car to the hold of *Quinalt Victory* was well under way. Marston's expertise had been of immense value, he would be told. He encountered Captain Kinne himself on the pier and the usually stern Kinne recognised him and thanked him for his assistance.

Powerful electric vapour-lights had been rigged to illuminate the operation once the sun had set and their peculiar glare gave the faces of the men on the pier, both white and coloured, a ghostly look.

Marston walked to the end of the pier. When he turned back toward the centre of activity he saw that all eyes were fixed on the delicate work at the *Quinalt Victory*. He checked his wristwatch and saw that it was ten o'clock. Bright moonlight was reflected off the surface of the Bay.

Instead of climbing down the ladder to the water's surface, Marston left his clothing in its usual neat pile, stood on the edge of the pier, and dived into the Bay. He swam to the seabed, taking delicious water in and passing it through his gills, letting his eyes grow accustomed to the faint phosphorescence that provided illumination in this world.

He turned to observe the hull of the *Quinalt Victory*. He was astonished at the number of human-like forms moving around the ship, gesturing meaningfully to one another, attaching something, something, to the metal hull of the *Quinalt Victory*.

Marston swam toward the ship, curious as to what the creatures were doing. This was the first time he had seen them using anything that looked like machinery. As he drew closer several of the creatures turned and swam toward him. As they approached he realised that they were like him in every way. The wide mouth and triangular teeth, the splayed limbs, the webbed hands and feet, the hooked claws, the oversized eyes and flattened noses.

How had he managed to pass among men until now? How had his alienness gone undetected? The scarf and dark glasses had helped but surely he would be caught out soon if he tried to continue his masquerade as human. He raised a hand and gestured, showing these aquatic beings that he was one of them, telling them in their own language, a language which he was just beginning to comprehend, that he was not a human, not a land-dweller.

He was not the enemy.

He was shocked by a brilliant flash from the *Quinalt Victory,* a glare that seemed as bright as the sun. Marston felt a shock wave, felt its unimaginable, crushing pressure as it reached him. Then, even before he could react, there was a second flash, this one brighter than a thousand suns, and a second shock wave infinitely greater than the first. But he felt it for only the most fleeting of moments, and then he felt nothing more.

HISTORIC NOTE

At 10:20 p.m., Monday, July 17, 1944, a huge explosion occurred at Port Chicago, California. Two ships were moored at the loading pier of the naval station there. The *E.A.Bryan* was fully loaded and ready to leave for the Pacific theatre of operations with a huge cargo of high explosives and military equipment. The *Quinalt Victory*, a brand-new vessel built at the Kaiser Shipyard in nearby Richmond, California, was preparing to take on its own cargo.

Some 320 individuals were killed in the explosion, most of them African-American stevedores. An additional 400 persons were injured. A common form of injury was blindness caused by flying splinters of window-glass in naval barracks. The main explosion was preceded by a rumble or smaller explosion, reports differing, which drew many off-duty stevedores to the windows to see what had caused the sound.

The brilliant flash, the roar of the explosion, and the shaking of the earth that resulted, were seen, heard, and felt as far away as the cities of Berkeley, Oakland, and San Francisco.

The *Bryan*, the *Quinalt Victory*, the loading pier, the railroad spur running along the pier, and the ammunition train that was parked on the pier at the time, were all totally destroyed. The town of Port Chicago was obliterated and a visitor to its site today will find only a few forlorn street markers to show where once a community thrived.

While official statements about the disaster aver only to the high explosives which had been loaded in the *E.A.Bryan*, critics in later years suggested that the explosion was nuclear in nature. In the summer of 1944 the atomic bomb was top secret and the very existence of the Manhattan Project was shrouded in layers of security. But once the bomb was dropped on Hiroshima and Nagasaki, speculation began that more than dynamite had been involved in the Port Chicago disaster.

If the Port Chicago explosion was indeed nuclear in nature, further speculation is divided between those who believe the explosion was accidental in origin, or was in fact a test by the United States government to measure the effects of a nuclear bomb. Certainly the weapons base at Port Chicago would have made a fine test subject, with ships, a railroad spur, temporary and permanent buildings, and many hundreds of expendable human subjects.

Perhaps the Port Chicago explosion was a nuclear accident? If so, it represented a major setback to the American nuclear weapons project. The successful Alamogordo test did not take place until July 16, 1945, one day short of a year after the Port Chicago explosion. Nuclear weapons were exploded in the air over Hiroshima and Nagasaki the following month, bringing about the end of the Second World War and providing an object lesson for Josef Stalin.

Where the Port Chicago naval weapons depot once stood, there is now the Concord Naval Weapons Station, a major loading area for the United States Pacific Fleet. The storage of nuclear weapons in barrow-like bunkers at the naval weapons station, while not officially acknowledged by the US government, is one of the most ill-kept secrets of our era.

VOICES IN THE WATER

by BASIL COPPER

I

I
T WAS LATE February when Roberts bought the mill. He was a successful artist and had long been trying to get out of London. The mill was a big place and one advantage was that it had already been partly converted into living accommodation. A lot more needed to be done in the way of renovation, but the price was right and Roberts snapped it up.

Another motivation was that his great friend Kent, an author, lived only a mile or so away. In earlier years Roberts had illustrated a number of Kent's books and a lasting friendship had been formed during that period.

The estate agent, Cedric Smithson, a big, bluff man with an iron-grey moustache, who had first taken Roberts on a guided tour, was enthusiastic about the possibilities. It was not just the usual estate agent's purchasing ploy, so Roberts was quick to catch the other's reference points. It was also fortunate that central heating had already been installed throughout. Roberts had gathered that the previous owner had intended to make the mill his permanent residence, but his wife had left him for another man, and in the face of this personal disaster he had lost all heart in the project and had returned to London.

Another attraction for Roberts, apart from the size of the place, which would easily lend itself to further accommodation for friends as well as a large studio and another area which would provide an elegant gallery for viewing sessions for his wealthy clients, was the enormous north-facing window in the area he intended to create his studio. All in all, the facilities already existing would provide a cosy home during the bitter winters Sussex sometimes endured.

So the artist had speedily summoned his wife from their London flat and to his relief she also had become enthusiastic about the place. With its enormous beams and four-inch thick wooden floors it would become a showplace once time and money had been expended on its refurbishment.

Through the good offices of Smithson, Roberts engaged some excellent local craftsmen and stayed on to supervise the work which occupied several months, so that it was not until early July that the couple were able to take up permanent occupation.

Another major benefit for Roberts was that a large stream ran beneath the building, as might be expected as it had been a working mill until about thirty years previously. The stream—though it was more a small river—ran foaming between the massive piles and from a vantage point, obtained via an enormous wooden hatch immediately above the race, he could savour the roar and power of the clear white water which swirled through beneath.

He was told by Smithson that the enormous mill-wheel, which was still in situation, had been rendered inoperable for years and that gratings had been installed to prevent any driftwood or foliage that might come down the stream from causing any damage beneath the building.

Once the hatch was raised and Roberts was able to look down on his first visit to the place, he was impressed with the roar of the water and the great power it would have exerted on the machinery in its heyday. But once the hatch was closed the movement of the water was muffled and, in any case, the living quarters were far above so that the surge of the stream was quite unobtrusive.

During the early days of Roberts' ownership, his wife, Gilda, who acted as his secretary and agent, stayed in London to supervise the business side of the artist's work—keeping in touch with clients in New York, Paris and Amsterdam, for her husband was now becoming a sought-after and celebrated painter, after long years of struggle and relative penury.

At this time Roberts had made his studio in the largest lower room of the mill and installed himself in a living room above, where Kent often visited him for drinks and a chat. Or, as the weather got better, the pair walked the short distance to the local pub, The Three Horseshoes, for white wine and the occasional meal. Kent, a strongly built man with an open countenance and black, curly hair, was almost as enthusiastic as Roberts about the new project and gave his friend valuable advice on the conversion and guided him in the direction of reliable specialist craftsmen.

One evening, when the weather was a little warmer and Roberts had finished work for the day on his latest commission, the two men sat in the vast living room with its massive beams and huge stone fireplace.

Roberts suddenly said, "Do you remember that canvas I did some years ago—the one I called 'Faces in the Fire'?"

Kent, who wore grey slacks and a tweed hacking jacket, was slumped with his legs over the huge arms of the chair opposite. He sat up and wrinkled his brow as he put down his glass on a small table at his side. "You mean the one that was featured in that *Town and Country* magazine? An oil wasn't it? I think those people did a very good colour shot. The publicity couldn't have done you any harm."

Roberts gave a short laugh. "You're right about that. It was a bit of an experiment, but Gilda got me a thousand guineas for that one. A wealthy Dutchman bought it and thought it a bargain at the price. Gilda is a very smart girl when it comes to extolling my wares."

Kent nodded. "She is that. But why do you ask about that work now?"

Roberts was re-filling his glass at a sideboard and didn't answer for a moment. Then he came back to sit facing his friend. "Well, it's more in your line than mine," he began. "You're the one with the fantastic imagination that you put into those novels of yours. I must have caught something of that from you. It was just a study—you know the sort of thing. In winter if you have a fire, you can stare at it and sometimes it seems as if you can detect faces in the flames."

"Oh, that," Kent said. "I quite understand. But I don't know why you're asking…"

Roberts held up his hand to interrupt him. "There's something similar at work in my imagination here," he said. "It's to do with the movement of the water. Oh, not up here, of course, where we can't hear it at all. But when you open the hatch down below, to look at the water, it can be quite fascinating."

Kent shook his head. "I don't get what you're driving at."

"Well, I know it sounds rather silly," Roberts began haltingly. "But it sometimes seems as though I can hear voices in the water."

"Oh, I see," Kent replied. "I've noticed it myself when wandering along the stream in winters past. It can be quite hypnotic. Don't tell me you're going to try to paint something along those lines? Mighty difficult, I should imagine."

Roberts shook his head, smiling. "Just a thought. Have another drink."

And the conversation passed on to other topics.

II

As spring lengthened into summer so did the work on the house progress. Gilda came down from London for several weeks, supervising the delivery of their furniture. She took over one of the top bedrooms for her office, where telephone, word processor and fax machines were installed. There was a magnificent view of the village from there and the silver thread of the stream making its way down to the building, which they had decided to call The Mill House. Furthermore, she had obtained a very good price for their London flat, with the result that Roberts, perhaps for the first time in his life, was becoming quite an affluent person. Of course he realised it was all down to Gilda, for without her he would never have received such sums for his artwork.

The couple had become quite friendly with the Smithsons also, and on one memorable evening they came to the house together with Kent and his fiancée, and they had a great housewarming party which went on until 3:00 a.m.

Roberts was spending more time in the studio down below and the faint, though constant, fret of the water made a soothing background to his painstaking and meticulous draughtsmanship. They had had a telephone installed there, and Gilda would call him at 12:30 p.m. each day and he would ascend to the main house for pre-lunch drinks, and after the meal they would wander along the stream for an hour or so before Roberts resumed his work.

By this time they had a number of friends in the village, most of whom were extremely pleased at the renovation work, as they felt the mill in its new guise greatly enhanced the neighbourhood. Workmen were still putting finishing touches to certain rooms in the house, and the quiet tapping as they went about their business made a pleasing background to Roberts' thoughts. His latest canvas was coming along well. An international financier had given him half-a-dozen preliminary sittings and now he was finishing off the portrait from photographs.

He had promised Gilda they would have a break in the autumn, when he had finished his current commissions; perhaps to Venice, where she had never been, but it all depended on his workload, which was growing year by year, thanks to her expert business training.

Kent came round to view progress shortly before the work on the building was concluded. He followed his host from room to room, entirely concurring with his friend's enthusiasm.

"You certainly got a bargain here," Kent said when the tour was over and they were settled in the huge living room. But he noticed, as he spoke, that a shadow seemed to pass across Roberts' face and he realised that the artist was extremely tired.

Gilda was away again, doing a tour of major galleries, carrying with her colour slides of Roberts' latest works, and he sensed that his friend had been working too hard. He caught the glance the other gave him. "Been overdoing it?" he said. "Not a sensible thing…"

Roberts gave a light laugh, which didn't deceive his friend. "Not really. It's just the long hours in the studio standing at the easel. It's very tiring work, you know. Not like writers. Sitting on a soft cushion all day dreaming up impossible plots."

Kent returned his smile. "There's a little bit more to it than that," he said good-naturedly.

"Of course, old chap. You know I was only joking. Stay to dinner. A nice lady comes in from the village when Gilda's away."

After the meal the two men sat smoking and talking in the great room that Roberts' craftsmen had created from what had been two smaller chambers which had been roughly partitioned for some commercial purpose by a previous owner when the place had been a working mill. Apparently the building had been constructed as far back as the sixteenth century, and a vast beam which ran across the whole fireplace wall carried the roughly carved date by some long dead carpenter: 1545.

When Kent's pipe had been drawn to his satisfaction and the whisky glasses had been filled, the two men were more relaxed and forthcoming than when Mrs Summers, who acted as the artist's housekeeper, had supervised the meal.

"How long did you say?" Kent asked.

He was referring to the final stages of renovation of the mill. There were various finishing touches that would be carried out by specialist craftsmen, such as wrought ironwork and light fittings in period with the age of the house.

Roberts sat back in his big carved oak chair with a satisfied expression on his face. "About three months should see it through," he said. "All in all there have been few problems. Far less than I had imagined."

"I know it's a delicate matter," his friend said diffidently. "You mentioned it before, but has the cost over-run...?"

Roberts shook his head. "Most remarkable, really. Nowhere near as much as I had anticipated. More than covered by the income generated by Gilda on her travels around Europe and the States.

"That's good to hear," Kent replied. "I'm glad I steered you toward the purchase. You must be sitting on a small fortune here. I suppose you won't ever think of selling?"

Roberts reached out for his glass. "No. I've discussed it with Gilda. I think we've settled here for life. I can't imagine we would ever find such a place full of history and at such a reasonable price. I can't thank you enough."

"Only too glad to have such a close friend near at hand," Kent said.

This conversation was to come back to haunt him.

III

The author was busy on a new collection of short stories and did not see Roberts again until three weeks later, when they ran into one another in the bar of The Three Horseshoes. Gilda was over for a few days, so it was a pleasant surprise for Kent and they decided to have dinner together at a local restaurant. It was a convivial evening, and when the three left the restaurant Kent had promised to visit the mill the following Monday to see some further improvements. Gilda was off on her travels again before then, so they said goodbye in the car park.

Kent arrived in the afternoon in question in a state of anticipation but, to his surprise, Roberts seemed withdrawn and vague regarding the invitation. He was, however, full of enthusiasm about a new painting he was engaged on, though when Kent questioned him further he remained tight-lipped about its subject and demurring whenever Kent questioned him more closely. But he did promise that he would reveal more about it at a later date. Roberts also gently declined Kent's repeated requests to visit the studio to see the work in progress.

"Later," he said. "It is something completely new for me, and I'm sure it will create a sensation when I first exhibit it."

But after dinner that night, long after Mrs Summers had gone, he unburdened himself of a subject that had obviously been slightly troubling him. It seemed so trivial at first that Kent could not believe it.

"The water?" he said. "I don't understand."

Roberts interrupted him peremptorily. "The mill-race," he said tautly. "It's beginning to get on my nerves."

Kent gave the other a deprecatory smile. "But you can't hear it," he said. "These walls are enormously thick. It's a long way down, and it's only a small stream…"

Roberts cut in abruptly. "I'm talking about the studio. It's just above the stream."

Kent just could not get his friend's drift. "What are you driving at? The floor is made of very thick timbers. The stream runs eight feet underneath. And it's not a very fast-flowing river, if one can call it that. I'm at a loss to know what's troubling you. We're old friends. You can be perfectly frank with me. You were so pleased and happy to have found such a wonderful place…"

Roberts gave him a twisted smile. "I know it sounds idiotic. It's difficult to explain…"

"Try me," Kent insisted.

Roberts gave a hopeless shrug. "It seems to depress," he said. "I'm here alone most of the time. Half of my day is spent down there. And with Gilda away…"

Kent reached out and put his hand on his friend's shoulder in a reassuring gesture. "I do understand," he said gently. "But there's something more, isn't there?"

Roberts turned a suddenly haggard face toward him. "Yes," he said simply. "There's something in the water."

IV

Kent went away an hour later greatly troubled at his friend's state of mind. His first thought had been to make a joke about taking more water with it, but he realised there was something far more serious than was evident. Roberts would not enlarge on the subject that was troubling him, and Kent did not like to probe any further.

However, things had apparently returned to normal toward the end of June when Roberts threw a party on the lawn of his restored property for friends, neighbours and the craftsmen who had worked so hard and expertly on the project.

Mingling with the guests were the local vicar and the librarian of the village Arts Centre, Roberts' London agent and a sprinkling of local notables. Some of the artist's canvases were on display in a conservatory erected as an adjunct to the mill house, and the local press had sent a reporter and photographer to cover the event.

All in all it was a most successful gathering, Kent thought. The only notable absentee being Gilda, who was still negotiating terms with purchasers in Holland, though she did make a phone call during the celebrations, which was relayed by loudspeaker to the assembled guests.

When Kent came away he was considerably reassured as to Roberts' state of mind. His friend was almost ebullient and greatly looking forward to a very successful future. Though Kent did not question Roberts about the things that had obviously been worrying his friend—he was far too tactful for that—he was greatly reassured by the artist's restored balance and felt secure in the knowledge that he had now recovered his normal state of mind.

But two things came back to Kent long afterward. When the vicar was at the garden party he expressed a wish to bless the house. He was about to anoint the huge crown post with holy water when he gave a sudden exclamation and dropped the vessel on to the floor before he was able to perform the ceremony. He explained that he suffered from arthritis of the hands and had received a sudden twinge of pain and the incident passed off.

The other occurrence was of a lighter nature and concerned Roberts suddenly spotting a young couple, who had evidently come down the stream in a canoe and had been prevented from making any further progress by the mill building. They were standing on the bank watching the party with great interest. Roberts immediately invited them to join in and they were soon the centre of interest. The wife was a very beautiful blonde girl of about twenty-five, with her husband equally handsome. Kent was vividly reminded of a famous classical painting of a Greek god and goddess whose title he had forgotten.

But some while afterward, the canoe had been found floating upside down in the stream several miles further up and there was no sign of its occupants. There were several boat yards in that area with various craft for hire and, as so many people congregated there in the summer months, no one was able to assist the police in their inquiries. The river was dragged but nothing was found. It eventually transpired through further press reports that the girl was a married woman who had run off with her lover. People in the village were extremely interested, but when the couple were last heard of in Canada the matter was soon forgotten.

Kent was busy on the new short story collection for some weeks, though he and Roberts kept in close touch by telephone. Gilda was back temporarily anyway, and whenever they did speak Roberts seemed relaxed and happy.

Gradually Kent began to lose the faint feeling of anxiety he had felt about the house, transmitted, of course, through Roberts' uneasiness and one or two strange remarks he had made about the constant fret of the water beneath the building. But that was only to be expected of a property of that age and size. Though it was true that the rushing of the stream beneath was obtrusive on the lower level, it was completely quiet on what might be termed the ground floor and on the upper levels, where bedrooms and living accommodation were situated.

Things went on in their usual placid fashion in the quiet surroundings of the village and it was almost the end of July when Kent arrived once more for an evening of conversation and an excellent dinner prepared by Roberts' housekeeper, Mrs Summers.

It was a beautiful evening and the two men sat drinking white wine while comfortably settled in window seats, thoroughly at ease with one another. There was a purple haze over the neighbouring fields, and that sort of absolute stillness one finds towards nightfall in late summer.

The silence was broken only by the occasional sound of birdsong, as the flocks returned to the far stands of trees, and now and then the contented lowing of cattle on their grazing grounds.

"A touch of Thomas Gray here," Kent observed at length.

The other's answering smile showed him that the poetic allusion had not been lost. "Worth all the sweat and turmoil," Roberts said as he refilled his friend's glass.

Kent nodded, and the two men stretched out their legs and looked out through the big picture window at the distant view, in one of those rare moments of contentment. But shortly they were roused from their reverie by the shrill bell Mrs Summers used when announcing that the meal was ready.

"Come along, gentlemen," she said good-naturedly, peering around the door lintel. "I'm sure you don't want it to be spoiled and neither do I."

"That woman's becoming quite a slave-driver," Roberts said with a short laugh as soon as she had withdrawn.

"A treasure, you mean," Kent rejoined. "You've now got two in your life."

"True," agreed Roberts, getting up and putting down his empty glass. "The only snag is that Gilda's away so much, and you'll be settled by September, don't forget."

He was referring to Kent's impending marriage, and his guest got up also, giving him a mock-rueful expression. "Bound and shackled, like yourself," he said. "Goodbye to the carefree bachelor life."

Roberts laughed. "You don't know what you're missing," he said.

The meal, as usual, was excellent. When the two were having coffee and cognac, and Mrs Summers had left for her nearby home, the phone rang in the adjoining room where Roberts kept filing cabinets and records of his business affairs. He excused himself and hurried off into his office.

He came back rubbing his hands. "That was Gilda, drumming up business in New York. Twelve thousand for two fairly small oils."

Kent gave a low whistle. "Congratulations. Perhaps Gilda could take me on as a client?"

Roberts shook his head. "Nothing doing. In any case, you're very successful from what I read about your print runs. Twenty thousand a time, if my information is correct."

The two men laughed conspiratorially and the talk passed to other matters.

V

From Roberts' Personal Diary.

Kent was here tonight. We had a pleasant and a long conversation after Mrs Summers had left. But I dare not broach the subject which is now my main concern. I know I am alone here most of the time, yet it is not just the creaking and movements of ancient timbers that one gets in a mediaeval house. It is the constant rush of the water. My studio is directly above the mill-race and though it is a relatively small stream yet the constriction as it passes between the brick walls magnifies the sound. There is a huge hatch just above, about eight feet from the surface, and when I open it and look down it sounds as though I can hear voices. They seem to be calling me. Or is this just fanciful?

If I mentioned this to Kent he would question my sanity. And I dare not broach the subject to Gilda. She is so down-to-earth. It seems that I must face this thing alone.

I could, of course, move the studio upstairs. But there is this great window which lets in the northern light and which I must have when creating my canvases. It seemed to have been made for me. Perhaps I should have thick rubber covering installed over the floor and equally thick carpeting over that to muffle the sound? It is something I shall have to think about if this continues…

VI

When Kent had occasion to visit the mill a few days later to call on Roberts, he found the haggard face on the artist again.

The lunch had been cleared away and Mrs Summers was just leaving, though she would be back again at tea-time. It was a practical arrangement as she lived only a few hundred yards away.

"He is in the study, Mr Kent," she said. "I should go up without ringing, if I were you." She paused, a troubled expression on her placid features. "I'm sure I can speak frankly with you, Mr Kent, as you're such an old friend."

"Of course, Mrs Summers," Kent said, hesitating with his hand on the great iron front door latch.

"Something is bothering your friend. I can't just put my finger on it but he keeps looking around as though something is standing behind him. It's a strange enough old place and full of atmosphere and odd corners but it's cheerful enough, and that won't account for it. I know he's alone a lot and painters are queer folk anyway…" Here she broke off and gave Kent a wry look. "I'm sure you won't take my remarks amiss, but as you're his best friend and all, I feel I can be frank with you, as I've already said."

"Naturally," Kent said. "No offence taken and I'm glad you've spoken to me. Though I'm not here very often, I've sensed that there was something wrong. I believe he often does speak to himself when he's wrestling with some weighty problem to do with his work. But I'll have a talk with him now if it will set your mind at rest."

The housekeeper's face lit up immediately. "I'm glad to hear you say so, Mr Kent. We must all rely on our friends in this difficult world." And to Kent's surprise she wrung his hand effusively and went on her way down the garden path with a lighter step.

Kent had taken the gist of her remarks seriously and, after locking the front door behind him, he made sure of making a good deal of noise as he ascended the great wooden staircase.

Roberts waited on the landing to greet him and led the way into the study, evident relief on his features. "I saw you were talking to Mrs Summers," he said. "I was watching from the window that juts out over the front entrance. She's a good sort and I suppose she's been telling you something about my strange behaviour."

"She didn't put it quite like that," Kent said awkwardly. "But she is a little concerned about you. Isn't it time we had a frank talk? You've changed in some subtle way since you've been down here and you can't deny it."

Dark shadows clouded the other's face as he sat down at his desk and fiddled with a paperweight as though to control his nerves.

Now that he was up closer, Kent could see that Roberts' eyes had dark smudges beneath them that hadn't been there before. "Talking may help," he told Roberts gently. "And it may do some good."

Roberts moved awkwardly in his swivel chair so that a great bar of sunlight fell across his features, enabling Kent to see more clearly the effects of nervous tension on his friend's face.

Roberts made a hopeless gesture with his hands. "I hardly know where to begin."

"Just tell it as you remember it," Kent said.

"I'm a pretty sane, strong-willed person, as you know," the artist said. "And this is something completely outside my experience.

I don't believe in the supernatural, but some while back I started hearing voices. I work a great deal in the studio, as you know, and the faint fret of the water beneath the building was very soothing at the beginning."

Kent leaned forward in his chair as his friend broke off. "Yes?" he prompted. "And then, after a while, something happened?"

Roberts nodded. "You won't believe this, but I started hearing voices, as though coming from the water." He caught the other's disbelieving glance. "I don't mean actual voices. But they were sounding in my head. They were asking me to come down."

"Down where?"

"Down below. Into the water. I know you will think me mad and that my experiences are the result of some mental aberration, but it isn't so. I'm as sane you are." He stared at Kent grimly. "You don't believe me?"

Kent inclined his head. "Of course I believe you. But the strain of your long hours of work… Might it not be some mental stress…?"

"It's not a mental problem. I went to see an eminent specialist in London, one of the most highly recommended in Europe. He gave me the most exhaustive tests and I spent several hours with him. He could find nothing wrong—no trace of pathological disease—and gave me a clean bill of health in every way."

"Then what is the problem?" Kent asked slowly.

Roberts' face was set in a hard mask. "Something terribly real. There's something evil in this house which is reaching out to claim me for some purpose."

Kent rose from the chair. "You can't really mean that?" he said incredulously.

Roberts got up too. "I certainly do. This constant repetition in my head. *Come to us.* An invitation to what? It will really drive me mad if something isn't done." He sat down again abruptly. "Several times I opened the hatch and stared down into the water. There was nothing, of course, but the constant rush seemed like distorted laughter."

Kent felt a sudden *frisson* of something he couldn't clearly define. Not fear, but coldness as though his friend's words had struck a chill to the soul, if such a thing were possible. Then he became businesslike. "Let's go down below and look at this sinister hatch of which you speak."

Roberts became agitated. "Please don't say that. It may sound like provocation."

Kent chose to ignore this extraordinary statement. He said nothing further, but followed his host down to the studio.

The room was a huge chamber and Kent had not seen it before in its final form. Though it was in close proximity to the water, it was quite warm as Roberts had installed central heating here also in case damp from the stream might affect his canvases.

There was an enormous wooden hatch, bound with iron bands, about six feet square, in the far corner. Owing to the huge weight, it was raised by a steel cable fastened to a metal ring, which ran through a pulley block bolted to a massive beam above and raised by a small metal windlass secured to the floor. The cable ran almost noiselessly through the pulley block as Roberts turned the handle of the windlass and then secured it with the brake as soon as it was fully open.

There was a sudden rush of cold air, mingled with various odours that Kent found difficult to place. It was true that the stream which ran foaming and clear about eight or ten feet below made a disturbing sound as it raced through, and such was its power that Kent could feel a faint vibration beneath his feet, as the water swirled round the piles which supported the building. He guessed that in the dim past flat-bottomed barges had rested beneath to take sacks of corn on board. Sunlight filtering through made a dappled surface of the wavelets below, and now and then the silver belly of a small fish slid in and out of view on its way downstream to the distant sea.

He turned to Roberts, the latter surveying him with a hopeful expression on his face. "I can see nothing unusual. A powerful surge round the building from time to time, but that is quite normal."

"Ah, but you are never here at night," Roberts said.

Kent gave him a blank look. "You don't mean to say that you paint down here at night? I thought natural light was necessary for all artists?" He broke off at the expression on the other's face.

"I do some of my best work at night," Roberts said. Then he changed his manner to one more placatory. "What I mean to say is that I re-touch portraits and so on, and make plans for future canvases." And with that he turned on his heel and led the way upstairs.

Kent declined his friend's invitation to tea. When he left the mill house he was a very troubled man.

VII

From Roberts' Personal Diary.

Is Kent right and that I am becoming over-imaginative in being alone so long in this huge house?

Or am I going mad? God forbid. But these events, though somewhat intangible, are nevertheless real in the still of the night. Still of the night? I use the term loosely for, goodness only knows, the house is never silent. The creaking of the beams, the furtive movements as though there are muffled footfalls in various rooms, and the distant trickle of water. For in truth one can hear the stream quite clearly, especially at night as we sleep with the windows open in this current hot weather. And the voices! Dear God, the voices! For these insistent whispers in my ears seem to say: *Come to us! The water is beautifully clear and cool. Stay with us in the rippling embrace of the flow, which has existed throughout all eternity. Iä! Iä! Cthulhu fhtagn!*

I put my pillow over my ears, but the voices still continue, which proves that they are inside my head. Sweet Jesus, where will it all end? We could leave this place, but I am convinced these cursed voices would still continue to plague me. For I have heard them when staying in my London hotel. This agony cannot continue much longer…

VIII

For a fortnight Roberts worked furiously on a new painting, and his labours completely absorbed him for his dread fantasies seemed to fade away. He was more cheerful altogether when he met Kent for lunch at The Three Horseshoes, which was a great relief to his old friend.

In addition, Gilda had rung several times, once from Chicago and on another occasion from Washington. She was making the rounds of private art galleries and dealers and the prospects were extremely good.

Mrs Summers had also noted the change in her employer and was greatly relieved when Kent ran across her in the village one afternoon.

Kent had a book launch in London the following day, so he was not present when certain events unfolded. He stayed on for three more days with his fiancée and her family in St. John's Wood.

The night he arrived back in the village it was quite late so he did not call on Roberts. Not that it would have made any difference to the outcome. Roberts had been in a good mood that brilliantly sunny day and had even attended a cricket match on the village green. But after dinner he felt some of the old malaise creeping over him. The housekeeper had long gone home and he could not settle to his accounts in the study.

It was a bright, clear night with the moon riding high, and he had the windows open to the faint breeze. Then suddenly, without warning, he felt the same insidious voices in his ears. *Come to us! There is deep peace below. You are one of us and we are reclaiming you! It is good and peaceful where we are. We have slept for countless aeons and now we are gathering strength. Come down and be at peace for all time… Ph'nglui mglw'nafh Cthulhu R'lyeh wgah-nagl fhtagn!*

Roberts felt cold sweat pouring down his cheeks, despite the heat of the night, and although he clapped his hands over his ears the persistent coaxing went on as though inside his head.

Mechanically and blindly Roberts found himself descending to the ground floor, walking like a drunken man. Then he found himself in the studio and the insistent susurration of the water had now assumed a more soothing aspect. The voices in his head went on, caressingly, insistently, as though a lover was welcoming a long-awaited partner.

Roberts sank to his knees on the heavy wooden floor, found his hands operating the windlass. The hatch opened silently and then he was gazing down into the dark stream, which seemed to fascinate him.

Come! Eternal life awaits! Iä-R'lyeh! Cthulhu fhtagn! Iä! Iä! The words rose to a crescendo, and then it happened.

The darkness of the water parted and something white and obscene floated to the surface. Roberts found himself staring into a loathsome visage, neither human nor fish. A pair of large unblinking eyes glistened in the dim light as the thing surveyed him with an alien stare. Its huge slit mouth lined with jagged green teeth opened in an obscene smile. Then two webbed claws reached up and plucked him effortlessly down into oblivion. The water boiled white and Roberts let out scream after scream as the torrent turned briefly scarlet and the surge swept him under.

IX

Kent was roused from a deep sleep by the insistent jangling of the telephone on his bedside table. As he came to full consciousness he glanced at his wristwatch and saw it was 3:00 a.m. Thinking it might be Gilda, he picked up the phone, but it was a man's voice, full of urgency.

"Carson here, Mr Kent. Something terrible has happened at The Mill House. I know it's an unearthly hour, but could you come over here right away? It really is imperative."

At first Kent could not place the voice, but then he remembered it was a CID Inspector based at Lewes, who had read a number of his crime novels and had given him invaluable advice about police procedures. From that a friendship had evolved. "The Mill House?" Kent said, still half-asleep. "Is Roberts…"

Carson interrupted him. "It's about your friend," he said gently. "I understand his wife is in New York, so I thought of you. I hope you don't mind?"

"No, of course not, but I still don't understand."

"A local man was walking past the place at midnight when he heard terrible screams coming from the building," replied Carson. "He tried the bell and there were lights on in the house, but no one answered. The local police had a list of key holders and they had to get his housekeeper to open up. What they found was so shocking that they contacted us. You really must come. Now."

Kent was already out of bed. "I'll be there in a quarter of an hour," he said grimly.

X

When Kent arrived at the mill the place was a blaze of light. There were three police cars with their headlights on and an ambulance. Several police officers in uniform were clustered around the open front door, smoking.

After Kent had identified himself, he hurried upstairs and was met by Carson coming down. The Inspector was a big, impressive-looking man in his early forties, broad-shouldered and athletic.

"A bad business, Mr Kent," he muttered. "A bad business." He put his hand on the other's shoulder as they went up to Roberts' study. "I'm afraid your friend is dead."

At first Kent could not take this in and stammered something banal and fatuous.

"It's true," the CID man said, ushering Kent into the study and motioning toward the whisky bottle and glasses on the desk. "You'd better have a peg. I'm afraid you're going to need it."

"I can't understand it," Kent said bewilderedly. "He was all right when I last saw him a few days ago, though a little troubled in his mind." Now that the whisky was beginning to take effect, his faculties were beginning to function normally. "It wasn't suicide?"

Carson shook his head.

Kent gave him an incredulous look. "Not murder?"

"Not that either. At least not as we understand it," Carson said grimly. "As I said, you'd better drink the rest of that glass. You're going to need it."

Half-dazed, Kent was led downstairs. As they descended to the last level, just above the mill-race, cold damp air was on his face.

The place was full of light, from portable lamps set about the floor, which was wet and interspersed with reddish stains. The hatch was wide open and gaping, but it was the huddled mass under the green canvas sheet that arrested his attention. A police surgeon, a small sandy-haired man with gold pince-nez dominating his face and wearing a dirty white smock, was kneeling by the shrouded mass.

Two other plain-clothes men sat on stools at the far side of the room, smoking and with stolid expressions on their faces. Nobody spoke for a moment.

Kent licked suddenly dry lips but Carson's strong hand was beneath his elbow and steered him to the high stool that Roberts sometimes used when spending long hours before his easel. That too was in the far corner, its surface covered by a white sheet.

The surgeon stood up. "Quite outside my experience," he said in a terse voice. "We'll know more when we get him down to the mortuary... or perhaps not," he added after a slight pause.

"Are you ready?" Carson asked. "Just a formality and I'm sorry to have to put you through this, but it will save the widow much grief."

Kent could not suppress a shudder at the crumpled mass of eviscerated flesh with hands and legs slashed and gouged as though by razor-sharp knives. There was such a look of horror on what was left of the dead face that Kent remembered it for the rest of his life. His legs were giving way and he sank thankfully back on to the stool.

"Beats your novels, eh, Mr Kent?" Carson said. The two men were on Christian name terms, but Carson was on familiar ground now and using his official manner in the presence of his subordinates.

"No blood," revealed the surgeon, whose name was Snaith.

"The water would wash it down, surely," Kent said.

The little man shook his head. "Even in cases where bodies are recovered from water after being gashed, say, by the propeller of motor boats, they retain most of their blood."

"But who could have done this?" Kent asked desperately.

"Nothing human, that's for sure," Carson put in.

"So it's not murder?"

Snaith shook his head. "That's the damnable thing. How are we going to explain this to high authority?"

"But it must be murder," Kent went on.

Carson shook his head. "Quite impossible. The house was securely locked for the night. As I said on the phone, we had to get the key from the housekeeper. We made extensive searches from top to bottom of the mill. No one had been here apart from Roberts."

"But the water," Kent went on desperately. "Perhaps the mill wheel..."

One of the plain-clothes men stepped forward. "We had a frogman under there, sir. That wheel has been inoperable for at least thirty years. It is secured by steel bolts and great chains."

Kent persisted in his questions though he knew he was being ridiculous. He turned back to Carson. "Could something like a shark have escaped from an aquarium and come down the stream?"

The Inspector would have laughed had the situation not been so macabre and horrific in its implications. "Quite impossible. Even if you were correct, nothing large enough to have inflicted such terrible injuries. There are massive iron grilles each side of the mill. They go right down to the bed of the stream. The steel has no rust and the grilles would merely let small fish get through. The water's only about eight or ten feet deep anyway." He resumed his brisk manner. "You chaps carry on. We'll try to sort out all this mess later. Mr Kent has had a shock and it's necessary to get him back to normal surroundings."

A dazed Kent was led gently upstairs and into the familiar study where he took another tumbler of whisky with as little effect as though it had been water. His sane, everyday world had collapsed about him. He was seized by a sudden fit of trembling and almost fell into the leather chair to which Carson led him.

He was not to know at that stage of Roberts' obscene diary entries hidden in a recess of the desk or of the vile painting of some loathsome thing under the sheeted canvas in the studio.

And thereafter he could never bear the sound of running water.

ANOTHER FISH STORY

by KIM NEWMAN

IN THE SUMMER of 1968, while walking across America, he came across the skeleton fossil of something aquatic. All around, even in the apparent emptiness, were signs of the life that had passed this way. Million-year-old seashells were strewn across the empty heart of California, along with flattened bullet casings from the ragged edge of the Wild West and occasional sticks of weathered furniture. The sturdier pieces were pioneer jetsam, dumped by exhausted covered wagons during a long dry desert stretch on the road to El Dorado. The more recent items had been thrown off overloaded trucks in the '30s, by Okies rattling towards orange groves and federal work programs.

He squatted over the bones. The sands parted, disclosing the whole of the creature. The scuttle-shaped skull was all saucer-sized eye-sockets and triangular, saw-toothed jaw. The long body was like something fished out of an ash-can by a cartoon cat—fans of rib-spindles tapering to a flat tail. What looked like arm-bones fixed to the dorsal spine by complex plates that were evolving towards becoming shoulders. Stranded when the seas receded from the Mojave, the thing had lain ever closer to the surface, waiting to be revealed by sand-riffling winds. Uncovered as he was walking to it, the fossil—exposed to the thin, dry air—was quickly resolving into sand and scraps.

Finally, only an arm remained. Short and stubby like an alligator leg, it had distinct, barb-tipped fingers. It pointed like a sign-post, to the West, to the Pacific, to the city-stain seeping out from the original blot of *El Pueblo de Nuestra Senora de la Reyna de los Angeles de Rio Porciunculo*. He expected these route-marks. He'd been following them since he first crawled out of a muddy river in England. This one scratched at him.

Even in the desert, he could smell river-mud, taste foul water, feel the tidal pull.

For a moment, he was under waters. Cars, upside down above him, descended gently like dead, settling sharks. People floated like broken dolls just under the shimmering, sunlit ceiling-surface. An enormous pressure squeezed in on him, jamming thumbs against his open eyes, forcing liquid salt into mouth and nose. A tubular serpent, the size of a streamlined train, slithered over the desert-bed towards him, eyes like turquoise-shaded searchlights, shifting rocks out of its way with muscular arms.

Gone. Over.

The insight passed. He gasped reflexively for air.

"Atlantis will rise, Sunset Boulevard will fall," Cass Elliott was singing on a single that would be released in October. Like so many doomed visionaries in her generation, Mama Cass was tuned into the vibrations. Of course, she didn't know there really had been a sunken city off Santa Monica, as recently as 1942. Not Atlantis, but the Sister City. A battle had been fought there in a World War that was not in the official histories. A War that wasn't as over as its human victors liked to think.

He looked where the finger pointed.

The landscape would change. Scrub rather than sand, mountains rather than flats. More people, less quiet.

He took steps.

He was on a world-wide walkabout, buying things, picking up skills and scars, making deals wherever he sojourned, becoming what he would be. Already, he had many interests, many businesses. An empire would need his attention soon, and he would be its prisoner as much as its master. These few years, maybe only months, were his alone. He carried no money, no identification but a British passport in the name of a new-born dead in the blitz. He wore unscuffed purple suede boots, tight white thigh-fly britches with a black zig-zag across them, a white Nehru jacket and silver-mirrored sunglasses. A white silk aviator scarf wrapped burnoose-style about his head, turbanning his longish hair and keeping the grit out of his mouth and nose.

Behind him, across America, across the world, he left a trail. He thought of it as dropping pebbles in pools. Ripples spread from each pebble, some hardly noticed yet but nascent whirlpools, some enormous splashes no one thought to connect with the passing Englishman.

It was a good time to be young, even for him. His signs were everywhere. Number One in the pop charts back home was 'Fire', by The Crazy World of Arthur Brown. "I am the God of Hellfire," chanted Arthur. There were such Gods, he understood. He walked through the world, all along the watchtower, sprung from the songs— an Urban Spaceman, Quinn the Eskimo, this wheel on fire, melting away like ice in the sun, on white horses, in disguise with glasses.

In recent months, he'd seen *Hair* on Broadway and *2001: A Space Odyssey* at an Alabama Drive-In. He knew all about the Age of Aquarius and the Ultimate Trip. He'd sabotaged Abbie Hoffman's magic ring with a subtle counter-casting, ensuring that the Pentagon remained unlevitated. He knew exactly where he'd been when Martin Luther King was shot. Ditto, Andy Warhol, Robert Kennedy and the VC summarily executed by Colonel Loan on the *Huntley-Brinkley Report*. He'd rapped with Panthers and Guardsmen, Birchers and Yippies. To his satisfaction, he'd sewn up the next three elections, and decided the music children would listen to until the Eve of Destruction.

He'd eaten in a lot of McDonald's, cheerfully dropping cartons and bags like appleseeds. The Golden Arches were just showing up on every Main Street, and he felt Ronald should be encouraged. He liked the little floods of McLitter that washed away from the clown's doorways, perfumed with the stench of their special sauce.

He kept walking.

Behind him, his footprints filled in. The pointing hand, so nearly human, sank under the sands, duty discharged.

At this stage of his career, the Devil put in the hours, wore down the shoe-leather, sweated out details. He was the start-up Mephisto, the journeyman tempter, the mysterious stranger passing through, the new gun in town. You didn't need to make an appointment and crawl as a supplicant; if needs be, Derek Leech came to you.

Happily.

Miles later and days away, he found a ship's anchor propped on a cairn of stones, iron-red with lichen-like rust, blades crusted with empty shells. An almost illegible plaque read *Sumatra Queen*.

Leech knew this was where he was needed.

It wasn't real wilderness, just pretend. In the hills close to Chatsworth, a town soon to be swallowed by Los Angeles, this was the Saturday matinee West. Poverty Row prairie, Monogram mountains. A brief location hike up from Gower Gulch, the longest-lasting game of Cowboys and Indians in the world had been played.

A red arch stood by the cairn, as if a cathedral had been smitten, leaving only its entrance standing. A hook in the arch might once have held a bell or a hangman's noose or a giant shoe.

He walked under it, eyes on the hook.

Wheelruts in sandy scrub showed the way. Horses had been along this route too, recently.

A smell tickled in his nose, triggering salivary glands. Leech hadn't had a Big Mac in days. He unwound the scarf from his head and knotted it around his neck. From beside the road, he picked a dungball, skin baked hard as a gob-stopper. He ate it like an apple. Inside, it was moist. He spat out strands of grass.

He felt the vibrations, before he heard the motors.

Several vehicles, engines exposed like sit-astride mowers, bumping over rough terrain on balloon tyres. Fuel emissions belching from mortar-like tubes. Girls yelping with a fairground Dodg'em thrill.

He stood still, waiting.

The first dune buggy appeared, leaping over an incline like a roaring cat, landing awkwardly, squirming in dirt as its wheels aligned, then heading towards him in a charge. A teenage girl in a denim halter-top drove, struggling with the wheel, blonde hair streaming, a bruise on her forehead. Standing like a tank commander in the front passenger seat, hands on the roll-bar, was an undersized, big-eared man with a middling crop of beard, long hair bound in a bandanna. He wore ragged jeans and a too-big combat jacket. On a rosary around his scraggy neck was strung an Iron Cross, the *Pour le Mérite* and a rhinestone-studded swastika. He signalled vainly with a set of binoculars (one lens broken), then kicked his chauffeuse to get her attention.

The buggy squiggled in the track and halted in front of Leech.

Another zoomed out of long grass, driven by an intense young man, passengered by three messy girls. A third was around somewhere, to judge from the noise and the gasoline smell.

Leech tossed aside his unfinished meal.

"You must be hungry, pilgrim," said the commander.

"Not now."

The commander flashed a grin, briefly showing sharp, bad teeth, hollowing his cheeks, emphasising his eyes. Leech recognised the wet gaze of a man who has spent time practising his stares. Long, hard jail years looking into a mirror, plumbing black depths.

"Welcome to Charlie Country," said his driver.

Leech met the man's look. Charlie's welcome.

Seconds—a minute?—passed. Neither had a weapon, but this was a gunfighters' eye-lock, a probing and a testing, will playfully thrown up against a wall, bouncing back with surprising ferocity.

Leech was almost amused by the Charlie's presumption. Despite his hippie aspect, he was ten years older than the kids—well into hard thirties, at once leathery and shifty, a convict confident the bulls can't hang a jailyard shivving at his cell-door, an arrested grown-up settling for status as an idol for children ignored by adults. The rest of his tribe looked to their *jefé*, awaiting orders.

Charlie Country. In Vietnam, that might have meant something.

In the end, something sparked. Charlie raised one hand, open, beside his face. He made a monocle of his thumb and forefinger, three other fingers splayed like a coxcomb.

In Britain, the gesture was associated with Patrick McGoohan's "Be seeing you" on *The Prisoner*. Leech returned the salute, completing it by closing his hand into a fist.

"What's that all about?" whined his driver.

Not taking his eyes off Leech, Charlie said, "Sign of the fish, Sadie."

The girl shrugged, no wiser.

"Before the crucifix became the pre-eminent symbol of Christianity, Jesus' early followers greeted each other with the sign of the fish," Leech told them. "His first disciples were net-folk, remember. 'I will make you fishers of men.' Originally, the Galilean came as a lakeside spirit. He could walk on water, turn water to wine. He had command over fish, multiplying them to feed the five thousand. The wounds in his side might have been gills."

"Like a professor he speaks," said the driver of the second buggy.

"Or Terence Stamp," said a girl. "Are you British?"

Leech conceded that he was.

"You're a long way from Carnaby Street, Mr. Fish."

As a matter of fact, Leech owned quite a bit of that thoroughfare. He did not volunteer the information.

"Is he The One Who Will…?" began Charlie's driver, cut off with a gesture.

"Maybe, maybe not. One sign is a start, but that's all it is. A man can easily make a sign."

Leech showed his open hands, like a magician before a trick.

"Let's take you to Old Lady Marsh," said Charlie. "She'll have a thing or two to say. You'll like her. She was in pictures, a long time ago. Sleeping partner in the Ranch. You might call her the Family's spiritual advisor."

"Marsh," said Leech. "Yes, that's the name. Thank you, Charles."

"Hop into Unit Number Two. Squeaky, hustle down to make room for the gent. You can get back to the bunkhouse on your own two legs. Do you good."

A sour-faced girl crawled off the buggy. Barefoot, she looked at the flint-studded scrub as if about to complain, then thought better of it.

"Are you waitin' on an engraved invitation, Mr. Fish?"

Leech climbed into the passenger's seat, displacing two girls who shoved themselves back, clinging to the overhead bar, fitting their legs in behind the seat, plopping bottoms on orange-painted metal fixtures. To judge from the squealing, the metal was hot as griddles.

"You are comfortable?" asked the kid in the driver's seat.

Leech nodded.

"Cool," he said, jamming the ignition. "I'm Constant. My accent, it is German."

The young man's blond hair was held by a beaded leather headband. Leech had a glimpse of an earnest schoolboy in East Berlin, poring over Karl May's books about Winnetou the Warrior and Old Shatterhand, vowing that he would be a blood brother to the Apache in the West of the Teuton Soul.

Constant did a tight turn, calculated to show off, and drove off the track, bumping onto an irregular slope, pitting gears against gravity. Charlie kicked Sadie the chauffeuse, who did her best to follow.

Leech looked back. Atop the slope, 'Squeaky' stood forlorn, hair stringy, faded dress above her scabby knees.

"You will respect the way Charlie has this place ordered," said Constant. "He is the Cat That Has Got the Cream."

The buggies roared down through a culvert, overleaping obstacles. One of the girls thumped her nose against the roll-bar. Her blood spotted Leech's scarf. He took it off and pressed the spots to his tongue.

Images fizzed. Blood on a wall. Words in the blood.

HEALTER SKELTER

He shook the images from his mind.

Emerging from the culvert, the buggies burst into a clearing and circled, scattering a knot of people who'd been conferring, raising a ruckus in a corral of horses which neighed in panic, spitting up dirt and dust.

Leech saw two men locked in a wrestling hold, the bloated quarter-century-on sequel to the Wolf Man pushed against a wooden fence by a filled-out remnant of Riff of the Jets. Riff wore biker denims and orange-lensed glasses. He had a chain wrapped around the neck of the sagging lycanthrope.

The buggies halted, engines droning down and sputtering.

* * *

A man in a cowboy hat angrily shouted "Cut, cut, cut!"

Another man, in a black shirt and eyeshade, insisted "No, no, no, Al, we can use it, keep shooting. We can work round it. Film is money."

Al, the director, swatted the insister with his hat.

"Here on the Ranch, they make the motion pictures," said Constant.

Leech had guessed as much. A posse of stuntmen had been chasing outlaws all over this country since the Silents. Every rock had been filmed so often that the stone soul was stripped away.

Hoppy and Gene and Rinty and Rex were gone. Trigger was stuffed and mounted. The lights had come up and the audience fled home to the goggle box. The only Westerns that got shot these days were skin-flicks in chaps or slo-mo massacres, another sign of impending apocalypse.

But Riff and the Wolf Man were still working. Just.

The film company looked at the Beach Buggy Korps, warily hostile. Leech realised this was the latest of a campaign of skirmishes.

"What's this all about, Charlie?" demanded the director. "We've told you to keep away from the set. Sam even goddamn paid you."

Al pulled the insister, Sam, into a grip and pointed his head at Charlie.

Charlie ignored the fuss, quite enjoying it.

A kid who'd been holding up a big hoop with white fabric stretched across it felt an ache in his arms and let the reflector sag. A European-looking man operating a big old Mickey Mouse-eared camera swivelled his lens across the scene, snatching footage.

Riff took a fat hand-rolled cigarette from his top pocket, and flipped a Zippo. He sucked in smoke, held it for a wine-bibber's moment of relish, and exhaled, then nodded his satisfaction to himself.

"Tana leaves, Junior?" said Riff, offering the joint to his wrestling partner.

The Wolf Man didn't need dope to be out of it.

Here he was, Junior: Lennie Talbot, Kharis the Caveman, Count Alucard—the Son of the Phantom. His baggy eyes were still looking for the rabbits, as he wondered what had happened to the 1940s.

Where were Boris and Bela and Bud and Lou? While Joni Mitchell sang about getting back to the garden, Junior fumbled about sets like this, desperate for readmission to the Inner Sanctum.

"Who the Holy Hades is this clown?" Al thumbed at Leech.

Leech looked across the set at Junior. Bloated belly barely cinched by the single button of a stained blue shirt, grey ruff of whiskers, chilli stains on his jeans, yak-hair clumps stuck to his cheeks and forehead, he was up well past the Late, Late Show.

The Wolf Man looked at Leech in terror.

Sometimes, dumb animals have very good instincts.

"This is Mr. Fish," Charlie told Al. "He's from England."

"Like the Beatles," said one of the girls.

Charlie thought about that. "Yeah," he said, "like the Beatles. Being for the benefit of Mr. Fish…"

Leech got out of the buggy.

Everyone was looking at him. The kerfuffle quieted, except for the turning of the camera.

Al noticed and made a cut-throat gesture. The cameraman stopped turning.

"Hell of a waste," spat the director.

In front of the ranch-house were three more dune buggies, out of commission. A sunburned boy, naked but for cut-off denims and a sombrero, worked on the vehicles. A couple more girls sat around, occasionally passing the boy the wrong spanner from a box of tools.

"When will you have Units Three, Four and One combat-ready, Tex?"

Tex shrugged at Charlie.

"Be lucky to Frankenstein together one working bug from these heaps of shit, Chuck."

"Not good enough, my man. The storm's coming. We have to be ready."

"Then schlep down to Santa Monica and steal… *requisition*… some more goddamn rolling stock. Rip off an owner's manual, while you're at it. These configurations are a joke."

"I'll take it under advisement," said Charlie.

Tex gave his commander a salute.

Everyone looked at Leech, then at Charlie for the nod that meant the newcomer should be treated with respect. Chain of command was more rigid here than at Khe Sanh.

All the buggies were painted. At one time, they had been given elaborate psychedelic patterns; then, a policy decision decreed they be redone in sandy desert camouflage. But the first job had been done properly, while the second was botched—vibrant flowers, butterflies and peace-signs shone through the thin diarrhoea-khaki topcoat.

The ranch-house was the basic derelict adobe and wood hacienda. One carelessly flicked roach and the place was an inferno. Round here, they must take pot-shots at safety inspectors.

On the porch was propped a giant fibre-glass golliwog, a fat grinning racial caricature holding up a cone surmounted by a whipped swirl and a red ball cherry. Chocko the Ice Cream Clown had originally been fixed to one of the 'requisitioned' buggies. Someone had written 'PIG' in lipstick on Chocko's forehead. Someone else had holed his eyes and cheek with 2.2 rifle bullets. A hand-axe stuck out of his shoulder like a flung tomahawk.

"That's the Enemy, man," said Charlie. "Got to Know Your Enemy."

Leech looked at the fallen idol.

"You don't like clowns?"

Charlie nodded. Leech thought of his ally, Ronald.

"Chocko's coming, man," said Charlie. "We have to be in a state of eternal preparedness. Their world, the dress-up-and-play world, is over. No more movies, no more movie stars. It's just us, the Family. And Chocko. We're major players in the coming deluge. Helter Skelter, like in the song. It's been revealed to me. But you know all that."

Funnily enough, Leech did.

He had seen the seas again, the seas that would come from the sundered earth. The seventh flood. The last wave.

Charlie would welcome the waters.

He was undecided on the whole water thing. If pushed, he preferred the fire. And he sensed more interesting apocalypses in the offing, stirring in the scatter of McDonald's boxes and chewed-out bubblegum pop. Still, he saw himself as a public servant; it was down to others to make the choices. Whatever was wanted, he would do his best to deliver.

"Old Lady Marsh don't make motion pictures any more. No need. Picture Show's closed. Just some folk don't know it yet."

"Chuck offered to be in their movie," explained Tex. "Said he'd do one of those nude love scenes, man. No dice."

"That's not the way it is," said Charlie, suddenly defensive, furtive. "My thing is the *music*. I'm going to communicate through my album. Pass on my revelation. Kids groove on records more than movies."

Tex shrugged. Charlie needed him, so he had a certain license. Within limits.

Charlie looked back, away from the house. The film company was turning over again. Riff was pretending to chain-whip Junior.

"Something's got to change," said Charlie.

"Helter skelter," said Leech.

Charlie's eyes shone.

"Yeah," he said, "you dig."

Inside the house, sections were roped off with crudely lettered PELIGROSO signs. Daylight seeped through ill-fitting boards over glassless windows. Everything was slightly damp and salty, as if there'd been rain days ago. The adobe seemed sodden, pulpy. Green moss grew on the floor. A plastic garden hose snaked through the house, pulsing, leading up the main staircase.

"The Old Lady likes to keep the waters flowing."

Charlie led Leech upstairs.

On the landing, a squat idol sat on an occasional table—a buddha with cephalopod mouth-parts.

"Know that fellow, Mr. Fish?"

"Dagon, God of the Philistines."

"Score one for the Kwiz Kid. Dagon. That's one of the names. Old Lady Marsh had this church, way back in the '40s. Esoteric Order of Dagon. Ever hear of it?"

Leech had.

"She wants me to take it up again, open store-front chapels on all the piers. Not my scene, man. No churches, not this time. I've got my own priorities. She thinks *infiltration*, but I know these are the times for catastrophe. But she's still a fighter. Janice Marsh. Remember her in *Nefertiti*?'

They came to a door, kept ajar by the hose.

Away from his Family, Charlie was different. The man never relaxed, but he dropped the Rasputin act, stuttered out thoughts as soon as they sprung to him, kept up a running commentary. He was less a Warrior of the Apocalypse than a Holocaust Hustler, working all the angles, sucking up to whoever might help him. Charlie needed followers, but was desperate also for sponsorship, a break.

Charlie opened the door.

"Miss Marsh," he said, deferential.

Large, round eyes gleamed inside the dark room.

Janice Marsh sat in a tin bathtub, tarpaulin tied around her wattled throat like a bib, a bulbous turban around her skull. From under the tarp came quiet splashing and slopping. The hose fed into the bath and an overspill pipe, patched together with hammered-out tin-cans, led away to a hole in the wall, dribbling outside.

Only her flattish nose and lipless mouth showed, overshadowed by the fine-lashed eyes. In old age, she had smoothed rather than wrinkled. Her skin was a mottled, greenish colour.

"This cat's from England," said Charlie.

Leech noticed Charlie hung back in the doorway, not entering the room. This woman made him nervous.

"We've been in the desert, Miss Marsh," said Charlie. "Sweeping Quadrant Twelve. Scoped out a promising cave, but it led nowhere. Sadie got her ass stuck in a hole, but we hauled her out. That chick's our mineshaft canary."

Janice Marsh nodded, chin-pouch inflating like a frog's.

"There's more desert," said Charlie. "We'll read the signs soon. It will be found. We can't be kept from it."

Leech walked into the dark and sat, unbidden, on a stool by the bathtub.

Janice Marsh looked at him. Sounds frothed through her mouth, rattling in slits that might have been gills.

Leech returned her greeting.

"You speak that jazz?" exclaimed Charlie. "Far out."

Leech and Janice Marsh talked. She was interesting, if given to rambles as her mind drifted out to sea. It was all about water. Here in the desert, close to the thirstiest city in America, the value of water was known. She told him what the Family were looking for, directed him to unroll some scrolls that were kept on a low-table under a fizzing desk-lamp. The charts were the original mappings of California, made by Fray Junipero Serra before there were enough human landmarks to get a European bearing.

Charlie shouldered close to Leech, and pulled a magic marker out of his top-pocket.

The vellum was divided into numbered squares, thick modern lines blacked over the faded, precious sketch-marks. Several squares were shaded with diagonal lines. Charlie added diagonals to the square marked '12'.

Leech winced.

"What's up, man?"

"Nothing," he told Charlie.

He knew what things were worth; that, if anything, was his special talent. But he knew such values were out of step with the times. He did not want to be thought a breadhead. Not until the 1980s, when he had an itchy feeling that it'd be mandatory. If there was to be a 1980s.

"This is the surface chart, you dig," said Charlie, rapping knuckles on the map. "We're about here, where I've marked the Ranch. There are other maps, showing what's underneath."

Charlie rolled the map, to disclose another. The top map had holes cut out, marking points of convergence. The lower chart was marked with inter-linked balloon-shapes, some filled in with blue pigment that had become pale with age.

"Dig the holes, man. This shows the ways down below."

A third layer of map was almost all blue. Drawn in were fishy, squiddy shapes. And symbols Leech understood.

"And here's the prize. The Sea of California. Freshwater, deep under the desert. Primordial."

Janice Marsh burbled excitement.

"Home," she said, a recognisable English word.

"It's under us," said Charlie. "That's why we're out here. Looking. Before Chocko rises, the Family will have found the way down, got the old pumps working. Turn on the quake. With the flood, we'll win. It's the key to ending all this. It has properties. Some places—the cities, maybe, Chicago, Watts—it'll be fire that comes down. Here, it's the old, old way. It'll be water that comes up."

"You're building an Ark?"

"Uh uh, Arks are movie stuff. We're learning to *swim*. Going to be a part of the flood. You too, I think. We're going to drown Chocko. We're going to drown Hollywood. Call down the rains. Break the rock. When it's all over, there'll only be us. And maybe the Beach Boys. I'm tight with Dennis Wilson, man. He wants to produce my album. That's going to happen in the last days. My album will be a monster, like the *Double White*. Music will open everything up, knock everything down. Like at Jericho."

Leech saw that Charlie couldn't keep his thinking straight. He wanted an end to civilisation and a never-ending battle of Armageddon, but still thought he could fit in a career as a pop star.

Maybe.

This was Janice's game. She was the mother of this family.

"He came out of the desert," Charlie told the old woman. "You can see the signs on him. He's a dowser."

The big eyes turned to Leech.

"I've found things before," he admitted.

"Water?" she asked, splashing.

He shrugged. "On occasion."

Her slit mouth opened in a smile, showing rows of needle-sharp teeth.

"You're a hit, man," said Charlie. "You're in the Family."

Leech raised his hand. "That's an honour, Charles," he said, "but I can't accept. I provide services, for a fee to be negotiated, but I don't take permanent positions."

Charlie was puzzled for a moment, brows narrowed. Then he smiled. "If that's your scene, it's cool. But are you The One Who Will Open the Earth? Can you help us find the Subterranean Sea?"

Leech considered, and shook his head, "No. That's too deep for me."

Charlie made fists, bared teeth, instantly angry.

"But I know who can," soothed Leech.

The movie people were losing the light. As the sun sank, long shadows stretched on reddish scrub, rock-shapes twisted into ogres. The cinematographer shot furiously, gabbling in semi-Hungarian about "magic hour", while Sam and Al worried vocally that nothing would come out on the film.

Leech sat in a canvas folding-chair and watched.

Three young actresses, dressed like Red Indians, were pushing Junior around, tormenting him by withholding a bottle of firewater. Meanwhile, the movie moon—a shining fabric disc—was rising full, just like the real moon up above the frame-line.

The actresses weren't very good. Beside Sadie and Squeaky and Ouisch and the others, the Acid Squaws of the Family, they lacked authentic drop-out savagery. They were Vegas refugees, tottering on high heels, checking their make-up in every reflective surface.

Junior wasn't acting any more.

"Go for the bottle," urged Al.

Junior made a bear-lunge, missed a girl who pulled a face as his sweat-smell cloud enveloped her, and fell to his knees. He looked up like a puppy with progeria, eager to be patted for his trick.

There was water in Junior's eyes. Full moons shone in them.

Leech looked up. Even he felt the tidal tug.

"I don't freakin' believe this," stage-whispered Charlie, in Leech's ear. "That cat's gone."

Leech pointed again at Junior.

"You've tried human methods, Charles. Logic and maps. You need to try other means. Animals always find water. The moon pulls at the sea. That man has surrendered to his animal. He knows the call of the moon. Even a man who is pure in heart…"

"That was just in the movies."

"Nothing was ever *just* in the movies. Understand this. Celluloid writes itself into the unconscious, of its makers as much as its

115

consumers. Your revelations may come in music. His came in the cheap seats."

The Wolf Man howled happily, bottle in his hug. He took a swig and shook his greasy hair like a pelt.

The actresses edged away from him.

"Far out, man," said Charlie, doubtfully.

"Far out and deep down, Charles."

"That's a wrap for today," called Al.

"I could shoot twenty more minutes with this light," said the cameraman.

"You're nuts. This ain't art school in Budapest. Here in America, we shoot with light, not dark."

"I make it *fantastic*."

"We don't want fantastic. We want it on film so you can see it."

"Make a change from your last picture, then," sneered the cinematographer. He flung up his hands and walked away.

Al looked about as if he'd missed something.

"Who are you, mister?" he asked Leech. "Who are you *really*?"

"A student of human nature."

"Another weirdo, then."

He had a flash of the director's body, much older and shaggier, bent in half and shoved into a whirlpool bath, wet concrete sloshing over his face.

"Might I give you some free advice?" Leech asked. "Long-term advice. Be very careful when you're hiring odd-job men."

"Yup, a *weird* weirdo. The worst kind."

The director stalked off. Leech still felt eyes on him.

Sam, the producer, had stuck around the set. He did the negotiating. He also had a demented enthusiasm for the kind of pictures they made. Al would rather have been shooting on the studio lot with Barbra Streisand or William Holden. Sam liked anything that gave him a chance to hire forgotten names from the matinees he had loved as a kid.

"You're not with them? Charlie's Family?"

Leech said nothing.

"They're fruit-loops. Harmless, but a pain in the keister. The hours we've lost putting up with these kids. You're not like that. Why are you here?"

"As they say in the Westerns, 'just passing through.'"

"You like Westerns? Nobody does much any more, unless they're made in Spain by Italians. What's wrong with this picture? We'd love to be able to shoot only Westerns. Cowboys are a hell of a lot easier to deal with than Hells' Angels. Horses don't break down like bikes."

"Would you be interested in coming to an arrangement? The problems you've been having with the Family could be ended."

"What are you, their agent?"

"This isn't Danegeld, or a protection racket. This is a fair exchange of services."

"I pay you and your hippies don't fudge up any more scenes? I could just get a sheriff out here and run the whole crowd off, then we'd be back on schedule. I've come close to it more'n once."

"I'm not interested in money, for the moment. I would like to take an option on a day and a night of time from one of your contractees."

"Those girls are *actresses*, buddy, not whatever you might think they are. Each and every one of 'em is SAG."

"Not one of the actresses."

"Sheesh, I know you longhairs are into everything, but…"

"It's your werewolf I wish to sub-contract."

"My what? Oh, Junior. He's finished on this picture."

"But he owes you two days."

"How the hell did you know that? He does. I was going to have Al shoot stuff with him we could use in something else. There's this *Blood* picture we need to finish. *Blood of Whatever*. It's had so many titles, I can't keep them in my head. *Ghastly Horror… Dracula Meets Frankenstein… Fiend with the Psychotropic Brain… Blood a-Go-Go…* At the moment, it's mostly home movies shot at a dolphinarium. It could use monster scenes."

"I would like to pick up the time. As I said, a day and a night."

"Have you ever done any acting? I ask because our vampire is gone. He's an accountant and it's tax season. In long shot, you could pass for him. We could give you a horror star name, get you on the cover of *Famous Monsters*. How about 'Zoltan Lukoff'? 'Mongo Carnadyne'? 'Dexter DuCaine'?"

"I don't think I have screen presence."

"But you can call off the bimbos in the buggies? Damp down all activities so we can finish our flick and head home?"

"That can be arranged."

"And Junior isn't going to get hurt? This isn't some Satanic sacrifice deal? Say, that's a great title. *Satan's Sacrifice*. Must register it. Maybe *Satan's Bloody Sacrifice*. Anything with blood in the title will gross an extra twenty per-cent. That's free advice you can take to the bank and cash."

"I simply want help in finding something. Your man can do that."

"Pal, Junior can't find his own pants in the morning even if he's slept in them. He's still got it on film, but half the time he doesn't know what year it is. And, frankly, he's better off that way. He still thinks he's in *Of Mice and Men*."

"If you remade that, would you call it *Of Mice and Bloody Men*?"

Sam laughed. "*Of Naked Mice and Bloody Men*."

"Do we have a deal?"

"I'll talk to Junior."

"Thank you."

After dark, the two camps were pitched. Charlie's Family were around the ranch-house, clustering on the porch for a meal prepared and served by the girls, which was not received enthusiastically. Constant formulated elaborate sentences of polite and constructive culinary criticism which made head chef Lynette Alice, aka Squeaky, glare as if she wanted to drown him in soup.

Leech had another future moment, seeing between the seconds. Drowned bodies hung, arms out like B-movie monsters, faces pale and shrivelled. Underwater zombies dragged weighted boots across the ocean-floor, clothes flapping like torn flags. Finned priests called the faithful to prayer from the steps of sunken temples to Dagon and Chthulhu and the Fisherman Jesus.

Unnoticed, he spat out a stream of seawater which sank into the sand.

The Family scavenged their food, mostly by random shoplifting in markets, and were banned from all the places within an easy reach. Now they made do with whatever canned goods they had left over and, in some cases, food parcels picked up from the Chatsworth post office sent by suburban parents they despised but tapped all the time. Mom and Dad were a resource, Charlie said, like a seam of mineral in a rock, to be mined until it played out.

The situation was exacerbated by cooking smells wafting up from the film camp, down by the bunkhouse. The movie folk had a catering budget. Junior presided over a cauldron full of chilli, his secret family recipe doled out to the cast and crew on all his movies. Leech gathered some of Charlie's girls had exchanged blow-jobs for bowls of that chilli, which they then dutifully turned over to their lord and master in the hope that he'd let them lick out the crockery afterwards.

Everything was a matter of striking a deal. Service for payment.

Not hungry, he sat between the camps, considering the situation. He knew what Janice Marsh wanted, what Charlie wanted, what Al wanted and what Sam wanted. He saw arrangements that might satisfy them all.

But he had his own interests to consider.

The more concrete the coming flood was in his mind, the less congenial an apocalypse it seemed. It was unsubtle, an upheaval that epitomised the saw about throwing out the baby with the bath-water. He envisioned more intriguing pathways through the future. He had already made an investment in this world, in the ways that it worked and played, and he was reluctant to abandon his own long-range plans to hop aboard a Technicolor spectacular starring a cast of thousands, scripted by Lovecraft, directed by DeMille and produced by Mad Eyes Charlie and the Freakin' Family Band.

His favoured apocalypse was a tide of McLitter, a thousand channels of television noise, a complete scrambling of politics and entertainment, PROUD-TO-BE-A-BREADHEAD buttons, bright packaging around tasteless and nutrition-free product, audio-visual media devoid of anything approaching meaning, bellies swelling and

IQs atrophying. In his preferred world, as in the songs, people bowed and prayed to the neon god they made, worked for Matthew and Son, were dedicated followers of fashion and did what Simon said.

He was in a tricky position. It was a limitation on his business that he could rarely set his own goals. In one way, he was like Sam's vampire: he couldn't go anywhere without an invitation. Somehow, he must further his own cause, while living up to the letter of his agreements.

Fair enough.

On his porch, Charlie unslung a guitar and began to sing, pouring revelations over a twelve-bar blues. Adoring faces looked up at him, red-fringed by the firelight.

From the movie camp came an answering wail.

Not coyotes, but stuntmen—led by the raucous Riff, whose singing had been dubbed in *West Side Story*—howling at the moon, whistling over emptied Jack Daniel's bottles, clanging tin plates together.

Charlie's girls joined in his chorus.

The film folk fired off blank rounds, and sang songs from the Westerns they'd been in. 'Get Along Home, Cindy, Cindy'. 'Gunfight at O.K. Corrall'. 'The Code of the West'.

Charlie dropped his acoustic, and plugged in an electric. The chords sounded the same, but the ampage somehow got into his reedy voice, which came across louder.

He sang sea shanties.

That put the film folk off for a while.

Charlie sang about mermaids and sunken treasures and the rising, rising waters.

He wasn't worse than many acts Leech had signed to his record label. If it weren't for this apocalypse jazz, he might have tried to make a deal with Charlie for his music. He'd kept back the fact that he had pull in the industry. Apart from other considerations, it'd have made Charlie suspicious. The man was naïve about many things, but he had a canny showbiz streak. He scorned all the trappings of a doomed civilisation, but bought *Daily Variety* and *Billboard* on the sly. You don't find Phil Spector wandering in the desert eating horse-turds. At least, not so far.

As Charlie sang, Leech looked up at the moon.

* * *

A shadow fell over him, and he smelled the Wolf Man.

"Is your name George?" asked the big man, eyes eager.

"If you need it to be."

"I only ask because it seems to me you could be a George. You got that Georgey look, if you know what I mean."

"Sit down, my friend. We should talk."

"Gee, uh, okay."

Junior sat cross-legged, arranging his knees around his comfortable belly. Leech struck a match, put it to a pile of twigs threaded with grass. Flame showed up Junior's nervous, expectant grin, etched shadows into his open face.

Leech didn't meet many Innocents. Yet here was one.

As Junior saw Leech's face in the light, his expression was shadowed. Leech remembered how terrified the actor had been when he first saw him.

"Why do I frighten you?" he asked, genuinely interested.

"Don't like to say," said Junior, thumb creeping towards his mouth. "Sounds dumb."

"I don't make judgements. That's not part of my purpose."

"I think you might be my Dad."

Leech laughed. He was rarely surprised by people. When it happened, he was always pleased.

"Not like that. Not like you and my Mom… you know. It's like my Dad's in you, somewhere."

"Do I look like him, Creighton?"

Junior accepted Leech's use of his true name. "I can't remember what he really looked like. He was the Man of a Thousand Faces. He didn't have a real face for home use. He'd not have been pleased with the way this turned out, George. He didn't want this for me. He'd have been real mad. And when he was mad, then he showed his vampire face…"

Junior bared his teeth, trying to do his father in *London After Midnight*.

"It's never too late to change."

Junior shook his head, clearing it. "Gosh, that's a nice thought, George. Sam says you want me to do you a favour. Sam's a good guy. He looks out for me. Always has a spot for me in his pictures. He says no one else can do justice to the role of Groton the Mad Zombie. If you're okay with Sam, you're okay with me. No matter about my Dad. He's dead a long time and I don't have to do what he says no more. That's the truth, George."

"Yes."

"So how can I help you?"

The Buggy Korps scrambled in the morning for the big mission. Only two vehicles were all-terrain-ready. Two three-person crews would suffice.

Given temporary command of Unit Number Two, Leech picked Constant as his driver. The German boy helped Junior into his padded seat, complementing him on his performance as noble Chingachgook in a TV series of *The Last of the Mohicans* that had made it to East Germany in the 1950s.

This morning, Junior bubbled with enthusiasm, a big kid going to the zoo. He took a look at Chocko, who had recently been sloshed with red paint, and pantomimed cringing shock.

Leech knew the actor's father sometimes came home from work in clown make-up and terrified his young son.

The fear was still there.

Unit Number Two was scrambled before Charlie was out of his hammock.

They waited. Constant, sticking to a pre-arranged plan, shut down his face, covering a pettish irritation that others did not adhere to such a policy, especially others who were theoretically in a command position.

The Family Führer eventually rolled into the light, beard sticky as a glazed doughnut, scratching lazily. He grinned like a cornered cat and climbed up onto Unit Number One—actually, Unit Number Four with a hastily repainted number since the real Number One was a wreck. As crew, Charlie cut a couple of the girls out of the corral:

the thin and pale Squeaky, who always looked like she'd just been slapped, and a younger, prettier, stranger creature called Ouisch. Other girls glowered sullen resentment and envy at the chosen ones. Ouisch tossed her long dark hair smugly and blew a gum-bubble in triumph. There was muttering of discontent.

If he had been Charlie, Leech would have taken the boy who could fix the motors, not the girls who gave the best blow jobs. But it wasn't his place to give advice.

Charlie was pleased with his mastery over his girls, as if it were difficult to mind control American children. Leech thought that a weakness. Even as Charlie commanded the loyalty of the chicks, the few men in the Family grumbled. They got away with sniping resentment because their skills or contacts were needed. Of the group at the Ranch, only Constant had deal-making potential.

"Let's roll, Rat Patrol," decreed Charlie, waving.

The set-off was complicated by a squabble about protocol. Hitherto, in column outings—and two Units made a column— Charlie had to be in the lead vehicle. However, given that Junior was truffle-pig on this expedition, Unit Number One had to be in the rear, with Number Two out front.

Squeaky explained the rules, at length. Charlie shrugged, grinned and looked ready to doze.

Leech was distracted by a glint from an upper window. A gush of dirty water came from a pipe. Janice Marsh's fish-face loomed in shadows, eyes eager. Stranded and flapping in this desert, no wonder she was thirsty.

Constant counter-argued that this was a search operation, not a victory parade.

"We have rules or we're nothing, Kaptain Kraut," whined Squeaky.

It was easy to hear how she'd got her nickname.

"They should go first, Squeak," said Ouisch. "In case of mines. Or ambush. Charlie should keep back, safe."

"If we're going to change the rules, we should have a meeting."

Charlie punched Squeaky in the head. "Motion carried," he said.

Squeaky rubbed her nut, eyes crossed with anger. Charlie patted her, and she looked up at him, forcing adoration.

Constant turned the ignition—a screwdriver messily wired into the raped steering column—and the engine turned over, belching smoke.

Unit Number Two drove down the track, towards the arch.

Squeaky struggled to get Unit Number One moving.

"We would more efficient be if the others behind stayed, I think," said Constant.

Unit Number One came to life. There were cheers.

"Never mind, li'l buddy," said Junior. "Nice to have pretty girlies along on the trail."

"For some, it is nice."

The two-buggy column passed under the arch.

Junior's *feelings* took them up into the mountains. The buggies struggled with the gradient. These were horse-trails.

"This area, it has been searched thoroughly," said Constant.

"But I got a *powerful* feeling," said Junior.

Junior was eager to help. It had taken some convincing to make him believe in his powers of intuition, but now he had a firm faith in them. He realised he'd always had a supernatural ability to find things misplaced, like keys or watches. All his life, people had pointed it out.

Leech was confident. Junior was well cast as the One Who Will Open the Earth. It was in the prophecies.

Unit Number Two became wedged between rocks.

"This is as far as we can go in the buggy," said Constant.

"That's a real shame," said Junior, shaking his head, "'cause I've a rumbling in my guts that says we should be higher. What do you think, George? Should we keep on keeping on?"

Leech looked up. "If you hear the call."

"You know, George, I think I do. I really do. The call is calling."

"Then we go on."

Unit Number One appeared, and died. Steam hissed out of the radiator.

Charlie sent Ouisch over for a sit-rep.

Constant explained they would have to go on foot from now on.

"Some master driver you are, Schultzie," said the girl, giggling. "Charlie will have you punished for your failure. Severely."

Constant thought better of answering back.

Junior looked at the view, mopping the sweat off his forehead with a blue denim sleeve. Blotches of smog obscured much of the city spread out toward the grey-blue shine of the Pacific. Up here, the air was thin and at least clean.

"Looks like a train-set, George."

"The biggest a boy ever had," said Leech.

Constant had hiking boots and a back-pack with rope, implements and rations. He checked over his gear, professionally.

It had been Ouisch's job to bottle some water, but she'd got stoned last night and forgot. Junior had a hip-flask, but it wasn't full of water.

Leech could manage, but the others might suffer.

"If before we went into the high desert a choice had been presented of whether to go *with* water or *without*, I would have voted for 'with,'" said Constant. "But such a matter was not discussed."

Ouisch stuck her tongue out. She had tattooed a swastika on it with a blue ball-point pen. It was streaky.

Squeaky found a Coca-Cola bottle rolling around in Unit Number One, an inch of soupy liquid in the bottom. She turned it over to Charlie, who drank it down in a satisfied draught. He made as if to toss the bottle off the mountain like a grenade, but Leech took it from him.

"What's the deal, Mr. Fish? No one'll care about littering when Helter Skelter comes down."

"This can be used. Constant, some string, please."

Constant sorted through his pack. He came up with twine and a Swiss army knife.

"Cool blade," said Charlie. "I'd like one like that."

Squeaky and Ouisch looked death at Constant until he handed the knife over. Charlie opened up all the implements, until the knife looked like a triggered booby-trap. He cleaned under his nails with the bradawl.

Leech snapped his fingers. Charlie gave the knife over.

Leech cut a length of twine and tied one end around the bottle's wasp-waist. He dangled it like a plum-bob. The bottle circled slowly.

Junior took the bottle, getting the idea instantly.

Leech closed the knife and held it out on his open palm. Constant resentfully made fists by his sides. Charlie took the tool, snickering to himself. He felt its balance for a moment, then pitched it off the mountainside. The Swiss Army Knife made a long arc into the air and plunged, hundreds and hundreds of feet, bounced off a rock and fell further.

Long seconds later, the tumbling speck disappeared.

"Got to rid ourselves of the trappings, Kraut-Man."

Constant said nothing.

Junior had scrambled up the rocky incline, following the nose of the bottle. "Come on, guys," he called. "This is it. El Doradio. I can feel it in my bones. Don't stick around, slowcoaches."

Charlie was first to follow.

Squeaky, who had chosen to wear flip-flops rather than boots, volunteered to stay behind and guard the Units.

"Don't be a drag-hag, soldier," said Charlie. "Bring up the freakin' rear."

Leech kept pace.

From behind, yelps of pain came frequently.

Leech knew where to step, when to breathe, which rocks were solid enough to provide handholds and which would crumble or come away at a touch. Instinct told him how to hold his body so that gravity didn't tug him off the mountain. His inertia actually helped propel him upwards.

Charlie gave him a sideways look.

Though the man was thick-skinned and jail-tough, physical activity wasn't his favoured pursuit. He needed to make it seem as if he found the mountain path easy, but breathing the air up here was difficult for him. He had occasional coughing jags. Squeaky and Ouisch shouldered their sweet lord's weight and helped him, their own thin legs bending as he relaxed on their support, allowing himself to be lifted as if by angels.

Constant was careful, methodical and made his way on his own.

But Junior was out ahead, following his bottle, scrambling

between rocks and up nearly-sheer inclines. He stopped, stood on a rocky outcrop, and looked down at them, then bellowed for the sheer joy of being alive and in the wilderness.

The sound carried out over the mountains and echoed.

"Charlie," he shouted, "how about one of them songs of yours?"

"Yes, that is an idea good," said Constant, every word barbed. "An inspiration is needed for our mission."

Charlie could barely speak, much less sing 'The Happy Wanderer' in German.

Grimly, Squeaky and Ouisch harmonised a difficult version of 'The Mickey Mouse Marching Song'. Struggling with Charlie's dead weight, they found the will to carry on and even put some spit and vigour into the anthem.

Leech realised at once what Charlie had done.

The con had simply stolen the whole idea outright from Uncle Walt. He'd picked up these dreaming girls, children of post-war privilege raised in homes with buzzing refrigerators in the kitchen and finned automobiles in the garage, recruiting them a few years on from their first Mouseketeer phase, and electing himself Mickey.

Hey there ho there hi there...

When they chanted "Mickey Mouse... Mickey Mouse", Constant even croaked "Donald Duck" on the offbeat.

Like Junior, Leech was overwhelmed with the sheer joy of the century.

He loved these children, dangerous as they were, destructive as they would be. They had such open, yearning hearts. They would find many things to fill their voids and Leech saw that he could be there for them in the future, up to 2001 and beyond, on the generation's ultimate trip.

Unless the rains came first.

"Hey, George," yelled Junior. "I dropped my bottle down a hole."

Everyone stopped and shut up.

Leech listened.

"Aww, what a shame," said Junior. "I lost my bottle."

Leech held up a hand for silence.

Charlie was puzzled, and the girls sat him down.

Long seconds later, deep inside the mountain, he heard a splash. No one else caught the noise.

"It's found," he announced.

Only Ouisch was small enough to pass through the hole. Constant rigged up a rope cradle and lowered her. She waved bye-bye as she scraped into the mountain's throat. Constant measured off the rope in cubits, unrolling loops from his forearm.

Junior sat on the rock, swigging from his flask.

Squeaky glared pantomime evil at him and he offered the flask to Charlie.

"That's your poison, man," he said.

"You should drop acid," said Squeaky. "So you can learn from the wisdom of the mountain."

Junior laughed, big belly-shaking chuckles.

"You're funnin' me, girl. Ain't nothing dumber than a mountain."

Leech didn't add to the debate.

Constant came to end of the rope. Ouisch dangled fifty feet inside the rock.

"It's dark," she shouted up. "And wet. There's water all around. Water with things in it. Icky."

"Have you ever considered the etymology of the term 'icky'?" asked Leech. "Do you suppose this primal, playroom expression of disgust could be related to the Latin prefix 'ichthy', which translates literally as 'fishy'?"

"I was in a picture once, called *Manfish*," said Junior. "I got to be out on boats. I like boats."

"*Manfish*? Interesting name."

"It was the name of the boat in the movie. Not a monster, like that Black Lagoon thing. Universal wouldn't have me in that. I did *The Alligator People*, though. Swamp stuff. Big stiff suitcase-skinned gator-man."

"Man-fish," said Charlie, trying to hop on the conversation train. "I get it. I see where you're coming from, where you're going. The Old Lady. What's she, a mermaid? An old mermaid?"

"You mean she really looks like that?" yelped Squeaky. "The one time I saw her I was tripping. Man, that's messed up! Charlie, I think I'm scared."

Charlie cuffed Squeaky around the head.

"Ow, that hurt."

"Learn from the pain, child. It's the only way."

"You shouldn't ought to hit ladies, Mr. Man," said Junior. "It's not like with guys. Brawlin' is part of being a guy. But with ladies, it's, you know, not polite. Wrong. Even when you've got a snoutful, you don't whop on a woman."

"It's for my own good," said Squeaky, defending her master.

"Gosh, little lady, are you sure?"

"It's the only way I'll learn." Squeaky picked up a rock and hit herself in the head with it, raising a bruise. "I love you, Charlie," she said, handing him the bloody rock.

He kissed the stain, and Squeaky smiled as if she'd won a gold star for her homework and been made head cheerleader on the same morning.

Ouisch popped her head up out of the hole like a pantomime chimneysweep. She had adorable dirt on her cheeks.

"There's a way down," she said. "It's narrow here, but opens out. I think it's a, whatchumacallit, passage. The rocks feel smooth. We'll have to enbiggen the hole if you're all to get through."

Constant looked at the problem. "This stone, that stone, that stone," he said, pointing out loose outcrops around the lip of the hole. "They will come away."

Charlie was about to make fun of the German boy, but held back. Like Leech, he sensed that the kid knew what he was talking about.

"I study engineering," Constant said. "I thought I might build houses."

"Have to tear down before you can build up," said Charlie.

Constant and Squeaky wrestled with rocks, wrenching them loose, working faults into cracks. Ouisch slipped into the hole, to be out of the way.

Charlie didn't turn a hand to the work. He was here in a supervisory capacity.

Eventually the stones were rolled away.

"Strange, that is," said Constant as sun shone into the hole. "Those could be steps."

There were indeed stairs in the hole.

Constant, of course, had brought a battery flashlight. He shone it into the hole. Ouisch sat on a wet step.

The stairs were old, pre-human.

Charlie tapped Squeaky, pushed her a little. She eased herself into the hole, plopping down next to Ouisch.

"You light the way," he told Constant. "The girls will scout ahead. Reconnaissance."

"Nothing down there but water," said Junior. "Been there a long time."

"Maybe no people. But big blind fish."

The Family crowd descended the stairs, their light swallowed by the hole.

Leech and Junior lingered topside.

Charlie looked up. "You comin' along, Mr. Fish?"

Leech nodded. "It's all right," he told Junior. "We'll be safe in the dark."

Inside the mountain, everything was cold and wet. Natural tunnels had been shaped by intelligent (if webbed) hands at some point. The roofs were too low even for the girls to walk comfortably, but scarred patches of rock showed where paths had been cut, and the floor was smoothed by use. Sewer-like runnel-gutters trickled with fresh water. Somehow, no one liked to drink the stuff—though the others must all have a desert thirst.

They started to find carved designs on the rocks. At first, childish wavy lines with stylised fish swimming.

Charlie was excited by the nearness of the sea.

They could hear it, roaring below. Junior felt the pull of the water.

Leech heard the voices in the roar.

Like a bloodhound, Junior led them through triune junctions, down forking stairways, past stalactite-speared cave-dwellings, deeper into the three-dimensional maze inside the mountain.

"We're going to free the waters," said Charlie. "Let the deluge wash down onto the city. This mountain is like a big dam. It can be blown."

The mountain was more like a stopper jammed onto a bottle. Charlie was right about pressure building up. Leech felt it in his inner ears, his eyes, his teeth. Squeaky had a nosebleed. The air was thick, wet with vapour. Marble-like balls of water gathered on the rock roof and fell on them, splattering on clothes like liquid bullets. In a sense, they were already underwater.

It would take more than dynamite to loose the flood; indeed, it would take more than physics. However, Charlie was not too far off the mark in imagining what could be done by loosening a few key rocks. There was the San Andreas fault to play with. Constant would know which rocks to take out of the puzzle. A little directed spiritual energy, some sacrifices, and the Coast of California could shear away like a slice of pie. Then the stopper would be off, and the seas would rise, waking up the gill-people, the mer-folk, the squidface fellows. A decisive turn and a world war would be lost, by the straights, the over-thirties, the cops and docs and pols, the Man. Charlie and Chocko could stage their last war games, and the sea-birds would cheer *tekeli-li tekeli-li…*

Leech saw it all, like a coming attraction. And he wasn't sure he wanted to pay to see that movie.

Maybe on a re-run triple feature with drastically reduced admission, slipped in between *Night of the Living Dead* and *Planet of the Apes*.

Seriously, *Hello Dolly!* spoke to him more on his level.

"The Earth is hollow," said Charlie. "The Nazis knew that."

Constant winced at mention of Nazis. Too many Gestapo jokes had made him sensitive.

"Inside, there are the big primal forces, water and fire. They're here for us, space kiddettes. For the Family. This is where the Helter Skelter comes down."

The tunnel opened up into a cathedral.

They were on an upper level of a tiered array of galleries and balconies. Natural rock and blocky construction all seemed to have melted like wax, encrusted with salty matter. Stalactites hung in spiky curtains, stalagmites raised like obscene columns.

Below, black waters glistened.

Constant played feeble torchlight over the interior of the vast space.

"Far out, man," said Ouisch.

"Beautiful," said Junior.

There was an echo, like the wind in a pipe organ.

Greens and browns mingled in curtains of icy rock, colours unseen for centuries.

"Here's your story," said Constant.

He pointed the torch at a wall covered in an intricate carving. A sequence of images—an *underground comic*!—showed the mountain opening up, the desert fractured by a jagged crack, a populated flood gushing forth, a city swept into the sea. There was a face on the mountain, grinning in triumph—Charlie, with a swastika on his forehead, his beard and hair tangled like seaweed.

"So, is that your happy ending?" Leech asked.

For once, Charlie was struck dumb. Until now he had been riffing, a yarning jailbird puffing up his crimes and exploits, spinning sci-fi stories and channelling nonsense from the void. To keep himself amused as he marked off the days of his sentence.

"Man," he said, "it's all true."

This face proved it.

"This is the future. Helter Skelter."

Looking closer at the mural, the city wasn't exactly Los Angeles, but an Aztec-Atlantean analogue. Among the drowning humans were fishier bipeds. There were step-pyramids and Studebaker dealerships, temples of sacrifice and motion picture studios.

"It's *one* future," said Leech. "A possible, maybe probable future."

"And you've brought me to it, man. I knew you were the real deal!"

The phrase came back in an echo, "real deal… real deal".

"The real deal? Very perceptive. This is where we make the real deal, Charles. This is where we take the money or open the box, this is make-your-mind-up-time."

Charlie's elation was cut with puzzlement.

"I've dropped that tab," announced Ouisch.

Junior looked around. "Where? Let's see if we can pick it up."

Charlie took Constant's torch and shone it at Leech.

"You don't blink."

"No."

Charlie stuck the torch under his chin, demon-masking his features. He tried to snarl like his million-year-old carved portrait.

"But I'm the Man, now. The Man of the Mountain."

"I don't dispute that."

"The Old Lady has told me how it works," said Charlie, pointing to his head. "You think I don't get it, but I do. We've been stashing ordinance. The kraut's a demolition expert. He'll see where to place the charges. Bring this place down and let the waters out. I know that's not enough. This is an imaginary mountain as much as it is a physical one. That's why they've been filming crappy Westerns all over it for so long. This is a place of stories. And it has to be opened in the mind, has to be cracked on another plane. I've been working on the rituals. My album, that's one. And the blood sacrifices, the offerings of the pigs."

"I can't wait to off my first pig," said Ouisch, cutely wrinkling her nose.

"I'm going to be so freakin' *famous*."

"Famous ain't all that," put in Junior. "You think bein' famous will make things work out right, but it doesn't at all. Screws you up more, if you ask me."

"I didn't, Mummy Man," spat Charlie. "You had your shot, dragged your leg through the tombs…"

Squeaky began to sing, softly.

"We shall over-whelm, we shall over-whe-e-elm, we shall overwhelm some day-ay-ay…"

Charlie laughed.

"It's the end of their world. No more goddamn' movies. You know how much I hate the movies? The *lies* in the movies. Now, I get to wipe Hollywood off the map. Hell, I get to wipe the *map* off the map. I'll burn those old Spanish charts when we get back to the Ranch. No more call for them."

Constant was the only one paying attention to Leech. Smart boy.

"It'll be so *simple*," said Charlie. "So pure. All the pigs get offed. Me and Chocko do the last dance. I defeat the clowns, lay them down forever. Then we start all over. Get it right this time."

"Simple," said Leech. "Yes, that's the word."

"This happened before, right? With the Old Lady's people. The menfish. Then we came along, the menmen, and fouled it up again, played exactly the same tune. Not this time. This time, there's the Gospel According to Charlie."

"Hooray and Hallelujah," sang Ouisch, "you got it comin' to ya…"

The drip of water echoed enormously, like the ticking of a great clock.

"I do believe our interests part the ways here," said Leech. "You yearn for simplicity, like these children. You hate the movies, the storybooks, but you want cartoons, you want a big finish and a new episode next week. Wipe it all away and get back to the garden. It's easy because you don't have to think about it."

He hadn't lost Charlie, but he was scaring the man. Good.

"I like complexity," said Leech, relishing the echo. "I *love* it. There are so many more opportunities, so many more arrangements to be made. What *I* want is a rolling apocalypse, a transformation, a thousand victories a day, a spreading of interests, a permanent revolution. My natural habitat is civilisation. Your ultimate deluge might be amusing for a moment, but it'd pass. Even you'd get bored with children sitting around adoring you."

"You think?"

"I *know*, Charles."

Charlie looked at the faces of Ouisch and Squeaky, American girls, unquestioningly loyal, endlessly tiresome.

"No, Mr. Fish," he said, indicating the mural. "This is what I want. This is what I want to do."

"I brought you here. I showed you this."

"I know. You're part of the story too, aren't you? If the Mummy Man is the One Who Will Open the Earth, you're the Mysterious Guide."

"I'm not so mysterious."

"You're a part of this, you don't have a choice."

Charlie was excited but wheedling, persuasive but panicky. Having seen his preferred future, he was worried about losing it. Whenever the torch was away from the mural, he itched lest it should change in the dark.

"I promise you this, Charles, you will be famous."

Charlie thumped his chest. "Damn right. Good goddamn right!"

"But you might want to give this up. Write off this scripted Armageddon as just another fish story. You know, the one that got away. It was *this big*. I have other plans for the end of this century. And beyond. Have you ever noticed how it's only Gods who keep threatening to end the world? Father issues, if you ask me. Others, those of my party, promise things will continue as they are. Everyone gets what they deserve. You ain't seen nothin' yet because what you give is what you get."

Charlie shook his head. "I'm not there."

Squeaky and Ouisch were searching the mural, trying to find themselves in the crowded picture.

Charlie's eyes shone, ferocious.

"Our deal was to bring you here," said Leech, "to this sea. To this place of revelation. Our business is concluded. The service you requested has been done."

Junior raised a modest flipper, acknowledging his part.

"Yeah," said Charlie, distracted, flicking fingers at Junior, "muchas grassy-asses."

"You have recompensed our friend for his part in this expedition, by ensuring that his employers finish their shoot unimpeded. That deal is done and everyone is square. Now, let's talk about *getting out* of the mountain."

Charlie bit back a grin, surprised.

"What are you prepared to offer for that?"

"Don't be stupid, man," said Charlie. "We just go back on ourselves."

"Are you so confident? We took a great many turns and twists. Smooth rock and running water. We left no signs. Some of us might have a mind to sit by the sea for a spell, make some rods and go fishing."

"Good idea, George," said Junior. "Catch a marlin, I bet. Plenty good eating."

Charlie's eyes widened.

After a day or so, the torch batteries would die. He might wander blindly for months, *years*, down here, hopelessly lost, buried alive. Back at the Ranch, he'd not be missed much; Tex, or one of the others, maybe one of the girls, could be the new Head of the Family, and would perhaps do things better all round. The girls would be no use to him, in the end. Squeaky and Ouisch couldn't guide him out of this fish city, and he couldn't live off them for more than a few weeks. Charlie saw the story of the Lost Voyager as vividly as he had the Drowning of Los Angeles. It ended not with a huge face carved on a mountain and feared, but with forgotten bones, lying forever in wet darkness.

"I join you in fishing, I think," said Constant.

Charlie had lost Constant on the mountain. Later, Leech would formalise a deal with the boy. He had an ability to put things together or take them apart. Charlie had been depending on that. He should have taken the trouble to offer Constant something of equal value to retain his services.

"No, no, this can't be right."

"You show Charlie the way out, meanie," said Ouisch, shoving Junior.

"If you know what's good for you," said Squeaky.

"One word and you're out of here safe, Charles," said Leech. "But abandon the deluge. I want Los Angeles where it is. I want *civilisation* just where it is. I have plans, you dig?"

"You're scarin' me, man," said Charlie, nervy, strained, near tears.

Leech smiled. He knew he showed more teeth than seemed possible.

"Yes," he said, the last sound hissing in echo around the cavern. "I know."

Minutes passed. Junior hummed a happy tune, accompanied by musical echoes from the stalactites.

Leech looked at Charlie, out-staring his Satan glare, trumping his ace.

At last, in a tiny voice, Charlie said, "Take me home."

Leech was magnanimous. "But of course, Charles. Trust me, this way will suit you better. Pursue your interests, wage your war against the dream factory, and you will be remembered. Everyone will know your name."

"Yeah, man, whatever. Let's get going."

"Creighton," said Leech. "It's night up top. The moon is full. Do you think you can lead us to the moonlight?"

"Sure thing, George. I'm the Wolf Man, ahhh-*woooooo*!"

Janice Marsh had died while they were under the mountain. Her room stank and bad water sloshed on the carpets. The tarpaulin served as her shroud.

Leech hated to let her down, but she'd had too little to bring to the table. She had been a coelacanth, a living fossil.

Charlie announced that he was abandoning the search for the Subterranean Sea of California, that there were other paths to Helter Skelter. After all, was it not written that when you get to the bottom you start again at the top. He told his Family that his album would change the world when he got it together with Dennis, and he sang them a song about how the pigs would suffer.

Inside, Charlie was terrified. That would make him more dangerous.

But not as dangerous as Derek Leech.

Before he left the Ranch, in a requisitioned buggy with Constant at the wheel, Leech sat a while with Junior.

"You've contributed more than you know," he told Junior. "I don't often do this, but I feel you're owed. So, no deals, no contracts, just an offer. A no-strings offer. It will set things square between us. What do you want? What can I do for you?"

Leech had noticed how hoarse Junior's speech was, gruffer even than you'd expect after years of chilli and booze. His father had died of throat cancer, a silent movie star bereft of his voice. The same poison was just touching the son, extending tiny filaments of death around his larynx. If asked, Leech could call them off, take away the disease.

Or he could fix up a big budget star vehicle at Metro, a Lifetime Achievement Academy Award, a final marriage to Ava Gardner, a top-ten record with the Monkees, a hit TV series…

Junior thought a while, then hugged Leech.

"You've already done it, George. You've already granted my wish. You call me by my name. By my Mom's name. Not by *his*, not by 'Junior'. They had to starve me into taking it. That's all I ever wanted. My own name."

It was so simple. Leech respected that; those who asked only for a little respect, a little place of their own—they should get what they deserve, as much as those who came greedily to the feast, hoping for all you can eat.

"Goodbye, Creighton," he said.

Leech walked away from a happy man.

TAKE ME TO THE RIVER

by PAUL McAULEY

THE FIRST AND probably last Bristol Free Festival hadn't drawn anything like the numbers its blithely optimistic organisers had predicted, but even so, the crowd was four or five times as big as any Martin Feather had ever faced. Martin had been brought in as a last-minute replacement after the regular keyboard player in Sea Change, the semi-professional group headlining the bill, had broken his arm in a five-a-side football match. Last night's run-through had gone okay, but now, in the mouth of the beast, Martin was beginning to get the jitters. The rest of the band were happy to hang out backstage, passing around a fat spliff, drinking free beer, and bullshitting with a mini-skirted reporter from the *Bristol Evening Post*, but Martin was too wound-up to stay still, and after his third visit to the smelly Port-A-Loo he wandered around to the front of the stage to check out the action.

It was the hottest day yet in the hottest summer in living memory. More than three hundred people sprawled on drought-browned grass in front of the stage, and a couple of hundred more queued at ice-cream vans and deathburger carts or poked around stalls that sold vegetarian food, incense sticks and lumpy bits of hand-thrown pottery, hand-printed silk scarves and antique shawls and dresses. A fire-eater and a juggler entertained the festival-goers; a mime did his level best to piss them off. There was a fortune teller in a candy-striped tent. There were hippies and bikers, straight families and sullen groups of teenagers, small kids running around in face paint and dressing-up-box cowboy outfits and fairy princess dresses, naked toddlers, and a barechested sunburnt guy with long blond hair and white jeans who stood front and centre of the stage, arms held out crucifixion-style and face turned up to the blank blue sky, as he grokked the music. He'd been there all afternoon, assuming the same pose for the Trad Jazz group, the pair of lank-haired unisex folk singers, the steel band, a group of teenagers who'd come all the way from Yeovil to play Gene Vincent's greatest hits, and the reggae that the DJ played between sets. And now for Clouds of Memory, second-from-top on the bill, and currently bludgeoning their way through 'Paint It Black'.

Martin had joined Clouds of Memory a few months ago, but he'd quickly fallen out with the singer and lead guitarist, Simon Cowley, an untalented egomaniac who couldn't stay in key if his life depended on it. Martin still rankled over the way he'd been peremptorily fired after a gig in Yate and left to find his own way home (it hadn't helped that his girlfriend had dumped him in the same week), but watching his nemesis make a buffoon of himself didn't seem like a bad way to keep his mind off his stomach's flip-flops.

Simon Cowley ended 'Paint It Black' by wrenching an unsteady F chord from his guitar a whole beat behind the rest of the band, and stood centre-stage with one arm raised in triumph, as if the scattering of polite applause was a standing ovation. His shoulder-length blond hair was tangled across his face. He was wearing a red jumpsuit and white cowboy boots. He turned to the drummer and brought down his arm, kicking off the doomy opening chords of his self-penned set-closing epic, 'My Baby's Gone to UFO Heaven', and Martin saw Dr. John stepping through the people scattered at the fringe of the audience, heading straight towards him.

He should have known at once that it meant trouble. Dr. John was a small-time hustler who, after dropping out of Bristol University's Medical School, supplemented his dole by buying grass and hash at street-price in St. Paul's, Bristol's pocket ghetto, and selling it for a premium to students. They'd first met because Dr. John rented a rotten little flat above the club where Martin had been working. Dr. John had introduced Martin to the dubious delights of the Coronation Tap, and after Martin had set up his hole-in-the-wall secondhand record shop, Dr. John would stop by once or twice a week to sell LPs he'd found in junkshops or jumble sales, or had taken from students in exchange for twists of seeds and stems. He'd tell Martin to put on some reggae and turn it up, and do what he called the monkey dance. He'd flip through the stock boxes, pulling out albums and saying with mock-amazement, "Can you believe this shit? Can you believe anyone would actually pay money for it?" He'd look over the shoulders of browsing customers and tell them, "I wouldn't buy that, man. It'll make your ears bleed. It'll lower your IQ," or he'd read out the lyrics of prog rock songs in a plummy voice borrowed from Peter Sellers until Martin lost patience and told him to piss off. Then he'd shuffle towards the door, apologising loudly for upsetting the nice middle-class students, pausing before he stepped out, asking Martin if he'd see him at the Coronation Tap later on.

When he wasn't hustling dope or secondhand records, Dr. John spent most of his time in the Tap, sinking liver-crippling amounts of psychedelically strong scrumpy cider, bullshitting, and generally taking the piss. Like many people who aren't comfortable in their own skins, he was restless, took great delight in being obnoxious, and preferred other people's voices to his own. He would recite entire *Monty Python* sketches at the drop of a hat, or try to hold conversations in Captain Beefheart lyrics ("The past sure is tense, Martin! A big-eyed bean from Venus told me that. Know what I mean?"). His favourite film was *Get Carter*, and he could play Jack Carter for a whole evening. "A pint of scrumpy," he'd say to the landlord, "in a thin glass." Or he'd walk up to the biggest biker in the pub and tell him, "You're a big man, but you're in bad shape. With me, it's a full-time job. So behave yourself." Amazingly, he was never beaten up, although a burly student in a rugby shirt once threw a full pint of beer in his face after being told that his eyes were like piss-holes in snow.

Dr. John's scrumpy-fuelled exploits were legendary. The time he'd been arrested for walking down the middle of Whiteladies Road with a traffic cone on his head. The time he'd tried to demonstrate how stuntmen could fall flat on their faces, and had broken one of his front teeth on the pavement. The time he'd climbed into a tree and gone to sleep, waking up a couple of hours later and falling ten feet onto the roof of a car, leaving a dent the exact shape of his body and walking away without a bruise. The time he'd slipped on ice, fallen over, and smashed the bottle of whiskey in his pocket: a shard of glass had penetrated his thigh and damaged a nerve, leaving him with a slight but permanent limp. His life was like a cartoon. He was Tom in *Tom and Jerry*, Wile E. Coyote in *Roadrunner*. He was one of those people who bang their way from one pratfall to the next in the kind of downhill spiral that seems funny as long as you don't get too close.

Now he gimped up to Martin, a short, squat guy with a cloud of curly black hair and a wispy beard, wearing a filthy denim jacket, a Black Sabbath T-shirt, and patchwork flares, saying loudly, "Didn't you used to be in this band?"

"For about five minutes in April."

Dr. John sneered at the stage. "You're well out of it, man. Is that a gong I see, right there behind the drummer? It is, isn't it? Fucking poseurs."

"If they dumped Simon and found someone who could actually sing and play lead guitar, they might have the kernel of a good sound. Put the bass and drums front and centre, like a reggae set-up."

"Not that you're bitter or anything," Dr. John said. He pulled a clear glass bottle half-filled with a cloudy brown liquid from one pocket of his denim jacket, unscrewed the cap and took a long swallow, belched, and offered it to Martin.

Martin took a cautious sip and immediately spat it out. "Jesus. What is it?"

"Woke up on the floor of this strange flat this morning, man. I must have been invited to a party. I mixed myself a cocktail with what was left." Dr. John snatched back the bottle, took another pull, and smacked his lips. "You have to admit it has a certain vigour."

"It tastes like cough medicine. There's beer backstage, if you want some."

"Backstage? Were you playing, man? I'm sorry to have missed it."

"I'm on next. Playing with the headliners."

"Free beer, man, now I know you're a star."

"I'm only a stand-in, but I get all the perks."

On stage, Simon Cowley, his face screwed up inside a fall of blond hair, was hunched over his guitar and picking his way through an extended solo. When Martin had joined Clouds of Memory, he'd tried to get them interested in the raw new stuff coming out of New York and London—Television and the Ramones, Dr. Feelgood and the 101ers—but Simon had sneered and said it was nothing but three-chord pub rock with no trace of musical artistry whatsoever. 'Artistry' was one of Simon's favourite words. He was the kind of guy who spent Saturday afternoons in guitar shops, pissing off the assistants by playing note-by-note copies of Jimmy Page and Eric Clapton solos. He liked to drop quotes from Nietzsche and Hesse into casual conversation. He was a big fan of Eric Von Daniken. He subscribed to the muso's music paper, *Melody Maker*, and despised the achingly hip streetwise attitudes of the *New Musical Express*, which Martin read from cover to cover every week. The tension between them had simmered for a couple of weeks, until, while they were packing up after that gig in Yate, Simon had picked an argument with Martin and sacked him on the spot.

Dr. John took another swig of his cocktail and said, "Sabbath, man, they're the only ones who can do this kind of thing properly. Did I tell you about the gig at Colston Hall this spring?"

"Only about a hundred times."

"It wasn't loud enough, but that was the only thing wrong with it. A thousand kids belting out 'Paranoid' at the top of their lungs, it was a religious experience. But this, this is like…" He looked up at the sky for inspiration, failed to find it, and took another drink.

"It's prog rock crap," Martin said, "but Dancing Jesus likes it."

The barechested guy stood in the middle of the thin crowd, arms flung wide, face tilted to the blue sky, quivering all over.

Dr. John's lifted his upper lip in a sneering smile that showed off his broken tooth. "Where his head's at, man, he'd groove on anything. I sold him my last three tabs of acid and he dropped them all. Anyone's in UFO heaven, it's him."

"Made much money here?"

"I'm here for the vibe, man."

"Right."

"Truly. I'm down to seeds and stems until Tuesday or Wednesday, when this a guy I know is going to deliver some primo hash. Moroccan gold, man, the real no-camel-shit-whatsoever deal. This guy, his brother's a sailor, gets the stuff straight from the souk. I'll put you down for an eighth, seeing as you're a good pal and a professional musician and everything." Dr. John looked around and sidled closer and said, "Plus, you can help me out a little right now."

Martin was instantly wary. He said, "I'm on after this lot finishes."

"I've seen these fuckers play before, man. They're getting into the drum solo, and then there's the bass solo, that plonker's endless guitar wankery… You've got plenty of time. And it's a really simple favour."

"I bet."

"A lot easier than saving someone from a beating."

A few weeks ago, at a dub concert in a community hall in St. Paul's, a gang of Jamaican youths had decided to get territorial on Martin's bloodclat white ass. Dr. John and his dealer had chased them off, a heroic deed Dr. John had mentioned no more than fifty or sixty times since. Martin said, "I believe it was your friend Hector who actually saved me."

"But I alerted him to the situation, I asked him to help you out because you're a good friend of mine. And friends have to look after each other, right?"

Martin sighed. "If I do this thing for you, will you promise to never mention St. Paul's again?"

"Cross my heart and hope to die, man. See that girl?" Dr. John put his arm around Martin, enveloping him in a powerful odour compounded of stale booze, sweat, and pot smoke, and turned him around.

"What am I looking at?"

"The girl, man. Black hair, white dress."

She stood beside the St John's ambulance, in the narrow wedge of shadow it cast. Tall and willowy in a long white dress that clung to her curves, her arms bare and pale, her elfin face framed by a Louise Brooks bob of midnight-black hair.

"I've been watching her," Dr. John said.

"I don't think she's your type."

Regulars at the Tap sometimes speculated about Dr. John's sex life. Everyone agreed that he must have one, but no one could imagine what it could be like.

"She's dealing, man. Actually, she's not really dealing because there's no money changing hands, she's been handing out freebies all afternoon. What you can do for me is sashay over there and cop a sample of whatever it is she's holding. See, it really is an easy-peasey little favour."

"If it's so easy, why don't you do it?"

"Man, that would hardly be cool. I'd blow my reputation if I was seen taking a hand-out from some hippy chick."

"But I wouldn't."

"That's different, man. You're not in the business. You're a civilian. Go get a sample, okay? And talk to her, try to find out where she's getting her stuff from. A chick like that, she has to be fronting for someone. Maybe those guys who muscled into my business at the Student Union."

"The ones who put the Fear in you," Martin said.

One day at the beginning of the long, hot summer, Dr. John had walked into the Tap with two black eyes and a split lip, and insisted on showing everyone the stitches in his scalp whether they wanted to look or not. "Four fuckers beat me up round the back of the Student Union. Told me that it was their territory from now on. Some pockmarked guy with a goatee is working my spot now, turning the kids on to brown heroin by telling them that he's out of grass right now but if they'd like to try a sample of this little powder…" Dr. John had looked solemn for a moment, then had put on his *Get Carter* voice. "Still, look on the bright side. They're only fucking students. Maybe a bit of heroin will light up their immensely dull lives."

Now he told Martin, "I'm scared of nothing, man. Still, if she *is* working for them, and they see me talking to her… You see what I mean? But you're a civilian. They won't touch you."

"She looks like she's from some cult," Martin said. "Like the Hare Krishnas who were here earlier, handing out copies of George's favourite book."

"Don't knock the guys in orange, man, they serve a mean lentil curry to people who, because of the government's attitude to alternative lifestyles, often find themselves having to choose between eating and paying the rent. Just walk over there, cop a little of what's she's holding, and come right back. It'll take you all of thirty seconds, and I swear I won't mention saving your life ever again."

"I'll do it," Martin said, "as long as you stop making those puppy eyes at me."

He tried to affect a cool stroll as he moved through the crowd towards the girl. The closer he got, the less attractive she appeared. Her face was plastered in white powder, her Louise Brooks bob was a cheap nylon wig, and her skin was puffy and wrinkled, as if she'd spent a couple of days in a bath. Martin told her that he'd heard she had some good stuff, and she looked at him for a moment, a gaze so penetrating he felt she had seen through to the floor of his soul, before she shook her head and looked past him at something a million miles away.

Martin said, "You don't have anything for me? How about for my friends? They're playing next, and they could do with a little lift."

She was staring straight through him. As if, after she'd dismissed him, he'd ceased to exist. Her eyes were bloodshot and slightly bulging, rimmed with thick mascara that made them seem even bigger. Her white dress was badly waterstained, and a clammy odour rose from it.

"Maybe I'll see you around," Martin said, remembering how he'd felt when he'd suffered one of his numerous rejections at the school disco. It didn't help that a gang of teenage boys jeered and toasted him with bottles of cider as he walked away.

Dr. John was waiting for him backstage, a plastic pint glass in his hand.

"I see you found the free beer," Martin said.

"You really are a superstar, man. I mention your name and it's like magic, this beer suddenly appears. What did she slip you? What did she say?"

"She didn't say a word, and she didn't slip me anything either. It's probably some kind of scam involving herbal crap made from boiled nettle leaves or grass-type grass, and she realised that I'd see right through it."

"All the best gear is herbal," Dr. John said, and launched into a spiel about William Burroughs and a South American Indian drug that was blown into your nostrils through a yard-long pipe and took you on a magical mystery tour, stopping only to give Simon Cowley a shit-eating grin as he came off stage, saying, "Fab set, man. Reminded me of Herman's Hermits at their peak."

Simon looked at Martin and said, "Still hanging out with losers I see," and walked past, chin in the air.

Then Martin was busy setting up his keyboards while the two festival roadies took down Clouds of Memory's drums and mikes and assembled Sea Change's kit, and before he knew it the set had kicked off. The sun was setting and a hot wind was getting up, fluttering the stage's canvas roof, blowing the music towards the traffic that scuttled along the far edge of Clifton Downs. Martin concentrated fiercely on playing all the right notes in the right order in the right place, but whenever he had a few moment's rest he glanced towards the girl. Seeing her beyond the glare of the footlights, seeing her with a hairy hippy with a beer-drinker's belly, a couple of giggling girls who couldn't have been more than fifteen, a bearded boy in bellbottoms and a brown chalkstripe waistcoat, a woman in a summer dress and a chiffon scarf...

When he came off, sweating hard after two encores, the rhythm guitarist of Clouds of Memory got in his face, saying something about his loser friend spiking beer. Martin brushed him off and went to look for Dr. John. There was no sign of him, backstage or front. The crowd was beginning to drift away. Two men in black uniforms had opened the back doors of the ambulance and were packing away their first aid kit. The girl was gone.

Martin didn't think any more about it until early the next morning, when he was woken by the doorbell. It was Monday morning, ten to eight, already stiflingly hot, and Martin had a hangover from the post-gig pub session with the guys from Sea Change and their wives and girlfriends and hangers-on. When the bell rang he put a pillow over his head, but the bell just wouldn't quit, a steady drilling that resonated at the core of his headache. Clearly, some moron had SuperGlued his finger to the bell push, and at last Martin got up and padded into the living room and looked out of the window to see who it was.

Martin's flat was on the top floor of a house in the middle of Worcester Terrace, a row of Georgian houses that the professional middle classes were beginning to reclaim from decades of low rent squalor. Four storeys below, Dr. John stood like a smudge of soot on the clean white doorstep, looking up and waving cheerfully when Martin asked him if he'd lost his mind.

"I've had a bit of an adventure," he shouted.

Martin put his keys in a sock and threw them down. By the time his visitor had laboured up the stairs he was dressed and in the kitchen, making tea. Dr. John stood in the doorway, making a noise like a deflating set of bagpipes. He had turned a colour normally associated with aubergines or baboons' bottoms. When he had his breath back, he said, "You should find somewhere nearer the ground. I think I have altitude sickness."

"I should punch you in the snout."

"Whatever it is you think I did, I didn't do it." Dr. John flopped heavily onto one of the kitchen chairs. He had the bright eyes and clenched jaw of a speed buzz. There was fresh mud on the knees of his jeans. Grass stains on his denim jacket; a leafy twig in his bird's nest hair.

"Then you didn't spike Simon Cowley's beer."

"Oh, *that*." Dr. John opened a Virginia tobacco tin and took out a roll-up. "Yeah, I did that. You have bacon and eggs to go with this tea?"

"If I had any bacon I'd give you bacon and eggs if I had any eggs."

Dr. John lit the roll-up and looked around the little kitchen. "I see you have cornflakes."

"Knock yourself out. What did you spike him with?"

"The herbal shit I scored off that girl." Dr. John poured milk over the bowlful of cornflakes. "Is that hot chocolate I see by the kettle?"

"So you blew your reputation as a professional drug-dealer to check out this hippy chick."

Dr. John shook chocolate powder over his cornflakes. "My curiosity was piqued."

"Did she give you anything?"

"She handed it over without a word. Check it out." Dr. John fished something from the pocket of his denim jacket and showed it to Martin. It was the size of his thumbnail and crudely pressed from a greenish paste; it looked more like a bird-dropping than a pill. "Weird-looking shit, huh? So weird, in fact, that even *I* wouldn't take it without testing it first. So I broke off the smallest little sliver and dropped it in Mr. UFO's beer."

"Too much acid has fried your brains."

"But in the best possible way." Dr. John was bent over the bowl, spooning up chocolate powder/milk/cornflakes mix. The roll-up was still glued to the corner of his mouth. Although the window was open, his funky odour filled the kitchen. "So, did my freebie take your wanky friend to somewhere good?"

"Good enough for his pal to know he'd been spiked."

"It didn't give him fits, make him foam at the mouth, make him sing in tune?"

"I didn't hang around to find out. He just looked very spaced. Had a thousand yard stare and a stupid grin."

"Cool. Maybe I'll give it a test flight this afternoon. Make me some more tea, man, and I'll tell you about the girl."

Dr. John said that he had followed her across the Downs into the wild strip of woods along the edge of the Avon Gorge. "She was like an elf, man. Breezed through those fucking woods as if she was born to it."

"So she isn't the front for Turkish gangsters. She really is just some crazy hippy."

"She might have been crazy, but she really could move. Floated right down those steep narrow paths to the bottom of the gorge in about a minute flat. I got stuck halfway, saw her cross the road at the bottom, saw her climbing over the rail on the other side, down to the river." Dr. John lit a fresh roll-up and looked at Martin, suddenly serious. "You know how the Avon is almost dried up because of the drought? There's grass growing on the mud, and where grass isn't growing it's all dry and cracked. She walked over that shit, man, straight towards what's left of the river. Then a couple of lorries went past, and when they were gone she wasn't there any more."

"She jumped into the river? Come on."

"One moment she was walking across those mud flats, and then those bastard lorries came along, and she was gone, that's all I know."

"Let me get this straight. She was giving away some kind of drug for free, and then she was struck by a fit of remorse, so she walked down to the river and drowned herself."

Martin, used to Dr. John's fantastic stories, reckoned that about half of what he'd been told was true. He believed that his friend had tried to follow the girl and lost her in the woods; the rest was just the usual bullshit embellishment.

"I don't know what her motivation was, man. I only know what I saw."

"You didn't go look for her? Or call the police?"

"I was on this dead-end path halfway up the side of the fucking gorge. I couldn't go any further, all I could do was climb up and start over, and if she reappeared while I was finding a new way down I would have missed her. So I sat there and kept watch, but the light was going, and I didn't see her again, and after a bit I suppose I fell asleep. Woke up this morning covered in dew, with this bastard headache."

"Let me guess: while you were keeping a look-out for this girl, you finished off your party cocktail."

"It was my only sustenance, man. I wasn't about to start eating leaves."

"Well, look on the bright side. If she did drown herself, you don't have to worry that she'll steal your customers."

"You don't believe me. That's cool. But I viddied it, brother, with my own glazzies. She walked over the mud and then she... Shit!"

Dr. John's chair went over as he pushed away from the table. Martin turned, saw the bird on the stone ledge outside the window. His first thought was that it was a gull, but although it was the right mix of white and grey, it was twice the size of any ordinary gull, and sort of lop-sided, and stank horribly, like rotten meat and low-tide sewage. When he reached out to shut the window, it fixed him with a mad red eye and snapped at his hand, its sharp yellow bill splintering the window frame when he snatched his fingers away. Then it stretched its wings (one seemed longer than the other, and both had growths, bat-like claws, at their joints) and dropped away in a half-turn and floated out across the communal gardens of the terrace, a white speck dwindling away towards the docks.

Dr. John kept glancing up at the sky as he walked with Martin up the hill towards the centre of Clifton. He was convinced that the bird had something to do with the girl. "It was a spy, man. A mutant gull from the lower depths of wherever she came from."

"It had some sort of disease," Martin said.

Dr. John turned a full circle, his face tipped skywards, and said in a sonorous film trailer baritone, "A mutant gull on a mission from Hell."

"You see pigeons with parts of their feet missing all the time. It's something to do with walking on pavements."

Dr. John laughed. "You're so straight, man, they could use you as a ruler."

"Maybe it ate a bad kebab on a rubbish tip."

"Maybe it ate one of the Tap's mystery meat pies. I'm pretty sure they've fried *my* chromosomes." Dr. John did a lurching Frankenstein walk for a few steps, arms held straight out, eyes rolled back.

They parted by the tidy park landscaped around the ruins of a church that had been hit by a German bomb during Bristol's Blitz. Dr. John said he was going to go home and drop that pill and see where it took him.

"Don't be crazy," Martin said.

"It's all part of my ongoing exploration of inner space, man. Cheaper than TV and a lot more fun."

"It's probably made out of hemlock and lead paint. Weedkiller and rat snot."

"Don't be such a worrywart. There isn't a pill or powder I can't handle," Dr. John said, and sloped off across the grassy space, a squat stubborn figure listing slightly to the left.

* * *

The next day, lunchtime in the Coronation Tap, one of Dr. John's grebo pals lurched up to Martin and asked where the little fucker was hiding himself.

"I'm not his keeper," Martin said. He was having a quiet pint and a pastie, and thinking about whether to shut up shop for a couple of weeks and go on holiday. The only customer he'd had all morning had been a confused old lady who, after poking about in the bins for ten minutes, had asked him if he had any Ken Dodd records. Scotland, perhaps. Apparently it had rained somewhere in Scotland only yesterday.

The grebo peered at Martin through a shroud of long, lank hair. He was barefoot, barechested under his filthy afghan coat, and stank like a goat. "I got something for him. The stuff he's been waiting for. *You* know."

"Not really," Martin said, and remembered that Dr. John had mentioned something about expecting a delivery of hash.

"We had a deal, right, so I went round to his flat and he wasn't there, and I've been waiting two whole fucking hours here, and now I have to go down the social and sign on. When you see him, tell him I was looking for him," the grebo said, and lurched off without giving his name.

That evening, after he'd closed up his shop, Martin made a detour on the way home, to call on Dr. John. He told himself that his friend was probably in the middle of one of his forty-eight hour sleepathons, but there was no harm checking. Just in case. He leaned on Dr. John's doorbell for five minutes, listening to it trill two floors above him, then went down the whitewashed steps and rang the bell of the private members club in the basement. It was owned by Dr. John's landlord, Mr. Mavros, an after-hours drinking spot featuring sticky purple shagpile and red leatherette booths. Martin had worked behind its bar last year, when he'd been scraping together enough seed money for his record shop.

"I hope this doesn't mean trouble for me," Mr. Mavros said, after he had handed over the key to Dr. John's flat.

"He's ill," Martin lied. "I said I'd stop by and see if he needed anything. Soup or aspirin or whatever."

"He look ill when I see him," Mr. Mavros said. He was a thin, consumptive man with no hair on his head except for a splendid pair of thick black eyebrows. He wore red braces over his immaculate white shirt, and as usual a small cigar was plugged into the corner of his mouth. "He come back from somewhere when I was locking up this place, two o'clock in the morning. I say hello and he look straight past me. Into the distance, like he see something that isn't there. I know he drink, he smoke dope, but this was different. You tell him, Martin, if he start on the hard drugs, if he cause me trouble, that's it, I throw him out."

The door to Dr. John's tiny flat stood ajar. The bed-sitting room was hot and stale. Sunlight burned at the edges of the drawn curtains. The bed was piled with cushions and dirty clothes; the floor was strewn with clothes and broken-backed paperbacks, unsleeved records and record sleeves, empty cans and bottles, tin-foil takeaway cartons, and yellowing newspapers. In the filthy little kitchen, the tap was running over a stack of unwashed dishes and pots. Martin turned it off, heard something splash somewhere else in the flat. He called out, felt a jolt of nerves when there was another splash.

The bathroom was a windowless cubbyhole just big enough for bath and bog and wash-basin. The light was off, and it smelt like the seal pool in the zoo. The bath was brimful, and in the semi-darkness Martin could see a shape under the shivering surface of the water.

"John?"

A pale hand lifted like a lily; water cascaded over the edge of the tub. Martin jerked the light cord with a convulsive movement and in the sudden harsh glare of the unshielded bulb the boy in the bathtub—fully clothed, in the same brown, chalkstripe waistcoat he'd been wearing at the Free Festival—sat bolt upright, eyes wide, water running out of his nose and mouth.

Martin helped the boy out of the tub and got him onto the bed, but he wouldn't answer any of Martin's questions about Dr. John, and quickly fell into something deeper than sleep. He breathed with his mouth open, making a rasping gurgle, and didn't stir when Martin went through his pockets, finding nothing but a couple of pound notes wadded together in a knot of papier-mâché. Martin suddenly found that he couldn't bear to stay a moment longer with this unquiet sleeper in the hot, claustrophobic flat, and fled into the late-afternoon sunlight and the diesel dust and ordinary noise of traffic.

He sat on the bench beside a telephone box on the other side of the road and thought about his options. If he told Mr. Mavros what he'd found, the landlord would probably throw out the boy and change the lock on the door. And if he went to the police, they'd probably make a note of Dr. John's disappearance and forget all about it. He could always walk away, of course, but Dr. John was a friend who had helped him out of a tight spot, and he had a vague but nagging sense of duty.

Sooner or later, he thought, Dr. John would turn up, or the boy would wake up and slope off to wherever Dr. John was hanging out. All he had to do was wait. How hard could that be? He went around the corner, bought a parcel of fish and chips and a can of Coke, and returned to the bench. The blue sky darkened and the air grew hotter and thicker. A police car slowed as it went past and the driver took a lingering look at Martin, who had to suppress an impulse to wave when the car came back in the other direction ten minutes later. The streetlights flickered on. A little later, Mr. Mavros switched on the light over the door of his club, illuminating the board painted with its faintly sinister motto: THERE ARE NO STRANGERS HERE, ONLY FRIENDS WHO HAVEN'T MET.

Martin bought another Coke at the fish-and-chip shop, and when he returned to the bench saw something swoop down onto the roofline of the row of houses, joining the half dozen white birds that hadn't been there five minutes ago. They're only gulls, he told himself, there are plenty of gulls in Bristol. But he got the shivers anyway, flashing on the monster that had nearly amputated his fingers, and was about to turn tail and head for home when he saw the boy in the brown waistcoat ambling away down the street.

The boy must have crawled back into the bath before he left Dr. John's flat; he tracked wet footprints that grew smaller and smaller as Martin followed him through the villagey centre of Clifton towards the Avon Gorge, walking with a quickening pace as if drawn to some increasingly urgent siren song. By the time they'd reached the grassy space in front of Brunel's suspension bridge, Martin was jogging to keep up. The boy walked straight across the road, looking neither right nor left, and plunged into the bushes beside the public lavatories. Martin got up his nerve and followed, found a steep, narrow path, and climbed to the top.

The sky was cloudless and black. The moon, almost full, was setting. The stubby observatory tower that housed a camera obscura shone wanly. Beyond it, the boy and half a dozen other people stood at the rail along the edge of the gorge. Martin skulked behind the thin cover of a clump of laurel bushes. He had the airy feeling that something was about to happen, but didn't have the faintest idea what it would be. One of the giant, arch-pierced stone towers that supported the suspension bridge reared up behind his hiding place, and it seemed to him that the watchers at the rail were staring at the lamp-lit road that ran between bridge's white-painted chains and struts to the other side of the deep narrow gorge.

Martin settled behind the laurels, sipped warm Coke. Gradually, more people drifted across the moonlit grass to join the little congregation at the rail. A girl in a cotton dress came past Martin's hiding place, so close he could have reached out and touched her bare leg. No one spoke. They stood at the rail and stared at the bridge. They reminded Martin of the gulls on the roof. Whenever he checked his digital watch, cupping his right wrist with his left hand to hide its little light, far less time had passed than he had thought.

10:08.

10:32.

10:56.

He must have dozed, because the noise jerked him awake. The people lined up along the edge of the drop were chanting, a slow liturgical dirge of nonsense words rich in consonants. They bent against the rail, their arms outstretched, swaying like sea anemones in a current, reaching towards the bridge. Martin turned, and saw that two shadowy figures were walking along the road to the mid-point of the bridge, where the two downcurving arcs of white-painted suspension chains met. One was a man, the other the girl in the white dress. She embraced her companion for a moment, and then he broke away and clambered over the rail and without hesitation or ceremony stepped out into thin air and plummeted into darkness.

Martin stood up, his heart beating lightly and quickly, his whole skin tingling, and thought that he saw a brief green flash in the river directly below the bridge, a moment of heat lightning. The girl was walking along the bridge towards the other side of the gorge; the people at the rail were beginning to drift away, each moving in a different direction.

One of them had a cloud of bushy hair, and walked with a distinct list.

Martin chased after him, stumbling in the dark, making far too much noise as he dodged from one clump of bushes to the next, at last daring to cut across his path and grab him by the shoulders and turn him around. Dr. John tried to twist away, like a freshly caught fish flopping in a trawlerman's grasp. Martin held on and at last his friend quietened and stood still, his gaze fixed on something a thousand miles beyond Martin's left shoulder.

"Let's get out of this," Martin said, and took hold of Dr. John's right arm above the elbow and steered him through the streets of Clifton to Worcester Terrace. There was another brief struggle after Martin had opened the front door, but then Dr. John quietened again and allowed himself to be led up the four flights of stairs to Martin's flat. He stood in a kind of dazed slouch, blinking slowly in the bright light of the kitchen while Martin made coffee, taking no notice of the mug that Martin tried to put it in his hand.

Martin leaned against the counter by the sink and sipped his own coffee and asked Dr. John where he'd been, what had happened to him, what the fuck had just happened on the bridge.

"Someone jumped. I saw it. He climbed over the rail and let go."

Dr. John didn't even blink. Martin had to step hard on the impulse to slap him silly.

"It's something to do with the pill, isn't it? The green pill, and the girl who gave it to you. Don't try to deny it, I saw her with whoever it was that jumped."

Dr. John stood still and silent, face slack, shoulders slumped. Or not entirely still—one hand was slowly and slyly creeping towards the breast pocket of his denim jacket. Martin knocked it away and reached inside the pocket and pulled out the green pill and held it in front of Dr. John's face.

"What is this shit? What does it do to you?"

Dr. John's eyes tracked the pill as Martin moved it to and fro; his hand limply pawed the air.

"Don't be pathetic," Martin said. He thrust the pill into the pocket of his jeans and steered Dr. John into the living room and put him to bed on the sofa. Then he went out to the phone box at the end of the road, dialled 999 and told the operator that he'd seen someone jump from the Clifton Suspension Bridge, and hung up when she asked for his name.

When Martin went into the living room the next morning, Dr. John was fast asleep, curled into the back of the sofa and drooling into the cushion he was using as a pillow. After Martin had shaken him awake and poured a cup of tea into him, he claimed not to remember anything about the last night, saying, "Man, I was definitely out of my head."

"You don't know the half of it."

They were sitting at the kitchen table. Dr. John drank a mug of tea and devoured three slices of white bread smeared with butter and sprinkled with brown sugar while Martin told him about the boy in the bathtub, the people lined up at the railing above the Avon Gorge, and the girl who had escorted the man to the midpoint of the bridge, how she'd embraced him, how he'd stepped into thin air. Dr. John wore a funny little smile, as if he knew the secret that would make sense of everything, but when Martin had finished he shrugged and said, "People jump off the bridge all the time. They *queue up* to jump off. The police have to comb pieces of them out of the trees, scrape them off the road, dig them out of the mud…" He patted his pockets. "Got any fags?"

Martin found a packet his girlfriend had left behind.

"Silk Cut? They're not real cigarettes," Dr. John said, but tore off the filter off one and lit it and sat back and blew smoke at the ceiling.

Martin was tired of trying to crack Dr. John's bullshit insouciance, but decided to give it one more try. He leaned across the table and said as forcefully as he could, "Someone jumped off the bridge. I saw it."

"I believe you, man," Dr. John said, still smiling that sly little smile.

"If you don't remember anything at all, you really were out of your head. And I thought there wasn't a pill or powder you couldn't handle."

"It isn't that I don't remember anything, man. I just don't remember any of the shit you saw. That was just the pattern on the veil that hides the true reality of things. That hides what's really going on."

"So what was really going on?"

"It's kind of hard to explain."

"I want to understand."

"Are you worried about me, man? I'm touched."

"I saw someone throw himself off the suspension bridge. The girl who gave you that pill, the one in the white dress, was right there with him when he jumped. I think that guy got high on whatever it is she's peddling, just like you did, and she persuaded him to jump. I think she killed him. That's what I saw. How about you?"

Dr. John thought for a few moments. "What you have to understand is that the green shit doesn't do anything but put you in the right frame of mind. It takes you to the beach, and after that it's up to you. You have to wade out into the sea and give yourself up to it of your own free will. And if you can do that, the sea takes you right through the bottom of the world into this space that's deeper and darker than anywhere you've ever been. The womb of the world, the place where rock and water and air and everything else came from."

He developed a thousand-yard stare for a moment, then shook himself and smiled around the cigarette, showing his broken tooth.

"It's very dark and quiet, but it isn't lonely. It's like the floor of the collective unconscious. Not in the Jungian sense, but something deeper than that. You can lose yourself in it forever. You *dissolve*. This is hard, trying to explain how it is to someone who doesn't believe a word of it, but haven't you ever had that feeling when everything inside you and everything outside you, everything in the whole wide world, lines up perfectly, just for a moment? I remember when I was a kid, this one day in summer. Hot as it is now, but everything lush and green. Cow parsley and nettles growing taller than me along the edges of the road on the way up to the common. Farmers turned cows and sheep out to graze there, and the grass was short and wiry, and warm beneath you when you lay down, and the sun was a warm red weight on your closed eyelids. You lay there and felt the whole world holding you to itself, and you heard a lark singing somewhere above you in the sunlight and the warm wind. You couldn't see it, but it was singing its heart out above you, and everything dissolved into this one moment of pure happiness. You know what I'm saying? Well, if you take that feeling and make it a thousand times more intense and stretched that one moment out to infinity, it would be a little like where I went."

"Except that you were high. It didn't really happen, you only thought it did."

Dr. John looked straight at Martin, smiling that sly smile, and said, "You don't know what I'm talking about, do you? You're just a tourist, man. A day-tripper. You might have ventured onto the beach a couple of times, you might even have dipped a toe into the sea, but that's as far as you've ever dared to go. Because as far as you're concerned, drugs are *recreational*. Something you do for *fun*."

Martin felt a sharp flare of anger. He'd seen something awful, he believed that he had risked his life to rescue Dr. John, and his only reward was scorn and derision. "If you want to fuck yourself up," he said, "do a proper job and score some heroin from that guy who works for those gangsters who beat you up."

"I found something better," Dr. John said. "We all did. Something we didn't know we needed until we found it. You don't need it, man. That's why she turned you down. Even if you got hold of some of her stuff and got off on it, you wouldn't be able to take the next step. You wouldn't be able to surrender yourself. But we knew where it would take us before we'd even seen it. We ached for it. It's our Platonic ideal, man, the missing part we've been searching for all our lives."

"One of your little gang killed himself last night. He threw himself off the suspension bridge, right in front of my eyes. He committed suicide. Is that what you want?"

"Suicide? Is that what you think you saw?"

Dr. John looked straight at Martin again. For a moment, Martin glimpsed the worm of self-loathing that writhed behind the mask of his fatuous smile and flippant manner. He looked away, no longer angry, but embarrassed at having glimpsed something more intimate than mere nakedness.

"Something wants our worship," Dr. John said, "and we want oblivion. It isn't hard to understand. It's a very simple deal."

"If you take another of those pills, you could be the next one off that bridge," Martin said.

Dr. John stood up. "You have your nice little flat, man, and your nice little shop and your nice little gigs with loser pub rock bands. You have a nice little life, man. You've found your niche, and you cling to it like a limpet. Good for you. The only problem is, you can't understand why other people don't want to be like you."

Martin stood up too. "Stay here. Crash out as long as you like. Get your head straight."

Dr. John shook his head. "My friends are waiting for me."

"Don't go back to the river," Martin said, but Dr. John was already out of the door and clumping away downstairs.

Martin shut up shop early that afternoon and took a walk up to the observatory. Children ran about in the sweltering heat, watched by indulgent parents. People were sunbathing on suncrisped grass. There was a queue at the ice-cream stall by the entrance to the observatory tower. Someone was flying a kite. It was all horribly normal, but Martin was possessed by a restless sense that something bad was going to happen. As if a thunderstorm hung just beyond the horizon, waiting for the right wind to blow it his way. As if the world was suddenly all an eggshell above a nightmare void. He drifted back through Clifton village and ended up in the Coronation Tap and drank five pints of Directors and ate one of the pub's infamous mystery pies, and at closing time walked back to the suspension bridge and thrashed through bushes to the top of the rise.

There they were, leaning at the rail in the warm half-dark, staring into the abyss.

None of them so much as glanced at Martin as, his heart beating quickly and lightly, his whole skin tingling airily, he walked across the grass. They leaned at the rail and stared with intense impassivity at the gorge and the floodlit bow of the suspension bridge. The two women on either side of Dr. John didn't even blink when Martin tried to pull him away, tugging one arm and then the other, trying to prise his grip from the rail, finally getting him in a bear-hug and hauling as hard as he could. As they staggered backwards, a gull skimmed out of the dusky air and bombed them with a pint of hot wet birdshit. It stank like thousand-year-old fish doused in ammonia, and stung like battery acid when it ran into Martin's eyes. Half-blind, gasping, he let go of Dr. John and tried to wipe the stuff from his eyes and face, and another gull swooped past, spattering him with a fresh load, clipping him with the edge of a wing. Martin sat down hard, saw more gulls circling in the dark air, one of them much bigger than the rest. One dipped down and swooped towards him, its wings lifted in a V-shape. His nerve gave out then, and he scrambled to his feet and ran, had almost gained the shelter of the bushes when the bird hit him from behind, ripping its claws across his scalp and knocking him down. He was crawling towards the bushes, blinded by blood and birdshit, when another gull smashed into him, and the world swung around and flew away like a stone on the end of a string.

When Martin came to, the swollen disc of the full moon was setting beyond the trees on the other side of the gorge. Its cold light filled his eyes. The person standing over him was a shadow against it, reaching down, clasping his hand and helping him sit up.

"Christ," Simon Cowley said. "They really worked you over."

Martin's face and hair were caked in blood and gullshit. His skin burned and his eyes were swollen half-shut. He gingerly touched the deep lacerations in his scalp, winced, and took his hand away.

"Gulls," he said.

"Vicious little fuckers, aren't they? Especially the big one."

"What do you know about it? And what are you doing here?"

"I came here after your hippy friend spiked my beer. I woke up from a horrible dream and found myself standing at the rail over there, in the middle of a whole bunch of sleepwalkers. I've been coming back every night since. And every night someone has gone over the bridge into the river." Simon's long blond hair was unwashed and he stank of sweat and sickness. His eyes were black holes in his pale face. A khaki satchel—an old gas mask carrier—hung from his shoulder. He looked around and said in a hoarse whisper, "I think there's something in the river. I think it swam in from the sea on the last high tide, it's been trapped here ever since because the drought lowered the level of the river. It's been living on what they give it."

"They worship it," Martin said, remembering Dr. John's ravings.

"I think it draws them here and makes them jump off the suspension bridge. I think it eats them," Simon said, "because no one has reported finding any bodies. You'd think, after at least three people jumped off the bridge in as many days, one of them would have washed up. I went down there yesterday in daylight, and took a good look around. Nothing. It devours them. Snaps them up whole."

Martin got to his feet. Heavy black pain rolled inside his skull. His eyes were on fire and his lacerations felt like a crown of thorns. He said, "We should call the police."

"You saw what was down there. I know you did because I saw you here last night."

"I saw something. I don't know what it was."

"You think the police can do anything about something like this?" Simon cocked his head. "You hear that?"

"I hear it."

People were chanting, somewhere below the edge of the gorge.

"It's beginning," Simon said.

"What's beginning?"

"You can help me or stay here, I don't care," Simon said, and ran towards the path that led down the face of the gorge.

Martin chased after him. Everything was black and white in the moonlight. Bleached trees and boulders and slabs of rock loomed out of their own shadows. The day's heat beat up from bare rock. The black air was oven-baked. Martin sweated through his T-shirt and jeans. His feet slipped on sweat inside his Doc Martens. Sweat stung his swollen eyes, his lacerated scalp. He caught up with Simon at the beginning of a steep smooth chute of limestone that had been polished by generations of kids using it as a slide. At the foot of the gorge, people were crossing the road, shambling towards the girl in the white dress, who stood at the rail at the edge of the river. A passing car sounded its horn, swerved past them.

Simon didn't look around when Martin reached him. He said, "You see her? She's the locus of infection. She's been missing for two weeks, did you know that? I did some research, looked at back copies of the *Evening Post* for anything about people jumping from the bridge, and there she was. I think she jumped off the bridge and the thing in the river took her and changed her and sent her out to bring it food."

Below, people were climbing over the guard rail at the edge of the road. The river shone like a black silk ribbon between its wide banks of mud. White flakes—gulls—floated above one spot.

"We have to stop it right now," Simon said. "It's high tide tonight. I think it wants to take them all before it goes back to sea."

"All right. How are we going to stop it?"

"I'm going to blow it up. I stole two sticks of dynamite from work. Taped them together with a waterproof fuse. You distract them and I throw the dynamite and we run."

"Distract them?"

People were slogging across the mud towards the gyre of gulls. They had started up their chant again.

"Shout at them," Simon said. "Throw rocks. Try to take back your hippy friend, like you did just now. Whatever you like, as long as you get them to chase you. Then I'll chuck the dynamite in the river, right at the spot under those gulls."

"Suppose they won't chase me?"

In the high-contrast glare of the moonlight, Simon's grin made his face look like a skull. "I'll chuck it in anyway."

"You're crazy. You'll kill them all."

"They're already dead," Simon said, and turned away. Martin grabbed the canvas satchel, but Simon caught the strap as it slid past his wrist. For a moment, they were perfectly balanced, the satchel stretched between them; then a gull swooped out of the black air. Simon ducked, staggered, put his foot down on thin air and fell backwards. Martin sat down heavily, the canvas satchel in his lap, heard a rolling crackle as Simon crashed through bushes, saw the pale shape of the gull fall away as it plummeted after him.

Martin got to his feet and slung the satchel over his shoulder and went on down the path, fetched up breathless at the bottom, his headache pounding like a black strobe. An articulated lorry went past in a glare of headlights and a roar of hot wind and dust. Martin ran across the road, clambered over the guardrail, and dropped to a swale of grassy mud, breaking through a dry crust and sinking up to his knees.

He levered himself out and stumbled forwards. He could hear the tide running in the river, smell its rotten salty stink. Inky figures stood along the edge of the black water on either side of the girl's pale shadow. Gulls swooped around them. Their hands were raised above their heads and they were chanting their nonsense syllables.

Iä! Iä! Iä-R'lyeh!

There was a sudden splashing as hundreds of fish leapt out of the water, shards of silver flipping and thrashing around the line of men and women. Martin ran down a shallow breast of mud, shouting Dr. John's name, and something huge breached the river. Light beat up from it in complex labial folds, rotten, green, alive. Gulls swirled through the light and flared and winked out. Blazing faultlines shot across the mud in every direction; fish exploded in showers of scales and blood.

The people were perfectly silhouetted against the green glare. They were still chanting.

Cthulhu fhtagn! Iä! Iä!

Martin staggered towards them, feet sinking into foul mud, swollen eyes squeezed into slits, and locked his arms around Dr. John's neck. Dr. John fought back, but Martin was stronger and more desperate, and hauled his friend backwards, step by step. The light began to pulse like a heartbeat. A virulent jag cut straight in front of Martin and Dr. John. Mud exploded with popcorn cracks. Martin fell down, pulling Dr. John with him, and the giant gull swooped past, missing Martin's face by inches. Dr. John tried to pull away and Martin clung to him with the last of his strength, watched helplessly as the misshapen bird swept high through the throbbing green glare and turned and plummeted towards them like a dive bomber.

Someone gimped past—Simon Cowley, raising the broken branch he'd been using as a crutch. The bird screeched and slipped sideways, but Simon threw his make-shift spear and caught it square in its breast, and it exploded in a cloud of feathers and rotten meat. Something like a nest of snakes was thrashing in the centre of the light. A thick, living rope whipped across the line of men and women, knocking them down like nine-pins, sweeping them into the river. Simon threw himself flat as another ropey tentacle cracked through the air. For a moment it flexed above Martin, its tip crusted with feathery palps and snapping hooks, dripping a thin slime, and then it sinuously withdrew. The light was dying back into itself. Water rushed into the place where something huge and unendurable had opened a brief gap in the world, bubbled and steamed, and closed over.

Eighteen months later, Martin was with his friends in the middle of the crowd coming out of the Watershed at the end of a Clash concert, his ears ringing and sweat turning cold on his skin under his ripped T-shirt and Oxfam jacket and straight-legged Levis 501s, when someone caught his arm and called his name. Martin turned, saw a guy in a black dufflecoat, short blond hair and a pinched white face, and after a couple of seconds recognised Simon Cowley.

Martin told his friends that he'd catch up with them in the pub, and said to Simon, "I never thought you'd be into punk rock."

"I'm not really here for the music."

Martin grinned. He was still pumped up by the concert's energy. "You missed something tremendous."

"I heard about your friend."

"Come to gloat, have you? Come to say 'I told you so'?"

"Actually, I came to say I'm sorry."

"Oh. Right."

"I also heard you gave up your shop, you joined a group, you have a record deal…"

"Those people I was with? That's the group. And the deal, it's for a single with Rough Trade. Nothing major," Martin said, "but we all had three-day hangovers after we signed."

"Still, a record deal."

"Yeah. How about you? I mean, I heard you broke up Clouds of Memory…"

"I gave all that up." Simon hesitated, then said, almost shyly, "Want to see something?"

"You don't look well, Simon. What have you been doing since…"

Simon shrugged. "I've been working. I've been waking up every night from bad dreams."

"I get those too, sometimes." But Martin didn't want to talk about that; didn't want to talk about anything to do with those awful days in that long hot summer. "Well, it was nice to run into you—"

"I'd really like you to see this. Apart from me, you're the only person who'll understand what it means. Please? It'll only take a minute."

"Only a minute, then," Martin said, and with a sense of foreboding followed Simon to the quay on the other side of the Watershed. Black water lapped a few feet below the edge of the walkway, flexing its patchwork covering of chip papers and beer cans and plastic detergent bottles. Martin shivered in the icy breeze that cut across the water, shoved his hands into the pockets of his jacket, and said, "What are we looking for?"

Simon put a finger to his lips, pointed at the water.

They were like tadpoles grown to the size of late-term human embryos. They were pale and faintly luminous, with heavy heads and large, black, lidless eyes and small pursed mouths. Skinny arms folded under pulsing gill slits. Snakey, finned tails. They hung in the black water at different levels.

Martin stared at them, little chills chasing each other through his blood, and whispered, "What are they?"

"Ghosts, maybe. Or shells, some kind of energy cast off when, you know…"

When the people had been taken. When they had been consumed.

Snapped up. Devoured. No bodies had been found; fourteen people had simply disappeared, as people sometimes do. Most of them were like Dr. John, chancers on the edge of society, missed by no one but their landlords and dealers and parole officers. There'd been some fuss in the local news about a housewife and a schoolboy who'd both gone missing the same day, but no one had made the connection between the two, and the story soon slipped off the pages. And that might have been the end of it, except that six months later the flat below Dr. John's was flooded; when he went to investigate, Mr. Mavros found Dr. John lying fully clothed in his overflowing bath, dead of a heroin overdose. Dr. John's parents had disowned him long ago. Only Martin and Mr. Mavros had attended the cremation, and Martin had scattered the ashes off the suspension bridge. And that, he thought, really had been the end of it, except for the dreams. Except for these ghosts, pale in the black water.

"I think they come for the music," Simon said. "Or maybe for what the music does to people. A concert is a kind of collective act of worship, isn't it? Maybe they feed on it…"

There were six or seven or eight of them. They looked up at Martin and Simon through the water and the floating litter.

"There used to be more," Simon said.

"Isn't one of them sort of listing to the left?"

"What do you mean?"

"Maybe not. It doesn't matter."

Simon said, "I tried to catch one once. I borrowed a keep net from my dad. They slipped right through it."

Martin said, "Afterwards, I found one of those pills in my pocket."

"Did you take it?"

"What would be the point?"

He'd flushed it down the sink. It had dissolved reluctantly, frothing slimy bubbles like a salted slug and giving off a vile stink that had reminded him of gull-shit. Dr. John had been right: it hadn't been meant for him. Dr. John and the others had been on the road to oblivion long before they'd been snared by the monster or old god or whatever it was that had been briefly trapped in the tidal mud of the Avon. If it hadn't taken them, something else would: an unlit gas oven; a razorblade and a warm bath; a swan dive from the suspension bridge; an overdose.

Martin had brushed against it and lived, but he'd been changed, no doubt about it. He'd given up his second-hand record shop and his nice flat with its convenient location and its view across the communal gardens towards the green breast of Jacob's Hill, and moved into a squat with the rest of his new band. He was happy there and gave himself one hundred per cent to his music, even though he was pretty sure, despite the record deal, it wouldn't last. But that didn't matter. He was only twenty-six, for God's sake. There was plenty of time to move on, to try something else.

He stood with Simon in the dark and the chill wind and watched the ghostly things in the water fade away.

"Sometimes I can almost hear them, you know?" Simon said. "I can almost understand what they're trying to tell me."

"It might be an idea to try to forget about them."

Simon sighed, shivered inside his duffel coat, tried to smile. "I never thought I'd say this, but you're probably right."

"Want to come and have a drink with me?"

"I have to get the last bus home." Simon had that uncharacteristic shy look again. "I'm getting married in a couple of months. My fiancée will be waiting up for me."

"Congratulations," Martin said, and discovered that he meant it.

"Maybe we'll have that drink some other time," Simon said, and they shook hands at the edge of the water and went their different ways into the city, into the rest of their lives.

THE COMING

by HUGH B. CAVE

KEITH WALKER WAS one of five passengers in the Reverend Ralph Beckford's station wagon that Sunday afternoon as it began its low-gear descent down The Devil's Ladder into Deeprock Gorge. All the others had been present in the Reverend's church that morning and heard him preach about the coming. Keith had not heard about it until he called on Jennifer Skipworth after the service.

"Oh, now, come on," he'd said when Jennifer told him what they planned to do. "You can't be serious!"

"We are serious." The girl he was in love with stopped pacing her living room and faced him with her hands outstretched. "Keith, we are! Like the Reverend says, it's all in Revelations if you'll just take time to read between the lines. Darling, I'm not asking you to believe. Only to come with us."

"But why Deeprock Gorge?" Keith protested. "I went fishing there once with Mr. Powell"—Otis Powell was editor of the Innsmouth newspaper Keith worked for—"and it's got to be the most Godforsaken place in the whole of Massachusetts. It's even hard to get to."

"Howard has a house there."

"Oh." There were some houses in the gorge, Keith remembered.

Cabins, anyway. Maybe three or four of them, strung out along the banks of the stream. Weekend summer camps, he guessed they were.

"Howard Lindsay, you mean? The big guy who owns the paint factory?"

She nodded. "He's a deacon in our church."

"I see."

"Do you want to know who else is going?"

"Well, if I'm going to be one of them," Keith said. Which, of course, he would be, because he sure wasn't going to let her go on any such crazy mission without him. He had long believed that most of the folks who went to Reverend Beckford's church were a little daft. That they now believed Satan was about to take over the world didn't surprise him.

How they hoped to stop old Beelzebub from doing it did interest him, though, as a possible story for the paper. "You mean you're going there just to pray?"

"That's right, Keith. To pray."

"Then why not in the church? Why Deeprock Gorge, of all places?"

"Because Christ wrestled with Satan in a wilderness. Please, darling, try to understand."

She told him who would be going. Reverend Beckford, of course. Mary Sewell and her eleven-year-old son Davey. Howard Lindsay, who had recently bought the gorge, or at least the cabins in it, so his factory workers could use them weekends. "And, I hope, you. You will come, won't you, Keith? It'll only be for one night."

"Where you go, I go," he told her.

Jennifer lived with her parents in a house on the edge of town, and on the way back to his in-town bachelor apartment, Keith had stopped at the home of Otis Powell, his editor, and told Powell what was up. "It could be a pretty good story, don't you think: Reverend Beckford convincing all those good people the Devil is coming to take us over, and some of them going into the wilderness to pray for help?" He would go anyway, he knew, even if Powell laughed at him. But Powell said yes, it could be a story, so go ahead and good luck.

* * *

The Devil's Ladder behind them, the road along the river's edge was no more than a pair of ruts through dark grey sand and rocks. At times Keith thought they wouldn't get through. But there were tyre tracks, so other vehicles must have managed it, and presently, lo and behold, there was the cabin.

He helped Jennifer with the food they'd brought, and the Sewells with their gear—because Mary Sewell weighed at least 250 pounds—and by the time he carried his own things into the cabin, the others were already in the bedrooms, getting set up for the night. What they should do, Reverend Beckford said, was have a bite of something to eat because it was already past five o'clock, and then get busy on what they'd come here for.

There were two bedrooms in the place, along with a bathroom, a small kitchen, and a big front room with a fireplace. The Reverend, Howard Lindsay and Keith had one bedroom; Jennifer and Mary Sewell and Mary's boy Davey had the other. The beds were cot-size bunks built into the walls.

"Just what are you planning to do here, Reverend?" Keith asked while making up his bed. The Reverend was about fifty years old and easily six-foot-three but so skinny he might disappear through a floor-crack at any minute. A nice fellow, though, except he got so intense about things sometimes.

"Pray," he said.

"I see."

"No, you don't see. But you will, soon as we've eaten."

"There may be other people in some of the cabins along here," Keith pointed out. "You plan on asking them to pray with us?"

Howard Lindsay said, "Yes, some of my people are out here this weekend. I checked in town before we left." Lindsay was a broad-shouldered, brawny fellow, just the sort you'd expect to want a cabin in a wilderness. The paint factory he owned seemed to make him a good deal of money.

"It's a bit late to call on people this evening," the Reverend said. "I'll do it tomorrow."

Keith finished getting his bed ready and went into the kitchen, where Jennifer and fat Mary Sewell—Big Mary, folks called her—

were starting supper. They'd brought along food already cooked, Jennifer explained, because they hadn't known how much free time they might have with all the praying to be done. After lighting the propane stove so they could heat things, Keith turned on the faucet in the sink and reached for a glass to get himself a drink of water.

"Use that," Big Mary said, pointing to a plastic jug of store-bought water. "Deacon Lindsay says the river water's clean and we're crazy, but the way this poor world is headed, you can't trust nothing any more."

Keith said okay and drank bottled water and then went out to sit on the back steps and think about the story he would write. Noting how dark it was getting, he looked at his watch, then held his wrist to his ear to make sure the watch was still running. In town, with daylight-saving time in effect, darkness would still be a long way off. But here in the gorge, with its high, sheer walls shutting out the light, the day was already dying. Made a fellow feel a bit strange, like he was in another world. There'd be a near-full moon tonight, though, he remembered. The gorge should be something to see with moonlight pouring down into it.

He finished thinking and went back inside, where he helped set the table for a fine supper of Boston baked beans and ham and home-baked bread. After the Reverend asked a blessing that seemed a bit too long with everyone so hungry, they ate. Then the Reverend pushed his chair back and said, "We men ought to do the dishes, I expect, since you ladies did the cooking. But first let's get started on what we came here for."

He led them out to the river's edge, where it was almost totally dark now. Even the shallow, twenty-foot wide stream was more heard than seen as it rushed past over its bed of boulders. With the Reverend telling them what to do, they formed a circle and held hands. Then in his deep, throaty voice he began praying.

"Lord, look down on this troubled Earth, please, and see what's happening here. It isn't pretty. All over this once-beautiful planet people are doing things they shouldn't ought to be doing. Like polluting our rivers and lakes so we'll soon be short of drinking water. And wantonly killing off whole species of the wonderful creatures you put here to share your bounty with us. Look, Lord, at how people are stupidly cutting down the forests we need to keep clean the air we breathe, and how they are further making the air unbreathable by poisoning it with smokestacks and automobile exhausts.

"Lord, the few of us that see what's going on and want to put a stop to it need your help now in the worst way. Yes, we do. By ourselves we can't make much of a difference because we're so outnumbered by those who don't care. Take a good look at what's going on down here, Lord. See for yourself the ever-greater numbers of people using drugs—especially young people. Note the drug-related murders and the child abuse. See the number of people openly admitting they've turned away from you and are worshipping Satan.

"Lord, the Devil is on the warpath again, as you must know. We've got whole nations here that are stockpiling things like hydrogen bombs and planning to use chemical- and germ warfare against their innocent neighbours. It's frightening, I tell you. It's scaring the living daylights out of those of us who aren't too blind or selfish to see what it's likely to lead to. But Lord, you beat old Lucifer once before in a wilderness like this, and with your help we can whip him again. So look down on us here and tell us what to do, we beseech you. Tell us before it's too late. Amen."

Reverend Beckford prayed along those lines for another half-hour or so, then opened his eyes. "There," he said with a heavy sigh, "I'm sure we all feel some better already because we know He heard us. We can go inside now. But at daybreak we'll talk to Him again."

When the men had done the dishes by lamplight, Howard Lindsay built a fire and the group sat by the fireplace, talking. Mary Sewell's boy Davey played some hymns on a harmonica he'd brought along. The others exclaimed at how good he was and asked for more. Then the moon came up, filling the gorge with a shimmering mist of quicksilver, and Keith reached for Jennifer Skipworth's hand.

"How about a little walk?" Keith suggested.

She smiled at him and they went out together, telling the others they'd soon be back.

* * *

The moonlight must have been responsible for what happened then. For more than two years Keith had known he was in love but hadn't quite been sure he wanted to be tied down in marriage. After all, Jennifer Skipworth was a bit heavy on the church-going at times, even for Innsmouth, and even now, this expedition into Deeprock Gorge for a confrontation with Satan was on the spooky side. But before they had walked a hundred yards downriver he heard himself blurting it out. "Hey… why don't you and I stop fooling around and get married, huh? Like soon, I mean."

Then before she could answer, the moonlight did something else. Just ahead of them, at the water's edge, a stone moved. Or if not a stone, a living thing that looked like a stone. It suddenly turned itself into a beetle or bug or insect the size of a dinner plate and with a loud hissing sound went waddling into the water, where it vanished.

Jennifer froze in her tracks and gasped, "What was that?"

Keith forgot about wanting to be married. His fingers tightened their grip on her hand and he went slowly forward, one careful step at a time, pulling her after him, until they reached the place where the thing had been. Smelling something, he dropped to his knees, still cautiously, and sniffed at the empty pocket of black sand. It had an odour of—what? Spoiled meat?

"Must have been some animal," he said, rising. "A possum, maybe? But hurt, somehow. You want to go back?"

Jennifer thought about it. He'd asked her to marry him. The stupid possum or whatever it was had interrupted her answer. She wanted to marry this man. She wanted to tell him so, right here in this wilderness with the moon pouring its blessing down on them. "Let's go on a bit more," she said.

But then, right away, other things began to happen. Where the stream had been softly and romantically whispering along beside them, it acquired a new voice. Lots of new voices. Still holding Jennifer's hand, Keith stopped short and scowled at the water and said, "Now what the hell…?"

The night began to fill up with weird noises. With snarly sounds and hissings and whimperings apparently being made by strange, unaccountable shadow-shapes that were appearing in the water.

Every now and then one of the shapes surfaced enough to be halfway visible in the moonlight.

They were creepy-crawlies of one sort or another, Keith decided. Insects, bugs, water-spiders—about what you'd expect in such a stream. But they were bigger than any he'd ever seen before. Bigger than they had any right to be.

"Keith, what's happening?" Jennifer whispered, hanging onto him. "What's going on here?"

Keith didn't know how to answer her. As they stood there staring wide-eyed at the stream, the unnatural sounds got louder and they saw more shadow-shapes that didn't make any sense in such a place. It was as if the whole river had suddenly come alive in some weird, threatening way. As if many of the tiny, harmless creatures that normally lived in such streams had all at once grown in size and were either angry or confused about what had happened to them.

Then all at once Keith and Jennifer heard their names called and saw Reverend Beckford hurrying down the gorge toward them.

"Wait!" the Reverend shouted, waving at them. "Wait for me!" His yell bounced off the walls of the gorge in a string of echoes as, out of breath, he hurried to catch up to them. When he did that and got his breath back, he said, "I've decided to call on the people in the other cabins now, this evening, so they can join us at prayer in the morning. I'd be pleased if you two would come along."

"Reverend, look!" Jennifer cried, turning to point to the river. "Something's happening here!"

But it wasn't happening any more. Evidently the Reverend's yell had put a stop to it, the way a rock dropped into a pool would scatter a school of minnows. The oversized insects or whatever they were had fled, and the only sounds now to be heard were the normal ones made by any stream travelling over a rocky bed.

With the moonlight showing them where to put their feet, the three of them walked on down the gorge to the first of the other cabins. Smaller than the one they were using, it was built up against the cliff wall with a flight of steps leading up to a short veranda. They climbed the steps and the Reverend knocked politely on the door, but there was no response. Keith looked at his watch. The Reverend knocked again, louder, and Keith said with a frown, "They can't be in bed; it's only quarter to eight." Then he walked along the veranda and peered in through a window.

So far as he could see, no one was home. "Maybe they're at some other cabin," he said. "Most likely all the folks who use these cabins of Lindsay's are friends. Maybe they get together in the evenings."

The Reverend said he thought that was probably so, and the three of them went on down the gorge to the second house, but no one answered his knock there, either. At the third, which appeared to be the last, they were truly surprised when they found no one at home.

"They've got to be here somewhere," the Reverend said. "You heard what Howard Lindsay said: he checked in town before we came, and some of his factory people are out here this weekend."

"You suppose they all got together and went someplace for dinner?" Keith wondered aloud.

Jennifer shook her head. "That wouldn't make any sense. I mean, why would they come here for a weekend in the wilderness and then go somewhere to eat? There are no restaurants around here."

"Well, like Keith says, they're probably together somewhere," the Reverend said. "We'll just have to try again in the morning."

It had been a long walk and they were weary by the time they got back to Howard Lindsay's cabin. The others—Lindsay, Big Mary and the boy—were seated there in front of the fireplace. Reverend Beckford told about the empty cabins. Then Jennifer spoke of what she and Keith had heard and seen before he joined them.

"Noises? Shadow-things?" Howard Lindsay said with a scowl. "You sure you didn't just get carried away by your imagination? This gorge can be pretty spooky at night if you're new here."

"We heard what we heard," Jennifer insisted. "We saw things that weren't natural."

"Maybe he's here!" said young Davey Sewell.

"Maybe who's here?" his mother said. "What are you talking about?"

"Satan. What if he came because we prayed to Jesus to fight him again? He and Jesus fought in the Bible, didn't they?" The boy's face glowed with excitement. "Maybe he wants a rematch!"

"Now, now," Lindsay said, "what you two heard was just the

different sounds the river makes at night. I've heard them many a time." He lifted a big tumbler of water from the floor beside his chair and looked through it at the logs blazing in the fireplace. "I don't care if our river wants to screech like an owl or wail like a banshee," he said with a grin. "This is the best damn drinking water—begging your pardon, Reverend—in the whole of creation. I never can get enough of it when I'm here." He aimed his grin at Big Mary and Jennifer. "You women and your bottled stuff!" he snorted. "I bet if you was to have both kinds tested, you'd find that what I'm drinking is a whole sight better!"

Big Mary heaved herself up from her chair and said, "Well, you go right ahead and drink all you want of it, Deacon, but I'm dead beat and going to bed. Goodnight, all of you."

"If that goes for the rest of you, I believe I'll turn in, too," Reverend Beckford said, making it a question by hiking his eyebrows up.

They said it did, and the evening was finished.

Those bunk-beds in Howard Lindsay's cabin were not the most comfortable in the world. When Keith opened his eyes and saw by the moonlight in the room that the Reverend and Howard Lindsay were still asleep, he thought his aching back must have been what waked him. Then he heard a noise outside the window next to his bunk. Someone was out there walking around, it seemed.

Puzzled, he got up and stepped to the window and looked out.

With the moon directly overhead, Deeprock Gorge was almost as bright as day, except the light was sort of unreal. What was out there was even more unreal, though. Keith grabbed hold of the window ledge and felt his eyes bulging in their sockets.

"Lord Jesus!" he heard himself whisper—and he was not a church-going man.

Just outside the window stood a naked man holding what looked like a tree-limb. He was about to use the limb as a club to smash the window, it seemed; at any rate he was holding it aloft in both hands and looking at the window. But what he was was more terrible than anything he might be thinking of doing.

He was big. Big all over. And not just huge but lumpy, as if he was made of rubber and someone had blown too much air into him. As for his head, Keith stared at that in total disbelief.

It wasn't natural in any way. It was, in fact, a mass of enormous lumps or bumps that all but hid the eyes and most of the mouth. Massive, malformed swellings they were, from which the man's eyes blazed like twin red coals and the left side of his mouth—all that remained visible—was curled up over teeth that were like the fangs of a serpent.

As Keith stared at him, half-paralysed, the man took a step forward and voiced the sound that must have waked Keith in the first place: a long, loud snarl of rage or hate or fury that actually made the window rattle.

And he wasn't alone.

Coming up behind him, on his right, was a naked woman, and she too brandished a tree-limb club. She might have been a pretty woman once, but now she had the same lumps all over her body that the man had, and something even uglier. Big tufts of hair grew out of her cheeks and breasts and belly: long, black, bristly hair that made her look like some kind of wild animal. Or something that was in the process of becoming an animal but hadn't quite finished. She too was snarling or hissing or whatever the sound ought to be called… because it wasn't just one sound now, or coming from only those two throats. At least half a dozen other things that had been men and women came plodding into view even as Keith stood there petrified at the window. All of them had clubs.

"Lord Jesus," Keith whispered again, then spun himself around on one heel and let out a yell that seemed likely to tear the roof off the cabin. "Reverend!" he screamed. "Lindsay! Wake up, wake up! We're in big trouble!"

Even before the Reverend and Howard Lindsay reached his side to see what he meant, the thing outside nearest the window swung his tree-branch club and the window exploded.

The Reverend took one look at what was out there and began to pray in a low, shuddery voice. Howard Lindsay said, "Great God a'mighty!" and rushed to the door, calling back over his shoulder, "I'll get the others! We have to clear out of here!" When he came racing back he had a double-barrelled shotgun in his hands, and the women and young Davey were behind him. Big Mary looked ridiculous in a lace-trimmed pink nightgown, of all things, while Jennifer and Davey wore pyjamas.

All three were big-eyed with fright and had a right to be, because the things outside were all at the window now, or their hideous faces were, filling the room with their snarling and hissing, and the floor was littered with shards of glass, and the Reverend was still praying, and Keith Walker stood there helpless, not knowing what to do. Nothing Keith had learned as a newspaper reporter was any good to him now.

Howard Lindsay knew what to do, though. Maybe he was the type for this kind of thing—big, burly, and running a paint factory—or maybe having a weapon in his hands gave him confidence. As if he faced a crowd of angry, naked, no-longer-human people every night of his life, he thrust the gun out in front of him and charged the shattered window yelling, "Get out of here! Out!"

Whatever they were, they still had minds enough to know the gun was sure to kill some of them if he used it. As he rushed to the window they backed away from it, still making those unhuman noises. But they backed away only a little.

"Out!" Lindsay roared, thrusting the gun through the broken pane and waving it around so as to threaten all of them with it. "Get away from here or I'll use this on you!" And when they didn't retreat fast enough to please him, he aimed over their heads and fired off a blast.

They backed up a bit more, and when Lindsay saw that was all the retreating they were going to do, he swung himself around and yelled at those in the room with him. "Come on!" he bellowed. "We have to get out of here while they're deciding what to do!"

Waving the gun, he led a rush to the bedroom doorway and through the big front room to the veranda, and down the veranda steps to Reverend Beckford's station wagon.

They piled into the wagon, all of them—the men and Jennifer and young Davey still in their pyjamas, Big Mary in that ridiculous nightgown, and with Lindsay at the wheel, because the Reverend was still praying, they took off. And just in time, too, because even as they did, that crowd of naked, hideous, no-longer-human men and women came around the corner of the cabin in clumsy pursuit.

As mentioned before, that river road was a low-gear thing, especially for a vehicle so heavily loaded. Big man though he was, the paint-factory owner had trouble keeping the station wagon ahead of the yelling, screaming horrors that came lurching after it, brandishing their clubs. Then came the climb out of the gorge, up the steep stretch known as The Devil's Ladder.

Pointing its nose almost skyward, the old station wagon groaned like a living thing too weary to maintain such an effort. With Lindsay twisting the wheel to avoid boulders that could break an axle, it clawed its way up with the naked things gaining on it. "Faster!" Keith Walker kept yelling at the driver. "For God's sake, give it some gas before they catch us!"

Just as the machine reached the top of the climb, the first of its pursuers grabbed hold of its rear bumper. But like a marathoner glad to be on level ground after struggling up an exhausting grade, the station wagon suddenly doubled its speed and the creature lost its grip and went sprawling face down in the road. From low gear Lindsay shifted into second, then into third. The pursuit died away. Everyone in the car let out a long sigh of relief.

Then the station wagon clawed its way around a bend and Lindsay had to step hard on the brake pedal because the road was blocked by a truck.

It was not a truck that was coming or going. It only stood there in the road with its doors open and its tailgate down and two men standing nearby at the edge of the gorge, surrounded by rusty metal drums they must have unloaded from it. Even as the vehicle bearing the refugees from the gorge shivered to a stop, one of the men rolled a drum to the canyon's rim and kicked it off into space.

The truck, Keith Walker noticed, was unmarked. Which was strange because in this part of the state people who owned such vehicles usually painted their names or the names of their businesses on them in pretty big letters. Like Howard Lindsay's two trucks had LINDSAY PAINT COMPANY, INNSMOUTH, MASS and his phone number on them in letters about a foot high.

So why was Lindsay clawing his way out of the station wagon now and striding toward this truck as if he owned it? Why, after a frantic look behind to see if the naked people were in sight yet, was he yelling at the men as if they worked for him? And why was he shouting, "What do you think you're doing here? How long have you been coming here with this stuff, for God's sake?"

"We been comin' here from the start, boss," one of the men said. He didn't look too bright. In fact, neither of them did. "Ain't that what you told us to do, huh?"

"You bloody idiot, I didn't say Deeprock! I said Redrock! But never mind now. You're blocking the road. Get this damned truck out of here! Fast!" And again Lindsay turned to see if the monstrous things from the gorge were in sight.

They were. They had just rounded the bend of the road. And though obviously tired now from their struggle to climb The Devil's Ladder—or maybe from the condition they were in, with their awful bodies even more misshapen than before—they still brandished their clubs and shouted threats. What was it they wanted, Keith asked himself? Revenge?

The two men ran back to their truck, and Lindsay to the station wagon. As the big vehicle growled into motion and Howard Lindsay sent the station wagon lurching after it, Keith turned for a last look behind.

For the first time he noticed that one of the naked gorge creatures was only a child. A girl about Davey's age. Then, mercifully, another bend in the road hid them all from sight.

The station wagon was off the gorge road and on a two-lane blacktop before anyone spoke. The truck driver had pulled over to let it pass, and once again Keith had noticed there was no name on the truck. Turning on the seat, he looked hard at Howard Lindsay, who was still driving, and said, "What do you really make at that paint factory of yours, Lindsay?"

Lindsay shot him an angry glance, then concentrated fiercely on the road again. But his mouth tightened.

"Does it have anything to do with that dark-complexioned fellow who was in Innsmouth a while back, saying he wanted to learn the paint business? That fellow from—where was he from now? Iraq? Iran? Somewhere in the Middle East, I seem to remember. Does what you're making now have anything to do with that fellow, Lindsay?"

Lindsay said nothing.

"But I guess he didn't really want to learn about paint-making, did he?" Keith persisted. "What he wanted was to teach you how to make something. Those Middle East countries are big on things like germ warfare, aren't they? Was it something like that he persuaded you to make and ship to him as paint? And have you been dumping the leftovers or by-products into Deeprock Gorge? That's about the size of it, Lindsay... isn't it?"

As the station wagon sped along the blacktop on its way to town, Howard Lindsay still had nothing to say, so Keith kept repeating the questions. Reverend Beckford and the others also fired questions at the driver, but he only sucked at his lower lip and gripped the wheel harder. Then all at once he stopped sucking his lip and Keith noticed it was twice its normal size. His hands gripping the wheel were swelling, too.

The Reverend Ralph Beckford was saying sort of vaguely, "When we get to town, we should go directly to the police station, don't you think? Someone will have to go back there and get those people, even if they can't be saved. And we must warn people about the river, too. We must make sure nobody else goes there."

No one answered him. A puffy patch had appeared suddenly on Howard Lindsay's forehead and his left cheek had bulged out.

He put his foot on the brake and steered the vehicle to the side of the road, just barely getting it there before his swelling hands lost their hold on the wheel. When he'd brought it to a stop, he sat there for a few seconds with his head bowed. Then he looked up at the image of his face in the rear-view mirror—a face like those of the people in the gorge—and said plaintively, "I'm afraid someone else will have to drive the rest of the way."

And he began to cry.

EGGS

by STEVE RASNIC TEM

GO TO THE SHORES the washed-out billboard had ordered. Scott wondered why they hadn't repainted the sign, or torn it down, as is it made a poor advertisement for a vacation spot. He could detect traces of successive layers of advertising, the latest being a dark-haired woman in a bikini, lounging on the sand, her red lips pouting at passing drivers. Her lips were the only part of her still bright, blood-like in comparison to the rest. Her skin had faded into a series of pale, rough blotches. Her black hair had receded into greyish cobwebs, her bikini merely a sketch that made her more hideous than seductive. Her eyes had been torn out.

Other things were revealed by tattered windows in this top layer of billboard: a piece of thick rope, part of an ancient vessel, a darkened tentacle of squid or octopus. There were letters and words as well, peeking through the torn spaces or leaking into the thin top layers of paper, but they appeared backwards, part of some foreign alphabet he did not recognise.

It's like a dream of the beach, he had thought, *but someone else's dream and not your own.* He wondered at the peculiar perception. The dream of someone much like himself who never went to the beach, who knew it only from movies and guidebooks or ancient, crumbling billboards erected in weedy lots too far off the interstate to be inviting. In the dream there is no sensation of sand between the toes, clinging to the back, the gritty feel of it inside wet swimming trunks, because the dreamer has not walked in sand for a very long time now, not since he was eight, and there had been that last trip to a broken-down seedy pier a few weeks before his parents' divorce.

In the dream the beach is wide and hot, brilliantly overlit in the way dreams can be when something essential is about to occur. The heated glare makes the faces of his fellow swimmers almost impossible to see, and in any case he knows he would avert his eyes if a viewing seemed imminent.

Now and then someone wades offshore and does not return, but no one else appears to be alarmed.

The blue of the water is an unnatural blue, a neon blue, and he lets it ease up over his feet without protest, and does not object even when it begins to lick away at his ankles, or lap up over his knees, tendrils of it exploring his swimtrunks and rising up over each vertebrae of his spinal column. Only when it pulls him does he become alarmed, and he sees that the water is suddenly a deep, stagnant green, and he struggles back toward the shore, but his feet slip on the scummy surface of the submerged sand, and he is pulled farther away from the beach and from the bathers with their brilliant, formless faces, and soon he is no longer a part of that life, which is receding rapidly, as if it never was.

His marriage ended when Scott decided now would be a good time to have children.

"We never, *ever*, wanted to have children," Eileen said fiercely, as if he needed to be told, as if he was a crazy person now and had to be periodically reminded of the realities of life.

"Well, we never really agreed…" he began, weakly, knowing she would think it was just like a man to introduce irrelevant legalities. He used to think men and women were very much alike, that any perceived differences were simply a matter of sexual politics. He'd been naïve.

"We didn't *have* to agree. It's always been so *obvious* to both of us, from the very beginning."

"But things change. A lot of things have changed, and now I think I want children. You're only twenty-nine; it's not too late."

"Scott, I've stood by you. You can't say I haven't."

"And I'm grateful. I think children would be good for the both of us. They'll make us look forward."

"My god… Scott…"

"They'll make us look at things more positively. We're woefully short on positive outlook around here."

"My god, Scott. You have *cancer*. You want me to have kids, and then raise them by myself?"

He stared at her. She'd just told him he was going to die. Well, everyone was going to die, why was he being such a kid about it? She'd never acknowledged it before, not even when he himself had spoken it out loud. But she *didn't* know. Nobody knew. "No," he replied. "No" to every notion passing through her head. Then he'd left the room, and their marriage. It had been an unreasonable response on his part, but chaos had passed into his body, and he did not believe it would ever leave.

Infiltration, carcinoma… The men and women in their white coats had used the words so elegantly, as if reciting deeply felt poetry, or intoning prayers in some rare dialect before a congregation anxious for enlightenment. *Metastatic, diffusely spreading, degree of penetration, invasion.* Surgical resection with regional lymphadenectomy was the treatment of choice for stage two gastric cancer. He decided to forego the clinical trials, pretending to family and friends a cure had taken place.

And maybe it had. Who could know? Strangeness ran through his body, and in madness his body had begun to eat itself, but who could say that the strangeness would always be alien to him?

They continued to live together. She travelled with him to doctors, shopping, the occasional movie. She was loyal to the end, and it pained him that that wasn't enough. He'd left her in his head, and could not find his way back. And he wasn't even sure she knew.

Then this vacation together. She thought it would do him some good. She didn't say it would do "us" some good because he knew she wasn't really looking forward to spending time out in public with her dying husband. She was a good person; she was genuinely concerned about his welfare. She should get away before he poisoned her.

There'd been no warning. Symptoms had been insignificant. Sometimes a slight pain when he ate a little too much, but who hadn't felt that at one time or other? Now and then a little difficulty swallowing, but he'd always been too emotional, always on the verge of having that lump in his throat. Later on he thought he had an ulcer— he didn't relax enough. But who could relax, the way the world was?

And the way the world was, was indifferent.

He'd never brought up having children again. He knew it was the selfish urge of someone who was dying. No good for her, or for any potential children for that matter. What would he do with children anyway? What would *they* do?

They would watch him die. That, he realised, was what he wanted. The young bear witness to the passing of the old. That was the way it happened the world over.

And beyond that, there was this flesh of his that would continue to walk the careless and uncaring world. Egocentric reasoning, perhaps. After he'd been diagnosed, an elderly neighbour had dropped by to discuss his own terminal illness. He wanted Scott to know that things never really ended, that they simply changed into something else. "There is a reality beyond the everyday," the man had said. "We are all part of something larger. We are each one face of that which has many faces. What we see today, in this life, is only part of the story, no more than an illusion of the truth." Instead of being reassured, however, Scott had been terrified. *Flesh of my flesh, flesh of my flesh,* a voice had intoned in his evening's dream. Scott had never sought to be a part of anything.

The fear was a bad reason to have kids, but he couldn't quite let it go.

* * *

A child wasn't going to happen, but he could still imagine it—how it would look, the sound of its voice. There would be a strangeness about it, surely, but in this child the strangeness would be beautiful. In this child the strangeness would not be a frightening thing.

There had been no reason for him to get sick, no reason at all. He had done nothing wrong. He had exercised, he had watched what he ate. He'd been so careful with everything put into his mouth Eileen often said he appeared to be taking the sacrament. You just never could tell what they put into food these days. Some of it was never even meant to be food. Not for normal people. Now Eileen cooked with soy and they ate as much fish as possible, but he never could feel comfortable eating fish, wondering from what depths they came.

Every night at the Shores he would look out over the ocean, gaze down where the water lapped and drifted back, half-expecting some child to emerge from the waves after its long swim home.

"Beautiful... beautiful," he would say.

Then came the night she caught him during his admiration, heard him call the boggy green expanse beautiful. "That's crazy, Scott. Look at it—it's like floating rot. You can't swim in it—you can't even walk through it."

He turned to her with a small smile, the largest he could muster in these times. "Then maybe you can walk on it," he said, hoping to make her even angrier. "I see you've decided not to enjoy our little vacation after all."

She ran back into the room, crying. He still smiled—he couldn't get the smile off his face. But he felt terrible. He was a jerk, she should leave him. Why wasn't she leaving him?

He turned back to the great, dark, crumbling shore, the slow-moving tide a deep greenish-brown even in moonlight. Fertile, abundant with life, eating itself and eating itself until one day there would be no more. He wondered when Nature had stopped having rules.

The next morning he found the body of a large dog washed up on the shore, a sizeable piece chewed out of its side. Another morning it was a syringe placed upright in the sand like a crucifix. Still another day something long and serpentine had wriggled its way up and down the beach, leaving patterns like words, a drawn-out *nyarlathhhh…* followed by extended obliterations. He didn't show Eileen any of this. She stayed locked in their bedroom, crying. She loved him, and he no longer deserved her. He was worried about how he might treat her in the future—there seemed to be no rules for behaviour any more.

Finally one morning she came out for breakfast, her eyes red but dry. She brought along the morning newspaper, again *The Shores*. "It says here that the towns along this section of coast have had an unusually high birth rate over the past five years. Nobody can explain it."

He stared at her. The eggs in his mouth tasted funny, but most food did these days. He wasn't even sure he should be eating eggs. He'd paid little attention to the diet they'd handed him. Eileen would know, but now she was proffering up some sort of conversational gambit. He owed her a reply. "Any details about these births… um…" The egg clung to the inside of his mouth and would not go down. "Anomalies, that sort of thing?"

She seemed to be staring at his mouth. He wondered if she understood his problem with the bit of egg. It felt mobile against his tongue, as if alive. He thought he felt a vestige of pseudopod, tried to wrest the thought from his mind.

"What… what do you mean?" She stammered slightly, but was still in control. Obviously the wrong thing for him to say. But now he was stuck having to explain himself.

"Um… congenital malformations," said awkwardly about the egg. "Birth…" a hard swallow and it was down. "…defects."

"Oh," she said quietly, staring at him. He could feel the cold sweat trickling down his forehead. "There's nothing about that sort of thing at all."

"Then…" He took a quick swallow of juice, acid burn all the way down the oesophagus, whatever his stomach had become in flames. *God*, he thought, *ordinary food is poison to me now.* "The babies… they all turned out normal."

She smiled a little, and now it was he doing the staring. It was the first smile he'd seen on her in days—and it looked good. "Well, as normal as any of us *can* turn out, I suppose. I mean, the article didn't mention birth defect incidence, any of that… I, well it's been making me think—I've *been* thinking—oh, Scott, I've just decided you're right, we should have a child, we should have it now."

He should have refused, of course. People don't change their minds about something so important so quickly. But if he'd learned anything in recent months it was that intention mattered little, and desire mattered less. He smiled at her, then looked for something to do. He picked up his fork and played with the remains of the egg but could not bring himself to eat any more. He couldn't even touch the glass containing the yellow acid. Finally his hand rested on the newspaper she'd left folded on the table. He picked it up. "You're sure?" he asked, opening it.

"Well, I'm a little scared about it, I admit. I mean, who wouldn't be? A decision like this." She twisted her napkin, not quite able to meet his eyes. "But I'm… scared a lot of the time. I guess we both are."

He could tell she was waiting for confirmation from him. He wanted to help her out, but he just couldn't. "You've made me very happy," he said, and it seemed strangely false, formal. He covered by fussing with the paper. After an indecent pause, he said, "It says here there was another fish kill off Innsmouth."

He waited for her to say something. He kept his eyes on the paper. Finally, "Innsmouth?"

"You know, a few miles up the shore? We passed it on the way down here. It was the last city before the big billboard."

"I don't remember a billboard."

"Well, I thought I pointed it out. I meant to."

"Do they say what killed the fish?" He could hear the strain in her voice, but he couldn't take his eyes from the paper. There was a two-page spread on the fish kill, which seemed odd—they were just fish, after all. But there were a number of pictures: the dark corpses piled up like in those World War II newsreels, stretched out on the sand with all their wedge-shaped heads in a row, one old man holding a large fish in his lap as if it were his drowned child. In the background, in the sand, a filigree of dark lettering.

"No… no. Says here it's a mystery. 'Local biologists stumped,' it says. Hey," he smiled and looked up. "So how many places have their own, *local* biologist?"

"I… I don't know," she said softly. "Do you think we should let him swim?"

"Come again?"

"The baby, should we let him near the water?"

Eileen had wanted to leave their "filthy" city for years. Actually it was "those filthy people" she'd wanted to leave. Ironic that she insisted they remain at The Shores to have the baby, where the water was so polluted she was afraid to walk closer than fifty feet or so, and even then she held her swollen belly protectively and averted her face. After coming to this decision so reluctantly, she had no intention of going anywhere until it had come to completion. Scott supposed it was some sort of nesting instinct, but he found it completely unexpected from her. He himself didn't want her to walk there, but he would have been hard-pressed to explain why.

Even though Scott couldn't work, or couldn't bring himself to, they still had some savings, and Eileen had inheritance from her parents, so they'd be okay for at least a year or so. Scott couldn't imagine living much past the baby's birth. Not that he was sure he was going to die—he just couldn't imagine living.

The Shores was a lonely place past the tourist season. People they did business with every day—the grocer, the pharmacist, the manager of the beachfront cabin they'd moved to—had grown noticeably less friendly once Scott and Eileen revealed their plans. "Gets pretty cold and windy, especially if you're not used to it, especially if you're pregnant," the pharmacist had said when filling Scott's prescription of painkillers. "Don't know that I'd want to put my wife through that."

"We're not likely to have everything you're going to need," the grocer had added several hours later. "See, I order in limited quantity, because I usually know who my customers are going to be."

Only the withered and palsied doctor they'd found to guide Eileen through the pregnancy seemed friendly at all, but his garrulousness seemed to have more to do with Eileen's forthcoming "miracle of birth" than with the patient herself. "The cells, they're dividing, multiplying even as we speak. Amazing, isn't it!" He touched her exposed belly with thin fingers that shook and skittered about like a spider's legs on glass. "Right about now the little one has a webbed-looking hand, no different from what a pig's foot looks like, about this stage. And imagine, a few weeks back they both had fins." Scott watched anxiously as the doctor poked and prodded some more, then suddenly thrust his wrinkled ear up to Eileen's belly. "You can almost hear the little fellow say, 'I'm no pig, Doctor Linden! At least I don't *think* I am!'" He laughed. "Actually, he has no idea what he is right now, and who knows, maybe he'll fool us all!"

"Well, I hardly think so," Eileen offered, gently easing herself away from the doctor's head.

"What I'm saying, dear lady, is that the little one's body is in flux right now. If you were to observe this new face closely you would see a countenance of barely controlled chaos, fiercely set against the imposed orders of our everyday world. The nose must migrate from somewhere atop the head. The mouth and jaws travel out of the brachial arches. The eyes lie at the sides of his head like his cousin's, the fish. They creep up front in stealth, as if ashamed to declare their difference. The ears, why, who knows what songs they hear, songs that we…"

"Is she healthy, doctor?" Scott interrupted.

"Well, I can't say now if it's a she or a he, but perhaps with the ultrasound…"

"My wife, doctor. Is my wife okay?"

Dr. Linden looked up at Eileen's face quizzically, as if seeing it for the first time. "Oh, I imagine she is," he replied.

They always walked back from the doctor's office through the small street of shops, because Eileen insisted that some exercise was good for her pregnancy. Scott was doubtful; she looked pale, especially against this backdrop of dark, burnt-looking wooden structures, but she would not be dissuaded. Nor would she pause by any structure for a breather. Now and then they would see someone—usually a fisherman in his rubber slicker—but this was increasingly rare. There were no CLOSED or OPEN signs in any of the doors, although Scott sometimes could detect yellowish light in the distant recesses of a shop or two. He supposed the locals just knew, and strangers had to find out.

By mid-afternoon each day an artificial twilight had set in, due to cloud cover rolling in from the bay. He hurried her along as fast as he thought safe. Once the clouds came in, everything smelled like rotting fish.

Around her sixth month of pregnancy, they started finding the eggs. "Eggs" was what Eileen called them, and that was what she'd convinced herself they were, but Scott had serious doubts. They seemed too large, and too deliberate. "Someone makes these things, honey, or several someones do. Look, that one has a signature on it." He tugged on the object, jarring it loose from the sandy stretch in front of their cabin where they'd discovered it the previous day. It was heavier than it looked, another detail convincing him they were either carved or manufactured, perhaps part of some local festival. No doubt the locals worked on these things all year, in their garages and basements, bringing them out at a preordained time of the year, planting them like the objects of a giant's Easter egg hunt. He'd ask the manager of the cabins for confirmation, if he could ever find the fellow—they hadn't seen him in weeks.

The egg-shaped object had an odd centre of gravity. It shifted under his hands and he had to struggle to control it. Dangerously off-balance, he bumped into Eileen, almost knocking her down. "God, I'm sorry." He wheezed, and ridiculously felt on the verge of tears. "There, see? A signature." He played his fingers over the back of the egg where a line of squiggles had been pressed into its surface.

"Are you sure that's a signature, hon? It's pretty hard to read."

"You saw Dr. Linden's handwriting on your prescription didn't you? No better than this. In fact it looks damned similar, if you ask me. I wouldn't be surprised if this was one he made."

"If you're right about the local celebration."

"Well, celebration or not, someone is making these things. Now look at that one over there." He led her over to a bend in the gravel and shell road that wound through the spare trees behind the cabins. "Look at all that decorative filigree. You can't tell me that's random chance at work. Besides this one's a little bigger, and shaped a bit differently." He bent and placed her hand on the pattern. She jerked back as if shocked.

"It feels weird," she said, looking around nervously. "I see a few more over by those trees. I wonder how many of these things there are, anyway."

"Just a few, I think. I mean, how many locals can there be? Full-time residents of The Shores? Not more than three dozen, I would think."

But the number of "eggs" they found around the cabin and especially on their daily walks down the beach doubled, doubled again, and doubled again. Eileen stopped mentioning them, and after awhile even stopped looking at them as far as Scott could tell.

Scott could look at little else. The round tops of the eggs made a knobbed carpet from the back of the beach up the grassy slope to the rocks beyond, and he could see a scattering wedged precariously on the high cliffs above. Sometimes they had to veer out of the way of some glacier-like encroachment of eggs onto the beach, stepping into the mossy edges of the water more than once. He did so with trepidation; Eileen simply marched on with no change in expression.

Eileen was changing: her breasts swelling, her belly dropping lower, hips and pelvis spreading. Now and then he could see blotches, broken blood vessels in her face. She looked into the mirror with distaste; often she didn't look into the mirror at all. She was gorgeous. But if he looked only at her belly: the high, tight roundness of it all, he could think only of the eggs filling the landscape around them, and he had to look away as well.

Eileen had gone from asking him about his own health, his own pains and sensations, his own feelings from several times a day to once, to every week or two, to not at all. He thought it just as well. There was painful activity going on inside which his pills only vaguely and intermittently assuaged.

One evening he watched as the dark green tide drifted out of the bay and over the sand, farther than it ever had before, covering the grass and lower rocks, seeping through old abandoned beachfront structures whose torn walls were like shredded wounds, creeping almost all the way up to the access road to their cabin. The next morning he was still there on the deck, watching as the tide rolled out, leaving thousands upon thousands of new eggs behind.

"I *can't* leave. The baby will be here any day," she said. "I have to get ready."

"Eileen, look what's happening here. We have to get out!"

She held on to each side of her belly, swollen like an overripe fruit, extending her palms as if to shield the baby's ears from the argument. "I *don't know* what's happening here, Scott, and neither do you. I haven't known what was happening since you got the cancer. A lot of things are happening that are just completely out of our control, things we don't seem to be able to do one thing about. But I *can* control how I carry this baby, and I'm not going to risk leaving now. You don't what those things out there are, anyway."

"They're eggs, just like you said in the first place. Huge eggs, an enormous multitude of them. They'll be filling the roads soon, and then there'll be no way out of here."

"All the more reason not to risk the travel. Besides, what makes you think they'll harm us in any way? They're eggs, Scott. Just like this baby used to be. And now this big belly of mine is as firm and tight as one of those shells. Maybe you're feeling you're not quite ready for this—I can certainly understand that. But this baby *is* going to happen, Scott."

They hashed it over a couple more times before he gave up and left. He didn't want to upset her by pushing too hard. He was already upset enough for the both of them. His pain had increased over the last several days—there was this enormous pressure, and he'd been able to eat hardly a thing. Eileen's appetite, of course, had grown prodigious. He didn't think she'd even noticed when he hadn't touched his own food.

He was running into the little village to find the doctor, hoping maybe he could talk some sense into her. She'd always paid attention to doctors—she'd hung on every word his own doctors had said, treating them as if they were priests. He bounded onto the darkened sidewalk, running full speed into a tall figure in a damp raincoat.

The odour in his face was old and stale. He peered up into the damp face of his landlord, whose nostrils widened at Scott's proximity. The man's eyes appeared oddly wide and filmy, and his face had greyed since Scott had seen him last. Flecks of dry skin layered his cheeks. "Eileen," Scott began anxiously. "My wife, I can't get her to leave."

The man's voice was blubbery, a frothy translation. "No… one… asked you…"

"You're local, that might have some sort of authority with her. You can tell her about the eggs, what they really are."

"No… one… asked you… to stay…"

"But our child…"

"But… our… chill… dren…" His landlord pushed away.

The doctor's office was locked, though through the glass door Scott saw a bare bulb glowing yellow in the waiting room ceiling. Shadows slithered across the back wall that led to the examining rooms. He began to shout, then beat on the pane until it splintered. No response, and the shadows continued their distant dance. Cardboard file boxes were stacked around the room. One had spilled, the cascade of papers left to drift across the centre rug. Ultrasounds. Curved shapes, vague, radiating lines. Faces and almost faces in the thousands.

Scott turned away from the doctor's door and began beating on the door of the next shop in the row. After almost an hour Scott had been unable to rouse anyone out of any of the dark little shops. If anyone had heard him, they obviously didn't care to help. As he headed back toward the cabin he had to side-step a number of eggs which had not been in his path before. He kicked one out of the way, just for the hell of it. Heavy as stone. He yelped and stumbled, watching the egg rock back and forth before settling itself onto its broad side. Cloud cover had filled in every gap of sky since his departure. Distant lightning illuminated edges of thunderhead. As far as he could see before him a tide of eggs rose and fell over the hills and pastures, gathering beneath and climbing to the lower boughs of trees. Growing, developing, dividing and complicating in ways unimaginable, a chaos of life uncaring, far beyond anything he might possibly comprehend. *Infiltrating carcinoma, diffusely spreading metastases...* Sometimes knowing the truth was not better. Sometimes the truth made an irrelevance of our lives.

When it began raining he tried to walk a little faster, but a road to walk on became increasingly rare. Egg pushed against egg until all repositioned and spread from horizon to horizon until half the visible world had been filled in. Lightning flashes showed off the innate lustre of the shells, as increasing downpour made the curves change, lengthen and soften. He stepped up on their backs gingerly at first, going from egg to egg as if crossing a stream on oily round stones.

Then he heard Eileen's voice calling through the slam of rain and he stepped hard and smashed and pushed forward with shoes caught in the breaking shells. He fell again and again with hands in goo and fierce activity snapping at his fingers but no matter because Eileen was screaming now against the crash of the shores and sky.

Pain ripped through his belly so completely infiltrated now he could not distinguish between stomach and pain, pain and colon and oesophagus in a confusion of cells. Around him seethed an ocean of the newborn, sliding easily through shell wall, eye and claw-foot and tentacle, and all of them different, all of them distinguishable, a thousand faces of the thousand forms.

"Scott!" She screamed and he saw her rise up in tatters, their child but one more child who would never know or understand or care who its parents had been.

But still he ran and smashed and bled to hold these tatters of her in awe. He closed his eyes in a last pathetic attempt to shut out the truth as around him the chaos that was the true face of the world turned and ate of itself again and again, the new bearing but brief witness to the old as their flesh grows thin, thinner still, and dissolves.

FROM CABINET 34, DRAWER 6
by CAITLÍN R. KIERNAN

5:46 P.M.

THE OLD THEATRE on Asylum Street smells like stale popcorn and the spilled soft drinks that have soured on the sticky floors, and the woman sitting in the very back row, the woman with the cardboard box open in her lap, shuts her eyes. A precious few seconds free of the ridiculous things on the screen, just the theatre stink and the movie sounds—a scream and a splash, a gunshot—and then the man coughs again. Thin man in his navy-blue fedora and his threadbare gabardine jacket, the man with the name that sounds like an ice-cream flavour, and when she opens her eyes he's still sitting there in the row in front of her, looking at her expectantly over the back of his seat. The screen becomes a vast rectangular halo about his head, a hundred thousand shades of grey, and "Well," he says, "there you have it."

"I don't know what I'm seeing any more," she says and he nods his head very slowly, up and down, up and down, like a small, pale thing on the sea, and she looks up at the screen again.

The man in the rubber monster suit, the flicker, the soft, insectile flutter from the projector in the booth above her head.

"Just an old movie," Dr. Solomon Monalisa says knowingly, not bothering to whisper because there's no one else is in the theatre but the two of them, him and her, the skinny, antique man and the bookish woman with her cardboard box. "A silly old movie to scare children at Saturday afternoon matinees, to scare teenage girls—"

"Is that what it is? Is that the truth?"

"The *truth*," he says, smiles a tired sort of a smile and coughs again. A handkerchief from his breast pocket to wipe his thin lips clean, and then the man with the ice-cream name stares for a moment into his own spit and phlegm caught in folds of linen as though they were tea leaves and he could read the future there.

"Yes, I suppose that's what you would call it," he tells her, stuffing the soiled handkerchief back into his pocket. "You would call it that until something better comes along."

On screen, a cavern beneath the black Amazonian lake, glycerine mist and rifle smoke, and the creature's gills rise and fall, struggling for breath; its bulging eyes are as blank and empty as the glass eyes of a taxidermied fish.

"It's almost over," Dr. Solomon Monalisa says. "Are you staying for the end?"

"I might talk," the woman whispers, even though they are alone, and the creature roars, its plated, scaly flesh torn by bullets, by knives and spears; rivulets of dark blood leak from its latex hide, and the old man nods his head again.

"You might. You wouldn't be the first."

"Would someone try to stop me?"

"Someone already has, Miss Morrow."

And now it's her turn to nod, and she looks away from the movie screen, the man in the latex suit's big death scene up there, the creature drifting limp and lifeless to the bottom of its lonely, weedy lagoon. Lacey Morrow looks down at the box in her lap, and *If I'd never found the goddamned thing*, she thinks, *if someone else had found it instead of me.* All the things she would give away for that to be true, years or memories, her life if she could die without knowing the things she knows now.

"Well, there it is," Dr. Solomon Monalisa says again and the last frames flicker past before the screen goes white and the red velvet curtain comes down and the house lights come up. "Not quite as silly as I remember. Not a bad way to pass an afternoon."

"Will they mind if I sit here a little longer?" she asks and he shrugs his thin shoulders, stands and straightens the lapels of his jacket, fusses with the collar of his shirt.

"No," he says. "I shouldn't think they'd mind at all."

She doesn't watch him leave, keeps her eyes fixed on the box, and his shoes make small, uneven sounds against the sticky floor.

1:30 P.M.

Waking from an uneasy dream of childhood, a seashore and her sisters and something hanging in the sky, something terrible that she wouldn't look at no matter what they promised her. Lacey blinks and squints through the streaky train window at the Connecticut countryside rushing by, surely Connecticut by now, probably somewhere well past Springfield and headed for Hartford. Crazy quilt of fields and pasture land stitched together with October leaves, the fiery boughs of birch and beech and hickory to clothe red Jurassic sandstone, and then she catches sight of the winding, silver-grey ribbon of the river to the west, flashing bright beneath the morning sun. She rubs her eyes, blinks at all that sunlight and wishes that she hadn't dozed off. But trains almost always lull her to sleep, sooner or later, the steady, heartbeat rhythm of the wheels against the rails, steel-on-steel lullaby, and the more random rattle and clatter of the couplings for punctuation.

She checks to see that the cardboard box is still there on the empty aisle seat beside her, that her satchel is still stowed safely at her feet, and, reassured, Lacey glances quickly about the car, slightly embarrassed at having fallen asleep. That strangers have been watching her sleep and she might have snored or drooled or mumbled foolish things in her dreams, but the car is mostly empty, anyway—a teenage girl reading a paperback, a priest reading a newspaper—and she looks back to the window, her nightmare already fading in the warmth of the day. They're closer to the river now, and she can see a small boat—a fishing boat, perhaps—cutting a V-shaped wake on the water.

"Have yourself a nice little nap, then?" and Lacey turns, startled, clipping the corner of the box with her elbow and it almost tumbles to the floor before she can catch it. There's a woman in the seat directly behind her, someone she hadn't noticed only a moment before, painfully thin woman with tangled, oyster-white hair, neither very old nor very young, and she's staring at Lacey with watery blue eyes that seem to bulge slightly, intently, from their sockets. Her skin is dry and sallow, and there's a sickly, jaundiced tint to her cheeks. She's wearing a dingy black raincoat and a heavy sweater underneath, wool the colour of instant oatmeal, and her nubby fingernails are painted an incongruous flamingo pink.

"I didn't mean to frighten you," the woman says in her deliberate, gravel-voice, and Lacey shakes her head *no*, "No, it's okay. I guess I'm not quite awake, that's all."

"I was starting to think I'd have to wake you up myself," the woman says impatiently, still staring. "I'm only going as far as Hartford. I don't have the time to go any farther than that." As she talks, Lacey has begun to notice a very faint, fishy smell, fish or low-tide mud flats, brine and silt and stranded, suffocating sea creatures. The odour seems to be coming from the white-haired woman, her breath or her clothes, and Lacey pretends not to notice.

"You're sitting there thinking, 'Who's this lunatic?' ain't you? 'Who's this deranged woman and how can I get her to shut the hell up and leave me alone?'"

"No, I just don't—"

"Oh, yes you are," the woman says and she jabs an index finger at Lacey, candy-pink polish and her knuckles like dirty, old tree roots. "But that's okay. You don't know me from Adam. You aren't *supposed* to know me, Miss Morrow."

Lacey glances at the other passengers, the girl and the priest. Neither of them are looking her way, still busy with their reading, and if they've even noticed the white-haired woman they're pretending that they haven't. Not like she's their problem, and Lacey says a silent, agnostic's prayer that it isn't much farther to the Hartford station; she smiles and the woman makes a face like she's been insulted.

"It ain't *me* you got to be afraid of, Miss. Get that straight. I'm sticking my neck out, just talking to you."

"I'm very sorry," Lacey says, trying hard to sound sorry instead of nervous, instead of annoyed. "But I really don't have any idea what you're talking about."

"Me, I'm nothing but a messenger. A courier," the woman replies, lowering her voice almost to a whisper and glaring suspiciously towards the other two passengers. "Of course, that wouldn't make much difference, if you know what I mean."

"I don't have any idea what you mean."

"Well, you got the box right there," the woman says and now she's pointing over the back of Lacey's seat at the cardboard box with the Innsmouth fossil packed inside. "That makes you a courier, too. Hell, that almost makes you a goddamn holy prophet on Judgement Day. But you probably haven't thought of it that way, have you?"

"Maybe it would be better if we talked later," Lacey whispers, playing along, and the woman's probably perfectly harmless, but she puts one hand protectively on the box, anyway. "*They* might be listening," she says and nods her head towards the teenager and the priest. "They might hear something we don't want them to hear."

The woman makes an angry, hissing sound between her yellow teeth and runs the long fingers of her left hand quickly through her tangled white hair, slicking it back against her scalp, pulling a few strands loose and they lie like pearly threads on the shoulder of her black raincoat.

"You think you got it all figured out, don't you?" she growls. "Put some fancy letters after your name and you don't need to listen to anybody or anything, ain't that right? Can't nobody tell you no different, 'cause you've seen it *all*, from top to bottom, pole to pole—"

"Calm down, *please*," Lacey says, glancing towards the other passengers again, wishing one of them would look up so she could get their attention. "If you don't, I'm going to have to call the conductor. Don't make me do that."

"Goddamn stuck-up dyke," the woman snarls and she spits on the floor, turns her head and stares furiously out the window with her bulging blue eyes. "You think I'm crazy. Jesus, you just wait till you come out the other side and *then* let's see what the hell you think sane looks like."

"I didn't mean to upset you," Lacey says, standing, reaching for the satchel with her laptop. "Maybe I should just move to another seat."

"You *do* that, Miss Morrow. Won't be no skin off *my* nose. But you better take this with you," and the woman's left hand disappears inside her raincoat, reappears with a large, slightly crumpled manila envelope, and she holds it out to Lacey. "They told me you'd figure it out, so don't ask me no more questions. I've already said too goddamn much as it is."

Lacey sets her satchel down beside the cardboard box and stares at the envelope for a moment, yellow-brown paper and what looks like a grease stain at one corner.

"Well, go on ahead. It ain't got teeth. It ain't gonna bite you," the white-haired woman sneers, not taking her eyes off the window, the farms and houses and "Maybe if you take it," she says, "the crazy woman will leave you alone."

Lacey snatches the envelope, hastily gathers her things, the satchel and the box, and moves quickly up the centre aisle towards the front of the car. The priest and the girl don't even look up as she passes them. *Maybe they don't see me at all*, she thinks. *Maybe they haven't heard a thing.* The door to the next car is stuck and she's wrestling with the handle when the train lurches, sways suddenly to one side, and she almost drops the box, imagines the fossil inside shattering into a hundred pieces.

Stupid girl, stupid silly girl.

And she forces herself to be still, then, presses her forehead against the cool, aluminium door. She takes a deep breath of air that doesn't smell like dead fish, that only smells like diesel fumes and disinfectant, perfectly ordinary train smells, comforting familiarity, and the cadence of the rails is the most reassuring sound in the world.

Go on ahead. It ain't got teeth. It ain't gonna bite you, the white-haired woman said, nothing at all but a crazy lady that someone ought to be watching out for, not letting her ride about on trains harassing people. Lacey looks down at the grease-stained envelope in her hand, held tenuously between her right thumb and forefinger.

"Do you need me to help you with that?" and it's only the priest, scowling up at her from his newspaper; he sighs a loud, irritated sigh and points at the exit. "Would you like me to get the *door* for you?"

"Yes," she says. "Thank you, Father. I'd really appreciate it. My hands are full."

Lacey glances anxiously past him towards the back of the car, and there's no sign of the white-haired woman now, but the door at the other end is standing wide open.

"There," the priest says and she smiles and thanks him again.

"No problem," he says, and as she steps into the short, connecting corridor, he continues speaking in low, conspiratorial tones, "But don't wait too long to have a look at what's in that envelope she gave you. There may not be much time left." Then the door slides shut again and Lacey turns and runs to the crowded refuge of the next car.

Her twenty-fifth birthday, the stormy day in early July when Lacey Morrow found the Innsmouth fossil, working late and alone in the basement of the Pratt Museum. Almost everyone else gone home already, but nothing unusual about that. Lacey pouring over the contents of Cabinet 34, drawers of Devonian fishes collected from Blossburg, Pennsylvania and Chaleur Bay, Quebec, slabs of shale and sandstone the dusky colour of charcoal, the colour of cinnamon; ancient lungfish and the last of the jawless ostracoderms, lobe-finned *Eusthenopteron* and the boxy, armour plates of the antiarch *Bothriolepis*. Relics of an age come and gone hundreds of millions of years before the dinosaurs, a time when the earliest forests lined the shores of lakes and rivers teeming with strange and monstrous fish, and vertebrates had begun to take their first clumsy steps onto dry land. And that transition her sole, consuming obsession since Lacey was an undergraduate, that alchemy of flesh and bone—fins to feet, gills to lungs—the puzzles that filled her days and nights, that filled her dreams. Her last girlfriend walking out because she'd finally had enough of Lacey's all-night kitchen dissections, the meticulously mutilated sea bass and cod, eels and small sharks sliced up and left lying about until she found time to finish her notes and sketches. Dead things in plastic bags crammed into the freezer and the ice cubes starting to taste more like bad sushi, their Hitchcock Road apartment stinking of formalin and fish markets.

"If I grow fucking scales maybe I'll give you a call sometime," Julie growled, hauling her boxes of clothes and CDs from their front porch to the back of her banged-up little Honda. "If I ever meet up with a goddamn mermaid, I'll be sure to give her your number."

Lacey watched her drive away, feeling less than she knew she *ought* to feel, wishing she would cry because any normal person would cry, would at least be angry with herself or with Julie. But the tears never came, nor the anger, and after that she figured it was better to leave romantic entanglements for some later stage in her life, some faraway day when she could spare a spark of passion for anything except her studies. She kept a picture of Julie in a pewter frame beside her bed, though, so she could still pretend, from time to time, when she felt alone, when she awoke in the middle of the night and there was nothing but the sound of rain on the roof and the wind blowing cold through the streets of Amherst.

But that August afternoon she wasn't lonely, not with the tall rows of battleship-grey steel cabinets and their stony treasures stacked neatly around her, all the company she needed and no thoughts but the precise numbers from her digital callipers—the heights and widths of pelvic girdles and scapulocoracoids, relative lengths of pectoral fins and radials. Finishing up with a perfectly preserved porolepiform that she suspected might be a new species, and Lacey noticed the box pushed all the way to the very back of the drawer, half-hidden under a cardboard tray of shale and bone fragments. Something overlooked, even though she'd thought she knew the contents of those cabinets like the back of her hand and any further surprises would only be in the details.

"Well, hello there," she said to the box, carefully slipping it from its hiding place beneath the tray. "How'd I ever miss you, hmmm?" It wasn't a small box—only a couple of inches deep, but easily a foot and a half square, sagging just a bit at the centre from having supported the weight of the tray for who knows how many years. There was writing on one corner of the lid, spidery fountain-pen ink faded as brown as dead leaves: *from Naval dredgings, USS Cormorant (April, 1928), Lat. 42° 40" N., Long. 70° 43" W, NE. of old Innsmouth Harbour, Essex Co., Mass. ?Devonian.* But there was no catalogue or field number, no identification either, and then Lacey opened the box and stared amazed at the thing inside.

"Jesus," she whispered, swallowing a metallic taste like foil or a freshly filled tooth, adrenaline-silver aftertaste, and her first impression was that the thing was a hand, the articulated skeleton of a human hand lying palm-side up in the box, its fingers slightly curled and clutching at the ceiling or the bright fluorescent lights overhead. She set the box down on one of the larger Chaleur Bay slabs, stared at the tips of her own trembling fingers and the petrified bones resting in a bed of excelsior. They were dark, the waxy black of baker's chocolate, and shiny from a thick coating of varnish or shellac.

No, not human, but certainly the forelimb of *something*, something big, at least a third again larger than her own hand, and "Jesus," she whispered again. Lacey lifted the fossil from the excelsior, gently because there was no telling how stable it was, how many decades since anyone had even bothered to open the box. She counted almost all the elements of the manus—carpals and metacarpals, phalanges— and the lower part of the forearm, sturdy radius and ulna ending abruptly in a ragged break, the dull glint of gypsum or quartz flakes showing from the exposed interior of the fossil. There was bony webbing or spines preserved between the fingers, and the three that were complete ended in short, sharp ungual claws; a small patch of what appeared to be scales or dermal ossicles on the palm just below the fifth metacarpal, oval disks with deeply concave centres unlike anything she could remember ever having seen before. Here and there, small bits of greenish-grey limestone still clung to the bones, but most of the hard matrix had been scraped away.

Lacey sat down on a wooden stool near Cabinet 34, her dizzy head too full of questions and astonishment, heart racing, the giddy, breathless excitement of discovery, and she forced herself to shut her eyes for a moment. Gathering shreds of calm from the darkness behind her lids, counting backwards from thirty until her pulse began to return to normal; she opened her eyes again and turned the fossil over to examine the other side. The bone surface on the back of the hand was not so well preserved, weathered as though that side had been exposed to the forces of erosion for some time before it was collected, the smooth, cortical layer cracked and worn completely away in places. There was a lot more of the greenish limestone matrix on that side, too, and a small snail's shell embedded in the rock near the base of the middle finger.

"What *are* you?" she asked the fossil, as if it might tell her, as simple as that, and everything else forgotten now, all her fine coelacanths and rhipidistians, for this newest miracle. Lacey turned it over again, examining the palm-side more closely, the pebbly configuration of wrist bones, quickly identifying the ulnare, what she thought must be the intermedium, and when she finally glanced at her watch it was almost six-thirty. At least an hour since she opened the box and she'd have to hurry to make her seven o'clock lecture. She returned the hand to the excelsior, paused a moment for one last, lingering glimpse of the thing before putting the lid back on. Overhead, high above the exhibits halls and the slate-tiled roof of the Pratt Museum, a thunderclap boomed and echoed across the valley, and Lacey tried to remember if she'd left her umbrella in her apartment.

1:49 P.M.

Sitting next to a woman who smells like wintergreen candy and mothballs, the steady *clackclackclack* of razorwheels against the rails, and Lacey's been staring at the photograph from the manila envelope for almost five minutes now. A movie still, she thinks, the glossy black-and-white photograph creased and dog-eared at one corner, and it shows an old man with a white moustache standing with two Indians beside a rocky outcrop. Someplace warm, someplace tropical because there are palmetto fronds at one edge of the photograph. It isn't hot on the train, but Lacey's sweating anyway, her palms gone slick and clammy, tiny beads like nectar standing out on her forehead and upper lip. The old man in the photograph is holding something cradled in both hands, clutching it like a holy relic, a grail, the prize at the end of a life-long search.

...'cause you've seen it all, from top to bottom and pole to pole...

The man in the photograph is holding the Innsmouth fossil. Or he's holding a replica so perfect that it must have been cast from the original and it really doesn't make much difference, either way. She turns the picture over and there's a label stuck to the back— Copyright © 1954 Universal-International—typed with a typewriter that drops its "N's".

There was a letter in the envelope, as well. A faded photocopy of a letter, careless, sprawling handwriting that she can only just decipher:

Mr. Zacharias R. Gilman, Esq.
7 High Street
Ipswich, Mass.

15 January 1952

Mr. William Alland
Universal Studios
Los Angeles, Cal.

Dear Mr. Alland,

Sir, I have seen your fine horror picture "It Came From Outer Space" six times as of this writing and must say that I am in all ways impressed with your work. You have a true artist's eye for the uncanny and deserve to be proud of your endeavours. I am enclosing some newspaper clippings, which may be of some small interest to a mind such as yours, regarding certain peculiar things that have gone on hereabouts for years. Old people here talk about the "plagues" of 1846 but they will tell you it wasn't really no plague that set old Innsmouth on the road to ruin, if you've a mind to listen. They will tell you lots of things, Mr. Alland and I lie awake at night thinking about what might still go on out there at the reef. But you read the newspaper clippings for yourself, sir, and make of it what you will. I believe you might fashion a frightful film from these incidents. I will be at this address through May, should you wish to reply.

Respectfully, your avid admirer,
Zacharias Gilman

"Do you like old monster movies?" the wintergreen and mothball woman asks her and Lacey shakes her head no.

"Well, that photograph, that's a scene from—"

"I don't watch television," she says.

"Oh, no, I didn't mean made-for-TV movies. I meant real movies, the kind you see in theatres."

"I don't go to theatres, either."

"Oh," the woman says, sounding disappointed, and in a moment she turns away again and stares out the window at the autumn morning rushing by outside.

10:40 A.M.

"Well, I like it," Dr. Morgan says, finally. "It looks good on paper." He chews absently at the stem of his cheap pipe and puffs pungent, grey smoke clouds that smell like roasting apples. "And a binomen should look good. It should sound good, rolling off the tongue. Damn it, Lacey, it should almost *taste* good."

More than three months since she found the Innsmouth fossil tucked away in Cabinet 34, and Lacey sits with Dr. Jasper Morgan in his tiny, third-floor office; all the familiar, musty comforts of that small room with its high ceilings and ornate, moulded plaster walls hidden behind solid oak shelves stuffed with dustwashed books and fossils and all the careful clutter of an academic's life. A geologic map of Massachusetts framed and hanging slightly askew. Rheumy hiss and clank from the radiator below the window and if the glass wasn't steamed over, she could see across the rooftops of Amherst, south to the low, autumn-stained hills beyond the town, the weathered slopes of the Holyoke Range rising blue-grey in the hazy distance.

Three months that hardly seem like three full weeks to her, days and nights, dreams and waking all become a blur of questions and hardly any answers, the fossil become her secret, shared only with Dr. Morgan, and Dr. Hanisak over in the zoology department. Hers and hers alone until she could at least begin to get her bearings and a preliminary report on the specimen could be written. When she was ready and her paper had been accepted by the journal *Nature*, Dr.

Morgan arranged for the press conference at Yale, where she would sit in the shadow of Rudolph Zallinger's mural and Othniel Marsh's dinosaurs and reveal the Innsmouth fossil to the whole, wide world.

"I had to call it something," she replies. "Seemed a shame not to have some fun with it. I have a feeling that I'm never going to find anything like this again."

"Exactly," and Jasper Morgan leans back in his creaky, wooden chair, takes the pipe from his mouth and stares intently into the smouldering bowl. Like a gypsy with her polished crystal ball, old man with his glowing cinders, and "'Words,'" he says in the tone of voice he reserves for quoting anyone he holds in higher esteem than himself, "'are in themselves among the most interesting objects of study, and the names of animals and plants are worthy of more consideration than biologists are inclined to give them.' Unfortunately, no one seems to care very much about the aesthetics these days, no one but rusty old farts like me."

He slides the manuscript back across his desk to Lacey, seventeen double-spaced pages held together with a green plastic paper clip; she nods once, reading over the text again silently to herself. Her eyes drift across his wispy, red pencil marks: a missing comma here, there a spelling or date she should double-check.

"That's not true," Lacey says.

"What's not true?"

"That no one but you cares any more."

"No? Well, maybe not. But, please, allow me the conceit."

"Dr. Hanisak still thinks the name's too fanciful. She said I should have called it something more descriptive. She suggested *Eocarpus*."

"Of course she did. Hanisak has all the imagination of a stripped wing nut," and the palaeontologist slips his pipe back between his ivory-yellow teeth.

"*Grendelonyx innsmouthensis*," Lacey whispers, and it *does* taste good, the syllables smooth as good brandy.

"See? There you are. 'Grendel's claw from Innsmouth,'" Jasper Morgan mutters around his pipe. "What the hell could be more descriptive than that?"

Across campus, the steeple chimes begin to ring the hour—nine, ten, ten and three-quarters—later than Lacey had realised and she frowns at her watch, not ready to leave the sanctuary of the office and his company.

"Shit. I'll miss my train if I don't hurry," she says.

"Wish I were going with you. Wish I could be there to see their faces."

"I know, but I'll be fine. I'll call as soon as I get to New Haven," and she puts the manuscript back inside its folder and returns it to the battered black leather satchel that also holds her iBook and the CD with all the slides for the presentation, the photographs and cladograms, her character matrix and painstaking line drawings. Then Dr. Morgan smiles and shakes her hand, like they've only just met this morning, like it hasn't been years, and he sees her to the door. She carries the satchel in one hand and the sturdy cardboard box in the other. Last night she transferred the fossil from its original box to this one, replaced the excelsior with cotton and foam-rubber padding. Her future in this box, her box of wonders, and "Knock 'em dead, kiddo," he says and hugs her, wraps her tight in the reassuring scents of his tobacco and aftershave lotion, and Lacey hugs him back twice as hard.

"Don't you go losing that damned thing. That one's going to make you famous," he says and points at the cardboard box.

"Don't worry. It's not going to leave my sight, not even for a minute."

A few more words, encouragement and hurried last thoughts, and then Lacey walks alone down the long hallway past classrooms and tall display cabinets, doors to other offices, and she doesn't look back.

"I couldn't find it on the map," she said, watching the man's callused, oil-stained hands as he counted out her change, the five dollars and two nickels that were left of the twenty after he'd filled the Jeep's tank and replaced a windshield-wiper blade.

"Ain't on no maps," the man said. "Not no more. Ain't been on no maps since sometime way back in the '30s . Wasn't much left to put on a map after the Feds finished with the place."

"The Feds?" she asked. "What do they have to do with Innsmouth?" and the man stepped back from the car and eyed her more warily than before. Tall man with stooped shoulders and gooseberry-grey eyes, a nose that looked like it'd been broken more than once; he shrugged and shook his head.

"Hell, I don't know. You hear things, that's all. You hear all sorts of things. Most of it don't mean shit."

Lacey glanced at the digital clock on the dashboard, then up at the low purple-black clouds sailing by, the threat of more rain and nightfall not far behind it. Most of the day wasted on the drive from Amherst, a late start in a downpour, then a flat tyre on the Cambridge Turnpike, a flat tyre *and* a flat spare, and by the time she made Cape Ann it was almost four o'clock.

"What business you got up at Innsmouth, anyhow?" the man asked suspiciously.

"I'm a scientist," she said. "I'm looking for fossils."

"Is that a fact? Well, ma'am, I never heard of anyone finding any sort of fossils around here."

"That's because the rocks are wrong. All the rocks around the Cape are igneous and—"

"What's that mean, '*igneous*'?" he interrupts, pronouncing the last word suspiciously, like it's something that might bite if he's not careful.

"It means they formed when molten rock—magma or lava—cooled down and solidified. Around here, most of the igneous rocks are plutonic, which means they solidified deep underground."

"I never heard of no volcanoes around here."

"No," Lacey says. "There aren't any volcanoes around here, not now. It was a very long time ago."

The man watched her silently for a moment, rubbed at his stubbly chin as if trying to make up his mind whether or not to believe her.

"All these granite boulders around here, those are igneous rock. For fossils, you usually need sedimentary rocks, like sandstone or limestone."

"Well, if that's so, then what're *you* doing looking for them out here?"

"That's kind of a long story," she said impatiently, tired of this distrustful man and the stink of gasoline, just wanting to get back on the road again if he can't, or won't, tell her anything useful. "I wanted to see Innsmouth Harbour, that's all."

"Ain't much left to see," he said. "When I was a kid, back in the

'50s, there was still some of the refinery standing, a few buildings left along the waterfront. My old man, he used to tell me ghost stories to keep me away from them. But someone or another tore all that shit down years ago. You take the road up to Ipswich and Plum Island, then head east, if you really wanna see for yourself."

"Thank you," Lacey said, and she turned the key in the switch and wrestled the stick out of park.

"Anytime at all," the man replied. "You find anything interestin', let me know."

And as she pulled away from the gas station, lightning flashed bright across the northern sky, somewhere off towards Plum Island and the cold Atlantic Ocean.

3:15 P.M.

The train slips through the shadow cast by the I-84 overpass, brief ribbon of twilight from concrete and steel eclipse and then bright daylight again, and in a moment the Vermonter is pulling into the Hartford station. Lacey looks over her shoulder, trying not to *look* like she's looking, to see if they're still standing at the back of the car watching her, the priest and the oyster-haired crazy woman who gave her the envelope with the photograph and letter. And they are, one on each side of the aisle like mismatched gargoyle bookends. Ten minutes or so since she first noticed them back there, the priest with his newspaper folded and tucked beneath one arm and the oyster-haired woman staring at the floor and mumbling quietly to herself. The priest makes eye contact with Lacey and she turns away, looks quickly towards the front of the train again. A few of the passengers already on their feet, already retrieving bags and briefcases from overhead compartments, eager to be somewhere else, and the woman sitting next to Lacey asks if this is her stop.

"No," she says. "No, I'm going on to New Haven."

"Oh, do you have family there?" the woman asks. "Are you a student? My father went to Yale, but that was—"

"Will you watch my seat, please?" Lacey asks her and the woman frowns, but nods her head yes.

214

"Thanks. I won't be long. I just need to make a phone call."

Lacey gets up and the oyster-haired woman stops mumbling to herself and takes a hesitant step forward; the priest lays one hand on her shoulder and she halts, but glares at Lacey with her bulging eyes and holds up one palm like a crossing guard stopping traffic.

"I'll only be a moment," Lacey says.

"You can leave that here, too, if you like," the woman who smells like wintergreen and mothballs says and Lacey realises that she's still holding the box with the Innsmouth fossil.

"No. I'll be right back," Lacey tells her, gripping the box a little more tightly, and before the woman can say anything else, before the priest has a chance to change his mind and let the oyster-haired woman come after her, Lacey turns and pushes her way along the aisle towards the exit sign.

"Excuse me," she says, repeated like a prayer, a hasty mantra as she squeezes past impatient, unhelpful men and women. She accidentally steps on someone's foot and he tells her to slow the fuck down, just wait her turn, what the fuck's *wrong* with her, anyway. Then she's past the last of them and moving quickly down the steps, out of the train and standing safe on the wide and crowded platform. Glancing back at the tinted windows, she doesn't see the priest or the crazy woman who gave her the envelope. Lacey asks a porter pulling an empty luggage rack where she can find a pay phone and he points to the Amtrak terminal.

"Right through there," he says, "on your left, by the rest rooms." She thanks him and walks quickly across the platform towards the doors, the wide, electric doors sliding open and closed, spitting some people out and swallowing others whole.

"Miss Morrow!" the priest shouts, his voice small above the muttering crowd. "Please, wait! You don't understand!"

But Lacey doesn't wait, only a few more feet to the wide terminal doors and never mind the damned pay phones, she can always call Jasper Morgan *after* she finds a security guard or a cop.

"Please!" the priest shouts, and the wide doors slide open again.

It ain't me you got to be afraid of, Miss. Get that straight.

"You'll have to come with us now," a tall, pale man in a black suit and black sunglasses says as he steps through the doors onto the platform and the sun shines like broken diamonds off the barrel of the pistol in his left hand and the badge in his right. Lacey turns to run, but there's already someone there to stop her, a black woman almost as tall as the pale man with the gun. "You'll only make it worse on yourself," she says in a thick Caribbean accent, and Lacey looks back towards the train, desperately searching the crowd for the priest, and there's no sign of him anywhere.

After the gas station, Lacey followed Highway 1 south to Kent Corner and from there she took Haverhill Street to the 1A, gradually working her way south and east, winding towards Ipswich and the sea. The sky beaten black and blue by the storms and the day dissolving slowly into a premature North Shore night while lightning fingers flicked greedily across the land. At Ipswich, she asked directions again, this time from a girl working behind the counter of a convenience store. The girl had heard of Innsmouth, though she'd never seen the place for herself, had only picked up stories at school and from her parents—urban legends mostly, wild tales of witches and sea monsters and strange lights floating above the dunes. She sold Lacey a Diet Coke and a bag of Fritos and told her to take Argilla Road out of town and stay on it all the way down to the river. "Be careful," the girl said worriedly and Lacey smiled and promised that she would.

"Don't worry about me," she said. "I just want to have a quick look around."

And twenty minutes later she reached the dead end of Argilla Road, a locked gate and chain-link fence crowned with loops of razor wire, stretching east and west as far as she could see. A rusty Army Corps of Engineers sign hung on the gate, NO TRESPASSING. VIOLATORS WILL BE PROSECUTED AND THIS AREA PATROLLED BY ARMED GUARDS—DO NOT ENTER. She parked the Jeep in a sandy spot near the fence and sat for a few minutes staring at the sign, wondering how many years it had been there, how many decades, before she cut the engine and got out. The wind smelled like rain and the sea, ozone and the fainter, silty stink of the salt marshes, commingled smells of

life and sex and death; she sat on the cooling hood of the car with a
folded topographic map and finished the bag of Fritos. Below her
the land dropped quickly away to stunted trees, billowing swells of
goldenrod and spike grass, and a few stingy outcroppings of granite
poking up here and there through the sand. The Manuxet River
snaked along the bottom of the valley, wandering through thickets
of bullrush and silverweed, tumbling over a few low falls on its way
down to the mouth of Ipswich Bay.

But there was no indication that there had ever been a town of any
sort here, certainly no evidence that this deserted stretch of coastline
had once been the prosperous seaport of Innsmouth, with its mills
and factories, a gold refinery and bustling waterfront, its history
stretching back to the mid-17th century. So maybe she was in the
wrong place after all. Maybe the ruins of Innsmouth lay somewhere
farther east, or back towards Plum Island. Lacey watched two seagulls
struggling against the wind, raucous grey-white smudges drifting
in the low indigo sky. She glanced at the topo map and then north-
west towards a point marked CASTLE HILL, but there was no castle
there now, if indeed there ever had been, no buildings of any sort,
only a place where the land rose up one last time before ending in a
weathered string of steep granite cliffs.

She'd drawn a small red circle on the map just offshore, to indicate
the co-ordinates written on the lid of the old box from Cabinet 34—
Latitude 42° 40" N, Longitude 70° 43" W—and Lacey scanned the
horizon, wishing she'd remembered her binoculars, hanging useless
in her bedroom closet at home. But there was *something* out there, a
thin, dark line a mile or more beyond the breakwater, barely visible
above the stormy sea. Perhaps only her imagination—something she
needed to see—or a trick of the fading light, or both, and she glanced
back down at the map. Not far from her red circle were contour lines
indicating a high, narrow shoal hiding beneath the water and the
spot was labelled simply ALLEN'S REEF. If the tide were out and the
ocean calm, maybe there would be more to see, perhaps an aplitic or
pegmatitic dike cutting through the native granite, an ancient river of
magma frozen, crystallised, scrubbed smooth by the waves.

"What do you think you'll find out there?" Jasper Morgan had asked her the day before. He'd come by her office with the results of a microfossil analysis of the sediment sample she'd scraped from the Innsmouth fossil. "There sure as hell aren't any Devonian rocks on Cape Ann," he'd said. "It's all Ordovician, and igneous, to boot."

"I just want to see it," she'd replied, skimming the letter typed on Harvard stationary, describing the results of the analysis.

"So, what does it say?" Dr. Morgan had asked, but Lacey read all the way to the bottom of the page before answering him.

"The rock's siltstone, but we already knew that. The ostracodes say Early Devonian, probably Lochkovian. And that snail's definitely *Loxonema*. So, there you go. Devonian rocks somewhere off Cape Ann."

"Damn," he'd whispered, grinning and scratching his head, and they'd spent the next half-hour talking about the thing from Cabinet 34, more than a hundred million years older than anything with a forearm like that had a right to be. No getting around the fact that it looked a lot more like a hand, something built for grasping, than a forefoot, and "Maybe we ought to just put it *back* in that drawer," Jasper Morgan had said, shaking his head. "Do you have any idea what kind of shit storm this thing's gonna cause?"

"I think maybe I'm beginning to."

"You might as well have found a goddamn cell phone buried in an Egyptian pyramid."

Thunder rumbles somewhere nearby, off towards Rowley, and a few cold drops of rain; Lacey glanced down at the map and then out at the distant black line of Allen's Reef one last time. Such a long drive to find so little, the whole day wasted, the night and the time it would take her to drive back to Amherst. Money spent on gasoline that could have gone for rent and groceries, and she slid off the hood of the Jeep and was already folding the map closed when something moved out on the reef. The briefest glimpse from the corner of one eye, the impression of something big and dark, scuttling on long legs across the rocks before slipping back into the water. Another thunder clap, then, and this time lightning like God was taking pictures, but she didn't move, stared at the reef and the angry sea crashing over it.

"Just my imagination," she whispered. Or maybe it had been a bird, or a particularly high wave falling across the rocks, something perfectly familiar made strange by distance and shadow.

The thunder rolled away and there were no sounds left but the wind blowing through the tall grass and the falls gurgling near the mouth of the Manuxet River. In an instant, the rain became a torrent and her clothes were soaked straight through before she could get back inside the Jeep.

3:25 P.M.

Handcuffs and a blindfold tied too tightly around her face before the man and woman who aren't FBI agents shoved her into the back of a rust-green Ford van. And now she lies shivering on wet carpeting as they speed along streets that she can't see. The air around her is as cold as a late December night and thick with the gassy, soursweet stench of something dead, something that should have been buried a long, long time ago.

"I already *told* you why," the man in the black suit and sunglasses growls angrily, and Lacey thinks maybe there's fear in his voice, too. "She didn't *have* it, okay? And we couldn't risk going onto the train after it. Monalisa's people got to her first. I already fucking *told* you that."

And whatever is in the back of the van with her answers him in its ragged, drowning voice like her grandmother dying of pneumonia when Lacey was seven years old. There are almost words in there, broken bits and pieces of words, vowel shards and consonant shrapnel, and the woman with the Caribbean accent curses and mumbles something to herself in French.

"Please," Lacey begs them. "I don't know what you want. Tell me what the fuck you want and I'll give it to you."

"You think so?" the woman asks. "You think it would be that easy now? After all this shit and you just gonna hand it over and we just gonna go away and leave you alone? *Merde...*"

The van squeals around a corner without bothering to slow down and Lacey is thrown sideways into something that feels like a pile of wet rags. She tries to roll away from it, but strong hands hold her fast and icy fingers brush slowly across her throat, her chin, her lips. Skin like sandpaper and Jell-O, fingertips that may as well be icicles, and she bites at them but her teeth close on nothing at all, a mouthful of frigid air that tastes like raw fish and spoiled vegetables.

"We had strict fucking instructions to *avoid* a confrontation," the man says and the car takes another corner, pitching Lacey free of the rag pile again.

"You just shut up and drive this damn car," the woman says. "You gonna get us all killed. You gonna have the cops on us—"

"Then *you* better tell that slimy motherfucker back there to shut the hell up and stop threatening me," the man growls at the woman. "I'm just about ready to say *fuck* you and him both. Pop a fucking cap in his skull and take my chances with the Order."

The rag pile gurgles and then makes a hollow, gulping noise. Lacey thinks it's laughing, as close as it can ever come to laughing, and she wonders how long it's going to be before it touches her again, wonders if they'll kill her first, and which would be worse.

"Yeah, this is sure some real goddamn funny shit," the man grumbles.

Lacey presses her face against the soggy carpeting, eyes open but nothing there to see, rough fabric against her eyeballs, and she tries to wipe its touch from her skin. Nothing she'll ever be able to scrub off, though, she knows that, something that's stained straight through to her soul.

"Is it the fossil?" she asks. "Is this about the goddamn fossil?"

"Now you startin' to use that big ol' brain of yours, missy," the woman says. "You tell us where it's hid, who you gave it to, and maybe you gonna get to live just a little bit longer."

"She ain't gonna tell you jack shit," the man sneers.

The rag pile makes a fluttering, anxious sound, and Lacey tries to sit up, but the van swerves and bounces over something, a pothole or a speed bump, a fucking old lady crossing the street for all she knows, and she tumbles over on her face again.

"It's in the box," she snarls, rolling onto her back and she kicks out with her left foot and hits nothing but the metal side wall. The rag pile gurgles and sputters wildly and so Lacey kicks the van again, harder than before. "Haven't you even *opened* the goddamn box?"

"Bitch, ain't *nothin'* we want in that box," the woman says. "You already handed it off to Monalisa, didn't you?"

"Of course she fucking gave it to him. Jesus, what the fuck else do you *think* she did with it?"

"I *told* you to shut up and drive."

"*Fuck* you," and then a car horn blares and everything dissolves into the banshee wail of squealing brakes, tyres burning themselves down to naked, steelbelt bones, the impact hardly half a heartbeat later, and Lacey is thrown backwards into the gurgling rag pile. *Something soft, at least,* she thinks, wondering if she's dead already and just hasn't figured it all out yet, and the man in the sunglasses screams like a woman.

And there's light, a flood of clean, warm sunlight across her face before the gunfire—three shots—*blam, blam, blam.* The rag pile abruptly stops gurgling and someone takes her by the arm, someone pulling her out of the van, out of hell and back into the world again.

"I can't see," she says, and the blindfold falls away to leave her squinting and blinking at the rough brick walls of an alleyway, a sagging fire escape, the stink of a garbage dumpster but even that smells good after the van.

"Wow," the old man says, grinning scarecrow of an old man in a blue fedora and a shiny, gabardine suit, blue bow tie to match his hat. "I saw someone do that in a movie once. I never imagined it would actually work."

There's a huge revolver clutched in his bony right hand, the blindfold dangling from the fingers of his left, and his violet-grey eyes sparkle like amethysts and spring water.

"Professor Solomon Monalisa, at your service," he says, lets the blindfold fall to the ground and holds one twig-thin hand out to Lacey. "You had us all worried, Miss Morrow. You shouldn't have run like that."

Lacey stares at his outstretched hand, and there are sirens now.

"Oh, I'm sorry. I forgot about the handcuffs. I'm afraid we'll have to attend to those elsewhere, though. I don't think we should be here when the police show up and start asking questions, do you?"

"No," she says, and the old man takes her arm again and starts to lead her away from the wrecked van.

"Wait. The box," she says and tries to turn around, but he stops her and puts a hand across her eyes.

"What's back there, Miss Morrow, you don't want to see it."

"They have the box. The Innsmouth fossil—"

"*I* have the fossil," he says. "And it's quite safe, I assure you. Come now, Miss Morrow. We don't have much time."

And he leads her away from the van, down the long, narrow alley and there's a door back there, a tall wooden door with peeling red paint and he opens it with a silver key.

EXCERPT FROM *NEW AMERICAN MONSTERS: MORE THAN MYTH?* BY GERALD DURRELL (HILL AND WANG, NEW YORK, 1959)

…which is certainly enough to make us pause and wonder about the possibility of a connection between at least some of these sightings and the celluloid fantasies being churned out by Hollywood film-makers. If we insist upon objectivity and are willing to entertain the notion of unknown animals, we must also, it seems, be equally willing to entertain the possibility that a few of these beasts may exist as much in the realm of the psychologist as that of the biologist. I can think of no better example of what I mean than the strange and frightening reports from Massachusetts proceeding the release of *Creature from the Black Lagoon* six years ago.

As first reported in the *Ipswich Chronicle*, March 20th, 1954, there was a flurry of sightings, from Gloucester north to Newburyport, of one or more scaly man-like amphibians, monstrous things that menaced boaters and were blamed for the death of at least one swimmer. On the evening of March 19th, Mrs. Cordelia Eliot of Rowley was walking along the coast near the Annisquam Harbor Lighthouse, when she saw what she later described as a "horrible fishman" paddling about just off shore. She claims to have watched it for half an hour, until the sun set and she lost sight of the creature. Four days later, there was another sighting by two fishermen near the mouth of the Annisquam River, of a "frogman with bulging red eyes and scaly greenish-black skin" wading through the shallows. When one of the men fired a shotgun at it (I haven't yet concluded if the men routinely carried firearms on fishing trips) it slipped quietly away into deeper water.

But the lion's share of the sightings that spring seem to have occurred in the vicinity of the "ghost town" of Innsmouth at the mouth of the Castle Neck River (previously known by its Agawam Indian name, *Manuxet*, a name which still persists among local old-timers). Most of these encounters are merely brief glimpses of scaly man-like creatures, usually seen from a considerable distance, either swimming near the mouth of the river or walking along its muddy banks at low tide. But one remarkable, and disturbing, account, reported by numerous local papers, involves the death of a nine-year-old boy named Lester Sargent, who drowned while swimming with friends below a small waterfall on the lower Castle Neck River. His companions reported that the boy began screaming and a great amount of blood was visible in the water. There were attempts to reach the swimmer, but the would-be rescuers were driven back by "a monster with blood-red eyes and sharp teeth." The boy finally disappeared beneath the water and his mutilated and badly decomposed body turned up a week later on Crane Beach, a considerable distance from the falls where he disappeared. The Essex County coroner listed the cause of death as shark attack.

"I've seen plenty of sharks," Harold Mowry, one of the swimmers, told reporters. "This wasn't a shark, I swear. It had hands, with great long claws, and it dragged Lester right down and drowned him."

Another notable sighting occurred along the old Argilla Road near Ipswich on April 2nd. The Rev. Henry Waite and his wife, Elizabeth, both avid bird watchers, claimed to have observed a "monster" strolling along the east bank of the Castle Neck River for more than an hour, before it dove into the river and vanished in a swirl of bubbles. Mrs. Waite described it as "tall and dark, and it walked a little hunched over. Through the binoculars we could see its face quite plainly. It did *have* a face, you know, with protruding eyes like a fish, and gills. At one point it turned and seemed to be watching us. I admit I was afraid and asked Henry if we shouldn't go for the police. Have you ever seen that *Monster from the Black Lagoon* [sic] movie? Well, that's what it looked like."

The last of the sightings were made in early May and no further records of amphibious man-monsters near Cape Ann or Ipswich Bay are available. One report of April 27th claimed that a group of school children had, in fact, found the monster dead, but their discovery later proved to be nothing but the badly decomposed carcass of a basking shark. It is impossible, I think, not to draw connections with the release of the Universal-International horror flick on March 5th. The old bugaboo of "mass hysteria" raises its shaggy head once more…

10.23 A.M.

Late for her meeting with Jasper before the drive to the train station and Lacey rushes upstairs from the collections, is already halfway across the central rotunda of the Pratt Museum's exhibit hall when Dr. Mary Hanisak calls out her name. Lacey stops and stands in the skeletal shadows of the mammoth and mastodon, the stuffed Indian elephant, and Dr. Hanisak is walking quickly towards her, carrying the cardboard box with the Innsmouth fossil inside.

"Can you believe you almost forgot this thing?" she asks. "That would have been pretty embarrassing, don't you think?"

Lacey laughs a little too loudly, her voice echoing in the museum. "Yeah," she says. "It would have," and she takes the box from the woman, chubby little Dr. Hanisak like a storybook gnome, Dr. Hanisak whose speciality is the evolution of rodent teeth. The box is wrapped tight with packing tape so there's no danger of its coming open on the train.

"Then you're all set now?"

"Ready as I'm ever going to be."

"And you're *sure* you want to do this? I mean, it's awfully high profile. I expect you'll be in newspapers all over the world when the reporters get a look at what's in that box. You might even be on CNN. Aren't you scared?"

Lacey stares for a moment at the dusty bones of a sabre-tooth cat mounted near the mammoth's feet. "You bet," she says. "I'm terrified. But maybe it'll at least bring in some new funding for the museum. We could use it."

"Perhaps," Dr. Hanisak replies uncertainly and she folds her hands and stares at the box. "You never can tell how these things will turn out, in the end."

"I suppose not," Lacey says, and then she looks at her watch and thanks Dr. Hanisak again. "I really have to get going," she says and leaves the woman standing alone with the skeletons.

EXCERPT FROM *FAMOUS FILM MONSTERS AND THE MEN WHO MADE THEM* BY BEN BROWNING (THE CITADEL PRESS, SECAUCUS, NJ, 1972)

Certainly there are several interesting stories floating about Hollywood regarding producer William Alland's inspiration for the story. The one most often repeated, it would seem, recounts how Alland heard a tale during a dinner party at Orson Welles' home regarding an ancient race of "fish-men" called the *dhaghon* inhabiting remote portions of the Amazon River. Local natives believed these creatures rose from the depths once a year, after floods, and abducted virgins. Naturally, the person telling the story is said to have sworn to its veracity. Another, less plausible, source of inspiration may have been a tradition in some parts of Massachusetts, in and around Gloucester, of humanoid sea monsters said to haunt a particularly treacherous stretch of coast near Ipswich Bay known appropriately enough as the "Devil's Reef". Rumour has it Alland knew of these legends, but decided to change the story's setting from maritime New England to the Amazon because he preferred a more exotic and primeval locale. At any rate, one or another of these "fish stories" might have stuck with him and become the germ for the project he eventually pitched to Universal.

* * *

3:47 P.M.

Through the peeling red door and she follows the old man down long hallways dimly lit by bare, incandescent bulbs, wallpaper shreds, upstairs and downstairs, and finally, a door he opens with another silver key. A steel fire door painted all the uncountable maroon-brown shades of dried gore and butcheries and it swings open slow on ratcreaking hinges, pours the heavy scents of frigid air and formaldehyde at their feet. There's light in there, crimson light, and Lacey looks at Dr. Solomon Monalisa and he's smiling a doubtful, furtive smile.

"What am I going to see in there?"

"That's a matter of opinion," he says and holds one skinny arm out like a theatre usher leading her to an empty seat.

"I asked you a simple question. All I wanted was a simple answer."

"Yes, but there are no *simple* answers, are there?"

"What's waiting for me in there?"

"All things are but mirrors, Miss Morrow. They reflect our deepest preconceptions, our most cherished prejudices—"

"Never fucking mind," she says and steps quickly across the threshold into a room as cold as the back of the Ford van. And the room is almost empty, high concrete walls and a concrete ceiling far overhead, banks of darkroom red lights dangling on chains, and the tank, sitting alone in the centre of it all.

"You're a very lucky woman," Dr. Monalisa says and the steel door clicks shut behind her. "Have you any idea, my dear, how few scientists have had this privilege? Why, I could count them all on my left hand."

The tank is at least seven feet tall, sturdy aquarium glass held together with strips of rusted iron, filled with murky preservative gone bloody beneath the lights, and Lacey stares at the thing floating lifeless behind the glass.

"What do *you* see, Miss Morrow?"

"My god," she whispers and takes another step towards the tank.

"Now that's a curious answer."

Neither man nor fish, neither fish nor amphibian, long legs and longer arms, and its bald, misshapen skull is turned upwards, as if those blind white eyes are gazing longingly towards Heaven. Solomon Monalisa rattles his keys and slips the handcuffs from her aching wrists.

"*Grendelonyx innsmouthensis*—*that's* what I thought you'd see, Miss Morrow. Grendel's claw—"

"But it's impossible," she whispers.

"Quite," Dr. Solomon Monalisa says. "It is entirely, unquestionably impossible."

"Is it real?"

"Yes, of course it's real. Why would I show it to you otherwise."

Lacey nods her head and crosses the room to stand beside the tank, places one hand flat against the glass. She's surprised that it isn't cold to the touch. The creature inside looks pale and soft, but she knows that's only the work of time and the caustic, preserving chemicals.

"It got tangled in a fishing net, dragged kicking into the light of day," the old man says and his footsteps are very loud in the concrete room. "Way back in November '29, not too long after the Navy finished up with Innsmouth. I suspect it was wounded by the torpedoes," and he points to a deep gash near the thing's groin. "They kept it in a basement at the university in Arkham for a time, and then it went to Washington. They moved it here right after the war."

She almost asks him which war, and who "they" are, but she doubts he would tell her, not the truth, anyway, and she can't take her eyes off the beautiful, terrible, impossible creature in the tank—its splayed hands, the bony webbing between its fingers, the recurved, piercing claws. "Why are you showing me this?" she finally asks instead.

"It seemed a shame not to," he replies, his smile fading now, and he also touches the aquarium glass. "There are so few who can truly comprehend the…" and he pauses, furrowing his brow. "The *wonder*—yes, that's what I mean, the wonder of it all."

"You said you have the fossil."

"Oh, yes. We do. I do. Dr. Hanisak was kind enough to switch the boxes for us last night, while you were finishing up at the museum."

"Dr. Hanisak—"

"Shhhhhh," and Monalisa holds a wrinkled index finger to his lips. "Let's not ask *too* many questions, dear. I assure you, the fossil is safe and sound. I'll give it back to you very soon. Ah, and we have all your things from the train. You'll be wanting those back as well, I should think. But I wanted you to see our friend here first, before you see the film."

"What film?" she asks, remembering the photograph from the manila envelope, the letter, the nosy woman asking her if she liked old monster movies.

"What odd sort of childhood did you have, Miss Morrow? Weren't you allowed to watch television? Have you truly never seen it?"

"My mother didn't like us watching television," Lacey says. "We didn't even own a TV set. She bought us books, instead. I've never cared much for movies. I don't know what you're talking about."

"Then that may be the most remarkable part of it all. You may be the only adult in America who's never seen *Creature from the Black Lagoon*," and he chuckles softly to himself.

"I've heard of it."

"I should certainly hope so."

And at last she turns away from the dead thing floating in the tank and looks into Dr. Solomon Monalisa's sparkling eyes. "You're not going to kill me?" she asks him.

"Why would I have gone to all the trouble to save you from those thugs back there if I only wanted you dead? They'd surely have seen to that for me, once they figured out you didn't have the fossil any longer."

"I don't understand any of this," Lacey says and realises that she's started to cry.

"No," he says. "But you weren't meant to. No one was. It's a secret."

"What about my work—"

"Your article has been withdrawn from *Nature*. And Dr. Hanisak was good enough to cancel the press conference at the Peabody Museum."

"And now I'm just supposed to pretend I never saw any of this?"

"No, certainly not. You're just supposed to keep it to yourself."

"It doesn't make any sense. Jesus, why don't you just destroy the fossil? Why don't you destroy *this* thing?" and she slaps the glass hard with the palm of her hand. "If it's a goddamn secret, if no one's supposed to know, why don't you get rid of it *all*?"

"Could *you* destroy these things?" the old man asks her. "No, I didn't think so. Haven't you taken an oath, of sorts, to search for answers, even when the answers are uncomfortable, even when they're *impossible*? Well, you see, dear, so have I."

"It was just lying there in the cabinet. Anyone could have found it. Anyone at all."

"Indeed. The fossil has been missing for decades. We have no idea how it ever found its way to Amherst. But you will care for it now, yes?"

She doesn't answer him, because she doesn't want to say the words out loud, stares through her tears at the creature in the tank.

"Yes, I thought you would. You have an uncommon strength. Come along, Miss Morrow. We should be going now," he says and takes her hand. "The picture will be starting soon."

For David J. Schow, Keeper of the Black Lagoon

RAISED BY THE MOON

by RAMSEY CAMPBELL

IT WAS THE scenery that did for him. Having spent the afternoon in avoiding the motorway and enjoying the unhurried country route, Grant reached the foothills only to find the Cavalier refused to climb. He'd driven a mere few hundred yards up the first steep slope when the engine commenced groaning. He should have made time during the week to have it serviced, he thought, feeling like a child caught out by a teacher, except that teaching had shown him what was worse—to be a teacher caught out by a child. He dragged the lever into first gear and ground the accelerator under his heel. The car juddered less than a yard before helplessly backing towards its own smoke.

His surroundings grew derisively irrelevant: the hills quilted with fields, the mountains ridged with pines, the roundish moon trying out its whiteness in the otherwise blue sky. He managed to execute most of a turn as the car slithered backwards, and sent it downhill past a Range Rover loaded with a family whose children turned to display their tongues to him. The July heat buttered him as he swung the Cavalier onto a parched verge, where the engine hacked to itself while he glared at the map.

231

Half the page containing his location was crowded with the fingerprints of mountains. Only the coast was unhampered by their contours. He eased the car off the brown turf and nursed it several digressive miles to the coast road, where a signpost pointed left to Windhill, right to Baiting. Northward had looked as though it might bring him sooner inland to the motorway, and so he took the Baiting route.

He hadn't bargained for the hindrance of the wind. Along the jagged coastline all the trees leaned away from the jumpy sea as though desperate to grasp the land. Before long the barren seaward fields gave way to rocks and stony beaches, and there weren't even hedges to fend off the northwester. Whenever the gusts took a breath he smelled how overworked the engine was growing. Beside the road was evidence of the damage the wind could wreak: scattered planks of some construction which, to judge by a ruin a mile further on, had been a fishmonger's stall. Then the doggedly spiky hedge to his right winced inland, revealing an arc of cottages as white as the moon would be when the sky went out. Perhaps someone in the village could repair the car, or Grant would find a room for the night—preferably both.

The ends of the half-mile arc of cottages were joined across the inlet by a submerged wall or a path that divided the prancing sea from the less restless bay. The far end was marked by a lone block of colour, a red telephone box planted in the water by a trick of perspective. His glimpse of a glistening object crouched or heaped in front of it had to be another misperception; when he returned his attention to the view once he'd finished tussling with the wheel as a gust tried to shove the car across the road, he saw no sign of life.

The car was panting and shivering by the time he reached the first cottage. A vicious wind that smelled of fish stung his skin as he eased his rusty door shut and peered tearfully at the buildings opposite. He thought all the windows were curtained with net until he realised the whiteness was salt, which had also scoured the front doors pale. In the very first window a handwritten sign offered ROOM. The wind hustled him across the road, which was strewn with various conditions of seaweed, to the fish-faced knocker on a door that had once been black.

More of the salt that gritted under his fingers was lodged in the hinge. He had to dig his thumb into the gaping mouth to heave the fish-head high and slam it against the metal plate. He heard the blow fall flat in not much of a passage and a woman's voice demanding shrilly "Who wants us now?"

The nearest to a response was an irregular series of slow footsteps that ended behind the door, which was dragged wide by a man who filled most of the opening. Grant couldn't tell how much of his volume he owed to his cable-knit jersey and loose trousers, but the bulk of his face drooped like perished rubber from his cheekbones. Salt might account for the redness of his small eyes, though perhaps anxiety had turned his sparse hair and dense eyebrows white. He hugged himself and shivered and glanced past his visitor, presumably at the wind. Parting his thick lips with a tongue as ashen, he mumbled "Where have you come from?"

"Liverpool."

"Don't know it," the man said, and seemed ready to use that as an excuse to close the door.

A woman plodded out of the kitchen at the end of the cramped dingy hall. She looked as though marriage had transformed her into a version of the man, shorter but broader to compensate and with hair at least as white, not to mention clothes uncomfortably similar to his. "Bring him in," she urged.

"What are you looking for?" her husband muttered.

"Someone who can fix my car and a room if I'll need one."

"Twenty miles up the coast."

"I don't think it'll last that far. Won't they come here?"

"Of course they will if they're wanted, Tom. Let him in."

"You're staying, then."

"I expect I may have to. Can I phone first?"

"If you've the money you can give it a tackle."

"How much will it take?" When Tom's sole answer was a stare, Grant tried "How much do you want?"

"Me, nothing. Nor her either. Phone's up the road."

Grant was turning away, not without relief, when the woman said "Won't he need the number? Tommy and his Fiona."

"I know that. Did you get it?" Tom challenged Grant.

"I don't think—"

"Better start, then. Five. Three. Three. Five," Tom said and shut the door.

Grant gave in to an incredulous laugh that politeness required him to muffle. Perhaps another cottage might be more welcoming, he thought with dwindling conviction as he progressed along the seafront. He could hardly see through any of the windows, and such furniture as he could distinguish, by no means in every room, looked encrusted with more than dimness. The few shops might have belonged to fishmongers; one window displayed a dusty plastic lobster on a marble slab also bearing stains suggestive of the prints of large wet hands. The last shop must have been more general, given the debris scattered about the bare floor—distorted but unopened tins, a disordered newspaper whose single legible headline said FISH STOCKS DROP, and was there a dead cat in the darkest corner? Beyond two further cottages was the refuge of the phone box.

Perhaps refuge was too strong a word. Slime on the floor must indicate that it hadn't been out of reach of the last high tide. A fishy smell that had accompanied him along the seafront was also present, presumably borne by the wind that kept lancing the trapped heat with chill. Vandalism appeared to have invaded even this little community; the phone directory was strewn across the metal shelf below the coin-box in fragments so sodden they looked chewed. Grant had to adjust the rakish handset on its hook to obtain a tone before he dragged the indisposed dial to the numbers he'd repeated all the way to the box. He was trying to distinguish whether he was hearing static or simply the waves when a man's brusque practically Scottish voice said "Beach."

"You aren't a garage, then."

"Who says I'm not? Beach's Garage."

"I'm with you now," Grant said, though feeling much as he had when Tom translated his wife's mnemonic. "And you fix cars."

"I'd be on the scrapheap if I didn't."

"Good," Grant blurted, and to compensate "I mean, I've got one for you."

"Lucky me."

"It's a Cavalier that wouldn't go uphill."

"Can't say a word about it till I've seen it. All I want to know is where you are."

"Twenty miles south of you, they tell me."

"I don't need to ask who." After a pause during which Grant felt sought by the chill and the piscine smell, the repairman said "I can't be there before dark."

"You think I should take a room."

"I don't tell anybody what to do. Invited you in as well, did they?"

The man's thriftiness with language was affecting Grant much as unresponsive pupils did. "Shouldn't they have?" he retorted.

"They'll do their best for you, Tom and Fiona. They need the cash."

"How did you know who they were?"

"There's always some that won't be driven out of their homes. A couple, anyway."

"Driven."

When competing at brevity brought no answer, Grant was about to add to his words when the man said "You won't see many fish round Baiting any more."

Grant heard the basis of a geography lesson in this. "So they've had to adapt to living off tourists."

"And travellers and whatever else they catch." The repairman interrupted himself with a cough that might have been a mirthless laugh. "Anyway, that's their business. I'll be there first thing in the morning."

The phone commenced droning like a fly attracted by the fishy smell until Grant stubbed his thumb on the hook. He dug the crumpled number of the holiday cottage out of his jeans and dialled, rousing only a bell that repeated itself as insistently as the waves for surely longer than his fellow students could have disagreed over who should answer it, even if they sustained the argument with a drink and quite possibly a toke to boot. No doubt they were expecting him to arrive ahead of them and set about organising as usual. He dropped the receiver onto its prongs and forced open the arthritic door.

He might have returned to his car along the sea wall, the top of which was nearly two feet wide, if waves hadn't been spilling over much of its length. There appeared to be little else to describe to any class he would teach; rubble was piled so high in the occasional alleys between the cottages that he couldn't even see behind them. The bay within the wall swarmed with infant waves, obscuring his view of whatever he kept glimpsing beneath them: probably the tops of pillars reinforcing the wall, except that the objects were irregularly spaced—the tips of a natural rock formation the wall had followed, then, although the string of blurred shapes put him in mind of a series of reflections of the moon. He was no closer to identifying them by the time he reached the Cavalier.

He manhandled his suitcase through the gap the creaky boot vouchsafed him and tramped across the road. He was hesitating over reaching for the knocker when the cottage door sprang open. He was bracing himself to be confronted by the husband, which must be why the sight of the woman's upturned face was disconcerting. "Get in, then," she exhorted with what could have been intended as rough humour.

Perhaps she was eager to shut out the wind that was trying all the inner doors, unless she wanted to exclude the smell. More of that lingered once Grant slammed the door than he found inviting. "Let's have you up," the woman said.

She'd hardly set one shabbily slippered foot on the lowest of the narrow uncarpeted stairs that bisected the hall when she swung round to eye him. "First time away?"

"Nothing like."

"Just your case looks so new."

"My parents bought me a set of them when I started college."

"We never had any children. What's your name, anyway?" she added with a fierceness he hoped she was directing at herself. "You know ours."

"Bill Grant."

"Good and strong," she said, giving him a slow appreciative blink before stumping shapelessly upwards to thump the first door open with her buttocks. The rumpled sea widened beyond the small window as he followed her into the room. He'd passed a number of framed photographs on his way upstairs, and here above the sink was yet another grey image of a man, nondescript except for the fish he was measuring between his hands. As in the other pictures, he was her husband Tom. His presence helped the furniture—a barely even single bed, a barren dressing-table, a wardrobe no larger than a phone box—make the room feel yet more confined. "Anything like home?" Fiona said.

It did remind him somewhat of his bedroom when he was half his size. "Something," he admitted.

"You want to feel at home if you go anywhere. I know I would." Having stared at him as though to ensure some of her meaning remained, she reached up to grab his shoulders with her cold swollen hands as an aid to squeezing past him. "We'll call you when it's time to put our snouts in the trough," she said.

He listened to the series of receding creaks her descent extracted from the stairs, and then he relieved his suitcase of the items he would need for an overnight stay, feeling absurdly as if he was preparing for a swift escape. Once he'd ventured across the tiny strident landing to the bathroom, a tiled white cell occupied by three dripping sweaters pegged on a rope above the bath and by a chilly damp that clung to him, he sat next to his pyjamas on the bed to scribble notes for a geography lesson based on Baiting, then sidled between the sink and the foot of the bed to the window.

It seemed his powers of observation needed work. The whitish rounded underwater blobs were closer together and to the middle of the sea wall than he remembered, unless any of them had indeed been a version of the moon, which was presently invisible above the roof. Perhaps he would soon be able to identify them, since the waves were progressing towards relative calm. He left his bulky bunch of keys on the windowsill before lying down to listen to the insistent susurration, which was occasionally interrupted by a plop that led him to believe the sea was less uninhabited than the repairman had said. He grew tired of craning to catch sight of whatever kept leaving ripples inside the sea wall, and by the time Fiona called "Ready" up the stairs, an invitation reminiscent of the beginning of a game, he was shelving towards sleep.

He must be near to dreaming while awake, since he imagined that a face had edged out of hiding to watch him sit up. It might have been dour Tom's in the photograph, or the moon that had crept into view above the bay, possibly appending at least one blob to the cluster along the sea wall. "I'll be down," Grant shouted loud enough, he hoped, to finish wakening himself.

He wasn't expecting to eat in the kitchen, on a table whose unfolding scarcely left room for three hard straight chairs and a stained black range crowned with bubbling saucepans and, beneath a small window that grudgingly twilighted the room, a massive stone sink. He'd thought a fishy smell that had kept him company upstairs was carried by the wind, but now he realised it might also have been seeping up from the kitchen. He was exerting himself to look entertained when Tom frowned across the table at him. "She ought to have asked you to pay in advance."

"Oh, Tom, he's nothing but a youngster."

Grant was a little too much of one to appreciate being described that way. "Can I give you a cheque and a card?"

"And your name and address."

"Let's have you sitting down first," Fiona cried, stirring a pan that aggravated the smell.

Grant fumbled in the pocket of his jeans for the cheque book and card wallet. "How much am I going to owe you?"

Tom glowered at his soup-bowl as though ashamed to ask. "Thirty if you're here for breakfast."

"Of course he will be, Tom."

"If he isn't sick of it by then."

Grant wrote a cheque in his best blackboard handwriting and slid it with his guarantee card and driving licence across the table. "Grant's the word, eh?" Tom grumbled, poking at the cards with a thick flabby forefinger whose nail was bitten raw. "She said you were a student, right enough."

"I teach as well," Grant was provoked into retorting. "That'll be my life."

"So what are you planning to fill their dim little heads with?"

"I wouldn't mind telling them the story of your village."

"Few years since it's been that." Tom finished scrutinising the cheque and folded it twice to slip into his trousers pocket, then stared at or through his guest. "On a night like this there'd be so many fish we'd have to bring the nets in before dawn or have them snapped."

"Nights like this make me want to swim," Fiona said, and perhaps more relevantly "He used to like taking the boat out then."

She ladled soup into three decidedly various bowls, and watched with Tom while Grant committed his stained spoon to the viscous milky liquid. It explained the smell in the kitchen and tasted just not too strongly of it to be palatable. "There are still fish, then," he said, and when his hosts met this with identical small-eyed stares "Good. Good."

"We've given up the fishing. We've come to an arrangement," said Tom.

Grant sensed that was as much as he would say about it, presumably resenting the loss of his independence. Nobody spoke until the bowls were empty, nor indeed until Fiona had served three platefuls of flaccid whitish meat accompanied by heaps of mush, apparently potatoes and some previously green vegetable. More of the meat finished gently quivering to itself in an indistinguishable lump on a platter. Grant thought rather than hoped it might be tripe, but unless the taste of the soup had lodged in his mouth, the main course wasn't mammalian. Having been watched throughout two rubbery mouthfuls, he felt expected to say at least "That's good too. What is it?"

"All there is to eat round here," Tom said in a sudden dull rage.

"Now, Tom, it's not his fault."

"It's people's like his." Tom scowled at his dinner and then at the guest. "Want to know what you want to tell the sprats you're supposed to be teaching?"

"I believe I do, but if you'd like—"

"About time they were told to stop using cars for a start. And if the poor deprived mites can't live without them, tell them not to take them places they don't need to go."

"Saints, Tom, they're only youngsters."

"They'll grow up, won't they, if the world doesn't conk out first."

With renewed ire he said to Grant "They need to do without their fridges and their freezers and their microwaves and whatever else is upsetting things."

Grant felt both accused of too much urban living and uneasy about how the meat was stored. Since no refrigerator was visible, he hoped it was fresh. He fed himself mouthfuls to be done with it and dinner generally, but hadn't completed the labour when he swallowed in order to speak. "At least you aren't alone, then."

"It's in your cities people go off and leave each other," muttered Tom.

"No, I mean you aren't the only ones in your village. I got the idea from your friend Mr Beach you were."

Tom looked ready to deny any friendship, but it seemed he was preparing to demand "Calling him a liar, are you?"

"I wouldn't say a liar, just mistaken," Grant said, nodding at the wall the cottage shared with its neighbour. His hosts merely eyed him as though they couldn't hear the renewed sounds beyond the wall, a floundering and shuffling that brought to mind someone old or otherwise incapacitated. "Rats?" he was compelled to assume.

"We've seen a few of those in our time," said Tom, continuing to regard him.

If that was meant for wit, Grant found it offered no more than the least of the children he'd had to teach. Some acoustic effect made the rat sound much larger as it scuffed along the far side of the wall before receding into the other cottage. Rather than risk stirring it or his hosts up further, Grant concentrated on downing enough of his meal to allow him to push away his plate and mime fullness. He was certainly full of a taste not altogether reminiscent of fish; he felt as though he was trying to swim through it, or it through him. When he drank a glass of the pitcher of water that had been the solitary accompaniment to the meal, he thought the taste was in there too.

Fiona cleared the plates into the sink, and that was the end of dinner. "Shall I help?" Grant had been brought up to offer.

"That's her work."

Since Fiona smiled indulgently at that, Grant didn't feel entitled to disagree. "I'd better go and phone, then."

He imagined he saw a pale shape lurch away from the window

into the unspecific dimness—it must have been Fiona's reflection as she turned to blink at him. "He said you had."

"I ought to let my friends know I won't be seeing them tonight."

"They'll know when you don't, won't they? We don't want the waves carrying you off." Wiping her hands on a cloth that might have been part of someone's discarded garment, she pulled out a drawer beside the sink. "Stay in and we'll play a few games."

While the battered cardboard box she opened on the table was labelled LUDO, that wasn't quite what it contained. Rattling about on top of the familiar board inside the box were several fragments of a substance Grant told himself wasn't bone. "We make our own amusement round here," Fiona said. "We use whatever's sent us."

"He's not your lad."

"He could be."

The scrape of Grant's chair on the stone floor went some way towards expressing his discomfort. "I'll phone now," he said.

"Not driving, are you?" Tom enquired.

"Not at all." Grant couldn't be bothered resenting whatever the question implied. "I'm going to enjoy the walk."

"He'll be back soon for you to play with," Tom told his wife.

She turned to gaze out at the dark while Tom's stare weighed on their visitor, who stood up. "I won't need a key, will I?"

"We'll be waiting for you," Fiona mumbled.

Grant sensed tension as oppressive as a storm, and didn't thank the bare floorboards for amplifying his retreat along the hall. He seized the clammy latch and hauled the front door open. The night was almost stagnant. Subdued waves smoothed themselves out on the black water beyond the sea wall, inside which the bay chattered silently with whiteness beneath the incomplete mask of a moon a few days short of full. An odour he no longer thought it adequate to call fishy lingered in the humid air or inside him as he hurried towards the phone box.

The heat left over from the day more than kept pace with him. The infrequent jab of chill wind simply encouraged the smell. He wondered if an allergy to whatever he'd eaten was beginning to make itself felt in a recurrent sensation, expanding through him from his stomach, that his flesh was turning to rubber. The cottages had grown intensely present as chunks of moon fallen to earth, and seemed less deserted than he'd taken them to be: the moonlight showed that patches of some of the windows had been rubbed or breathed or even licked imperfectly clear. Once he thought faces rose like flotsam to watch him from the depths of three successive cottages, unless the same face was following him from house to ruined house. When he failed to restrain himself from looking, of course there was only moonlit dimness, and no dead cat in the general store. He did his best to scoff at himself as he reached the phone box.

Inside, the smell was lying in wait for him. He held the door open with his foot, though that admitted not only the infrequent wind but also more of the light that made his hand appear as pale as the receiver in it was black. His clumsy swollen fingers found the number in his pocket and held the scrap of paper against the inside of a frame that had once contained a mirror above the phone. Having managed to dial, he returned the paper to its niche against his unreasonably flabby thigh and clutched the receiver to his face with both hands. The fourth twosome of rings was parted by a clatter that let sounds of revelry at him, and belatedly a voice. "Who's this?"

For longer than a breath Grant felt as if he was being forced to stand up in class for a question he couldn't answer, and had to turn it back on the questioner. "It's Ian, isn't it?"

"Bill," Ian said, and shouted it to their friends. "Where have you got to?" he eventually thought to ask.

"I've broken down on the coast. I'm getting the car fixed tomorrow."

"When are we seeing you?"

"I told you, tomorrow," Grant said, though the notion felt remote in more ways than he could name.

"Have a drink for us, then, and we will for you. Won't we, you crew?"

The enthusiasm this aroused fell short of Grant, not least because he'd been reminded of the water accompanying dinner, a memory that revived the taste of the meal. "Don't get too pissed to drive tomorrow," Ian advised and made way for a chorus of drunken encouragement followed by the hungry buzz of the receiver.

Grant planted the receiver on its hook and shoved himself out of the box. Even if Baiting had boasted a pub, he would have made straight for his room; just now, supine was the only position that appealed to him. As the phone box shut with a muted thud that emphasised the desertion of the seafront, he set out along the top of the submerged wall.

It was broad enough for him to feel safe even if he wobbled—luckily for his career, however distant that seemed, teachers didn't have to be able to swim. He wouldn't have minded being able to progress at more than a shuffle towards the landmark of his car blackened by the moonlight, but the unsynchronised restlessness flanking him made him feel less than stable, as if he was advancing through some unfamiliar medium. The luminous reflection of the arc of cottages hung beneath them, a lower jaw whose unrest suggested it was eager to become a knowing grin. The shape of the bay must be causing ripples to resemble large slow bubbles above the huddle of round whitish shapes along the middle of the sea wall. He still couldn't make them out, nor how many images of the moon were tracking him on or just beneath the surface of the inlet. The closer he came to the halfway mark, the larger the bubbles appeared to grow. He was within a few yards of them, and feeling mesmerised by his own pace and by the whispers of the sea, when he heard a protracted stealthy wallowing behind him. He turned to find he had company on the far end of the wall.

It must be a swimmer, he told himself. Its glistening suggested it was wearing a wet suit rendered pallid by the moon; surely it couldn't be naked. Was the crouched figure making a joke of his progress? As it began to drag its feet, which struck him as unnecessarily large, along the wall, it looked no more at home on the path than he felt. Its head was bent low, and yet he had the disconcerting impression that it was presenting its face to him. It had shuffled several paces before he was able to grasp that he would rather outdistance it than see it in greater detail. He swung around and faltered just one step in the direction of his car. While his attention had been snared, another figure as squat and pale and dripping had set out for him from the opposite end of the wall.

He was paralysed by the spectacle of the pair converging effortfully but inexorably on him, the faces on their lowered heads indisputably towards him, until a movement let him peer in desperation at the farthest cottage. The front door had opened, and over the car roof he saw Tom. "Can you come and help me?" Grant shouted, stumbling towards him along the wall.

The cottages flattened and shrank his voice and sent him Tom's across the bay. "No need for that."

"There is," Grant pleaded. "That's in my way."

"Rude bugger."

Grant had to struggle to understand this meant him. It added itself to the sight of the advancing figure pallid as the underside of a dead fish. The closer it shuffled, the less it appeared to have for a face. "What are they?" he cried.

"They're all the moon brings us these days," Tom said, audibly holding Grant or people like him responsible, and stepped out of the cottage. He was naked, like the figures on the wall. The revelation arrested Grant while Tom plodded to the car. Indeed, he watched Tom unlock it and climb in before this sent him forward. "Stop that," he yelled. "What do you think you're doing? Get out of my car."

The Cavalier was no more likely to start first time for a naked driver than it ever did for him, he promised himself. Then it spluttered out a mass of fumes and performed a screeching U-turn. "Come back," Grant screamed. "You can't do that. You're polluting your environment."

No doubt his protests went unheard over the roaring of the engine. The sound took its time over dwindling once the coastline hid the car. The squat whitish shapes had halted once Grant had begun shouting. He strode at the figure crouched between him and the cottage and, since it didn't retreat, with as little effect at the other. He was repeating the manoeuvre, feeling like a puppet of his mounting panic, when that was aggravated by a burst of mirth. Fiona had appeared in the cottage doorway and was laughing at him. "Just jump in," she called across the water.

He didn't care how childish his answer sounded if she was capable of saving him. "I can't swim."

"What, a big strong lad like you?" Her heartiness increased as she declared "You can now. You can float, at any rate. Give it a try. We'll have to feed you up."

Beyond the spur of the coastline the sound of the car rose to a harsh note that was terminated by a massive splash. "That's the end of that," Fiona called. "You can be one of my big babies instead."

Grant's mind was refusing to encompass the implications of this when Tom came weltering like a half-submerged lump of the moon around the bay. Grant dashed along the sea wall, away from Fiona and Tom. He was almost at the middle section when he saw far too much in the water: not just the way that section could be opened as a gate, but the pallid roundish upturned faces that were clustered alongside. They must be holding their breath to have grown clear at last, their small flat unblinking eyes and, beneath the noseless nostrils, perfectly round mouths gaping in hunger that looked like surprise. As he wavered, terrified to pass above them, he had a final insight that he could have passed on to a classroom of pupils: the creatures must be waiting to open the gate and let in the tide and any fish it carried. "Don't mind them," Fiona shouted. "They don't mind we eat their dead. They even bring them now."

An upsurge of the fishy taste worse than nausea made Grant stagger along the wall. The waiting shape crouched forward, displaying the round-mouthed emotionless face altogether too high on its plump skull. Hands as whitish and as fat jerked up from the bay, snatching at Grant's feet. "That's the way, show him he's one of us," Fiona urged, casting off her clothes as she hurried to the water's edge.

She must have been encouraging Grant's tormentors to introduce him to the water. In a moment fingers caught his ankles and overbalanced him. His frantic instinctive response was to hurl himself away from them, into the open sea. Drowning seemed the most attractive prospect left to him.

The taste expanded through him, ousting the chill of the water with a sensation he was afraid to name. When he realised it was the experience of floating, he let out a howl that merely cleared his mouth of water. Too many pallid shapes for him to count were heaving themselves over the wall to surround him. He flailed his limbs and then tried holding them still, desperate to find a way of making himself sink. There was none. "Don't worry," Fiona shouted as she sloshed across the bay towards him, "you'll soon get used to our new member of the family," and, in what felt like the last of his sanity, Grant wondered if she was addressing his captors or Tom.

FAIR EXCHANGE

by MICHAEL MARSHALL SMITH

WE WERE IN some bloke's house the other night, nicking his stuff, and Bazza calls me over. We've been there twenty minutes already and if it was anyone else I'd tell them to shut up and get on with it, but Baz and I've been thieving together for years and I know he's not going to be wasting my time. So I put the telly by the back door with the rest of the gear (nice little telly, last-minute find up in the smaller bedroom) and head back to the front room. I been in there already, of course. First place you look. DVD player, CDs, stereo if it's any good, which isn't often. You'd be amazed how many people have crap stereos. Especially birds—still got some shit plastic midi-system their dad bought them down the High Street in 1987. (Still got LPs, too, half of them. No fucking use to me, are they? I'm not having it away with an armful of things that weigh a ton and aren't as good as CDs: where's the fucking point in that?)

I make my way to Baz's shadow against the curtains, and I see he's going through the drawers in the bureau. Sound tactic if you've got a minute. People always seem to think you won't look in a drawer— *Doh!*—and so in go the cheque books, cash, personal organiser, old mobile phone. Spare set of keys, if you're lucky: which case you bide

249

your time, hope they won't remember the keys were in there, then come back and make it a double feature when the insurance has put back everything you took. They've made it easy for you, haven't they. Pillocks. Anyway, I come up next to Baz, and he presents the drawers. They're empty. Completely and utterly devoid of stuff. No curry menus, no bent-up party photos, no balls of string or rubber bands, no knackered batteries for the telly remote. No dust, even. It's like someone opened the two drawers and sucked everything out with a Hoover.

"Baz, there's nothing there."

"That's what I'm saying."

It's not *that* exciting, don't see Jerry Bruckheimer making a film of it or nothing, but it's odd. I'll grant him that. It's not like the rest of the house is spick and span. There's stuff spilling out of cupboards, kitchen cabinets, old books sitting in piles on the floor. The carpet on the landing upstairs looks like something got spilt there and never cleared up, and the whole place is dusty and smells of mildew or something. And yet these two drawers, perfect for storing stuff— could even have been designed for the purpose, ha ha ha—are completely empty. Why? You'll never know. It's just some private thing. That's one of the weird bits about burglary. It's intimate. It's like being able to see what colour pants everyone is wearing. Actually you could do that too, if you wanted, but that's not what I meant. Not my cup of tea. Not professional, either.

"There was nothing in there at all?"

"Just this," Baz says, and holds something up so I can see it. "It was right at the back."

I took it from him. It's small, about the size and shape of the end of your thumb. Smooth, cold to the touch. "What is it?"

"Dunno," he shrugs. "Marble?"

"Fucking shit marble, Baz. It's not even fucking *round*."

Baz shrugs again and I say "Weird" and then it's time to go. You don't want to be hanging around any longer than necessary. Don't want to be in a burning hurry, either—that's when you can get careless or make too much noise or forget to look both ways as you slip out—but once you've found what you came for, you might as well be somewhere else.

So we go via the kitchen, grab the bin bag full of gear and slip out the back way. Stand outside the door a second, make sure no one's passing by, then walk out onto the street, calm as you like. Van's just around the corner. We stroll along the pavement, chatting normally, looking like we live in one of the other houses and walk this way every night. Get in the van—big white fucker, naturally, virtually invisible in London—and off we go.

It's fucking magic, that moment.

The one where you turn the van into the next street and suddenly you're just part of the evening traffic, and you know it's done and you're away and bar a fuck-up with the distribution of the goods it's like it never happened. I always light a fag right then, crack open the window, smell the London air coming in the van. Warm, cold, it's London. Best air in the world.

Weird thing, though. Even though it's not that big a deal, the business with the drawers was still niggling me a few hours later. You do see the odd thing or two in my business—stuff that don't quite make sense. Couple of months ago we're doing over a big old house, over Tufnell Park way, and either side of the mantelpiece there's a painting. Two little paintings, obviously done by the same bloke. Signed the same, for a start. Now, there's huge photos all over the mantelpiece, including some wedding ones, and it don't take a genius to work out that these two paintings are of the owners: one of the bloke, and the other of his missus. What's *that* about? For a start, you've already got all the photos. And why get two paintings, one of each of you? If you're going to get a painting done, surely you have the two of you together, looking all lovey-dovey and like you'll never, ever get divorced and stand screaming at each other in some brief's office arguing about bits of furniture you only bought in the first place because they was there and you had the cash burning a hole in your pocket. Maybe that's it—you have the paintings done separate so you can split them when you break up. But if you're already thinking about that, then… Whatever. People are just weird. Baz wanted to draw moustaches on the paintings, but I wouldn't let him. They can't have been cheap. So we just did one on the wife.

Anyway, couple of hours in the Junction and everything's peachy. Already shifted most of the electrical goods to blokes we know are either keeping them for themselves or can be trusted to punt them on over the other side of town. Baz and I done a deal and he's going to keep the little telly for his sister's birthday. Couple bits of jewellery Baz found will go to Mr. Pzlowsky, a pro fence I use over in Bow. He don't talk to no one—can barely understand what the old fucker's saying, anyway—and can be trusted to only rob us short-sighted, not actually blind.

So the only thing left is the little thing I've got in my pocket. I get it out, look at it. Funny thing is, I don't really remember slipping it in there. Like I said, it's small, and it looks like it must be made of glass. It's so shiny, and transparent in parts, that it can't be anything else. But it's got colours and textures in it too—kind of pinks and salmon, and some threads of dark green. And it feels… it feels almost wet, even though it had been in my pocket for ages. I suppose it's just some special kind of glass or stone or something.

"Wozzat?"

I look up and see Clive is racking up at the pool table a couple of yards away. "What's what?"

"What you got in your hand, twatface."

I'm not trying to be funny, I don't mind Clive, I'm just surprised he's noticed it from over there.

I hold it up. "Dunno," I said. "What do you think?"

He comes over, chalking up his cue, takes a look. "Dunno," he agrees. "Hold on though, tell you what it looks a bit like."

"What's that?"

"My sister-in-law went on holiday last year. Bali. Over, you know, in Polynesia."

"Polynesia? Where the fuck's that?"

"Dunno," he admitted. "Fucking long flight though, by all accounts. Think they said it was in the South Seas or something. Dunno where that is either. Anyway, she brought our mum back something looked a bit like that. Said it was coral, I think."

"You reckon?"

He leaned forward, looked at it more closely. "Yeah. Could be. Polished up, or something. Tell you what, though. It weren't half as nice as your one. Where'd you get it?"

"Ah," I said. "That would be telling."

He nodded. "You nicked it. Well, I reckon that's worth something, I do."

And he wanders off to the table, where some bloke's waiting for him to break.

"Nice one," I said, and took another look at the thing.

Even though I'm sitting right in the back of the pub, snug into the wood panelling there, this little piece of coral or stone or glass or whatever seems to have a glow about it. Suppose it's catching a glint from the long light over the pool table, but the light coming off it seems like it's almost green. Could be the baize, I suppose, but... I dunno. Probably had a Stella too many.

I slipped it back in my pocket. I reckoned Clive was probably right, and it most likely was worth something.

Funny thing, though. I didn't like the idea of getting rid of it.

Next few days just sort of go by. Nothing much going on. Baz had to head East to visit some mate in the London Hospital, so he goes over and does the business with Mr. Pzlowsky. Usually I'd do it because people have been known to take advantage of Bazza, but me and the Pole had words over it a year ago and he plays fair with him now. Fair as he plays with anyone, that is. The handful of jewellery we got from the house with the empty drawers gets us a few hundred quid, which is better than either of us expected. Old silver, apparently. American.

We play pool, we play darts, we watch television. You know how it is. Had a row with me bird, Jackie: she caught sight of the little coral thing (I'd just put it down next to the sink for a minute while I changed trousers) and seemed to think it was for her. Usually I do come back with a little something for the old trout, granted, but on this occasion I hadn't. Pissed me off a bit, to be honest. She just sits at home all evening on her fat arse, doing nothing, and then when I come home she expects I'll have some little present for her. Anyway, whatever. It got sorted out.

Couple days later Baz and I go out on the game again. Nothing mega, just out for a walk, trying back doors, side doors, garden gates, usual kind of stuff. What the coppers call "opportunistic" crime. Actually, we call it that too.

"Fancy a bit of opportunistic, Baz?" I'll say.

He'll neck the last of his pint. "Go on, then. Run out of cash anyway."

We were only out an hour or so, and came back to the pub with maybe three, four hundred quid worth of stuff. Usual bits of jewellery, plus a Palm V, two external hard drives, three phones, wallet full of cash and even a pot of spare change (might as well, plenty of quid coins in there). That's the thing about this business: you've got to know what you're doing. Got to be able to have a quick look at rings and necklaces, and know whether they're worth the nicking. Glance at a small plastic case, realise there's a pricey little personal organiser inside. See things like those portable hard drives, which don't look like anything, and know that if you wipe them clean you can get forty apiece for them in City pubs, more for the ones with more megs or gigs or whatever (it's written on the back). Understand which phones are hard to clone or shift and so not worth the bother. Know that a big old pot of change can be well worth it, and also that if you tip it into a plastic bag it makes a bloody good cosh in case you meet someone on the way out.

The other thing is the mental attitude. I remember having a barney with an old boyfriend of Baz's sister, couple years ago. She'd met him in some wine bar up West and he was a right smartarse, well up himself, fucking student or something it was.

He comes right out and asks me: "How can you do it?"

Not "do", notice, I'd've understood that (and I don't mind giving out some tips): but "can". How *can* I do it? And this from some little wanker who's being put through college by mummy and daddy, who didn't have a lazy girlfriend to support, and who was a right old slowcoach when it came to doing his round at the bar. Annoying thing was, after I'd discussed it with him for a bit (I say "discussed":

there was a bit of pushing and shoving at the start), I could sort of see his point.

According to him, it was a matter of attitude. If someone came round and turned me mum's place over, I'd be after their fucking blood. I knew that already, of course, he wasn't teaching me nothing there: I suppose the thing I hadn't really clocked was this mental attitude thing. I know that mum's got some bits and pieces that she'd be right upset if they was nicked. Not even because they're worth much, but just because they mean something to her. From me old man, whatever. If I turn someone's place over, though, I don't know what means what to them. Could be that old ring was a gift from their Gran, whereas to me it's just a tenner from Mr. Pzlowsky if I'm lucky. That tatty organiser could have phone numbers on it they don't have anywhere else. Or maybe it was a big deal that their dad bought them a little telly, it's the first one of their own they've had, and if I nick it then they're always going to be on their second, or third, or tenth.

The point is I don't know all that. I don't know anything about these people and their lives, and I don't really care. To me, they're just fucking cattle, to be honest. What's theirs is mine. Fair enough, maybe it's not a great mental attitude. But that's thieving for you. Nobody said it was a job for Mother Teresa.

Anyway, we're back in the Junction and a few more beers down (haven't even shifted anything on yet, still working through the change pot) when who should walk in the door but the Pole. Mr. Pzlowsky, as I live and breath. He comes in the door, looks around and sees us, and makes his way through the crowd.

Baz and I just stare at him. I've never seen the Pole anywhere except in his shop. Tell the truth, I thought he had no actual legs; just spent the day propped up behind his counter raking in the cash. He's an old bloke, sixties, and he smokes like a chimney and I'm frankly fucking amazed he's made it all the way here.

And also: why?

"I'd like a word with you," he says, when he gets to us.

"Buy us a beer, then," I go.

I'm a bit pissed off at him, truth be known. He's crossing a line. I don't want no one in the pub to know where we shift our gear. As it happens it's just me and Baz there at that moment, but you never know when Clive's going to come in, or any of the others.

He looks at me, then turns right around and goes back to the bar. "Two Stellas," I shout after him, and he just scowls.

Baz and I turn to look at each other. "What's going on?" Baz asks.

"Fucked if I know."

As I watch the Pole at the bar, I'm thinking it through. My first thought is he's come because there's a problem with something we've sold him, he's had the old Bill knocking on his door. But now I'm not sure. If it was grief, he wouldn't be buying us a pint. He'd be in a hurry, and pissed off. "Have to wait and see."

Eventually Mr. Pzlowsky gets back to us with our drinks on a little tray. He sits down at our table, his back to the rest of the pub, and I start to relax. Whatever he's here for, he's playing by the rules. He's drinking neat gin, no ice. Ugh.

"Cheers," I say. "So: what's up?"

He lights one of his weird little cigarettes, coughs. "I have something for you."

"Sounds interesting," I say. "What?"

He reaches in his jacket pocket and pulls out a brown envelope. Puts it on the table, pushes it across. I pick it up, look inside.

Fifties. Ten of them. Five hundred quid. A "monkey", as they say on television, though no fucker I know does.

"Fuck's this?"

"A bonus," he says, and I can hear Baz's brain fizzing. I can actually hear his thoughts. A bonus from the Pole, he's thinking: What the fuck is going on?

"A bonus, from the Pole?" I say, on his behalf. "What the fuck is going on?"

"This is what it is," he says, speaking quietly and drawing in close. I won't do his accent, but trust me—you have to concentrate. "It is from that jewellery you bring me last week. The silver. The American silver. I have one of my clients in this afternoon, he is the one sometimes buys unusual things, and I decide I will show this silver to him. So I get one of these things out—I always show just one first, you understand, because it can be more expensive that way.

He looks at it, and suddenly I am on high alert. This is because I am experienced, see, I know what is what in my trade. I see it in his eyes when he sees the piece: he really wants this thing, yes? I was going to say two hundred to him, maybe two hundred fifty, this is what I think it was worth. But when I see his face, I think a moment, and I say seven hundred fifty! Is a joke, a little bit, but also I think maybe I see what is in his eyes again, and we'll see."

"And?"

"He says 'done', just like that, and he asks me if I have some more. I almost fall off my stool, I tell you truthfully."

I nearly fell off my own stool, right there in the pub. Seven hundred and fifty fucking notes! Fuck me!

The Pole, sees my face, laughs. "Yes! And this is just the smallest one, you understand? So I say yes, I have some more, and his eyes are like saucers immediately. In all the time I do this thing, only a very few times do I see this look in a man's face which says 'I will pay whatever you want'. So I bring them out, one by one. You bring me five of them, you remember. He buys them all."

Baz gapes. "All of them? For seven-fifty each?"

The Pole goes all sly, and winks. "At least," he says, and I knew there and then that one or two of them went for a lot more than that. There's quiet for a moment, as we all sip our drinks. I know Baz is trying to do the sums in his head, and not having much luck. I've already done them, and I'm a bit pissed off we didn't realise what we had. Fuck knows what the Pole is thinking.

He finishes his gin in a quick swallow and gets up. "So, thank you, boys. Is a good find. He tell me is turn of the century American silver, from East Coast somewhere, he tell me the name, I forget it, something like Portsmouth, I think. And… well, the man says to me that if I find any more of this thing, he will buy it. Straight away. So… think of me, okay?"

And he winked again, and shuffled his way out through the crowd until we couldn't see him any more.

"Fuck me," Baz says, when he's gone.

"Fuck me is right," I say. I open the envelope, take out four of the fifties, and give them to him. "There's your half."

"Cheers. Mind you," Baz says, over his beer, "he's still a fucker. How much did all that add up to?"

"Minimum of seven-fifty each, that's three grand seven-fifty," I said. "But from that fucker's face, I'm thinking he got five, six grand at least. And if he got that off some bloke who knows it's nicked, then in the shops you got to double or treble it. Probably more."

"Sheesh. Still, good for him. He didn't have to see us right."

"Yeah," I said, because he wasn't completely wrong. The Pole could have kept quiet about his windfall. His deal with us was done. "But you know what that cash is really about?"

Baz looked at me, shook his head. He's a lovely bloke, don't get me wrong. He's my best mate. But the stuff in his head is mainly just padding to stop his eyeballs falling in. "What it means is," I said, "he's very fucking keen to get some more. In fact, probably says he was lying about the seven-fifty for the cheapest. He got more. Maybe much more. He got *so* much dosh for them, in fact, it was worth admitting he did well, and paying us a bonus so we go to him if we find any more."

"Better keep our eyes open, then," Baz said, cheerfully. "More beer?"

"Cheers," I said.

I watched him lurch off to the bar. My hand slipped into my pocket, and I found my cold little friend. The bit of polished stone, coral, glass, whatever. I knew then that Clive had been right. My little piece was probably worth a lot of money. The bits of jewellery had been all right, but nowhere near as pretty as my stone.

I wasn't selling it though, no way. I had got too used to the feel of it in my hand. Twenty, thirty times a day I'd hold it. I liked the way it fitted between my fingers. Longer I had it, better it seemed to fit. Sometimes, if I held it up to my face, I thought I could smell it too. Couldn't put my finger on what it smelled of, but it was nice, comforting. The Pole wasn't getting hold of it. Not Jackie neither.

It was mine.

On the Sunday Baz goes on holiday. He's off to Tenerife for the week. This is fine by me, because I need time to plan.

Now Baz, he thinks we've just got to keep an eye out for this stuff, that it's something like a particular DVD player or whatever. I know different. If it's this fucking valuable, then it's not something we're just going to find in some gaff in Kentish Town, mixed in with all the shit from Ratners or Argos or wherever. This isn't just common-or-garden thieving we're looking at. This is nicking to order, which is a different kind of skill. Happens all the time, of course: you pass the word to the right bloke in the right pub that you want some particular BMW, or a new Mini in cream, and they'll go do the business for you. There's big money in it. Not my area, normally, but this is different. We do all right with the usual gear, but if me and Baz can take some more of this silver to the Pole, we can do very nicely indeed. It's worth making an effort.

So on the Monday night, I'm out on the streets by myself. It's about ten-thirty. I park the van around the corner, and I take a stroll down the street where the house is, the house where we found the stuff. Couldn't remember which one it was at first, but in the end I worked it out. All the other houses in this street, they've been done up. Windowsills painted, bricks re-pointed, new tiles on the path, that kind of thing. Scaffolding on a couple others. Lot of people have moved in recently, the area's coming up. But this particular house, it looks a bit more knackered. I'm thinking the people have been there a while, which makes sense, what with it being so untidy inside. Could be they're foreign. You get that, sometimes. People moved in just after the war or whatever, when it was dirt-cheap. House gets passed on to the children, and then bingo, suddenly they're sitting on a gold mine. Could be they're Yanks, even—which would explain the old silver being from the US originally.

I walk past the house and see the curtains are drawn and the lights are on. Lot of people do that when they go out, but if you take lights to mean there's no one at home, you'll being doing time so fast your feet won't touch the ground. Me, I've never been inside. Not intending to be, either. And I'm not planning on doing the job solo anyhow. It's a big house. It's a two-person manoeuvre—not least because it was Baz who picked up the bits of silver in the first place. I don't know where he found them, but it's got to be the first place to look. Quicker you're in and out, the better.

I walk the street one way, then go around the corner and have a fag. Then I walk back past the house. I'm trying to remember the exact layout, because we've been in a few other houses since. I'm glancing across at the front window on the second floor when I see a shape, a shadow on the curtain. I smile to myself, glad I'm not so stupid as to have had a go tonight. And loyal, of course—I want Baz in on it, and he's not back until Sunday.

I slow the pace, keep an eye on this shadow. Never know, it might be a bird with her tits out. Don't see nothing of note, though. Curtains are too tightly drawn, and it's that thing where the light's behind them and they get magnified till they're just some huge blob.

The light goes off, and I realise mostly likely that's the kid just gone to bed. That tells me that room was where the little telly was from, and the whole floor clicks in my head.

I walked back to the van, feeling very professional indeed.

Next night I'm busy, and the one after. Not nicking. The Tuesday was our "anniversary" (or so Jackie says; far as I can see I don't understand why we have them when we're not even fucking engaged, and anyway—anniversary of what? We met at a party, got pissed, shagged in one of the bedrooms on a pile of coats, and that was that). Either way we ended up going up West and having a meal and then getting bladdered at a club. Wednesday night I'm not going fucking anywhere. I felt like shit.

So it's Thursday when I'm outside the house again.

I was there a little earlier, about quarter to nine. You look a bit less suspicious, being out on the street at that time; but on the other hand there's more people around to see you loitering about. I walked past the house first, seeing the curtains are drawn again. Can't work out whether the lights are on full or not: there's still a bit of light in the sky.

I'd actually slowed down, almost stopped, when I heard footsteps coming up the street. I started moving again, sharpish. You don't want the neighbours catching someone staring at a house. There's some right nosey fuckers. They'll call the old Bill quick as you like. Course the Bill won't do much, most of the time, but if they think there's lads scouting for opportunistics then sometimes they'll get someone to drive down the street every now and then, when they're bored.

So I started walking again, and as I look I see there are some people coming up the street towards me. Three of them. Actually, they're still about thirty yards away, which is a surprise. Sounded like they were closer than that. I just walk towards them. I didn't actually whistle—nobody whistles much these days, which I think is a bit of a shame—but I was as casual as you like.

Just as I'm coming up to them, them up to me, the streetlights click on. One of these lights is there just as we're passing each other, and suddenly there's these big shadows thrown across my path. I look across and see there's two of them in front, a man and a woman. The woman's wearing a big floppy hat—must have been to some fancy do—and the bloke happens to be looking across her, towards the street. She's in shadow, he's turned the other way, so I don't see either of their faces, which is fine by me. If I haven't seen theirs then they haven't seen mine, if you know what I mean.

I'm just stepping past them, and I mean around, really, because they're both pretty big, when suddenly someone *was* looking at me.

It was the girl, walking behind them. As I'm passing her, her head turns, and she looks right at me.

I look away quickly, and then they're gone.

All I'm left with is an image of the girl's face, of it slowly turning to look at me. To be honest, she was a bit of a shocker. Not scarred or nothing, just really big-faced. With them eyes look like they're sticking out too far, make you look a bit simple.

But she was young, and I think she smiled.

I walked down to the corner, steady as you like. As I turned around it I glanced back, just quickly. I saw two things. I see the three of them are going into the house. They weren't neighbours, after all. They're the people from the actual house. The people with the jewellery. The people I'm going to be nicking from.

The second thing I notice is that the streetlight we passed isn't lit any more.

* * *

I'm a bit unsettled, the next day, to be honest. Don't know why. It isn't like me. Normally I'm a pretty chilled bloke, take things as they come and all that. But I find myself in the pub at lunchtime, which I don't usually do—not on a weekday, anyway, unless it's a Bank Holiday—and by the afternoon I'm pretty lagered up. I sit by myself, in a table at the back, keep knocking them back. Clive pops in about three and I had a couple more with him, but it was quiet. I didn't say much, and in the end he got up and started playing pool with some bloke. It was quite funny actually, some posh wanker in there by mistake, fancied playing for money. Clive reeled him in like a kipper.

So I'm sitting there, thinking, trying to work out why I feel weird. Could be that it's because I've seen the people I'm going to be nicking from. Usually it's not that way. It's just bits of gear, lying around in someone else's house. They're mine to do what I want with. All I see is how much they're worth. Now I know that the jewellery is going to belong to that woman in the hat. And I know that Baz's sister is watching a telly that belonged to the girl who looked at me. All right, so she was a minger, but it's bad enough being ugly without people nicking your prize possession.

That could be another thing, of course. She'd seen me. No reason for her to think some bloke in the street is the one who turned them over, but I don't like it. Like I didn't like Mr. Pzlowsky being in the Junction. You don't want anyone to be able to make those connections.

I'm thinking that's it, just them having seen me, and I'm beginning to feel bit more relaxed. I've got another pint in front of me, and I've got my stone in my right hand. It's snuggled in there, in my palm, fingers curled around it, and that's helping too. It's like worry beads, or something: I just feel better when it's there.

And then I realise that there's something else on my mind. I want to find that jewellery. But I don't necessarily want to hand it on.

The Pole is still gagging for it, I know. He's rung me twice, asking if I've got any more, and that tells me there's serious money involved. But now I think about it properly, with my stone in my hand and no Baz sitting there next to me, jabbering on, I realise I want the stuff for myself. I didn't actually handle it, the last time. Baz found it, kept it, sold it to the Pole.

If a little bit of stone feels like this one does, though, what would the silver feel like? I don't know—but I want to know.

And that's why, on the Saturday night, I went around there. Alone.

I parked up at 5:00, and walked past once an hour. I walked up, down, on both sides of the street. Unless someone's sitting watching the whole time, I'm just another bloke. Or so I tell myself, anyway. The truth is that I'm just going to do it whatever.

It's a Saturday night. Very least, the young girl is going to go out. Maybe the mum and dad too, out for a meal, to the cinema, whatever. Worst case, I'll just wait until they've all gone to bed, and try the back door. I don't like doing it that way. Avoid it if I can. You never know if you're going to run into some have-a-go-hero who fancies getting his picture in the local paper. Clive had one of those, couple years back. Had to smack the guy for ages before he went down. Didn't do any nicking for three months after that. It puts you right off your stride. Risky, too. Burglary is one thing. Grievous Bodily Harm is something else. The coppers know the score. Bit of nicking is inevitable. The insurance is going to pay anyway, so no one gets too exercised. But with GBH, they're on your case big-time. I didn't want to go into the house with people in it. But by the time I'd walked past it three times, I knew I was going to if I had to.

Then, at half-past seven, the front door opens.

I'm sitting in the van, tucked around the corner, but I can see the house in the rear-view mirror. The front door opens and the girl comes out. She walks to the end of the path, turns left, and goes off up the street.

One down, I think. Now: how many to go?

I tell you, an hour is a long time to wait. It's a long time if you're just sitting there smoking, nothing but a little stone for company, watching a house in the mirror until your neck starts to ache.

At quarter-past eight I see the curtains in the downstairs being drawn. Hello, I thought. It's not dark yet. Nothing happens for another twenty minutes.

Then I see the door opening. Two people come out. She's wearing a big old hat again. It's a bit far away, and I can't see his face, but I see he's got long hair. I see also just how fucking big they are. Fat, but tall too. A real family of beauties, that's for sure.

They fuck around at the door for a while, and then they walk up the path, and they turn right too.

Bingo. Fucking bingo. I've had a result.

I give them fifteen minutes. Long enough to get on the bus or down the tube, long enough that they won't suddenly turn up again because one of them forgot their phone or wallet. Also, enough for the light to go just a little bit more, so it's going to be a bit darker, and I won't stick out so much.

Then I get out of the van, and walk over to the house. First thing I do is walk straight down the front path, give a little ring on the door. Okay, so I've only seen three of them before, but you never know. Could be another kid, or some old dear. I ring it a couple of times. Nothing happens.

So then I go around the side, the way we got in last time. It's a bit of a squeeze, past three big old bins. Fuck knows what was in them—smelled fucking terrible. Round the back there's the second door. Last time it was unlocked, but I'm not reckoning on that kind of luck twice. Certainly not after it got them burgled. I try it, and sure enough, it didn't budge.

So I get myself up close to the glass panel in the door, and look through the dusty little panes. Some people, soon as they get burgled, they'll have a system put in. Bolting the stable door. It's why you've got to be careful if you find some keys the first time and go back a couple weeks later. Can't see any sign of wires.

So I take the old T-shirt out of my pocket, wrap it around my fist. One quick thump.

It makes a noise, of course. But London is noisy. I wait to see if anybody's light goes on. I can be back out on the street and away in literally seconds.

Nothing happens. No lights. No one shouts "Oi!"

I reach my hand in through the window and would you fucking believe it: they've only left the key in the lock. I love people, I really do. They're so fucking *stupid*. Two seconds later, I'm inside.

Now's here the point I wish Baz is with me. He's not bright, but he's got a good memory for places. He'd remember exactly where he'd found everything. I don't have a clue, but I've got a hunch.

The bureau with the empty drawer. The place where I got my stone. Well, Baz found it, of course. But it's mine now.

I walk through the kitchen without a second glance. Did it properly last time. The main light's on in the living room, and I can see it's even more untidy than last time. The sofa is covered in all kinds of shit. Old books, bits of clothes. A big old map. Looks *very* old, in fact, and I make a mental note to take that when I go. Could be the Pole's contact would be interested in that too.

I stand in front of the bureau. My heart is going like a fucking jackhammer. Partly it's doing a job by myself. Mainly I just really, really want to find something. I want the jewellery. More even than that, I want another stone.

I look through the drawers. One by one. Methodical. I take everything out, look through it carefully. There's nothing. I'm pissed off, getting jittery. I've always known it might be that there just isn't any more of the stuff. But now I'm getting afraid.

In the end I go to the drawer I know is empty, and I pull it out. It's still empty. I'm about to shove it closed again, when I notice something. A smell. I look around the room, but at first I can't tell what's making it. Could be a plate with some old food on it, I think, lost under a pile of books somewhere. Then I realise it's coming from the drawer. I don't know how to describe it, but it's definitely there. It's not strong, but…

Then I get it, I think. It's air. It's a different kind of air. It's not like London. It's like… the sea. Sea air, like you'd get down on the front in some pissy little town on the coast, the kind people don't go to any more and didn't have much to recommend it in the first place. Some little town or village with old stone buildings, cobbled streets, thatched roofs. A place where there's lots of shadows, maybe a big old deserted factory or something on a hill overlooking the town; where you hear odd footsteps down narrow streets and alleys in the dark afternoons and when the birds cry out in the night the sound is stretched and cramped and echoes as if it is bouncing off things you cannot see.

That kind of place. A place like that.

I lean down to the drawer, stick my nose in, give it another good sniff. No doubt about it—the smell's definitely coming from inside. I don't like it. I don't like it at all. So I slam it shut.

And that's when I realise.

When the drawer bangs closed, I hear a little noise. Not just the slam, but something else.

Slowly, I pull it back out again. I put my hand inside, and feel towards the back. My arm won't go in as far as it should.

The drawer's got a false back.

I pull it and pull it, but I can't get it to come out. So I get the screwdriver out of my back pocket and slip it inside. I angle my hand around and get the tip into the join right at the back. I'm feeling hot, and starting to sweat. Fucking tricky to get any pull on it, but I give it a good yank.

There's a splintering sound, and my hand whacks into the other side. I let go of the screwdriver and feel with my fingers. An inch of the wooden back has come away. There's something behind it, for sure. A little space. I can tell because my fingertips feel a little cold, as if there's a breeze coming from in there. Can't be, of course, but it tells me what I need to know.

Something's behind there. Could be the jewellery I came for. Could be even better. Could be another stone. Another stone that smells like the sea. So I get the screwdriver in position again. Get it good and tight against the side, and get ready to give it an almighty pull.

And that's when I feel the soft breath on the back of my neck, and her hands coming gently around my waist; and one of the others turning off the lights.

It *is* just a question of attitude, it turns out. The student tosser had it right. It's all a matter of how you see the people you're doing over, whether you think about them at all, or if you just see what you can get from them. What you *need*.

I gave them Baz, on the Sunday night. They didn't make me watch, but I heard. An hour later there was just a stain on the carpet, like the one we'd seen upstairs. They gave me another one of the stones, even prettier than the one I had before. It's beautiful.

Fair exchange is no robbery. I'm giving them Jackie next.

THE TAINT

by BRIAN LUMLEY

JAMES JAMIESON LOOKED through binoculars at the lone figure on the beach—a male figure, at the rim of the sea—and said, "That's pretty much what I would have wanted to do, when I was his age. Beachcombing, or writing books; maybe poetry? Or just bumming my way around the world. But my folks had other ideas. Just as well, I suppose. 'No future in poetry, son. Or in daydreaming or beachcombing.' That was my father, a doctor in his own right. Like father like son, right?" Lowering his binoculars, he smiled at the others with him. "Still, I think I would have enjoyed it."

"Beachcombing, in the summer? Oh, I could understand that well enough!" John Tremain, the middle-aged headmaster at the technical college in St. Austell, answered him. "The smell of the sea, the curved horizon way out there, sea breezes in your hair, and the wailing of the gulls? Better than the yelping of brats any time—oh yes! The sun's sparkle on the sea and warm sand between your toes—it's very seductive. But this late in the season, *and* in my career?" He shook his head. "Thanks, but no thanks. You won't find me with my hands in my pockets, sauntering along the tidemark and picking over the seaweed."

He paused, shrugged, and continued, "Not now, anyway. But on the other hand, when I was a young fellow teaching arts and crafts: carpentry and joinery, woodcraft in general—I mean, working *with* woods as opposed to surviving in them—now would have been the ideal time for a stroll on the beach. And I used to do quite a bit of it. Yes, indeed. For it's autumn when the best pieces get washed ashore."

"Pieces?" Jilly White came back from wherever her thoughts had momentarily wandered, blinked her pretty but clouded green eyes at Tremain, then glanced from face to face in search of a hint, a clue. "I'm sorry, John, but I wasn't quite…?"

"Driftwood," the teacher smiled. "All those twisted, sand-papered roots that get tumbled in with the tide when the wind's off the sea. Those bleached, knotted, gargoyle branches. It's a long time ago now, but—" He almost sighed, gave another shrug, and finished off, "But searching for driftwood was as close as I ever got to being a beachcomber."

And Doreen, his tall, slender, haughty but not unattractive wife, said, "You've visited with us often enough, Jilly. Surely you must have noticed John's carvings? They were all driftwood originally, washed up on the beach there."

And now they all looked at Jilly…

There were four of them, five if you included Jilly White's daughter, Anne, curled up with a book in the lee of a sand-dune some twenty-five yards down the beach and out of earshot. Above her, a crest of crabgrass like some buried sand-giant's eyebrow framed the girl where her curled body described a malformed eye in the dune's hollow. And that was where Jilly White's mind had been: on her fifteen-year-old daughter, there in the lee of the dune; and on the muffled, shuffling beachcomber on the far side of the dunes, near the water's edge where the waves frothed and the sand was dark and damp.

All of them were well wrapped against a breeze off the sea that wasn't so much harsh as constant, unremitting. Only endure it long enough, it would cool your ears and start to find a way through your clothes. It was getting like that now; not yet the end of September, but the breeze made it feel a lot later.

"John's carvings?" said Jilly, who was still a little distant despite that she was right there with the others on Doctor (or ex-Doctor)

James Jamieson's veranda overlooking the beach. But now, suddenly, she snapped to. "Oh, his *carvings*! The driftwood! Why, yes, of course I've noticed them—and admired them, honestly—John's driftwood carvings. Silly of me, really. I'm sorry, John, but when you said 'pieces' I must have been thinking of something broken. Broken in pieces, you know?"

And Jamieson thought: *She looks rather fragile herself. Not yet broken but certainly brittle... as if she might snap quite easily.* And taking some of the attention, the weight off Jilly, he said, "Scrimshaw, eh? How interesting. I'd enjoy to see your work some time."

"Any time at all," Tremain answered. "But, er, while it's a bit rude of me to correct you, er, James, it isn't scrimshaw."

"Oh?" The old man looked taken aback. "It isn't?"

The headmaster opened his mouth to explain, but before he could utter another word his wife, Doreen, cut in with, "Scrimshaw is the art or handicraft of old-time sailors, Doctor." She could be a little stiff with first names. "Well, art of a sort, anyway." And tut-tutting— apparently annoyed by the breeze—she paused to brush back some ruffled, dowdy-looking strands of hair from her forehead before explaining further. "Scrimshaw is the name they've given to those odd designs that they carve on shells and old whalebones and such."

"Ah!" Jamieson exclaimed. "But of course it is!" And glancing at Jilly, now huddling to herself, shivering a little and looking pale, he smiled warmly and said, "So you see, Jilly my dear, you're not alone in mixing things up this afternoon. What with driftwood and scrimshaw and the wind—which is picking up I think, and blowing our brains about—why, it's easy to lose track of things and fall out with the facts. Maybe we should go inside, eh? A glass of cognac will do us the world of good, and I'll treat you to something I've newly discovered: a nice slice of homemade game pie from that bakery in the village. Then I'll be satisfied that I've at least fed and watered you, and warmed your bones, before I let you go off home."

But as his visitors trooped indoors, the ex-Doctor quickly took up his binoculars to scan the beach again. In this off-the-beaten-track sort of place, one wouldn't really expect to see a great many people on the shore; none, at this time of year. The beachcomber was still there, however; hunched over and with his head down, he shambled slowly along. And it appeared that Anne, Jilly's bookish, reserved if not exactly retiring daughter, had finally noticed him. What's more, she had stood up and was making her way down the beach toward him.

Jamieson gave a start as Jilly touched his arm. And: "It's all right," she said quietly, (perhaps even confidentially, the doctor thought). "It's nothing you should feel concerned about. Young Geoff and Anne, they're just friends. They went to school together… well, for a while anyway. The infants, you know?"

"Oh dear!" Jamieson blinked his slightly rheumy old eyes at her. "I do hope you don't think I was spying on them—I mean, on your daughter. And as for this, er, Geoff?"

"It's all right," she said again, tugging him inside. "It's quite all right. You've probably bumped into him in the village and he may well have sparked some professional interest in you. That's only natural, after all. But he's really quite harmless, I assure you…"

Eating slowly, perhaps to avoid conversation, Jilly wasn't done with her food when the Tremains were ready to go. "Anyway," she said, "I'll have to wait for Anne. She won't be long…knows better than to be out when the light starts failing."

"You don't mind her walking with the village idiot?" John's words sounded much too harsh; he was probably biting his lip as he turned his face away and Doreen helped him on with his coat.

"Ignore my husband," Doreen twisted her face into something that didn't quite equal a smile. "According to him all children are idiots. It seems that's what being a teacher does to you."

Jilly said, "Personally, I prefer to think of the boy as an unfortunate. And of course in a small seaside village he stands out like a sore thumb. I'm glad he has a… a friend in Anne."

And John half relented. "You're right, of course. And maybe I'm in the wrong profession. But it's much like Doreen says. If you work all day with kids, especially bolshy teenagers, and in this day and age when you daren't even frown at the little sods let alone slap their backsides—"

At the door, Doreen lifted her chin. "I don't recall saying anything like that. Nothing as rude as that, anyway."

"Oh, you know what I mean!" John said testily, trailing her outside, and colliding with her where she'd paused on the front doorstep. Then—in unison but almost as an afterthought—they stuck their heads back inside to thank Jamieson for his hospitality.

"Not at all," their host answered. "And I'll be dropping in on you soon, to have a look at those carvings."

"Please do," John told him.

And Doreen added, "Evenings or weekends, you'll be welcome. We're so glad that you've settled in here, Doctor."

"Oh, call me James, for goodness sake!" Jamieson waved them goodbye, closed the door, turned to Jilly and raised an enquiring, bushy grey eyebrow.

She shrugged. "A bit pompous maybe, but they're neighbours. And it does get lonely out here."

They went to the bay window in the end wall and watched the Tremains drive off down the road to their home less than a mile away. Jilly lived half a mile beyond that, and the tiny village—a huddle of old fishermen's houses, really—stood some four or five hundred yards farther yet, just out of sight behind the rising, rocky promontory called South Point. On the far side of the village, a twin promontory, North Point, formed a bay, with the harbour lying sheltered in the bight.

For a moment more Jamieson watched the Tremains's car speed into the distance, then turned a glance of covert admiration on Jilly. She noticed it, however, cocked her head on one side and said, "Oh? Is there something…?"

Caught out and feeling just a little uncomfortable now, the old man said, "My dear, I hope you won't mind me saying so, but you're a very attractive woman. And even though I'm a comparative stranger here, a newcomer, I can't say I've come across too many eligible bachelors in the village."

Now Jilly frowned. Her lips began to frame a question—or perhaps a sharp retort, an angry outburst—but he beat her to it.

"I'm sorry, I'm so sorry!" He held up his hands. "It's none of my business, I know. And I keep forgetting that your husband… that he—"

"—Died less than eighteen months ago, yes," Jilly said.

The old man sighed. "My bedside manner hasn't improved any with age," he said. "I retired here for what I thought would be solitude—an absence of everything that's gone before—only to find that I can't seem to leave my practice behind me! To my patients I was a healer, a father confessor, a friend, a champion. I didn't realise it would be so hard not to continue being those things."

She shook her pretty head, smiled wanly and said, "James, I don't mind your compliments, your concern, or your curiosity. I find it refreshing that there are still people who… who care about anyone. Or anything for that matter!"

"But you frowned."

"Not at what you said," she answered, "but the way you said it. Your accent, really."

"My accent?"

"Very similar to my husband's. He was an American, too, you know."

"No, I didn't know that. And he had a similar accent? A New England accent, you say?" Suddenly there was a new, a different note of concern in Jamieson's voice, unlike the fatherly interest he'd taken in Jilly earlier. "And may I ask where he hailed from, your husband? His home town?"

"George was from Massachusetts, a town on or near the coast— pretty much like this place, I suppose—called, er, Ipswich? Or maybe Arkham or Innsmouth. He would talk about all three, so I can't be certain. And I admit to being a dunce where American geography is concerned. But I'm sure I have his birth certificate somewhere in the house, if you're that interested?"

Sitting down, the old man bade Jilly do the same. "Interested?" he said. "Well, perhaps not. Let sleeping dogs lie, eh?"

"Sleeping dogs?" Now she was frowning again.

And he sighed before answering. "Well, I did practice for a few months—*just* a few months—in Innsmouth. A very strange place, Jilly, even for this day and age. But no, you don't want to know about that."

"But now you've got *me* interested," she said. "I mean, what was so strange about the place?"

"Well, if you must know, it was mainly the people—degenerate, inbred, often retarded—in fact much like young Geoff. I have bumped into him, yes, and there's that about the boy… there's a certain look to him…" But there the old man paused, probably because he'd seen how Jilly's hands fluttered, trembling on the arms of her chair. Seeing where he was looking, she put her hands in her lap, clasping them until her fingers went white. It was obvious that something he had said had disturbed her considerably. And so:

"Let's change the subject," he said, sitting up straighter. "And let me apologise again for being so personal. But a woman like you— still young and attractive, in a place like this—surely you should be looking to the future now, realising that it's time to go, time to get out of here. Because while you're here there are always going to be memories. But there's an old saying that goes 'out of sight—'"

"'—Out of mind?'" She finished it for him.

"Something like that." He nodded. "A chance to start again, in a place, some town or city, that *does* have its fair share of eligible bachelors…" And then he smiled, however wryly. "But there I go, being personal again!"

Jilly didn't return his smile but told him, "I do intend to get away, I have intended it, but there are several things that stop me. For one, it's such a short time since George… well, since he…"

"I understand." Jamieson nodded. "You haven't yet found the time or the energy to get around to it."

"And two, it's not going to be easy to sell up—not for a decent price, anyway. I mean, look how cheaply you were able to secure this place."

Again the old man nodded. "When people die or move away, no one moves in, right? Well, except for old cheapskates like me."

"And all perfectly understandable," said Jilly. "There's no school in the village, and no work; the fishing has been unproductive for years now, though of late it has seemed to pick up just a little. As for amenities: the nearest supermarket is in St. Austell! And when the weather gets bad the old road out of the village is like a death-trap; it's always getting potholed or washed out. So there's no real reason why anyone would want to come here. A few holidaymakers, maybe, in the summer season, and the very rare occasion when someone like you might want to retire here. But apart from that…"

"Yes?" He prompted her, slyly. "But apart from that? Jilly, almost everything you've said seems to me contradictory. You've given some very excellent reasons why you *shouldn't* stay, and a few pretty bad ones why you *should*. Or haven't I heard them all yet?"

She shrank down into herself a little, and Jamieson saw her hands go back to the arms of her chair, fluttering there like a pair of nervous birds…

"It's my daughter," she said after a while. "It's Anne. I think we'll have to stay here a little longer, if only for her sake."

"Oh?"

"Yes. She's… she's doing piano with Miss Harding in the village, and twice a week she studies languages at night school in St. Austell. She loves it; she's quite a little interpreter, you know, and I feel I have to let her continue."

"Languages, you say?" The old man's eyebrows went up. "Well, she'll find plenty of work as an interpreter—or as a teacher, for that matter."

"Yes, I think so, too!" said Jilly, more energetically now. "It's her future, and she has a very real talent. Why, she even reads sign!"

"I'm sorry?"

"Sign language, as used by the deaf and dumb."

"Oh, yes, of course. But no, er, higher education?"

"She had the grades," said Jilly, protectively. "She would have no trouble getting into university. But what some desire, others put aside. And to be totally honest… well, she's not the communal type. She wouldn't be happy away from home."

Again Jamieson's nod of understanding. "A bit of a loner," he said.

"She's a young girl," Jilly quickly replied, "and so was I, once upon a time. And I know that we all go through our phases. She's unsettled enough—I mean, what with her father's death and all—so any move will just have to wait. And that's that."

Now, having firmly indicated that she no longer desired to talk about her daughter, it was Jilly's turn to change the subject. And in doing so she returned to a previous topic.

"You know," she said, after a moment, "despite that you'll probably think it's a morbid sort of fascination, I can't help being interested in what you were saying about Innsmouth—the way its denizens were, well, strange."

Denizens, Jamieson repeated her, but silently, to himself. *Yes, I suppose you could describe them that way.*

He might have answered her. But a moment earlier, as Jilly had spoken the last few words, so the veranda door had glided open to admit Anne. There she stood framed against the evening, her hair blowing in the unrelenting sea breeze, her huge green eyes gazing enquiringly into the room. But her face was oh-so-pale, and her gaze cold and unsmiling. Maybe she'd been out in the wind too long and the chill had finally got to her.

Sliding the door shut behind her, and going to the fire to warm herself she said, "What was that you were saying, Mother? Something about strange denizens?"

But Jilly shrugged it off. "Mr. Jamieson and I were engaged in a private conversation, dear, and you shouldn't be so nosy."

That was that; Anne's return had called a halt to any more talk. But when Jamieson drew the veranda curtains he couldn't help noticing that hulking, shambling, head-down figure silhouetted against the sand dunes; the shape of Geoff, casting long ugly shadows as he headed back toward the village.

Following which it was time to drive Anne and Jilly home…

There was a week of bad weather. James Jamieson would sit in a chair by his sliding patio window and gaze out across the decking of the veranda, across the dunes and beach, at the roaring, rearing ocean. But no matter the driving rain and pounding surf, the roiling sky split by flashes of lightning and shuddering to drum rolls of thunder, sooner or later there would be a hulking figure on the sands: "Young Geoff," as Jilly White had seen fit to call him, the "unfortunate" youth from the village.

Sometimes the boy—or young man, whatever—would be seen shambling along the tidemark; at others he'd walk too close to the turbulent water, and end up sloshing through the foam when waves cast their spume across his route. Jamieson made a point of watching him through his expensive high-resolution binoculars, and now and then he would bring Geoff's face into sharper focus.

The sloping forehead and almost bald head; the wide, fleshy mouth, bulging eyes and scaly bump of a chin, with the bristles of a stubby beard poking through; the youth's skin—its roughness in general, with those odd folds or wattles—especially the loose flaps between his ears and his collar...

One afternoon toward the end of the week, when the weather was calmer, Jamieson also spied John Tremain on the beach. The link road must have washed out again, relieving the headmaster of his duties for a day or so and allowing him time to indulge his hobby. And sure enough as he walked the tidemark, he would stoop now and then to examine this or that piece of old driftwood. But at the same time "the village idiot" was also on the beach, and their paths crossed. Jamieson watched it all unfold in the cross hairs of his binoculars:

Tremain, crouching over a dark patch of seaweed, and Geoff coming over the dunes on a collision course. Then the meeting; the headmaster seeing the youth and jerking upright, lurching backward from the advancing figure and apparently threatening him with the knobby end of a stripped branch! The other coming to an awkward halt, and standing there with his arms and hands flapping uselessly, his flabby mouth opening and closing as if in silent protest.

But was it revulsion, hatred, or stark terror on Tremain's part? Or simply shock? Jamieson couldn't make up his mind. But whichever, it appeared that Tremain's dislike of "bolshy" teenagers went twice for those who weren't so much bolshy as, well, unfortunate.

That, however, was all there was to it; hardly a confrontation as such, and over and done with as quickly as that. Then Tremain scuttling for home, and Geoff standing there, watching him go. The end. But at least it had served to remind Jamieson of his promise to go and see John's driftwood carvings—which was one reason at least why he should pay a return visit...

* * *

At the weekend Jamieson called the Tremains on the telephone to check that the invitation was still open, and on Sunday evening he drove the solitary mile to his neighbour's place, parking by the side of the road. Since he, the Whites and the Tremains had the only properties on this stretch of potholed road, it wasn't likely that he'd be causing any traffic problems.

"Saw you on the beach the other day," he told John when he was seated and had a drink in his hand. "Beachcombing, hey?"

The other nodded. "It seems our talking about it must have sparked me off again. I found one or two rather nice pieces."

"You certainly have an eye for it," the old man commented, his flattery very deliberate. "Why, I can see you have several 'nice pieces'—expertly finished pieces, that is—right here. But if you'll forgive my saying so, it seems to me these aren't so much carvings as wind-, sea-, and sand-sculptures really, which you have somehow managed to revitalise with sandpaper and varnish, imagination and infinite skill. So much so that you've returned them to a new, dramatic life of their own!"

"Really?" Tremain was taken aback; he didn't see Jamieson's flattery for what it really was, as a means to an end, a way to ingratiate himself into the Tremains's confidence. For Jamieson found himself in such a close-knit microcosm of isolated community society that he felt sure the headmaster and his wife would have knowledge of almost everything that had gone on here; they would have the answers to questions he couldn't possibly put to Jilly, not in her condition.

For the old man suspected—indeed, he more than suspected—that Jilly White's circumstances had brought her to the verge of nervous exhaustion. But what exactly were her circumstances? As yet there were loose ends here, which Jamieson must at least attempt to tie up before making any firm decision or taking any definite course of action.

Which was why the ex-Doctor was here at the Tremains's this evening. They were after all his and Jilly's closest neighbours and closest in status, too. Whereas the people of the village—while they might well be the salt of the earth—were of a very different order indeed. And close-mouthed? Oh, he'd get nothing out of them.

And so back to the driftwood:

"Yes, really," the old man finally answered John Tremain's pleased if surprised inquiry. "I mean, this table we're sitting at, drinking from: a table of driftwood—but see how the grain stands out, the fine polish!" In fact the table was quite ugly. Jamieson pointed across the room. "And who could fail to admire your plant stand there, so black it looks lacquered."

"Yacht varnish," Tremain was all puffed up now. "As for why it's so black, it's ebony."

"*Diospyros*," said Doreen Tremain, entering from the kitchen with a tray of food. "A very heavy wood, and tropical. Goodness only knows how long it was in the sea, to finally get washed up here."

"Amazing!" Jamieson declared. "And not just the stand. Your knowledge of woods—and indeed of most things, as I've noted—does both of you great credit."

And now she preened and fussed no less than her husband. "I do so hope you like turbot, er, James?"

"*Psetta maxima*," said Jamieson, not to be outdone. "If it's fish, dear lady, then you need have no fear. I'm not the one to turn my nose up at a good piece of fish."

"I got it from Tom Foster in the village," she answered. "I like his fish, if not his company." And she wrinkled her nose.

"Tom Foster?" Jamieson repeated her, shaking his head. "No, I don't think I know him."

"And you don't want to," said John, helping the old man up, and showing him to the dining table. "Tom might be a good fisherman, but that's all he's good for. Him and his Gypsy wife."

Sitting down, Jamieson blinked his rheumy eyes at the other and enquired, "His Gypsy wife?"

"She's not a Gypsy," Doreen shook her head. "No, not Romany at all, despite her looks. It seems her great-grandmother was a Polynesian woman. Oh, there are plenty such throwbacks in Devon and Cornwall, descendants of women brought back from the Indies and South Pacific when the old sailing ships plied their trade. Anyway, the Fosters are the ones who have charge of that young Geoff person. But there again, I suppose we should be thankful that someone is taking care of him."

"*Huh!*" John Tremain grunted. "Surely his mother is the one who should be taking care of him. Or better far his father, except we all know that's no longer possible."

"And never would have been," Doreen added. "Well, not without all sorts of complications, accusations, and difficulties in general."

Watching the fish being served, Jamieson said, "I'm afraid you've quite lost me. Do you think you could… I mean, would you mind explaining?"

The Tremains looked at each other, then at the old man.

"Oh?" he said. "Do I sense some dark secret here, one from which I'm excluded? But that's okay—if I don't need to know, then I don't need to know. After all, I am new around here."

"No," said Doreen, "it's not that. It's just that—"

"It's sort of delicate," her husband said. "Or not exactly delicate, not any longer, but not the kind of thing people like to talk about. Especially when it's your neighbour, or your ex-neighbour, who is concerned."

"My *ex*-neighbour?" Jamieson frowned. "George White? He was *your* neighbour, yes, but never mine. So, what's the mystery?"

"You've not sensed anything?" This was Doreen again. "With poor Jilly? You've not wondered why she and Anne always seem to be sticking up for—"

"For that damned idiot in the village?" John saw his opportunity to jump in and finish it for her.

And the old man slowly nodded. "I think I begin to see," he said. "There's some connection between George White, Jilly and Anne, and—"

"And Geoff, yes," said Doreen. "But do you think we should finish eating first? I see no reason why we can't tell you all about it. You are or were a doctor, after all—and we're sure you've heard of similar or worse cases—but I'd hate the food to spoil."

And so they ate in relative silence. Doreen Tremain's cooking couldn't be faulted, and her choice of white wine was of a similar high quality…

* * *

"It was fifteen, sixteen years ago," John Tremain began, "and we were relative newcomers here, just as you are now. In those days this was a prosperous little place; the fish were plentiful and the village booming; in the summer there were people on the beaches and in the shops. Nowadays—there's only the post office, the pub, and the bakery. The post office doubles as a general store and does most of the business, and you can still buy a few fresh fish on the quayside before what's left gets shipped inland. And that's about it right now. But back then:

"They were even building a few new homes here, extending the village, as it were. This house and yours, they were the result. That's why they're newish places. But the road got no further than your place and hasn't been repaired to any great extent since. Jilly and George's place was maybe twenty years older; standing closer to the village, it wasn't as isolated. As for the other houses they'd planned to build on this road, they just didn't happen. Prices of raw materials were rocketing, the summers weren't much good any more, and fish stocks had begun a rapid decline.

"The Whites had been here for a year or two. They had met and married in Newquay, and moved here for the same reason we did: the housing was cheaper than in the towns. George didn't seem to have a job. He'd inherited some fabulous art items in gold and was gradually selling them off to a dealer in Truro. And Jilly was doing some freelance editing for local publishers."

Now Doreen took over. "As for George's gold: it was jewellery, and quite remarkable. I had a brooch off him that I wear now and then. It's unique, I think. Beautiful but very strange. Perhaps you'd like to see it?"

"Certainly," said the old man. "Indeed I would." While she went to fetch it, John continued the story.

"Anyway, Jilly was heavy with Anne at the time, but George wasn't a home body. They had a car—the same wreck she's got now, more off the road than on it—which he used to get into St. Austell, Truro, Newquay, and goodness knows where else. He would be away for two or three days at a time, often for whole weekends. Which wasn't fair on Jilly who was very close to her time. But look, let me cut a long story short.

"Apparently George had been a bit of a louse for quite some time. In fact as soon as Jilly had declared her pregnancy, that was when he'd commenced his… well, his—

"—Womanising?" The old man sat up straighter in his chair. "Are you saying he was something of a rake?"

By now Doreen had returned with a small jewellery box. "Oh, George White was much more than *something* of a rake," she said. "He was a great deal of a rake, in fact a roué! And all through poor Jilly's pregnancy he'd been, you know, doing it in most of the towns around."

"Really?" said Jamieson. "But you can't know that for sure, now can you?"

"Ah, but we can," said John, "for he was seen! Some of the locals had seen him going into… well, 'houses of ill repute', shall we put it that way? And a handful of the village's single men, whose morals also weren't all they might be, learned about George's reputation in those same, er, houses. But you'll know, James—and I'm sure that in your capacity as a doctor you *will* know—it's a sad but true fact that you do actually reap what you sow. And in George White's case, that was true in more ways than one."

"Which is where this becomes even more indelicate," Doreen got to her feet. "And I have things to do in the kitchen. So if you'll excuse me…" And leaving her jewellery box on the table she left the room and closed the door behind her. Then:

"George caught something," said John, quietly.

"He what?"

"Well, that's the only way I can explain it. He caught this bloody awful disease, presumably from some woman with whom he'd, er, associated. But that wasn't all."

"There's more?" Jamieson shook his head. "Poor Jilly."

"Poor Jilly, indeed! For little Anne was only a few months old when this slut from Newquay arrived in the village with her loathsome child—a baby she blamed on George White."

"Ah!" Jamieson nodded knowingly. "And the child was Geoff, right?"

"Of course. That same cretin, adopted by the Fosters, who shambles around the village even now. A retarded youth of some fifteen years—but who looks like and has the strength of an eighteen-

Anne's half-brother. And because I'm quite fond of Jilly, I find that…
that *creature* perfectly unbearable!"

"Not to mention dangerous," said Jamieson.

"Eh? What's that?" The other looked startled.

"I was out on my veranda," said the old man. "It was just the other
day, and I saw you with… with that young man. You seemed to be
engaged in some sort of confrontation."

"But that's it exactly!" said Tremain. "He's suddenly there—he
comes upon you, out of nowhere—and God only knows what goes
on in that misshapen head of his. Enough to scare the life out of a
man, coming over the dunes like that, and blowing like a stranded
fish! A damn great fish, yes, that's what he reminds me of. *Ugh!* And
it's how Tom Foster uses him, too!"

"What? Foster uses him?" Jamieson seemed totally engrossed. "In
what way? Are we talking about physical abuse?"

"No, no, nothing that bad!" Tremain held up his hands. "No, but
have you seen that retard swim? My God, if he had more than half
a brain he'd be training for the Olympics! What? Why, he's like a
porpoise in the water! *That's* how Foster uses him."

"I'm afraid I'm still not with you," Jamieson admitted, his
expression one of complete bafflement. "You're saying that this Foster
somehow uses the boy to catch fish?"

"Yes." The other nodded. "And if the weather hadn't been so bad
recently you wouldn't have seen nearly so much of the idiot on the
beach. No, for he'd have been out with Tom Foster in his boat. The
lad swims—in all weathers, apparently—to bring in the fish for that
degenerate who looks after him."

Jamieson laughed out loud, then stopped abruptly and asked,
"But… do you actually believe that? That a man can herd fish? I
mean, that's quite incredible!"

"Oh?" Tremain answered. "You think so? Then don't just take
my word for it but the next time you're in town go have a drink in
the Sailor's Rest. Get talking with any of the local fishermen and ask
them how come Foster always gets the best catches."

"But herding fish—" the old man began to protest.

And Tremain cut him off: "Now, I didn't say that. I said he brings them in—somehow attracts them." Then he offered a weak grin. "Yes, I'm well aware that sounds almost as silly. But—" He pursed his lips, shrugged and fell silent.

"So," said Jamieson. "Some truths, some rumours. But as far as I'm concerned, I still don't know it all. For instance, what was this awful disease you say George White contracted? What do you mean by 'awful'? All venereal diseases are pretty awful."

"Well, I suppose they are," Tremain answered. "But not like this one. There's awful and awful, but this was hideous. And he passed it down to his idiot child, too."

"He did what?"

"The way 'young Geoff' looks now, that was how George White looked in the months before he—"

"Died?"

"No." The other shook his head, grimly. "It's not as simple as that. George didn't just die, he took his own life." And:

"Ah!" said the old man. "So it was suicide."

Tremain nodded. "And I know this is a dreadful thing to say, but with a man like that—with his sexual appetites—surely it's just as well. A disease like that… why, he was a walking time bomb!"

"My goodness!" Jamieson exclaimed. "Was it never diagnosed? Can we put a name to it? Who was his doctor?"

"He wouldn't see a doctor. The more Jilly pressed him to do so, the more he retreated into himself. And only she could tell you what life must have been like with him, during his last few weeks. But since she'd already stuck it out for fifteen or more years, watching it gradually come out in him during all of that time… God, how strong she must have been!"

"Terrible, terrible!" said Jamieson—and then he frowned. "Yet Jilly and *her* child, I mean Anne—apparently they didn't come down with anything."

"No, and we can thank God for that!" said Tremain. "I think we'll have to assume that as soon as Jilly knew how sick George was, she—or they—stopped… well, you know what I mean."

"Yes." Jamieson nodded. "I do know: they were man and wife

in name only. But if both Anne and Geoff were born within a few months of each other—and if young Geoff was, well, *defective* from birth—then Anne is a very fortunate young woman indeed."

"Exactly," said Tremain. "And is it any wonder her mother's nerves are so bad? My wife and I, we've known the White's a lot longer than you, James, and I can assure you that there's never been a woman more watchful of her child than Jilly is of Anne."

"Watchful?"

Doreen had come back in, and she said, "Oh, yes. That girl, she can't cough or catch a cold, or even develop a pimple without having her mother fussing all over her. Why, Anne's skin is flawless, but if you should see them on the beach together next summer—and if Anne's skin gets a little red or rough from the sun and the sand—you watch Jilly's reaction."

And Tremain concurred. "It's a wonder Jilly so much as lets that kid out of the house…"

The subject changed; the conversation moved on; half an hour or so later Jamieson looked at his watch. "Almost time I was on my way," he said. "There are some programmes I want to watch on TV tonight." He turned to Doreen. "Before I go, however, you might like to show me that brooch of yours. You were, er, busy in the kitchen for a while when we were talking and I didn't much like to open the box in your absence."

"Yes," she said. "It was very thoughtful of you to wait for me." She opened the small velvet-lined box and passed it across to him. The brooch was pinned to a pad in the bottom of the box and the old man let it lie there, simply turning the box in his hand and looking at the brooch from all angles.

"You're absolutely right." He nodded after a moment or two. "Without a doubt it has a certain beauty, but it's also a very odd piece. And it's not the first time I've seen gold worked in this style. But you know…" Here he paused and frowned, apparently uncertain how best to continue.

"Oh?" she said. "Is something wrong?"

"Well—" he began to answer, then paused again and bit his lip. "Well, it's just that… I don't know. Perhaps I shouldn't mention it."

Doreen took back the box and brooch, and said, "But now you really *must* mention it! You have to! Do you think there's something wrong with the brooch? But then, what could be wrong with it? Some kind of fake, maybe? Poor quality gold? Or not gold at all!" Her voice was more strident, more high-pitched, moment by moment. "Is that it, James? Have I been cheated?"

"At the price, whatever it was you paid? Probably not. It's the meaning of the thing. It's what it stands for. Doreen, this isn't a lucky item."

"It's unlucky? In what way?"

"Well, anthropology was a hobby of mine no less than driftwood art is your husband's. And as for the odd style and native workmanship we see here… I believe you'll find this brooch is from the South Seas, where it was probably crafted by a tribal witch doctor."

"What? A witch doctor?" Doreen's hand went to her throat.

"Oh, yes." Jamieson nodded. "And having fashioned it from an alloy of local gold and some other lustrous metal, the idea would have been to lay a curse upon it, then to ensure it fell into the hands of an enemy. A kind of sympathetic magic—or in the poor victim's case, quite unsympathetic."

Now Doreen took the box back, and staring hard at its contents said, "To be honest, I've never much liked this thing. I only bought it out of some misguided sense of loyalty to Jilly, so that I could tell myself that at least some money was finding its way into that household. What with George's philandering and all, they couldn't have been very well off."

Her husband took the box off her, peered at the brooch for a few moments, and said, "I think you must be right, James. It isn't a very pleasant sort of thing at all. It's quite unearthly, really. These weird arabesques, not of any terrestrial foliage but more of…what? Interwoven seaweeds, kelp, suckered tentacles? And these scalloped edges you see in certain shells. I mean, it's undeniably striking in its looks—well, until you look closer. And then, why, you're absolutely right! It's somehow crude, as if crafted by some primitive islander."

He handed the box back to his wife who said, "I'll sell it at once! I believe I know the jewellers where George White got rid of those other pieces." And glancing at the old man: "It's not that I'm superstitious, you understand, but better not to risk it. You never know where this thing's been."

"Dear lady, you're so right," Jamieson said. "But myself, having an interest in this sort of thing—and being a doctor of an entirely different stamp—I find the piece fascinating So if you do decide to sell it, don't take it to a dealer but offer it to me first. And whatever you paid for it, I think we can safely say you won't be the worse off."

"Why, that's so very kind of you!" she said, seeing him to the door. "But are you sure?"

"Absolutely," the old man answered. "Give me a ring in the morning when you've had time to think it over, and let me know what I owe you."

With which the Tremains walked him to his car...

The winter came in quickly and savagely, keeping almost everyone in the village to their houses. With the fishermen's boats sheltering within the harbour wall, only the old Sailor's Rest was doing anything like good business.

Driving his car to work at the college in St. Austell over frequently washed-out and ever potholed roads, headmaster John Tremain cursed the day he'd bought his place (a) for its cheapness and (b) for its "seclusion and wild dramatic beauty". The seclusion was fine and dandy but he could do without the wildness of winters like this one, and of drama he'd had more than enough. Come spring and the first half-decent offer he got, he and Doreen would be out of here for a more convenient place in St. Austell. It would be more expensive, but what the hell... he'd sell the car, cycle to work, and save money on petrol and repairs.

As for the Whites: Jilly and Anne were more or less housebound, but they did have a regular visitor in the old American gentleman. James Jamieson had seemed to take to them almost as family, and never turned up on their doorstep without bringing some gift or other with him. Often as not it was food: a fresh pie from the bakery, a loaf of bread and slab of cheese, maybe a bottle of good wine. All to the good, for Jilly's old car was well past reliable, and Anne had to attend her piano and language lessons. Jamieson would drive the girl to and fro without complaint, and wouldn't accept a penny for all his kindness.

Also, when Anne went down with a sore throat, which served to drive her mother frantic with worry, Jamieson gave the girl a thorough examination and diagnosed a mild case of laryngitis. His remedy—one aspirin three times daily, and between times a good gargle with a spoonful of salt in water—worked wonders, for mother and daughter both! But his ministrations didn't stop there. For having now seen Jilly on several occasions when her nervous condition was at its worst, the old man had in fact prescribed for her, too; though not without protesting that in fact he shouldn't for he'd retired from all that. Nevertheless, the pills he made up for her did the trick, calming her nerves like nothing she'd tried before. They couldn't entirely relieve her obsession or anxieties with regard to Anne, however, though now when she felt compelled to fuss and fret her hands wouldn't shake so badly, and her at best fluffy mind would stay focussed for longer. Moreover, now that certain repetitive nightmares of long-standing no longer visited her quite so frequently, Jilly was pleased to declare that she was sleeping better...

Occasionally, when the weather was a little kinder, Anne would walk to her piano lesson at Miss Harding's thatched cottage on the far side of the village. Jilly would usually accompany her daughter part way, and use the occasion to visit the bakery or collect groceries at the post office. The winter being a hard one, such times were rare; more often than not, James Jamieson would arrive in his car in time to give Anne a lift. It got so that Jilly even expected him, and Anne—normally so retiring—had come to regard him as some kind of father or grandfather figure.

One day in mid-January, when the wind drove the waves high up the beach, and stinging hail came sleeting almost horizontally off the sea, the old man and his young passenger arrived at Miss Harding's place to find an agitated Tom Foster waiting for them—in fact waiting for Jamieson.

The old man had bumped into Foster once or twice before in the Sailor's Rest, and had found him a surly, bearded, weather-beaten brute with a gravelly voice and a habit of slamming his empty mug on the bar by way of catching the barman's attention and ordering another drink. He had few friends among the other fishermen and was as much a loner as any man Jamieson had ever known. Yet now, today, he was in need of a friend—or rather, in need of a doctor.

The village spinster, Miss Julia Harding, had kept Foster waiting in the small conservatory that fronted her cottage; he wasn't the sort of person she would allow in the house proper. But Foster, still shaking rain from his lank hair, and pacing to and fro—a few paces each way, which was all the conservatory allowed—pounced on Jamieson as soon as the old man was ushered into view by Miss Harding.

"It's the boy," he rasped, grabbing Jamieson's arm. "Can't get no sleep, the way um itches. I know'd you'd be comin' with the lass fer the teachin', and so I waited. But I do wish you'd come see the boy. I'd consider it a real favour, and Tom Foster dun't forget um that does um a favour. But it's more fer young Geoff'n fer me. Um's skin be raw from scratchin', so it be. And I got no car fer gettin' um inter the city… beside which, um dun't want no big city doctor. But um won't fuss any with you, if you'll come see um."

"I don't any longer practice…" The old man appeared at a loss what to do or say.

But Anne took his other arm. "Please go," she said. "Oh do *please* go and see Geoff! And I'll go with you."

Miss Harding wagged her finger at Anne, and said, "Oh? And what of your lesson, young lady?" But then, looking for support from Tom Foster and Jamieson, and seeing none, she immediately shook her head in self-denial. "No, no—whatever was I thinking? If something ails that poor lad, it's surely more important than a piano lesson. It must be, for Mr. Foster here, well, he's hardly one to get himself all stirred up on a mere whim—nor for anything much else, except maybe his fishing—and not even that on a bad day!"

"That I'm not," growled Foster, either ignoring or failing to recognise the spinster's jibe for what it really was. And to Jamieson: "Will you come?"

"Well," the old man sighed, "I don't suppose it can do any harm to see the boy, and I always carry my old medicine bag in the back of the car…not that there's a lot of medicine in it these days. But—" He threw up his hands, took Anne and Foster back out to his car, and drove them to the latter's house where it stood facing the sea across the harbour wall in Fore Street.

Tom Foster's wife, a small, black-haired, dark-complexioned woman, but not nearly as gnarled or surly as her husband, wiped her hands on her apron to clasp Jamieson's hand as she let them into the house. She said nothing but simply indicated a bedroom door where it stood ajar.

Geoff was inside, a bulky shape under a coarse blanket, and the room bore the unmistakable odour of fish—but then, so did the entire house. Wrinkling his nose, Jamieson glanced at Anne, but she didn't seem to have noticed the fish stink; all she was interested in was Geoff's welfare. As she approached the bed so its occupant seemed to sense her presence; the youth's bulbous, ugly head came out from under the blanket, and he stared at her with luminous green eyes. But:

"No, no, lass!" Tom Foster grunted. "I knows you be friends but you can't be in 'ere. Um's naked under that blanket, and um ain't nice ter look at what wi' um's scratchin' and all. So out you goes and Ma Foster'll see ter you in the front." And coarse brute of a man that he was, he gentled her out of the room.

As Foster closed the door behind her, so Jamieson drew up a chair close to the bed, and said, "Now then, young man, try not to be alarmed. I'm here to see what the trouble is." With which he began to turn back the blanket. A squat hand, short-fingered and thickly webbed, at once grasped the top edge of the blanket and held it fast. The old man saw blood under the sharp fingernails, the trembling of the unfortunate's entire body under the blanket, and the terror in his huge, moist, oh-so-deep eyes.

Foster immediately stepped forward. "Now, dun't you take on so, lad," he said. "This un's a doctor, um be. A friend ter the lass and 'er Ma. If you let um, um'll see ter your scratchin.'"

The thing called Geoff (for close-up he was scarcely human) opened his mouth and Jamieson saw his teeth, small but as sharp as needles. There was no threat in it, however—just a popping of those pouty lips, a soundless pleading almost—as the hand slowly relaxed its grip, allowing the old man to turn back the cover without further hindrance.

Despite that Foster was hovering over the old man, watching him closely, he saw no evidence of shock at what was uncovered: that scaly body—which even five years ago a specialist in St. Austell had called the worst case of ichthyosis he'd ever seen, now twice as bad at least—that body under a heavily wattled neck and sloping but powerful shoulders, and the raw, red areas on the forearms and under the ribcage where the rough grey skin had been torn. And as the old man opened his bag and called for hot water and a clean towel, Foster nodded his satisfaction. He had done the right thing sure enough, and Jamieson was a doctor good and true who would care for a life even if it were such as this one under the blanket.

But as Foster turned away to answer Jamieson's request, the old man took his arm and said, "Tom, do you care for him?"

"Eh?" Foster grunted. "Why, me and my old girl, we've cared fer um fer fifteen years! And in fifteen years you can get used ter things, even them things that never gets no better but only worse. And as fer folks—even poorly made 'uns such as the boy—why, in time you can even get fond of 'em, so you can!"

Jamieson nodded and said, "Then look after him better." And he let Foster go…

Anne saw the wet, pink-splotched towels when Mrs Foster brought them out of Geoff's room. And then Tom Foster allowed her in.

The old man was putting his things back into his bag as she hurried to the bedside. There was a clean white sheet under the blanket now, and it was tucked up under Geoff's blob of a chin. The youth's neck was bandaged to hold a dressing under his left ear; his right arm lay on top of the blanket, the forearm bandaged where a red stain was evidence of some small seepage.

"What was it?" Anne snatched a breath, touching her hand to her lips and staring at Jamieson wide-eyed, her face drawn and pale, even paler than usual. "Oh, what was it?"

"A skin disorder," he told her. "Something parasitic—like lice or scabies—but I think I got all of it. No need to worry about it, however. It must have been uncomfortable for him, but it certainly wasn't deadly. Geoff will recover, I assure you."

And Tom Foster said, "Anythin' I can do fer you, Mr. Jamieson, sir, jus' you ask. I dun't forget um who's done me or mine a favour—no, not never."

"Well, Tom," Jamieson answered, "I might come to you for a nice piece of fish some time, and that would be payment enough for what little I've done here. Right now, though, we've other things to talk about." He turned to the girl. "Anne, if you'll wait in the car?"

Anne had sat down in the chair by the bed. She was holding Geoff's hand and they were looking at each other, and Jamieson couldn't help noticing a striking similarity in the deep green colour of their eyes... but *only* in their colour. It was true that Anne's eyes were slightly, almost unnoticeably protuberant, but as for the other's...

...In his current physical condition, and despite that his eyes were huge and bulging, even more so than was usual, still the old man had to grant them the dubious distinction of being Geoff's most human feature!

And now the youth had taken his hand from the girl's, and his stubby fingers were moving rapidly, urgently, making signs which she appeared to understand and began answering in a like fashion. This "conversation" lasted only a moment or so longer, until Geoff turned his watery gaze on Jamieson and twisted his face into what had to be his version of a smile. At which Anne said:

"He says I'm to thank you for him. So thank you." Then she stood up and left the room and the house...

Inside the front door, Jamieson spoke to Tom Foster in lowered tones. "Do you know what I dug out and scraped off him?"

"How'd I know that?" the other protested. "You be the doctor."

"Oh?" said the old man. "And you be the fisherman, but you tell me you've never seen such as that before? Very well, then I'll tell you: they were fish-lice, Tom. Copepods, small crustaceans that live on fish as parasites. Now then, Mr. Fisherman—tell me you've never seen fish-lice before."

The other looked away, then slowly nodded. "I've seen 'em, sure enough. Usually on plaice or flounder, flatties or bottom-feeders. But on a man? In the flesh of a man?" And now he shook his head. "I jus' dint want ter believe it, that's all."

"Well, now you can believe it," said Jamieson. "And the only way he could have got them was by frequent periods of immersion in the sea. They got under his skin where it's especially scaly and fed there like ticks on a dog. They were dug in quite deep, so I know he's had them for a long time."

"Oh? And are you sayin' I ain't looked after um, then?" Tom was angry now. "Well, I'm tellin' you as how I dint see 'em on um afore! And anyways, you answer me this—if um's had 'em so long, why'd they wait ter flare up now, eh?"

The old man nodded. "Oh, I think I can tell you that, Tom. It's because his skin was all dried out. And because they need it damp, they started digging in for the moisture in his blood. So all of a sudden the boy was itching and hurting. And when he scratched, the hurt only got worse. That's what happened here. So now then, you can tell me something: when were you last out at sea, Tom? *Not recently*, I'll wager!"

"Ah-*hah*!" The other narrowed his eyes, thrust his chin out. "So then, Mr. Jamieson. You've been alistenin' ter rumours, eh? And what did them waggin' village tongues tell you… that Tom Foster makes um's poor dumb freak swim fer um? And that um gets um ter chase up the fish fer um? *Hah!*" He shook his head. "Well it ain't so! That 'un swims 'cos um *likes* ter swim, and 'cos um *wants* ter swim—and in all weathers if I dun't be watchin' um! That's all there be ter such tall stories. But if you be askin' does um know where the best fish can be found? Then you're damn right um do, and that's why I gets the best catch—always! So then, what else can I tell you?"

"Nothing, Tom," said Jamieson. "But there is something you can do for that youth. If he wants to swim, let him—you don't need to let the village see it. And if he gets… well, infested again, you saw me working and know what to do. But whatever you do, you mustn't let him dry out like that again. No, for it seems to me his skin needs that salt water…"

It had stopped hailing, and protected by the building Anne was waiting just outside the door. Since the door had been standing ajar, she must have heard the old man's and Foster's conversation. But she said nothing until they were in the car. Then:

"He had fish-lice?" It wasn't a shocked exclamation, just a simple enquiry.

And starting up the car Jamieson answered, "Oh, people are prone to all kinds of strange infections and infestations. I've heard it said that AIDS—a disease caused by immune deficiency—came from monkeys; and there's that terrible CJD that you can get from eating contaminated or incorrectly processed beef. And how about psittacosis? From parrots, of all things! As for that poor boy: well, what can I say? He likes to swim."

"It's very strange," she said, as Jamieson drove out of the village, "but my father… he didn't like the sea. Not at all. He had those books about it—about the sea and other things—and yet was afraid of it. He used to say it lured him. They say he killed himself, suicide, and perhaps he did; but at least he did it his way. I remember he once said to me, 'If a time comes when I must go, it won't take me alive'. Toward the end he used to say all sorts of things that didn't make a lot of sense, but I think he was talking about the sea."

"And what makes you think that?" Jamieson asked her, glancing at her out of the corner of his eye, and aware that she was watching him, probably to gauge his reaction.

"Well, because of the way he did it… jumped off the cliff at South Point, down onto the rocks. He washed up on the beach, all broken up."

"How awful!" The old man swung the car onto the lonely road to Jilly White's house. "And yet you and your mother, you continue to live right here, almost on the beach itself."

"I think that's because she needs to be sure about certain things," the girl answered. "Needs to be sure of me, perhaps?"

Jamieson saw Jilly standing on the doorstep and stopped the car outside the house. He would have liked to carry on talking, to have the girl clarify her last cryptic remark, or learn more about the books she'd mentioned—her father's books, about the sea. But Jilly was already coming forward. And now Anne touched the old man's arm and said, "It's best she doesn't know we were at the Fosters'. If she knew about Geoff's fish-lice, it might only set her off again."

Then, lifting her voice a little as she got out of the car, she said, "Thanks again for the ride." And in a whisper added, "And for what you did for Geoff…"

The winter dragged on. Jamieson spent some of the time driving, visiting the local towns, even going as far afield as Falmouth and Penzance. And to break the boredom a little, usually there would be a weekly "social evening" alternating between Jilly's, the Tremains's, and Jamieson's place. The old man even managed to inveigle Jilly into joining him and the Tremains in a visit to the dilapidated Sailor's Rest one night.

On that occasion Anne went with them. She was under-age for drinking—even for being in the pub—but the proprietor knew her, of course, and served her orange juice; and in any case it wasn't as if the place was about to be raided.

Their table was close to a great open fireplace where logs popped and hissed, and the pub being mainly empty, the service couldn't be faulted. In an atmosphere that was quietly mellow, the country food bought fresh from the village bakery was very good. Even Jilly appeared clear-headed and in good spirits for once, and as for the Tremains: putting their customary, frequently unwarranted snobbery aside, they were on their very best behaviour.

That was the up-side, but the down-side was on its way. It came as the evening drew to a close in the forms of the fisherman Tom Foster, and that of his ward the shambling Geoff, when the pair came in from the cold and took gloomy corner seats at a small table. It was doubtful that they had noticed the party seated near the fire on the far side of the room, but Foster's narrowed eyes had certainly scanned the bar area before he ushered his ward and companion to their more discreet seats.

And as suddenly as that the evening turned sour. "Checking that his enemies aren't in," said Tremain under his breath. "I can understand that. He's probably afraid they'll report him."

"His enemies?" said Jamieson. "The other village fishermen, you mean? Report him for what?"

"See for yourself," said the other, indicating the barman, who was on his way to Foster's corner with a tray. "A pint for Tom, and a half for that… for young Geoff. He lets that boy drink here—alcohol, mind— and him no older than Anne here. I mean, it's one thing to have that… well, that poor unfortunate in the village, but quite another to deliberately addle what few brains he's got with strong drink!"

Anne, visibly stiffening in her chair, at once spoke up in the youth's defence. "Geoff isn't stupid," she said. "He can't speak very well, and he's different, but he isn't stupid." And staring pointedly at Tremain, "He isn't ignorant, either."

The headmaster's mouth fell open. "Well, I…!" But before he could say more:

"John, you asked for that," Doreen told him. "You're aware that Anne is that youth's friend. Why, she's probably the only friend he's got! You should mind what you say."

"But I…" Tremain began to protest, only to have Jamieson step in with:

"Oh, come, come! Let's not ruin the pleasant evening we're having. Surely our opinions can differ without that we have to fight over them? If Tom Foster does wrong, then he does wrong. But I say let that youth have whatever pleasures he can find."

"And I agree," said Doreen, glowering at her husband. "God only knows he'll find few enough!"

With which they fell silent, and that was that. Things had been said that couldn't be retracted, and as for the evening's cosy atmosphere and light-hearted conversation: suddenly everything had fallen flat. They tried to hang on to it but were too late. John Tremain took on a haughty, defensive attitude, while his wife turned cold and distant. Jilly retreated quietly into herself again, and young Anne's presence continued to register only by virtue of her physically being there— but as for her thoughts, they could be anywhere…

After that, such get-togethers were few and far between. Their friendship—the fact that the Tremains, Whites, and Jamieson stuck together at all—continued on a far less intimate level, surviving mainly out of necessity; being of the village's self-appointed upper crust, they couldn't bring themselves to mingle too freely with those on the lower rungs of the social ladder.

The old man was the odd-man-out—or rather the pig-in-the-middle; while he maintained contact with the Tremains, Jamieson never failed to assist Jilly and Anne White whenever the opportunity presented itself. Moreover, he visited the Sailor's Rest from time to time, building at least tentative friendships with several of the normally taciturn locals. The Tremains reckoned him either a fool or a saint, while the Whites—both of them—saw him as a godsend.

One evening in early March Jilly called the old man, ostensibly to tell him she was running low on medication, the pills which he'd prescribed and made up for her. But Jamieson sensed there was more than that to her call. The woman's voice hinted of loneliness, and the old man's intuition was that she wanted someone to talk to… or someone to talk to her.

He at once drove to her house.

Waiting for his knock, Jilly made him welcome with a glass of sherry. And after he had handed over a month's supply of her pills, and she had offered him a chair, she said, "I feel such an idiot calling you so late when I've had all day to remember my medication was getting low. I hope you don't mind?"

"Not at all, my dear," the old man answered. "If anything, I'm just a little concerned that you may be taking too many of those things. I mean, by my calculations you should still have a fortnight's supply at least. Of course, I could be wrong. My memory's not as keen as it used to be. But…?"

"Oh!" she said. And then, quickly recovering: "Ah! No—not at all—your memory's fine. I'm the one at fault. For like a fool I... well, I *spilled* some pills the other day, and didn't like to use them after they'd been on the floor."

"Very sensible, too!" he answered. "And anyway, I've let it go too long without asking you how you've been feeling. But you see, Jilly, I'm not getting any younger, and what used to be my bedside manner is all shot to pieces. I certainly wouldn't like to think those pills of mine were doing you any harm."

"Doing me harm? On the contrary," she replied. "I think I'm feeling better. I'm calmer—perhaps a little easier in my mind—but... Well, just a moment ago, James, you were complaining about your memory. *Huh!* I should be so lucky! No, I don't think it's your pills—though it could be a side-effect—but I do seem to stumble a lot. And I don't just mean in my speech or my memory, but also physically. My balance is off, and I sometimes feel quite weak. You may have noticed?"

"Side-effects, yes." He nodded. "You could be right. But in a remote place like this it's easy to get all vague and forgetful. I mean, who do you talk to? You see me occasionally—and of course there's Anne— but that's about it." He looked around the room, frowning. "Talking about Anne, where is she?"

"Sleeping." Jilly held a finger to her lips. "What with the weather improving and all, she's been doing a lot of walking on the beach. Walking and reading, and so intelligent! Haven't you ever wondered why she isn't at school? They had nothing more to teach her, that's why. She left school early, shortly after her father... after George... after he..." She paused, touched her hand to her brow, looked suddenly vague.

"Yes, I understand," said the old man, and waited.

In another moment Jilly blinked; and shaking her head as if to clear it, she said, "I'm sorry, what were you saying?"

"I was just wondering if there was anything else I could do for you," Jamieson answered. "Apart from delivering your pills, that is. Did you want to talk, perhaps? For after all, we could all of us use a little company, some friendly conversation from time to time."

"Talk?" she said—and then the cloud lifted from her brow. "Ah, *talk*! Now I remember! It was something you were telling me one time, but we were somehow interrupted. I think it was Anne. Yes, she came on the scene just as you were going to talk about... about... wasn't it that coastal town in America, the place that George came from, that you were telling me about?"

"Innsmouth?" said the old man. "Yes, I believe I recall the occasion. But I also recall how nervous you were. And Jilly, in my opinion—from what I've observed of you, er, in my capacity as a doctor or ex-doctor— it seems to me that odd or peculiar subjects have a very unsettling effect on you. Are you sure you want to hear about Innsmouth?"

"While it's true that certain subjects have a bad affect on me," she began slowly, "at the same time I'm fascinated by anything concerning my husband's history or his people. Especially the latter, his genealogy." She speeded up a little. "After all what do we really know of genetics—those traits we carry down the generations with us—traits passed on by our forebears? And I think to myself, perhaps I've been avoiding George's past for far too long. Things have happened here, James..." She clutched his arm. "Weird alterations, alienations, and I need to be sure they can't ever happen again, not to me or mine!" She was going full tilt now. "Or if they do happen, that I'll know what to do—what to do about—do about..."

But there Jilly stopped dead, with her mouth still open, as if she suddenly realised that she'd said too much, too quickly, and even too desperately.

And after a long moment's silence the old man quietly said, "Maybe I'd better ask you again, my dear: are you sure you want me to tell you about Innsmouth?"

She took a deep breath, deliberately stilled the twitching of her slender hands on the arms of her chair, and said "Yes, I really would like to know all about that place and its people."

"And after I've gone, leaving you on your own here tonight? What of your dreams, Jilly? For I feel I must warn you: you may well be courting nightmares."

"I want to know," she answered at once. "As for nightmares: you're right, I can do without them. But still I *have* to know."

"Anne has told me there are some books that belonged to her

father." Jamieson tried to reason with her. "Perhaps the answer you're seeking can be found in their pages?"

"George's books?" She shuddered. "Those ugly books! He used to bury himself in them. But when they were heaping the seaweed and burning it last summer, I asked Anne to throw them into the flames!" She offered a nervous, perhaps apologetic shrug. "What odds? I couldn't have read them anyway, for they weren't in English; they weren't in any easily recognisable language. But the worst thing was the way they felt. Why, just touching them made me feel queasy!"

The old man narrowed his eyes, nodded and said, "And do you really expect me to talk about Innsmouth, when the very thought of a few mouldy old books makes you look ill? And you asked the girl to burn them, without even knowing their value or what was in them? You know, it's probably a very good thing I came along when I did, Jilly. For it's fairly obvious that you're obsessed about something, and obsessions can all too easily turn to psychoses. Wherefore—"

"—You're done with me," she finished it for him, and fell back in her chair. "I'm ill with worry—or with my own, well, 'obsession' if you like—and you're not going to help me with it."

The old man took her hand, squeezed it, and shook his head. "Oh, Jilly!" he said. "You've got me all wrong. Psychology may be one of our more recently accepted medical sciences, but I'm not so ancient that I predate it in its entirety! Yes, I know a thing or two about the human psyche; more than enough to assure you that there's not much wrong with yours."

She looked bewildered, and so Jamieson continued, "You see, my dear, you're finally opening up, deliberately exposing yourself to whatever your problem is, taking your first major step toward getting rid of it. So of course I'm going to help you."

She sighed her relief, then checked herself and said, "But, if that involves telling me about Innsmouth—?"

"Then so be it," said the old man. "But I would ask you not to interrupt me once I start, for I'm very easily side-tracked." And after Jilly nodded her eager assent, he began…

* * *

"During my time at my practice in Innsmouth, I saw some strange sad cases. Many locals are inbred, to such an extent that their blood is tainted. I would very much like to be able to put that some other way, but no other way says it so succinctly. And the 'Innsmouth look'—a name given to the very weird, almost alien appearance of some of the town's inhabitants—is the principal symptom of that taint.

"However, among the many myths and legends I've heard about that place and those with 'the look', some of the more fanciful have it the other way round; they insist that it wasn't so much inbreeding that caused the taint as miscegenation… the *mixed* breeding between the town's old-time sea captains and the women of certain South Sea island tribes with which they often traded during their voyages. And what's more, the same legends have it that it wasn't only the native *women* with whom these degenerate old sea dogs associated, but… but I think it's best to leave that be for now, for tittle-tattle of that nature can so easily descend into sheer fantasy.

"Very well, but whatever the origin or source of the town's problems—the *real* source, that is—it's still possible that it may at least have some *connection* with those old sea-traders and the things they brought back with them from their ventures. Certainly some of them married and brought home native women—which in this day and age mightn't cause much of a stir, but in the mid-19th century was very much frowned upon—and in their turn these women must surely have brought some of their personal belongings and customs with them: a few native gewgaws, some items of clothing, their 'cuisine', of course… possibly even something of their, er, religions? Or perhaps 'religion' is too strong a word for what we should more properly accept as primitive native beliefs.

"In any case, that's as far back as I was able to trace the blood taint—if such it is—but as for the 'Innsmouth look' itself, and the horrible way it manifested itself in the town's inhabitants… well, I think the best way to describe that is as a disease; yes, and perhaps more than one disease at that.

"As to the form or forms this affliction takes," (now Jamieson began to lie, or at least to step aside from the truth,) "well, if I didn't know any better, I might say that there's a fairly representative example or specimen, as it were, right here in our own backyard: that poor unfortunate youth who lives with the Fosters, Anne's friend, young Geoff. Of course, I don't know of any connection—and can't see how there could possibly be one—but that youth would seem to have something much akin to the Innsmouth stigma, if not the self-same affliction. Just take a look at his condition:

"The unwholesome scaliness of the skin, far worse than any mere ichthyosis; the strange, shambling gait; the eyes, larger than normal and increasingly difficult to close; the speech—where such exists at all—or the guttural gruntings that pass for speech; and those gross anomalies or distortions of facial arrangement giving rise to fishy or froggy looks... and all of these features present in young Geoff. Why, John Tremain tells me that the youth reminds him of nothing so much as a stranded fish! And if somehow there is something of the Innsmouth taint in him... well then, is it any wonder that such dreadful fantasies came into being in the first place? I think not..."

Pausing, the old man stared hard at Jilly. During his discourse she had turned very pale, sunk down into her chair, and gripped its arms with white-knuckled hands. And for the first time he noticed grey in her hair, at the temples. She had not, however, given way to those twitches and jerks normally associated with her nervous condition, and all of her attention was still rapt upon him.

Now Jamieson waited for Jilly's reaction to what he'd told her so far, and in a little while she found her voice and said, "You mentioned certain gewgaws that the native women might have brought with them from those South Sea islands. Did you perhaps mean jewellery, and if so have you ever seen any of it? I mean, what *kind* of gewgaws, exactly? Can you describe them for me?"

For a moment the old man frowned, then said, "Ah!" and nodded his understanding. "But I think we may be talking at cross purposes, Jilly. For where those native women are concerned—in connection with their belongings—I actually *meant* gewgaws: bangles and necklaces made from seashells, and ornaments carved out of coconut shells... that sort of thing. But it's entirely possible I know what *you* mean by gewgaws... for of course I've seen that brooch that Mrs. Tremain purchased from your husband. Oh yes; and since I have a special interest in such items, I bought it back from her! But in fact the only genuine 'gewgaws' in the tales I've heard were the cheap trinkets which those old sea captains offered the islanders in so-called 'trade'. Trade? Daylight robbery, more like! While the gewgaws that *you* seem to be interested in have to be what those poor savages parted with in exchange for those worthless beads and all that useless frippery— by which I mean the quaintly worked jewellery, but *real jewellery,* in precious golden alloy, that Innsmouth's seafarers as good as stole from the natives! And you ask have I actually seen such? Indeed I have, and not just the piece I bought from Doreen Tremain…"

The old man had seemed to be growing more and more excited, carried away by his subject, apparently. But now, calming down, he paused to collect his thoughts and settled himself deeper in his chair before continuing. And:

"There now," he finally said. "Didn't I warn you that I was easily side-tracked? And wouldn't you know it, but now I've completely lost the thread!"

"I had asked you about that native jewellery," she reminded him. "I thought maybe you could describe it for me, or at least tell me where you saw it. And there was something else you said—something about the old sea captains and… and *things* they associated with other than the natives?—that I somehow found, well, interesting."

"Ah!" the old man answered. "But I can assure you, my dear, that last was sheer fantasy. And as for the jewellery… where did I see it? Why, in Innsmouth itself, where else? In a museum there—well, a sort of museum—but more properly a shrine, or a site of remembrance, really. I suppose I could tell you about it if you still wish it? And if you're sure none of this is too troubling for you?" The way he looked at her, his gaze was very penetrating. But having come this far, Jilly wasn't about to be put off.

"I do wish it," she nodded. "And I promise you I'll try not… not to be troubled. So do please go on."

The old man nodded and stroked his chin, and after a while carried on with his story.

"Anthropology, the study of man's origins and ways of life, was always something of a hobby of mine," he began. "And crumbling old Innsmouth, despite its many drawbacks, was not without its sources—its own often fascinating history and background—which as yet I've so poorly delineated.

"Some of the women—I can't really call them ladies—who attended my practice were of the blood. Not necessarily tainted blood but native blood, certainly. Despite the many generations separating them from their dusky forebears, still there was that of the South Sea islands in them. And it was a handful of these patients of mine, my clients, so to speak, that led to my enquiries after the jewellery they wore… the odd clasp or brooch, a wrist bangle or necklace. I saw quite a few, all displaying a uniform, somehow rude style of workmanship, and all very similarly adorned or embellished.

"But as for a detailed description, that's rather difficult. Floral? No, not really. Arabesque? That would more properly fit the picture; weird foliage and other plant forms, curiously and intricately intertwined… but not foliage of the land. It was oceanic: seaweeds and sea grasses, with rare conches and fishes hidden in the design—particularly fishes—forming what may only be described as an unearthly piscine or perhaps batrachian depiction. And occasionally, as a backdrop to the seaweeds and grasses, there were hinted buildings: strange, squat pyramids, and oddly angled towers. It was as if the unknown craftsman—who or whatever—had attempted to convey the lost Atlantis or some other watery civilisation…"

The old man paused again, then said, "There. As a description, however inadequate, that will have to suffice. Of course, I was never so close to the Innsmouth women that I was able to study their clasps and brooches in any great detail, but I did enquire of them as to their origin. Ah, but they were a close-mouthed lot and would say very little… well, except for one, who was younger and less typical of her kind; and she directed me to the museum.

"In its heyday it had been a church—that was before the tainted blood had moved in and the more orthodox religions out—a squat-towered stone church, yes, but long since desanctified. It stood close to another once-grand building: a pillared hall of considerable size, still bearing upon its pediment the faded legend, ESOTERIC ORDER OF DAGON.

"Dagon, eh? But here a point of great interest:

"Many years ago, this great hall, too, had been a place of worship... or obeisance of some sort, certainly. And how was this for an anthropological puzzle? For of course the fish-god Dagon—half-man, half-fish—had been a deity of the Philistines, later to be adopted by the Phoenicians who called him Oannes. And yet these Polynesian islanders, thousands of miles away around the world, had offered up their sacrifices—or at least their prayers—to the self-same god. And in the Innsmouth of the 1820s their descendants were carrying on that same tradition! But you know, my dear, and silly as it may seem, I can't help wondering if perhaps they're doing it still... I mean today, even now.

"But there you go, I've side-tracked myself again! So where was I? Ah, yes! The old church, or rather the museum.

"The place was Gothic in its looks, with shuttered windows and a disproportionately high basement. And it was there in the half-sunken basement—the museum proper—that the 'exhibits' were housed. There under dusty glass in unlocked boxwood cases, I saw such a fabulous collection of golden jewellery and ornaments... why, it amazed me that there were no labels to describe the treasure, and more so that there was no curator to guard it against thieves or to enlighten casual visitors with its story! Not that there were many visitors. Indeed, on such occasions as I was there I saw no one—not even a church mouse.

"But that jewellery, made of those strange golden alloys... oh, it was truly fascinating! As was a small, apparently specialised library of some hundreds of books; all of them antiques, and all quietly rotting away on damp, easily-accessible shelves. Apart from one or two titles of particularly unpleasant connotation, I recognised nothing that I saw; and, since most of those titles were in any case beyond me, I never so much as paused to turn a page. But as with the exotic, alien jewellery—and *if* I had been a thief, of course—I'm sure I might have walked out of there with a fortune in rare and forbidden volumes under my coat, and no one to stop, accuse or search me. In fact, searching my memory, I believe I've heard mention that certain books and a quantity of jewellery were indeed stolen from the museum some twenty-odd years ago. Not that gold was ever of any great rarity in Innsmouth, for those old sea captains had brought it home in such large amounts that back in the 1800s one of them had even opened up a refinery in order to purify his holdings! I tried to visit the refinery, too, only to find it in a state of total dereliction… as was much of the old town itself in the wake of a… well, of a rumoured epidemic, and subsequent government raids in 1927–28. But there, that's another story."

And fidgeting a very little—seeming suddenly reticent—Jamieson brought his narrative to an abrupt halt, saying, "And there you have it, my dear. With regard to your question about the strange jewellery… well, I've tried to answer it as best possible. So, er, what else can I tell you? Nothing, I fear…"

But now it was Jilly White's eyes searching the old man's face, and not the other way about. For she had noticed several vague allusions and some major omissions in his narrative, for which she required explanations.

"About the jewellery… yes, I believe I understand," she said. "But you've said some other things that aren't nearly so clear. In fact you seemed to be avoiding certain subjects. And I w-w-want… I *wan-w-w*…!" She slammed her arms down on the arms of her chair, trying to control her stammering. "I *want* to know! About—how did you put it?—the *associations* of those old sea captains with something other than the island women, which you said was sheer fantasy. But fantasy or not, I want to know. And about… about their beliefs… their religion and d-d-*dedication* to Dagon. Also, w-w-with regard to that foreign jewellery, you said something about its craftsman, '*who or whatever!*' Now what did you mean by that? And that epidemic you mentioned: what was all that about? What, an epidemic that warranted government raids? James—if you're my friend at all— surely you m-m-*must* see that I have to know!"

"I can see that I've upset you," he answered, reaching out and touching her hand. "And I believe I know what it is that's so unsettling for you. You're trying to connect all of this to George, aren't you? You think that his blood, too, was tainted. Jilly, it may be so, but it's not your fault. And if the taint is in fact a disease, it probably wasn't his fault either. You can't blame yourself that your husband may have been some kind of… of carrier. And even if he was, surely his influence is at an end now? You mustn't go on believing that it… that it isn't over yet."

"Then convince me otherwise," she answered, a little calmer now that she could speak openly of what was on her mind. "Tell me about these things, so that I'll better understand them and be able to make up my own mind."

Jamieson nodded. "Oh, I can tell you," he said, "if only by repeating old wives tales—myths and rumours—and fishermen's stories of mermaids and the like. But the state of your nerves, I'd really rather not."

"My nerves, yes," she said. "Wait." And she fetched a glass of water and took two of her pills. "There, and now you can see that I'm following doctor's orders. Now *you* must follow my orders and tell me." And leaning forward in her chair, she gripped his forearms. "Please. If not for my sake… for Anne's?"

And knowing her meaning, how could he refuse her?

"Very well," the old man answered. "But my dear, this thing you're worrying about, it is—it *has* to be—a horrible disease, and nothing more. So don't go mixing fantasy and reality, for that way lies madness."

And after a moment's thought he told her the rest of it…

"The stories I've heard… well, they were incredible. Legends born of primitive innocence and native ignorance both. You see, with regard to Dagon, those islanders had their own myths which had been handed down from generation to generation. Their blood and looks being so debased, and the taint having such a hold on them— probably since time immemorial—they reasoned that they had been created in the image of their maker, the fish-god himself, Dagon.

"Indeed they told those old sea captains just such stories, and also that in return for worshipping Dagon they'd been given all the wealth of the oceans in the abundance of fish they were able to catch, and in the strange golden alloy, which was probably washed out of their mountains in rainy-season streams. It would be the native priests, of course—their witch doctors, priests of Dagon or his 'esoteric order'— who secretly worked the gold into the jewellery whose remnants we occasionally see today.

"But the modern legend—the one you'll hear in Innsmouth and its environs—is that in return for the good fishing and the gold, the natives gave of their children to the sea, or to man-like beings who lived in the sea: the so-called 'Deep Ones', servitors of Dagon and other alleged, er, 'deities' of the deep, such as Great Cthulhu and Mother Hydra. And the same legend has it that Innsmouth's sea captains, in their lust for alien gold, the favours of mainly forgotten gods out of doubtful myths, and the promise of life everlasting, followed suit in the sacrifice of *their* young to Dagon and the Deep Ones. Except they were not sacrifices as such but matings! Thus in *both* legends, it became possible to blame the 'Innsmouth look' or taint on this miscegenation: the mingling of Deep One and clean human blood. But of course no such matings took place because there's no such thing as a merman! Nor was there ever, but that didn't stop a handful of the more degenerate Innsmouth people from adopting the cult, as witness that weathered, white-pillared hall dedicated to the Esoteric Order of Dagon.

"Which leaves only the so-called 'epidemic' of 1927–28…

"Well, seventy years ago our society was far less tolerant. And sad to say that when stories leaked out of Innsmouth of the sheer scale of the taint—the numbers of inbred, diseased and malformed people living there—the federal government's reaction was excessive in the extreme. But there's little doubt that it would have been the same if AIDS had been found there in the same period: panic, and a knee-jerk reaction, yes. And so there followed a vast series of raids and many arrests, and a burning and dynamiting of large numbers of rotting old houses along the waterfront. But no criminal charges were brought and no one was committed for trial; just vague statements about malignant diseases, and the covert dispersal of a great many detainees into various naval and military prisons.

"Thus old Innsmouth was depopulated, and these seventy-odd years later its recovery is still only very sluggish. There is, however, a modern laboratory there now, where pathologists and other scientists—some of them Innsmouth people themselves—continue to study the taint and to offer what help they may to the descendants of survivors of those frenzied federal raids. I worked there myself, however briefly, but it was disheartening work to say the least. I saw sufferers in every stage of degeneration, and could only offer the most basic assistance to any of them. For among the doctors and other specialists there… well, the general consensus is that there's no hope for a cure as yet for those with the Innsmouth blood. And until or unless the taint is allowed to die out by gradual dispersion or depletion of that diseased foreign gene pool, there shall always be those with the Innsmouth look…"

Jilly was as calm as Jamieson had ever seen her now—too calm, he thought—like the calm before a storm. Her eyes were unblinking and had a distant quality, but her look was reflective rather than vague or vacant. And finally, after a few long moments of silence, the old man prompted her, "What now, Jilly? Is something still bothering you?"

Her gaze focussed on him and she said, "Yes. I think there is one more thing. You said something about everlasting life—that the Innsmouth seafarers had been promised everlasting life if they embraced the worship of Dagon and these other cult figures. But… what if they reneged on the cult, turned back from such worship? You see, toward the end George frequently rambled in his sleep, and I'd often hear him say that he didn't *want* to live forever, not like that. He meant his condition, of course. But I can't believe—no, no, I *can*! I *do*!—that *he* believed in s-s-such things. So, do you think—I mean, is it p-p-possible—that my husband was once a m-member of that old Innsmouth c-c-cult? And could there be anything of t-truth in it? I mean, anything at all?"

Jamieson shook his head. "Anything to it? Only in his mind, my dear. For you see, as George's condition worsened, it would have been more than a merely physical thing. He would have been doing what you are doing: looking for an explanation where none exists. And having had to do with those cultists—and knowing the legends—he might have come to believe that certain things were true. But as for you, you mustn't. You simply mustn't!"

BRIAN LUMLEY

"B-b-but that tainted blood," she said, her voice a whisper now, as if from far away. "His blood, and Geoff's blood, and… and w-w-what of Anne's?"

"Jilly, now I want you to listen." The old man took hold of her arms, grasping her very firmly. And of all the lies or half-truths he had told her in the past half-hour, the next would be his biggest deceit of all. "Jilly, I have known you and Anne—especially Anne—for quite a while now, and from my knowledge of the Innsmouth taint, and also from what I know and have seen of your daughter, I would be glad to stake my reputation on the fact that she is as normal as you or I."

At which she sighed, relaxing a little in her chair…

And taking that as his signal to depart, Jamieson stood up. "I must be off," he said. "It's late and I've some things to do before bed." Then, as he made his way to the door, he said: "Do give my regards to Anne, won't you? It's a shame I missed her—or perhaps not, since we needed to have our talk."

Jilly had followed him—rather stumblingly, he thought—and at the door said, "I really d-d-don't know how to thank you. My mind feels so much more at ease now. But then it always does after I-I-I've spoken with you." She waited until he'd got into his car, and waved him a shaky goodbye before closing the door.

Pulling away from the house, the old man noticed an almost furtive flicker of movement in the drapes of an upstairs window. It was Anne's bedroom; and very briefly he saw her face—those huge eyes of hers—in the gap of partly drawn-aside curtains. At which he wondered how long she had been awake; even wondered if she had been asleep! And if not, how much she'd overheard.

Or had she perhaps already known it all…?

The long winter with its various ailments—Anne White's laryngitis, and Doreen Tremain's 'flu—merged slowly into spring; green shoots became flowers in village gardens or window-boxes; lowering skies brightened, becoming bluer day to day.

But among these changes were others, not nearly so natural and far less benign, and old Jamieson was witness to them all.

He would see the beachcomber—"young Geoff", indeed, as if he were just another village youth—shambling along the tidemark. But he wasn't like other youths, and he was ailing.

Jamieson watched him in his binoculars, that tired shambler on the shore: his slow lurching, feet flip-flopping, shoulders sloping, head down and collar up. And despite that the weather was much improved, he no longer went out to sea. Oh, he *looked* at the sea—constantly pausing to lift his ugly head and gaze out across that wide wet horizon—gaze longingly, the old man thought, as he attempted to read something of emotion into the near-distant visage—but the youth's great former ability in the water, and his untried but suspected strength on dry land, these seemed absent now. Plainly put, he was in decline.

The old man had heard rumours in the village pub. The fishing was much improved but Tom Foster wasn't doing as well as in previous years; he'd lost his good luck charm, the backward boy who guided his boat to the best fishing grounds. At least, that was how they saw it, the other fishermen, but it was Tom Foster himself who had told the old man the truth of it one evening in the Sailor's Rest.

"It's the boy," he said, concernedly. "Um's not umself. Um says the sea lures um, and um's afeared of it. Oh, um walks the shore and watches all the whitecaps, the seahorses come rollin' in, but um ain't about ter go aridin' on 'em. I dun't know what um means, but um keeps complainin' as how um 'ain't ready', and doubts um ever will be, but if um 'goes now' it'll be the end of um. Lord only knows where um's thinkin' of goin'! And truth is, um sickens. So while I knows um'd come out with me if I was ter ask um, I won't fer um's sake. The only good thing: um lies in the bath a lot, keeps umself well soaked in fresh water so um's skin dun't suffer much and there be no more of them fish-lice."

And the leathery old seaman had shrugged—though in no way negligently—as he finished his pint, and then his ruminations with the words, "No more sea swimmin', no more fish-lice—it's as simple as that. But as fer the rest of it… I worries about um, that I do."

"Answer me one question," the old man had begged of Foster then. "Tell me, why did you take him in? You had no obligation in that respect. I mean, it wasn't as if the youth—the child—was of your blood. He was a foundling, and there were, well, complications right from the start."

Foster had nodded. "It were my woman, the missus, who took ter um. Her great-granny had told of just such young 'uns when um were a little 'un out in the islands. And Ma Foster felt fer um, um did. Me too, 'ventually, seein' as how we've had um all this time. But we always knew who um's dad were. No big secret that, fer um were here plain ter see. Gone now, though, but um did used ter pay um's share."

"George White gave you money?"

"Fer Geoff's upkeep, yes." Foster had readily admitted it. "That's a fact. The poor bugger were sellin' off bits of precious stuff—jewell'ry and such—in all the towns around. Fer the lad, true enough, but also fer um's own pleasure... or so I've heard it said. But that's none of my business..."

Then there was poor Jilly White. She, too—her health—was very obviously in decline. Her nightmares were of constant concern, having grown repetitive and increasingly weird to the point of grotesque. Also, her speech and mobility were suffering badly; she stuttered, often repeated herself, occasionally fell while negotiating the most simple routines both in and out of doors. Indeed, she had become something of a prisoner in her own home; she only rarely ventured down onto the beach, to sit with her daughter in the weak but welcome spring sunshine.

As to her dreams:

It had been a long-drawn-out process, but Jamieson had been patient; he had managed to extract something of the nightmarish contents of Jilly's dreams from the lady herself, the rest from Anne during the return journey from a language lesson trip into St. Austell. Unsurprisingly, all of the worst dreams were centred upon George White, Jilly's ex-husband; not on his suicide, as might at least in some part be expected, but on his disease: its progression and acceleration toward the end.

In particular she dreamed of frogs or the batrachia in general, and of fish... but *not* as creatures of Nature. The horror of these visitations was that they were completely alien, gross mutations or hybrids of man and monster. And the man was George White, his human face and something of his form transposed upon those of the amphibia and fishes alike—and all too often upon beings who had the physical components of both genera *and more*! In short, Jilly dreamed of Deep Ones, where George was a member of that aquatic society!

And Anne White told of how her mother mumbled and gibbered, gasping her horror of "great wet eyes that wouldn't or couldn't close"; or "scales as sharp and rough as a file"; or "the flaps in George's neck, going right through to the inside and pulsing like... like *gills* when he snorted or choked in his sleep!" But these things with regard to her mother's nightmares weren't all that Anne had spoken of on the occasion of that revealing drive home from her language lesson. For she had also been perfectly open in telling Jamieson:

"I know you saw me at my window that time when you brought her pills and spoke to my mother at length, the night you told her about Innsmouth. I heard you start to talk, got out of bed, and sat listening at the head of the stairs. I was as quiet as could be and must have heard almost everything you said."

And Jamieson had nodded. "Things she probably wouldn't have spoken of if she'd known you were awake? Did it... bother you, our conversation?"

"Perhaps a little... but no, not really," she had answered. "I know more than my mother gives me credit for. But about what you told her, in connection with my father and what she dreamed about him, well, there is something I'd like to know—without that you need to repeat it to her."

"Oh?"

"Yes. You said that you'd seen those sick Innsmouth people, 'in every stage of degeneration'. And I wondered..."

"...You wondered just what those stages were?" The old man had prompted her, and then gone on: "Well, there are stages and there are states. It usually depends on how they start out. The taint might occur from birth, or it might come much later. Some scarcely develop the Innsmouth look at all... while others are born with it."

"Like Geoff?"

"Like him, yes." Again Jamieson nodded. "It rather depends on the strength of the Innsmouth blood in the parents… or in at least one of them, obviously. Or in the ancestral blood line in general."

And then, out of the blue and without any hesitation, she'd said, "I know that Geoff is my half-brother. It's why my mother let's us be friends. She feels guilty for my father's sake—in his place, I mean. And so she thinks of Geoff as 'family'. Well, of a sort."

"And you? How do you think of him?"

"As my brother, do you mean?" She had offered an indecisive shake of her head. "I'm not really sure. In a way, I suppose. I don't find him horrible, if that's what you mean."

"No, of course not, and neither do I!" The old man had been quick to answer. "As a doctor, I've grown used to accepting too many abnormalities in people to be repulsed by any of them."

"Abnormalities?" Anne had cocked her head a little, favouring Jamieson with a curious, perhaps challenging look. And:

"Differences, then," he had told her.

And after a moment's silence she'd said, "Go on, then. Tell me about them: these states or stages."

"There are those born with the look, as I've mentioned," he had answered, "and those who gradually develop it, some of whom stay mostly, well, *normal*-looking. There are plenty of those in Innsmouth right now. Also, there is always a handful who retain their, er, agreeable—their acceptably, well, *human*—features for a great many years, changing only towards the end, when the metamorphosis occurs very rapidly indeed. At the hospital where I worked, some of the geneticists—Innsmouth people themselves—were trying to alter certain genes in their patients; if not to kill off the process entirely, at least to prolong the human looks of those who were likely to suffer the change."

"'Human-looking', and 'metamorphosis', and 'geneticists', Anne had nodded, thoughtfully. "But with those words—and the way you explained it—it doesn't sound so much a disease as a, well, a 'metamorphosis', yes; and that *is* your own word! Like a pupa into a butterfly, or rather a tadpole into a frog. Except, instead of a tadpole…"

But there she'd frowned, broken off and sat back musing in her seat. "It's all very puzzling, but I think the answers are coming and that I'm beginning to understand." Then, sitting up straight again until she strained against her safety belt, she had said. "But look—we're almost home!" And urgently turning to stare at Jamieson's profile: "We're through the village and there are still some things I wanted to ask—just one or two more, that's all."

At which the old man had slowed down, allowing her time to speak, and prompting her, "Go on then, ask away."

"This cult of Dagon," she had said then. "This religion or 'Esoteric Order' in Innsmouth—does it still exist? I mean, do they still worship? And if so, what if someone with the look or the blood—what if he doesn't want to be one of them—what if he reneges and… and runs away? My mother asked you much the same question, I know. But you didn't quite answer her."

"I think," Jamieson had said then, bringing his vehicle to a halt outside the Whites' house, "I think that would be quite bad for this hypothetical person. What would he do, if or when the change came upon him? With no one to help him; none of his own kind, that is."

Anne's mother had come to the door of the house, and stood there all pale and uncertain. But Anne, getting out of the car, had looked at the old man with her penetrating gaze, and he had seen that it was all coming together for her—and that indeed she knew more than her mother had given her credit for…

In the second week of May things came to a head.

The first handful of tourists and early holidaymakers were in the village, staying at two or three cheap bed-and-breakfast places; and these city folk were making their way down onto the beaches each day, albeit muffled against the still occasionally brisk weather.

And in the lenses of Jamieson's binoculars, the gnarled Tom Foster and his malformed ward had also been seen—as often as not arguing, apparently—the younger one pulling himself away, and the elder dragging after him, shaking his head and pointing back imploringly the way they'd come. And despite that the ill-favoured youth was failing, he yet retained enough strength to power him stumblingly, stubbornly on, leaving his foster-father panting and cursing in his wake. But when the youth was alone—fluttering there like a stumpy scarecrow on the sands, with his few wisps of coarse hair blowing back from his head in the wind off the ocean—then as always he would be seen gazing out over the troubled waters, as if transfixed by their vast expanse...

It happened on a reasonably warm Sunday afternoon that the Tremains, Jamieson, and Anne White were on the beach together, or rather at the same time. And so was young Geoff.

For ease of walking the old man held to firmer ground set back from the dunes, on a heading that would take him past the Tremains's house as he visited Jilly White's place. Doreen and John Tremain were taking the air maybe two hundred yards ahead of Jamieson; with their backs to him, they hadn't as yet observed him. And Anne was a small dot in the distance, huddled with a book in the lee of a grass-crested dune, a favourite location of hers, just one hundred or so yards this side of her mother's house. Today she stayed close to home out of necessity, for the simple reason that Jilly had taken to her bed four days ago as the result of some sort of physical or mental collapse, if not a complete nervous breakdown.

There were a very few holidaymakers on the beach... fewer still in bathing costumes, daring the water for the first time. But closer to the sea than the rest—coming from the direction of the village and avoiding the small family groups—there was young Geoff. Jamieson had his binoculars with him; he paused to focus on the youth, finding himself mildly concerned on noting his poor condition.

He was stumbling very badly now; his flabby mouth had fallen fully open, and his bulbous chin wobbled on his chest. Even at this distance, the youth's eyes seemed filmed over, and the scaly skin of his face was grey. He seemed to be gasping at the air, and his broad, rounded shoulders went up and down with the heaving of his chest.

As the old man watched, so that strange figure tore off its shapeless jacket and threw it aside, then angled its route even closer to the band of damp sand at the sea's rim. Some children paddling and splashing there, laughing as they jumped the small waves in six inches of water, noticed Geoff's approach. They at once quit their play and fell silent, backed away from him, and finally turned to run up the beach.

And sensing that something was about to happen here, Jamieson put on a little more speed. Likewise the Tremains; they too were walking faster, cresting the dunes, heading for the softer sands of the beach proper. Being that much closer to the youth, they had obviously witnessed his antics and noted his poor condition, and like the old man they'd sensed something strange in the air.

Anne, on the other hand, remained seated, reading in the scoop of her dune, as yet unaware of the drama taking shape close by.

Jamieson, no longer showing any sign of his age or possible infirmity, put on yet more speed; he was anxious to be as close as possible to whatever was happening here. He only paused when he heard a weird cry—a strange, ululant howling—following which he hurried on and crested the dunes in the prints left by the Tremains. Then, from that slightly higher elevation, and at a distance of less than one hundred and fifty yards, he scanned the scene ahead.

Having heard the weird howling, Anne was on her feet now at the crest of her dune, looking down across the beach. And there was her half-brother, up to his knees in the water, tearing off his shirt and dropping his ragged trousers, making these nerve-jangling noises as he howled, hissed, and shrieked at the sea!

Anne ran down across the beach; the Tremains hurried after, and Jamieson raced to catch up. He was vaguely aware that Jilly White had appeared on the decking at the back of her house, and was standing or staggering there in her dressing-gown. White as a ghost, clutching at the handrail with one shaking hand, Jilly held the other to her mouth.

Anne was into the water now, wading out toward the demented— or tormented—youth. John Tremain had kicked off his shoes; he tested the water, hoisted the cuffs of his trousers uselessly, and went splashing toward the pair. And meanwhile Jamieson, puffing and panting with the effort, had closed in on the scene as a whole.

Geoff had stopped hissing and howling; he grasped at Anne's hand, held it tight, pointed urgently out to sea. Then, releasing her, he made signs: *Come with me, sister, for I have to go! I am not ready, but still I must go! It calls to me… the sea is calling and I can no longer resist… I must go!*

Then he saw her uncertainty, her denial, stopped making his signs, and began dragging her deeper into the water. But it was now clear that he was deranged, unhinged, and his teeth gleamed the yellowy-white of fish-bone as he recommenced his gibbering, his howling, his awful cries of supplication… his liturgy to the unknown lords of the sea.

Jamieson was much closer now, and Tremain closer still. The headmaster grabbed at Anne, tried to fight the youth off. Geoff released Anne's hand and turned on Tremain, fastening his sharp teeth on the other's shoulder and biting through his thin shirt. Tremain gave a cry of pain! Lurching backwards, he stumbled and fell into the water, which momentarily covered his head.

But the youth saw what he had done—knew he'd done wrong and with Tremain's blood staining his face, and streaming from his gaping circle of a mouth, he appeared to regain his senses… at least partly. And shaking his head, Geoff signalled his farewell to Anne, waddled a foot deeper into the water's surge, let himself fall forward and began to swim.

He swam, and it was at once apparent that this was his natural element. And seeing him go, Jamieson thought, *Alas that he isn't equipped for it…*

Tremain had dragged himself to the beach; Anne had returned to where the water reached her knees, and watched Geoff's progress as his form diminished with distance. Jamieson helped John Tremain up out of the shallows, dampened a handkerchief in salt water, applied it to the raw, bleeding area between the other's neck and shoulder. Doreen Tremain hurried forward, wringing her hands and asking what she should do.

"Take him home," said the old man. "Keep my handkerchief on the wound to staunch the bleeding. Treat it with an antiseptic, then pad and bandage it. When John recovers from the shock take him into St. Austell for shots: anti-tetanus, and whatever else is prescribed. But don't delay. Do you understand?" She nodded, helped her husband up the beach and away.

Anne was at the water's rim. Soaked from the waist down and shocked to her core—panting and gasping—she stared at the old man with her mouth wide open. And turning her head, looking out to sea, she said, "Geoff… Geoff!"

"Let's get you home," said Jamieson, taking her hand.

"But Geoff… what of Geoff?"

"We'll call the coastguard." The old man nodded reassuringly, and threw his jacket round her shoulders.

"He said… said he wasn't ready." She allowed him to lead her from the water.

"None of us were," Jamieson muttered under his breath. "Not for this."

Halfway up the beach toward the house, they heard a gurgling cry. It was Jilly White, staggering on the decking of her ocean-facing patio, one hand on the rail, the other pointing at the sky, the horizon, the sea, the beach… and finally at her daughter and Jamieson. Her drawn face went through a variety of changes; vacant one moment, it showed total horror in the next, and finally nothing as her eyes rolled up like white marbles.

Then, as her knees gave way beneath her, Jilly crumpled to the decking and lay there jerking, drooling, and mouthing incoherently…

The coastguard found no sign of Geoff, despite that their boat could be seen slicing through the off-shore water all that day, and then on Monday from dawn till dark. A doctor—a specialist from St. Austell—gave Jilly White a thorough examination, and during a quiet, private discussion with Jamieson out of earshot of Anne, readily agreed with the old man's diagnosis. Of course Anne asked about it after the specialist had left, but Jamieson told her it could wait until all had settled down somewhat; and in any case things being as they were, for the moment incapable of improvement, Jilly's best interests lay in resting. He, Jamieson himself, would remain in attendance, and with Anne's help he would care for her mother until other decisions were made if such should become necessary.

In the event, however, the old man didn't expect or receive too much help from Anne; no, for she was out on the beach, walking its length mile upon mile, watching the sea and only coming home to eat and sleep when she was exhausted. This remained her routine for four days, until Geoff's bloated body was washed up on a shingle beach some miles down the coast.

Then Anne slept, and slept, a day and a night.

And the next morning—after visiting her mother's bedside and finding her sleeping, however fitfully—Anne went to the old man in the hollow of her dune, and sat down with him in the sand on the first truly warm day of the year.

He was in shirt-sleeves, grey slacks, canvas shoes; dressed for the fine weather. And he had her book in his lap, unopened. Handing it over, he said, "I found it right here where you left it the other day. I was going to return it to you. You're lucky no one else stumbled on it, and that it hasn't rained."

She took the heavy old book and put it down away from him, asking, "Did you look at it?"

He shook his head. "It's your property. For all I know you might have written in it. I believe in privacy, both for myself and for others."

She took his hand and leaned against him, letting him know that come what may they were friends. "Thank you for everything that you've done, especially for my mother," she said. "I mean, I'm so glad you came here, to the village. Even knowing you *had* to come—" (a sly sideways glance at him) "—still I'm glad. You've been here just a few months, yet I feel like I've known you, oh, for a very long time."

"I'll take that as a compliment," Jamieson answered her.

"I feel I can talk to you," she quickly went on. "I've felt that way since the first time I saw you. And after you treated Geoff when he was sick… well, then I knew it was so."

"And indeed we do talk," said the old man. "Nothing really deep, or not *too* deep, not yet—or until now?—but we talk. Perhaps it's a question of trust, of a sort of kinship?"

"Yes." She nodded. "I know I can tell you things, secrets. I've needed to tell someone things. I'd like to have been able to tell my mother, but she wouldn't have listened. Her nerves. She used to get worried, shake her head, walk away. Or rather, she would stumble away. Which has been getting worse every day. But you… you're very different."

He smiled. "Ah, well, but that's always been my lot. As I believe I once told Jilly, sometimes I'm seen as a father confessor. Sort of odd, really, because I'm not a Catholic."

"Then what are you?" Anne tilted her head on one side. "I mean, what's your religion? Are you an atheist?"

"Something like that." Jamieson shrugged. "Actually, I do have certain beliefs. But I'm not one to believe in a conventional god, if that's what you're asking. And you? What do you believe in?"

"I believe in the things my father told me," she answered dreamily. "Some beautiful things, some ugly, and some strange as the strangest myths and fables in the strangest books. But of course *you* know what I mean, even if I'm not sure myself." As she spoke, she took up her book and hugged it to her chest. Bound in antique leather, dark as old oak and glossy with age, the book's title, glimpsed between Anne's spread fingers, consisted of just three ornately tooled letters: *E.O.D.*

"Well," said Jamieson, "and here you are with just such a book. One of your strange books, perhaps? Certainly its title is very odd. Your mother once told me she gave you such books to burn…"

She looked at the book in her hands and said, "My father's books? There were some she wanted rid of, yes. But I couldn't just burn them. This is one of them. I've read them a lot and tried to make sense of them. Sometimes I thought I understood them; at others I was at a loss. But I knew they were important and now I know why." And then, suddenly galvanised, gripping his arm below the elbow. "Can we please stop pretending? I know almost everything now… so won't you please tell me the rest? And I swear to you—whatever you tell me—it will be safe with me. I think you must know that by now."

The old man nodded and gently disengaged himself. "I think I can do that, yes. That is, as long as you're not going to be frightened by it, and provided you won't run away… like your father."

"He was very afraid, wasn't he?" she said. "But I'll never understand why he stole the books and the Innsmouth jewellery. If he hadn't taken them, maybe they'd have just let him go."

"I think that perhaps he planned to sell those books," the old man answered. "In order to support himself, naturally. For of course he would have known that they were very rare and valuable. But after he fled Innsmouth, changed his name, got back a little self-confidence and started to think clearly, he must also have realised that wherever the books surfaced they would be a sure link—a clue, a pointer—to his whereabouts. And so he kept them."

"And yet he sold the jewellery." She frowned.

"Because gold is different than books." Jamieson smiled. "It becomes very personal; the people who buy jewellery wear it, of course, but they also guard it very closely and they don't keep it on library shelves or places where others might wonder about it. Also, your father was careful not to spread it too thickly. Some here, some there; never too much in any one place. Perhaps at one time he'd reasoned that just like the books he shouldn't sell the jewellery—but then came the time when he had to."

"Yet the people of the Esoteric Order weren't any too careful with it," she said, questioningly.

"Because they consider Innsmouth their town and safe," Jamieson answered. "And also because their members rarely betray a trust. Which in turn is because there are penalties for any who do."

"Penalties?"

"There are laws, Anne. Doesn't every society have laws?"

Her huge eyes studied his, and Jamieson felt the trust they conveyed… a mutual trust, passing in both directions. And he said, "So is there anything else I should tell you right now?"

"A great many things," Anne answered, musingly. "It's just that I'm not quite sure how to ask about them. I have to think things through." But in the next moment she was alert again:

"You say my father changed his name?"

"Oh yes, as part of the merry chase he's led us—led me—all these years. But the jewellery did in the end let him down. All winter long, when I've been out and about, I've been buying it back in the towns around. I have most of it now. As for your father's name: actually, he wasn't a White but a Waite, from a long line—a very, *very* long line—of Innsmouth Waites. One of his ancestors, and mine, sailed with Obed Marsh on the Polynesian trade routes. But as for myself… well, chronologically I'm a lot closer to those old seafarers than poor George was."

She blinked, shook her head in bewilderment; the first time the old man had seen her caught unawares, which made him smile. And: "You're a Waite, too?" she said. "But… Jamieson?"

"Well, actually it's Jamie's son." He corrected her. "Jamie Waite's son, out of old Innsmouth. Have I shocked you? Is it so awful to discover that the kinship you've felt is real?"

And after the briefest pause, while once again she studied his face: "No," she answered, and shook her head. "I think I've probably guessed it—some of it—all along. And Geoff, poor Geoff… Why, it would also make you kin to him, and I think he knew it, too! It was in his eyes when he looked at you."

"Geoff?" The old man's face fell and he gave a sad shake of his head. "What a pity. But he was a hopeless case who couldn't ever have developed fully. His gills were rudimentary, useless, unformed, atrophied. Atavisms, throwbacks in bloodlines that we hoped had been successfully conditioned out, still occur occasionally. That poor boy was in one such 'state', trapped between his ancestral heritage and his—or his father's—scientifically engineered or altered genes. And instead of cojoining, the two facets fought."

"A throwback," she said, softly. "What a horrible description!"

And the old man shrugged, sighed, and said, "Yes. Yet what else can we call him, the way Geoff was, and the way he looked? But one day, my dear, our ambassadors—our agents—will walk among people and look no different from them, and be completely accepted by them. Until eventually we Deep Ones will be the one race, the true amphibious race which nature always intended. We were the first… why, we *came* from the sea, the cradle of life itself! Given time, and the land and sea both shall be ours."

"Ambassadors…" Anne repeated him, letting it all sink in. "But in actual fact agents. Spies and fifth columnists."

"Our advance guard." He nodded. "And who knows—you may be one of them? Indeed, that's my intention."

She stroked her throat, looked suddenly alarmed. "But Geoff and me, we were of an age, of a blood. And if his—his gills? —those flaps were gills? But…" Again she stroked her throat, searchingly now. Until he caught at her hand.

"Yours are on the inside, like mine. A genetic modification which reproduced itself perfectly in you, just as in me. That's why your father's desertion was so disappointing to us, and one of the reasons why I had to track him down: to see how he would spawn, and if he'd spawn true. In your case he did. In Geoff's, he didn't."

"My gills?" Yet again she stroked her throat, and then remembered something. "Ah! My *laryngitis*! When my throat hurt last December, and you examined me! Two or three aspirins a day was your advice to my mother, and I should gargle four or five times daily with a spoonful of salt dissolved in warm water."

"You wouldn't let anyone else see you." The old man reminded her. "And why was that, I wonder? Why me?"

"Because I didn't *want* any other doctor looking at me," she replied. "I didn't want anyone else examining me. Just you."

"Kinship," he said. "And you made the right choice. But you needn't worry. Your gills—at present the merest of pink slits at the base of your windpipe—are as perfect as in any foetal or infant land-born Deep One. And they'll stay that way for... oh, a long time—as long or even longer than mine have stayed that way, and will until I'm ready—when they'll wear through. For a month or so then they'll feel tender as their development progresses, with fleshy canals like empty veins that will carry air to your land lungs. At which time you'll be as much at home in the sea as you are now on dry land. And that will be *wonderful,* my dear!"

"You want me to... to come with you? To be a... a...?"

"But you already are! There's a certain faint but distinct odour about you, Anne. Yes, and I have it, too, and so did your half-brother. But you can dilute it with pills we've developed, and then dispel it utterly with a dab of special cologne."

A much longer silence, and again she took his bare forearms in her hands, stroking down from the elbow. His skin felt quite smooth in that direction. But when she stroked upwards from the wrist...

"Yes," she said, "I suppose I am. My skin is like yours... the scales don't show. They're fine and pink and golden. But if I'm to come with you, what of my mother? You still haven't told me what's wrong with her."

And now, finally, after all these truths, the old man must tell a lie. He must, because the truth was one she'd never accept—or rather she would—and all faith gone. But there had been no other way. And so:

"Your mother," the old man hung his head, averted his gaze, started again. "Your mother, your own dear Jilly… I'm afraid she won't last much longer." That much at least was the truth.

But Anne's hand had flown to her mouth, and so he hurriedly continued. "She has CJD, Anne—Creutzfeldt–Jacob disease—the so-called mad cow disease, at a very advanced stage." (That was another truth, but not the whole truth.)

Anne's mouth had fallen open. "Does she know?"

"But how can I tell her? And how can you? She may never be herself again. And if or when she were herself, she would only worry about what will become of you. And there's no way we can tell her about… well, you know what I mean. But Anne, don't look at me like that, for there's nothing that can be done for her. There's no known cure, no hospital can help her. I wanted her to have her time here, with you. And of course I'm here to help in the final stages. That specialist from St. Austell, he agrees with me."

Finally the girl found her voice. "Then your pills were of no use to her."

"A placebo." *Now* Jamieson lied. "They were sugar pills, to give her some relief by making her *think* I was helping her."

No, not so… and no help for Jilly, who would never have let her daughter go; whose daughter never *would* have gone while her mother lived. And those pills filled with synthetic prions—rogue proteins indistinguishable from the human form of the insidious bovine disease, developed in a laboratory in shadowy old Innsmouth—eating away at Jilly's brain even now, faster and faster.

Anne's hand fell from her face. "How long?"

He shook his head. "Not long. After witnessing what happened the other day, not long at all. Days, maybe? No more than a month at best. But we shall be here, you and I. And Anne, we can make up for what she'll miss. Your years, like mine… oh, you shall have years without number!"

"It's true, then?" Anne looked at him, and Jamieson looked back but saw no sign of tears in her eyes, which was perfectly normal. "It's true that we go on—that our lives go on—for a long time? But not everlasting, surely?"

He shook his head. "Not everlasting, no—though it sometimes feels that way! I often lose count of my years. But I am your ancestor, yes."

Anne sighed and stood up. And brushing sand from her dress, she took his hand, helping him to his feet. "Shall we go and be with my mother… grandfather?"

Now his smile was broad indeed—a smile he showed only to close intimates—which displayed his small, sharp, fish-like teeth. And:

"Grandfather?" he said. "Ah, no. In fact I'm your *father's* great-great-grandfather! And as for yourself, Anne… well you must add another 'great.'"

And hand in hand they walked up the beach to the house. The young girl and the old—the *very* old—man…?

AFTERWORD

RANDY BROECKER was born and lives in Chicago, Illinois. Inspired by the pulp magazines and EC comics he read as a child, his first published artwork appeared in Rich Hauser's legendary 1960s EC fanzine, *Spa-Fon*.

Many years later, a meeting with publisher Donald M. Grant at the second World Fantasy Convention eventually led in 1979 to *The Black Wolf* and his first hardcover illustrations. Since then his work has appeared in books produced by PS Publishing, Robinson Publishing, Carroll & Graf, Fedogan & Bremer, Cemetery Dance, Underwood-Miller, Sarob Press, Pumpkin Books, American Fantasy, Highland Press and other imprints on both sides of the Atlantic.

He was Artist Guest of Honour at the 2002 World Horror Convention and is the author of the World Fantasy Award-nominated study *Fantasy of the 20th Century: An Illustrated History* from Collector's Press, which also formed part of a three-in-one omnibus entitled *Art of Imagination: 20th Century Visions of Science Fiction, Horror, and Fantasy*.

"In the best of Lovecraft's writing there is a feverish intensity not unlike that displayed in the work of Richard Upton Pickman, that painter of the perverse whose work I also happen to admire," reveals Broecker.

"Both have the ability to convince one of the existence of the strange and wondrous horrors that they present so realistically. Horrors that I have enjoyed encountering for quite awhile now, and when given the opportunity like this to present my own interpretations, I confess that wild batrachians wouldn't keep me away."

RAMSEY CAMPBELL was born in Liverpool, where he still lives with his wife Jenny. His first book, a collection of stories entitled *The Inhabitant of the Lake and Less Welcome Tenants*, was published by August Derleth's legendary Arkham House imprint in 1964, since when his novels have included *The Doll Who Ate His Mother*, *The Face That Must Die*, *The Nameless*, *Incarnate*, *The Hungry Moon*, *Ancient Images*, *The Count of Eleven*, *The Long Lost*, *Pact of the Fathers*, *The Darkest Part of the Woods*, *The Grin of the Dark*, *Thieving Fear*, *Creatures of the Pool*, *The Seven Days of Cain*, and the movie tie-in *Solomon Kane*.

His short fiction has been collected in such volumes as *Demons by Daylight*, *The Height of the Scream*, *Dark Companions*, *Scared Stiff*, *Waking Nightmares*, *Cold Print*, *Alone with the Horrors*, *Ghosts and Grisly Things*, *Told by the Dead*, and *Just Behind You*. He has also edited a number of anthologies, including *New Terrors*, *New Tales of the Cthulhu Mythos*, *Fine Frights: Stories That Scared Me*, *Uncanny Banquet*, *Meddling with Ghosts*, and *Gathering the Bones: Original Stories from the World's Masters of Horror* (with Dennis Etchison and Jack Dann).

PS Publishing recently published the novels *Ghosts Know*, *The Kind Folk* and a new Lovecraftian novella, *The Last Revelation of Gla'aki*, along with the definitive edition of his early Arkham House collection, *Inhabitant of the Lake*, which includes all the first drafts of the stories, along with new illustrations by Randy Broecker. Forthcoming from the author is the novel *Bad Thoughts*, the collection *Holes for Faces*, and another novella, *The Pretence*.

Now well in to his fifth decade as one of the world's most respected authors of horror fiction, Ramsey Campbell has won multiple World Fantasy Awards, British Fantasy Awards and Bram Stoker Awards, and is a recipient of the World Horror Convention Grand Master Award, the Horror Writers Association Lifetime Achievement Award, the Howie Award of the H. P. Lovecraft Film Festival for Lifetime Achievement, and the International Horror Guild's Living Legend Award. He is also President of the Society of Fantastic Films.

"H. P. Lovecraft remains one of the crucial writers in the field," Campbell explains. "He united the American tradition of weird fiction—Poe, Bierce, Chambers—with the British—Machen, Blackwood, M. R. James. He devoted his career to attempting to find the perfect form for the weird tale, and the sheer range of his work (from the documentary to the delirious) is often overlooked. Few writers in the field are more worth re-reading: certainly I find different qualities on different occasions. I recently read 'The Outsider' to my wife Jenny to both our pleasures. I still try to capture the Lovecraftian sense of cosmic awe in some of my tales.

"'Raised by the Moon' was suggested by the boating lake at West Kirby. It's much like the area contained by the submerged wall in the story, although the town is nothing like the surroundings. Perhaps the creatures in the tale are distant cousins of the Deep Ones—we might call them the Shallowers."

Campbell's early story 'The Church in the High Street' appears in *Shadows Over Innsmouth*.

HUGH BARNETT CAVE (1910–2004) was born in Chester, England, he emigrated to America with his family when he was five. Cave sold his first story, 'Island Ordeal', to *Brief Stories* in 1929, and went on to publish around 800 pieces of fiction (often under various bylines) to such pulp magazines as *Weird Tales*, *Strange Tales*, *Ghost Stories*, *Black Book Detective Magazine*, *Spicy Mystery Stories* and the so-called "shudder" or "weird menace" pulps, *Horror Stories* and *Terror Tales*, amongst many other titles.

The author then left the field for almost three decades, moving to Haiti and later Jamaica, where he established a coffee plantation and wrote two highly praised travel books, *Haiti: Highroad to Adventure* and *Four Paths to Paradise: A Book About Jamaica*. He also continued to write for the "slick" magazines, such as *Collier's*, *Cosmopolitan*, *Esquire*, *The Saturday Evening Post* and many other titles.

In 1977, Karl Edward Wagner's Carcosa imprint published a hefty volume of Cave's best horror tales, *Murgunstrumm and Others*, which won the World Fantasy Award, and he returned to the genre with new stories and a string of modern horror novels (most of them involving voodoo or the walking dead): *Legion of the Dead*, *The Nebulon Horror*, *The Evil*, *Shades of Evil*, *Disciples of Dread*, *The Lower Deep*, *Lucifer's Eye*, *Isle of the Whisperers*, *The Dawning*, *The Evil Returns* and *The Restless Dead*.

The Horror Writers of America presented Cave with their highest honour, the Lifetime Achievement Award, in 1991, and in 1997 he was given a Special World Fantasy Award when he attended the World Fantasy Convention in London as a Guest of Honour. Milt Thomas' biography, *Cave of a Thousand Tales: The Life & Times of Hugh B. Cave*, was published by Arkham House the week after the author's death.

'The Coming' was originally written back in the early 1990s for *Shadows Over Innsmouth*. When that volume became an all-British line-up, the author took out the Lovecraftian references and later sold it to another anthology. It appears here as Cave originally intended.

BASIL COPPER (1924–2013) was born in London, and for thirty years he worked as a journalist and editor of a local newspaper before becoming a full-time writer in 1970.

His first story in the horror field, 'The Spider', was published in 1964 in *The Fifth Pan Book of Horror Stories*, since when his short fiction has appeared in numerous anthologies, been extensively adapted for radio, and collected in *Not After Nightfall*, *Here Be Daemons*, *From Evil's Pillow*, *And Afterward the Dark*, *Voices of Doom*, *When Footsteps Echo*, *Whispers in the Night*, *Cold Hand on My Shoulder* and *Knife in the Back*.

One of the author's most reprinted stories, 'Camera Obscura', was adapted for a 1971 episode of the anthology television series *Rod Serling's Night Gallery*.

Besides publishing two non-fiction studies of the vampire and werewolf legends, his other books include the novels *The Great White Space*, *The Curse of the Fleers*, *Necropolis*, *House of the Wolf* and *The Black Death*. He also wrote more than fifty hardboiled thrillers about Los Angeles private detective Mike Faraday, and continued the adventures of August Derleth's Holmes-like consulting detective Solar Pons in several volumes, including the novel *Solar Pons versus The Devil's Claw*.

More recently, PS Publishing has produced the non-fiction study *Basil Copper: A Life in Books*, and a massive two-volume set of *Darkness, Mist & Shadow: The Collected Macabre Tales of Basil Copper*. A restored version of Copper's 1976 novel *The Curse of the Fleers* appeared from the same imprint in 2012.

"I have already paid public tribute to August Derleth on both sides of the Atlantic in my own non-fiction studies," explained the author, "so I would prefer to paint a more intimate picture of a good-humoured, generous and loveable human being in these random recollections. I am on record as saying he was a Renaissance man. This was literally true, and his huge appetite for literature and life kept him at his desk under an incredible workload that would have consumed lesser men, for decade after decade.

"Like Lovecraft, he passed almost unnoticed except for the gigantic ripples in the small, rather esoteric world he had chosen to make his own. His reputation can only increase and appreciate as the years go by, while Arkham House itself in its prosperous and steady continuance is a living memorial to his courage and his life-work."

Copper's novella 'Beyond the Reef' originally appeared in *Shadows Over Innsmouth* and was subsequently reprinted as a single hardcover volume in Germany. In a reversal of Hugh B. Cave's story in the present volume, 'Voices in the Water' was initially written as a non-Lovecraftian ghost story, but the Innsmouth references were added for its first appearance here.

LES EDWARDS studied at the Hornsey College of Art from 1968–72. On leaving, he began to work as a freelance illustrator, and swiftly established himself as a stalwart of the UK illustration scene.

In a career spanning four decades he has painted a great number of covers, including those for such anthology series as *The Mayflower Book of Black Magic*, *The Fontana Book of Horror*, *The Star Book of Horror*, *The Reign of Terror*, *The Year's Best Horror Stories* and *The Mammoth Book of Best New Horror*. More recently, he has illustrated the best-selling H. P. Lovecraft collections *Necronomicon: The Best Weird Tales of H. P. Lovecraft* and *Eldritch Tales: A Miscellany of the Macabre*, *The Complete Chronicles of Conan* and *Conan's Brethren* by Robert E. Howard, and *Curious Warnings: The Great Ghost Stories of M. R. James*.

In recent years the artist has also taken to painting under the pseudonym "Edward Miller" in order to produce a different kind of work in a more romantic style. This work has also become popular, and he now pursues both careers with equal enthusiasm.

In 1995 he was Artist Guest of Honour at the World Science Fiction Convention and in 2010 he was Artist Guest of Honour at the World Horror Convention. He has been voted Best Artist by the British Fantasy Society on seven occasions, and has been nominated in that category every year since 1994. He has also been nominated for five Chesley Awards and for the World Fantasy Award for Best Artist five times, with his alter-ego, "Edward Miller", winning it in 2008.

"If you are a fan of the fantastic," explains the artist, "then it is not possible to ignore the work of the strange author from Providence. Somehow he has become permanent. He endures. Even the word 'Lovecraftian' has slipped into the language, although there might be strange ambiguities as to what it actually means. For some it refers to the literary style, which, let's face it, is a barrier which some readers never surmount. For others, it has to do with bulging gelatinous masses, the chanting of barbarous names and huge, ancient and tentacled beings.

"For me it is to do with a sense of dread; with the knowledge that the universe is, at best, indifferent and more likely, inimical, and that our grip on sanity is slight. It is to do with the feeling that if you scratch away the surface of our carefully preserved reality you will find madness staring back. And however hard Lovecraft tries, however he strives for that one elusive, perfect word, you know that he will never quite be able to convey the true and awful horror that's in his imagination. It's a feeling I share.

"But what sets Lovecraft, and a very few others, apart is that those feelings remain long after the story is finished. The best horror stories have this quality which sets them apart from the merely adequate, if enjoyable, chiller, and sets 'Horror' as a genre apart from other literature. It is why the best of Lovecraft's stories are always worth returning to."

BOB EGGLETON was fascinated by science fiction and fantasy at an early age, especially the monster movies featuring Godzilla and other creatures. He attended Rhode Island College and left to pursue a career in commercial illustration and fine art.

His artwork has appeared on countless book and magazine covers, comics, posters, prints, trading cards, stationary, drink coasters and jigsaw puzzles, and has been collected in such volumes as *Alien Horizons: The Fantastic Art of Bob Eggleton* and *The Book of Sea Monsters* (both with Nigel Suckling), *Greetings from Earth: The Art of Bob Eggleton*, *Dragonhenge* and *The Stardragons* (both with John Grant), *Primal Darkness: The Gothic & Horror Art of Bob Eggleton* (with Shinichi Noda) and *Dragons' Domain: The Ultimate Dragon Painting Workshop*.

Best known for his spectacular dragons, depictions of Godzilla, and his artwork for Brian Lumley's "Necroscope" series, the artist's paintings of Cthulhu have been used, amongst other places, on the Arkham House anthology *Cthulhu 2000*, *Best of Weird Tales*, *The House of Cthulhu* and the premier issue of *H. P. Lovecraft's Magazine*.

A recipient of multiple Hugo and Chesley Awards for Best Artist, Eggleton has also worked on the conceptual design for a number of movies. An asteroid discovered in 1992 by Spacewatch at Kitt Peak has been named "13562 Bobeggleton" after the artist.

"H. P. Lovecraft has got to be the world's greatest writer of 'monsters' in his terrific stories," observes Eggleton. "His creatures are like no others in fiction, on the Earth or off it. I try to visualise them as real things, which drip with slime and shamble along. Things that, as Lovecraft himself would say, 'Cause men to die with the screams still in their throats.'"

JOHN STEPHEN GLASBY (1928–2011) graduated from Nottingham University with an honours degree in Chemistry. He started his career as a research chemist for ICI in 1952 and worked for them until his retirement.

Around the same time, he began a parallel career as an extraordinarily prolific writer of novels and short stories, producing more than 300 works in all genres over the next two decades, many under such shared house pseudonyms as "Rand Le Page", "Berl Cameron", "Victor La Salle" and "John E. Muller". His most noted personal pseudonym was "A. J. Merak". He subsequently published a new collection of ghost stories, *The Substance of Shade*, occult novel *The Dark Destroyer*, and the SF novel *Mystery of the Crater*.

More recently, Philip Harbottle compiled two collections of the Glasby's supernatural fiction, *The Lonely Shadows* and *The Dark Boatman*, while the author's son, Edmund Glasby, edited *The Thing in the Mist: Selected by John S. Glasby*, collecting eleven of the author's stories from Badger Books' digest horror magazine *Supernatural Stories*.

A long-time fan of the work of H. P. Lovecraft, in the early 1970s the author also submitted a collection of Cthulhu Mythos stories to August Derleth at Arkham House. Derleth suggested extensive revisions and improvements, which Glasby duly followed, but the publisher unfortunately died before the revised book could see print, and the manuscript was returned.

In his later years, Glasby returned to writing more supernatural stories in the Lovecraftian vein, and 'The Quest for Y'ha-Nthlei'—a direct sequel to Lovecraft's 'The Shadow Over Innsmouth'—was written especially for this volume.

CAITLÍN R. KIERNAN is the author of several novels, including *Low Red Moon*, *Daughter of Hounds*, *The Drowning Girl: A Memoir* and *The Red Tree*, which was nominated for both the Shirley Jackson and World Fantasy awards.

Since 2000, her shorter tales of the weird, fantastic and macabre have been collected in several volumes, including *Tales of Pain and Wonder*; *From Weird and Distant Shores*, *To Charles Fort with Love*, *Alabaster*, *A is for Alien* and *The Ammonite Violin & Others*. Subterranean Press has recently released a retrospective of her early writing, *Two Worlds and In Between: The Best of Caitlín R. Kiernan (Volume One)*.

"'From Cabinet 34, Drawer 6' probably started taking shape in 1996," recalls the author, "after David J. Schow sent me a beautiful reproduction of the Devonian-aged fossil hand shown in the opening scenes of *The Creature from the Black Lagoon*. Dave has the most awesome collection of Creature memorabilia anywhere on earth, I suspect. I sat the model atop a bookshelf in my office, and from time to time I'd think about it's plausibility as an *actual* fossil, about coming across it in some museum drawer somewhere, forgotten and dusty with an all but indecipherable label, and what implications to our ideas of vertebrate evolution such a fossil would have.

"And then, late in 2001, when I was doing research for my fourth novel, *Low Red Moon*, I began attempting to figure out where precisely Lovecraft had meant the town of Innsmouth to be located. I finally settled on Crane Beach and Ipswich Bay, west of Cape Ann. Anyway, the two things came together—the 'fossil' hand of the Creature, 'The Shadow Over Innsmouth'—and I stopped working on the novel just long enough to write this story. I borrowed Dr. Solomon Monalisa from one of my earlier stories, 'Onion.'"

"As for *why* I decided that Ipswich Bay was Lovecraft's Innsmouth Harbour, here's a quote from my online journal, from my entry for November 26, 2001:

Lovecraft indicates that the narrator's bus, after leaving Newburyport, is travelling south-east, following the coast. HPL writes: "Out the window I could see the blue water and the sandy line of Plum Island, and we presently drew very near the beach as our narrow road veered off from the main highway to Rowley and Ipswich." This definitely indicates that the direction of travel is, in fact, south-east. A little father along, "At last we lost sight of Plum Island and saw the vast expanse of the open Atlantic on our left." At this point the road on which the bus is travelling begins to climb to higher ground; at the crest of the rise, the passengers… beheld the outspread valley beyond, where the Manuxet joins the sea just north of the long line of cliffs that culminate in Kingsport Head [another HPL invention] and veer off towards Cape Ann… but for a moment all my attention was captured by the nearer panorama just below me. I had, I realised, come face to face with rumour-shadowed Innsmouth." The narrator must, at this point, be looking to the east or south-east.

For me, the key is finding the Manuxet River. Of course, there really is no Manuxet River, *per se*—it's yet another of HPL's geographical fictions, but there are many rivers between Plum Island and Cape Ann, winding, swampy things that eventually empty into Plum Island Sound or Ipswich Bay. The river closest to Plum Island (and the bus doesn't *seem* to travel very far from the point where the narrator loses sight of the island before reaching the crest of the hill from which Innsmouth is visible) is the Ipswich River. A little farther on, there's the Castle Neck River. It's the mouth of this river that I'm favouring at the moment as the location of Innsmouth, based on HPL's statement that the Manuxet "…turned southward to join the ocean at the breakwater's end." Now, as the sea lies to the north, most of the rivers along this part of the coast do not make southerly turns, but flow north and east to the Atlantic. Notably, the Castle Neck River does have a distinct south-east kink just as it enters the estuary at the north-west end of Ipswich Bay.

Of course, HPL obviously took considerable liberties with the local geography, and I suspect that he may have also shortened the distance between Cape Ann and Plum Island in his head, recalling some excursion or another and compressing or expanding distance as we all tend to do. So, blah, blah, blah, and in my story at least, Innsmouth Harbour is at the mouth of the Castle Neck River (i.e., the Manuxet)."

HOWARD PHILIPS LOVECRAFT (1890–1937) is one of the 20th century's most important and influential authors of supernatural fiction.

Born in Providence, Rhode Island, he lived most of his life there as a studious antiquarian who wrote mostly with no care for commercial reward. During his lifetime, the majority of Lovecraft's fiction, poetry and essays appeared in obscure amateur press journals or in the pages of the struggling pulp magazine *Weird Tales*.

Following the author's untimely death, August Derleth and Donald Wandrei founded the publishing imprint of Arkham House in 1939 with the initial idea of keeping all Lovecraft's work in print. Beginning with *The Outsider and Others*, his stories were collected in such hardcover volumes as *Beyond the Wall of Sleep*, *Marginalia*, *Something About Cats and Other Pieces*, *Dreams and Fancies*, *The Dunwich Horror and Others*, *At the Mountains of Madness and Other Novels*, *Dagon and Other Macabre Tales*, *3 Tales of Horror* and *The Horror in the Museum and Other Revisions*, along with several volumes of "posthumous collaborations" with Derleth, including *The Lurker at the Threshold*, *The Survivor and Others* and *The Watchers Out of Time and Others*.

During the decades since his death, Lovecraft has been acknowledged as a mainstream American writer second only to Edgar Allan Poe, while his relatively small body of work has influenced countless imitators and formed the basis of a world-wide industry of books, role-playing games, graphic novels, toys and movies based on his concepts.

Lovecraft was not adverse to testing early drafts his latest story out on friends and colleagues, as this extract from a letter written to fellow *Weird Tales* author Clark Ashton Smith and dated February 18, 1932, illustrates:

Glad to hear you liked 'The Shadow Over Innsmouth', and thanks tremendously for the suggestions concerning possible alteration. Your central idea of increasing emphasis on the narrator's taint runs parallel with D'Erlett's [August Derleth] main suggestion, and I shall certainly adopt it in any basic recasting I may give the tale. The notion of having the narrator captured is surely a vivid one containing vast possibilities—and if I don't use it, it will be only because my original conception (like most of my dream-ideas) centred so largely in the physical detachment of the narrator.

As Lovecraft's seminal story, 'The Shadow Over Innsmouth', kicked off *Shadows Over Innsmouth*, it is his surviving discarded draft of the tale that is featured in this volume. According to Lovecraft biographer and scholar S. T. Joshi, this "may be his second or even third attempt at the story, since he announces in several letters that he is using the plot as 'laboratory experimentation' by writing it out successively in different styles". The compressed and incomplete version of the story that appears in this book only survived because it was found on the reverse of pages containing the final draft.

BRIAN LUMLEY started his writing career by emulating the work of H. P. Lovecraft and has ended up with his own, highly enthusiastic, fan following for his world-wide best-selling series of "Necroscope" vampire books.

Born in the coal-mining town of Horden, County Durham, on England's north-east coast, Lumley joined the British Army when he was twenty-one and served in the Corps of Royal Military Police for twenty-two years, until his retirement in December 1980.

After discovering Lovecraft's stories while stationed in Berlin in the early 1960s, he decided to try his own hand at writing horror fiction, initially based around the influential Cthulhu Mythos. He sent his early efforts to editor August Derleth, and Arkham House published two collections of the author's stories, *The Caller of the Black* and *The Horror at Oakdene and Others*, along with the short novel, *Beneath the Moors*.

Lumley then continued Lovecraft's themes in such novels and collections as *The Burrowers Beneath*, *The Transition of Titus Crow*, *The Clock of Dreams*, *Spawn of the Winds*, *In the Moons of Borea*, *The Compleat Crow*, *Hero of Dreams*, *Ship of Dreams*, *Mad Moon of Dreams*, *Iced on Iran and Other Dreamquests*, *The House of Cthulhu and Other Tales of the Primal Land*, *Fruiting Bodies and Other Fungi* (which includes the British Fantasy Award-winning title story), *Return of the Deep Ones and Other Mythos Tales* and *Dagon's Bell and Other Discords*. The author's most recent book is a new collection of non-Lovecraftian horror stories, *No Sharks in the Med and Other Stories*, from Subterranean Press, and he has also completed a new "Necroscope" novella for the same publisher.

The Brian Lumley Companion was published in 2002 by Tor Books, and he is the winner of a *Fear* Magazine Award, a Lovecraft Film Festival Association "Howie", the World Horror Convention's Grand Master Award and, most recently, a recipient of the Horror Writers' Association's Lifetime Achievement Award, and another Lifetime Achievement Award from the World Fantasy Convention

"'The Taint' was written between December 2002 to January 2003, specifically for this book," explains Lumley. "It would be impossible to deny HPL's influence on the story, even if I wanted to, which I don't. Because H. P. Lovecraft's Deep Ones, those 'batrachian dwellers of fathomless ocean', which he employed so effectively in his story 'The Shadow Over Innsmouth', and hinted at in others of his stories, have always fascinated me. And not only me, but an entire generation of authors most of whom weren't even born until long after Lovecraft's tragically early death.

"Indeed, this present volume—and my story in it—probably wouldn't have come to pass but for the success of editor Steve Jones' initial foray into Deep Ones territory, *Shadows Over Innsmouth*. That first book—one might say the progenitor of the current volume, containing stories by Neil Gaiman, Kim Newman, Ramsey Campbell, Basil Copper and a host of others, including my own 'Dagon's Bell'— was surely more than adequate proof of the popularity of Lovecraftian themes among today's writers.

"Indeed, the urge to create something in this (but what to call it? This sub-genre?) was so powerful in me that back in 1978 I had written a 60,000-word novel, *The Return of the Deep Ones*, mainly to satisfy my own craving for something that was no longer available. Oh, yes, I used to write for myself in those days. So when I was approached about a tale for this companion volume... well, what could I do but write one?

"As for the novella: much like 'Dagon's Bell' and *The Return of the Deep Ones*, it's the result of my wondering—what if certain members of the Esoteric Order of Dagon somehow escaped and emigrated from degenerate old Innsmouth—that darkly mysterious seaport 'town of ill repute' inhabited by the changeling Deep Ones, those less than human, amphibious worshippers of Lord Cthulhu in his house in R'lyeh—to resurface elsewhere? For instance, in England.

"One of only a very few recent Mythos tales by my hand, apart from its unavoidable, indeed obligatory back-drop, this story escapes almost entirely from Lovecraft's literary influence to become wholly original, and I consider it on a par with 'Born of the Winds', written all of thirty years earlier.

"'The Taint' was originally published in a limited edition of *Weird Shadows Over Innsmouth* in time to launch the book at the World Fantasy Convention, Madison WI, in November 2005."

RICHARD A. LUPOFF was born in Brooklyn, New York, and for many years has lived in Berkeley, California, with his wife, Patricia. He spent a few years in the US Army in the late 1950s, never firing a shot in anger and never had one shot at him, neither of which he regrets. He has worked as both a print and broadcast journalist from his student days onward, and for fifty years has done a books-and-authors show on local radio station KPFA.

A novelist, short story writer, critic, screenwriter and anthologist, his many books include the novels *One Million Centuries*, *Sandworld*, *Sword of the Demon*, *The Return of Skull-Face* (with Robert E. Howard), *Space War Blues*, *Circumpolar!*, *Lovecraft's Book*, *Galaxy's End*, *Night of the Living Gator* and two *Buck Rogers* novelisations (under the byline "Addison E. Steele"). His short fiction has been collected in *The Ova Hamlet Papers, Before... 12:01... and After, Claremont Tales, Claremont Tales II* and *Quintet: The Cases of Chase and Delacroix.*

Lupoff's non-fiction titles include *Edgar Rice Burroughs: Master of Adventure, Barsoom: Edgar Rice Burroughs and the Martian Vision, Writer at Large* and *The Great American Paperback*, and he has edited *All in Color for a Dime* and *The Comic Book Book* (both with Don Thompson) and two volumes of *What If: Stories that Should have Won the Hugo.*

In 1963, he and Pat Lupoff won the Hugo Award for their fanzine *Xero*, and a 2004 compilation *The Best of Xero* was nominated for another Hugo. He is also a winner of the Edgar Rice Burroughs Lifetime Achievement Award and the Left Coast Crime Lifetime Achievement Award for mystery fiction.

A short film based on his story '12:01 P.M.' was an Academy Awards nominee in 1990 and was expanded into a feature three years later.

"I discovered H. P. Lovecraft when I was eleven years old," recalls Lupoff, "living in a small town in New Jersey, and forced to attend church services every Sunday. I wish I'd had the courage to protest this forced religiosity openly – of course, it didn't take – but I found other ways to maintain my independence.

"I made up my own, subversive versions of familiar hymns and sang them when called upon to participate. And I sneaked secular reading matter into church, hid it in my hymnal, and read happily while the preacher railed about Mortal Sin, the Day of Judgement, and the Fires of Hell.

"One week I stumbled across a little paperback anthology called *The Avon Ghost Reader*. As I remember, it had a deliciously lurid cover painting – a green, claw-like hand rising menacingly in the foreground, a spooky looking old mansion in the distance – and a marvellous selection of frightening stories, including 'The Dunwich Horror', by H. P. Lovecraft. At age eleven I had no understanding of the publishing industry and didn't realise that this story was a reprint and that its author had been dead for nearly twenty years.

"What I did understand was that I'd stumbled across an author of

unusual merit. I vowed to watch for his byline. My next reward was a
copy of another little paperback, *Weird Shadow Over Innsmouth*, and
I was totally hooked. I've been a Lovecraft fan for most of my life,
and I am delighted to see the Old Gentleman finally getting his due.
I'm equally gratified to have made my own small contribution to the
traditions of his work."

PAUL McAULEY was born in Stroud, Gloucestershire. A former
research biologist at Oxford University and UCLA, and a former
lecturer at St. Andrews University, he became a full-time writer
in 1996. McAuley sold a story to the SF digest *If* when he was just
nineteen, but the magazine folded before it could appear, and his first
published story appeared in *Asimov's Science Fiction* in 1984.

With his debut novel, *Four Hundred Billion Stars* (1988), he
became the first British writer to win the Philip K. Dick Memorial
Award and he established his reputation as one of the best young
science fiction writers in the field by winning the John W. Campbell
Memorial Award in 1995.

His other novels include *Secret Harmonies* (aka *Of the Fall*),
Eternal Light, *Red Dust*, *Pasquale's' Angel* (winner of the Sidewise
Award for Best Long Form Alternate History fiction), the Arthur
C. Clarke Award-winning *Fairyland*, *Child of the River*, *Ancients of
Days*, *Shrine of Stars*, *The Secret of Life*, *Whole Wide World*, *White
Devils*, *Mind's Eye*, *Players*, *Cowboy Angels*, *The Quiet War*, *Gardens
of the Sun* and *In the Mouth of the Whale*. The author's short fiction
is collected in *The King of the Hill and Other Stories*, *The Invisible
Country* and *Little Machines*, while his story 'The Temptation of Dr.
Stein' was awarded the 1995 British Fantasy Award.

"I lived in the city of Bristol, hard by the Avon river and the
Severn estuary in the west of England, for seven years. It was the first
place I lived after moving away from home, I studied for both my
undergraduate degree and Ph.D at the university, and I had my first
job there. So it was definitely an influence on my life, but like the best
spring water, it has spent a long time percolating through the strata of
my subconscious before becoming the source of a story.

"Not only is Bristol a port city whose port has more or less silted up, but ordinarily it rains there every other day. What better setting for a Lovecraftian homage?

"I sat my final examinations for my B.Sc (a joint degree in Botany and Zoology, if anyone is interested) during the summer of 1976, when 'Take Me to the River' is set, which really was as hot and as dry as any disaster imagined by J. G. Ballard. The drought mentioned in the story was real enough – reservoirs and lakes dried up, grass and trees turned brown, crops wilted, people were encouraged to ration water by sharing baths, and the sun burned every day in a pitiless sky that was either hard blue or headachy white. It ended when the government appointed a 'Minister of Drought', which worked a lot better than any rain dance or cloud seeding, but for a little while it really did seem that the world might end, or that strange, marvellous or fearsome creatures might hatch from the drying mud and foetid rivers."

KIM NEWMAN is a novelist, critic and broadcaster. His fiction includes *The Night Mayor*, *Bad Dreams*, *Jago*, the *Anno Dracula* novels and stories, *The Quorum*, *The Original Dr Shade and Other Stories*, *Life's Lottery*, *Back in the USSA* (with Eugene Byrne) and *The Man from the Diogenes Club*, all under his own name, and *The Vampire Genevieve* and *Orgy of the Blood Parasites* as "Jack Yeovil".

His non-fiction books include *Ghastly Beyond Belief* (with Neil Gaiman), *Horror: 100 Best Books* and *Horror: Another 100 Best Books* (both with Stephen Jones), *Wild West Movies*, *The BFI Companion to Horror*, *Millennium Movies* and BFI Classics studies of *Cat People* and *Doctor Who*.

He is a contributing editor to *Sight & Sound* and *Empire* magazines (contributing the latter's popular 'Video Dungeon' column), has written and broadcast widely on a range of topics, and scripted radio and television documentaries.

Newman's stories 'Week Woman' and 'Ubermensch' have been adapted into episodes of the TV series *The Hunger*, and the latter tale was also turned into an Australian short film in 2009. Following his Radio 4 play *Cry Babies*, he wrote an episode ('Phish Phood') for BBC

Radio 7's series *The Man in Black*, and he was a main contributor to the 2012 stage play *The Hallowe'en Sessions*. He has also directed and written a tiny film, *Missing Girl*.

The author's most recent books include expanded reissues of his acclaimed *Anno Dracula* series and the "Professor Moriarty" novel *The Hound of the d'Urbervilles* (all from Titan Books), along with a much-enlarged edition of *Nightmare Movies* (from Bloomsbury).

"For anyone following the loose interconnectedness of most of my stories, my contribution to this anthology is (obviously) a follow-up to 'The Big Fish' from *Shadows Over Innsmouth*. Returning to California twenty-six years on from the 1942 setting of the first fish story, we're going inland this time—because I suspected seaside tales might become over-familiar in this series, and decided it would be effective counter-programming to do something set in a desert.

"'Another Fish Story' also fills in a gap in the life and career of Derek Leech, who appears in my novel *The Quorum*, and several other stories and books of mine, including 'Seven Stars' (the serial from *Dark Detectives*). Most of the people in the story are real and you can look them up in showbiz gossip and true crime books.

"I subsequently wrote a third fish story, getting back to the beach this time, and 'Richard Riddle, Boy Detective in "The Case of the French Spy"' will be included in *Weirder Shadows Over Innsmouth*."

ALLAN SERVOSS' fascination with the works of H. P. Lovecraft began during his teenage years in Montana when he read a worn paperback copy of *The Case of Charles Dexter Ward*. He soon started ordering all he could find by Lovecraft from a small publishing house "out east" called Arkham House.

After graduating from college, he found himself living in Madison, Wisconsin, and in due time discovered that he lived just a short distance from Arkham House and August Derleth. A visit to Derleth's home (unannounced) led to a friendship between the two men during the editor/publisher's final year, and Servoss being invited to illustrate Gary Myers' Arkham volume *The House of the Worm*, which finally saw print in 1975. Except for also contributing to a few issues of *Whispers* magazine, that marked the artist's last dealing with weird illustration for nearly twenty-five years.

The intervening period was spent raising a family and teaching art until, in 2000, he was asked to produce a cover for the Arkham House edition of *In the Stone House* by Barry N. Malzberg.

Servoss has had his paintings and drawings displayed in many galleries and juried art exhibitions, illustrated books outside the weird genre, and seen his work reproduced in such periodicals as *American Artist Magazine*, *The Artist Magazine* and *International Artist*. *In His Library at R'lyeh, Dead Lovecraft Waits Dreaming...* is the title of a portfolio of the illustrator's work, he was featured in the recent Centipede Press volume *Artists Inspired by H. P. Lovecraft*, and he has enjoyed seeing HPL finally receiving the literary place in history he deserves.

MICHAEL MARSHALL SMITH was born in Knutsford, Cheshire, and grew up in the United States, South Africa and Australia. He currently lives in Santa Cruz, California, with his wife and son.

Smith's short fiction has appeared in numerous magazines and anthologies and, under his full name, he has published the modern SF novels *Only Forward*, *Spares* and *One of Us*. He is the only person to have won the British Fantasy Award for Best Short Story four times—along with the August Delerth, International Horror Guild and Philip K. Dick awards.

Writing as "Michael Marshall" he has published six international best-selling novels of suspense, including *The Straw Men* and *The Intruders*, currently in development with the BBC. His most recent novels are *Killer Move* and *We are Here*.

"I first read H. P. Lovecraft back when I was discovering horror fiction in the late 1980s. What I admire most about him—in addition to his endlessly foetid imagination, and his richly baroque prose style—is his certainty. His vision. So many writers of the macabre struggle to communicate true darkness, falling over themselves to sell you their slant on the universe. Lovecraft always seems in possession of a secret so black—and yet so unquestionable—that you are left hurrying in his wake, possessed by an awful fascination to be told what he so obviously already knows. Take it or leave it, he says: this is how it is. There are bad things out there. I know, I've seen them.

"There's another group of people with a very particular slant on the universe, one which enables them to behave as others do not. These are thieves. I'm convinced that the first profession was not prostitution, as is so often claimed, but thieving. Nicking things. Taking what belongs to others, and not caring about the consequences—somehow possessing a moral *carte blanche*. And in 'Fair Exchange' I wondered what might happen if someone of this profession got himself pulled into a world far darker than even he could comprehend."

STEVE RASNIC TEM was born in the heart of the Appalachian Mountains and lives with his wife, the writer Melanie Tem, in Colorado.

A prolific short story writer and poet, Tem's work has appeared in countless magazines, anthologies and chapbooks. His first novel, *Excavation*, appeared in 1987 and the following year he won the British Fantasy Award for his story 'Leaks'. His short fiction has been collected in *Ombres sur la route* (published in France), the International Horror Guild Award-winning *City Fishing* and *The Far Side of the Lake*.

The semi-autobiographical chapbook *The Man on the Ceiling*, co-written with his wife, won the World Fantasy Award, the Bram Stoker Award and the International Horror Guild Award, while another chapbook, *In These Final Days of Sales*, also won the Bram Stoker Award.

Tem's last novel was Deadfall Hotel from Solaris, to be followed by Blood Kin in 2014. His most recent collections are Ugly Behavior (New Pulp Press), Onion Songs (Chômu), and Celestial Inventories (ChiZine), a major compilation of his more recent strange fiction. Also in the pipeline is a PS Publishing novella, In the Lovecraft Museum.

As the author explains: "The seed for 'Eggs' came from a small sculpture I bought in Covent Garden on my first trip to England many years ago: an ugly little thing coming out of an egg-shaped stone. It sat on one of my bookcases gathering dust until one early morning, when some chance reflections brought it to my attention so that it might tell its tale.

"Although Lovecraft's stylistic approach is not one I'd care to emulate, the notion so dramatically embodied in his fiction that the world is this mysterious place we cannot even begin to understand is one with which I'm in profound sympathy. The characters in Lovecraft's work are alien even to their own lives—is there any theme more contemporary and vital than this?"

ACKNOWLEDGMENTS

Special thanks to Dorothy Lumley, Steve Saffel, Cath Trechman, Natalie Laverick, Philip Harbottle (Cosmos Literary Agency), Joshua Bilmes (JABberwocky Literary Agency), April Derleth (Arkham House Publishers, Inc.), Sara Broecker, Mandy Slater, Dwayne H. Olson, Michael Waltz, Bill Schafer (Subterranean Press), Bob Garcia, Bernie Wrightson and Anthony Sapienza, all the contributors, and, especially, my late and much lamented friend Philip J. Rahman for his support and belief in this and all my books for F&B.

ABOUT THE EDITOR

STEPHEN JONES is one of Britain's most acclaimed anthologists of horror and dark fantasy. He has more than 125 books to his credit, including *Shadows Over Innsmouth*, *H. P. Lovecraft's Book of Horror* (with Dave Carson), *H. P. Lovecraft's Book of the Supernatural*, *Necronomicon: The Best Weird Tales of H. P. Lovecraft* and *Eldritch Tales: A Miscellany of the Macabre*. He has won numerous awards for his work, including three World Fantasy Awards and four Bram Stoker Awards. You can visit his website at www.stephenjoneseditor.com.

SHADOWS OVER INNSMOUTH
Edited by Stephen Jones

Under the unblinking eye of World Fantasy Award-winning editor
Stephen Jones, sixteen of the finest modern authors, including
Neil Gaiman, Kim Newman, Ramsey Campbell and Brian Lumley
contribute stories to the canon of Cthulhu. Also featuring the story
that started it all, by the master of horror, H. P. Lovecraft.

"A fine assembly of talented writers... A superb anthology for
Lovecraft fans." *Science Fiction Chronicle*

"Horror abounds in *Shadows Over Innsmouth*." *Publishers Weekly*

"Good, slimy fun... There are a number of genuinely frightening
pieces here." *San Francisco Chronicle*

For more fantastic fiction, author events, exclusive excerpts, competitions, limited editions and more

VISIT OUR WEBSITE
titanbooks.com

LIKE US ON FACEBOOK
facebook.com/titanbooks

FOLLOW US ON TWITTER
@TitanBooks

EMAIL US
readerfeedback@titanemail.com